Sylvie Gallimore is a mother and grandmother, originally from Bristol, England, who has written all her life but waited until in her late 60s to actually write the novel that everyone says they all have in them.

The Poet's Trap had been an idea in her mind for many years—a collection of her poems in a book published in 1996 by Dorrance Publishing.co.inc of Pittsburgh, Pennsylvania (ISBN 0-8059-3330-1), had been the inspiration for *The Poet's Trap*. It was an incident as seen by several people, telling different viewpoints on the happening. The idea to combine poetry and a story, the two intertwining, has been a long time in her thoughts. Hopefully, the results are worth waiting for.

The Poet's Trap was released in 2016 and *The Southerly Curse (Before the Poet's Trap)* was originally intended to be three extra novels, but as there were so many times in the characters' lives that it was necessary to repeat incidents, it was decided to make the three books into one; combining already written books was quite a challenge but, hopefully, successful.

For the friends that I have lost since the short time it has taken me to write this latest novel, Pete Jeffery, Helena Woodward, Peter (Foxey) Foxworthy, Paul Emsley and my dear friend Julie.

For all my friends that still remain
And those that have gone ahead.
For those who did fulfil their dreams
And those with things unsaid.

Life is a work still in progress
And a race that's still to run
With ambitions still to be met
And battles still to be won.

I am trying hard to complete the task
Set for me at the start.
It has taken me longer than planned
So each of you take heart.

I believe that age is just a number.
Irrelevant, it's true.
It is never too late to fulfil a dream
If that dream is still with you.

Sylvie Gallimore

For my wonderful family—sons: Joe, Adam and Dan; my daughter-in-law, Blanca; and my beautiful grandsons: David, Rick and Aiden, who are dearer to me than life itself. Also, Charlotte and not forgetting my husband, Richard, who spends a lot of time alone whilst I write.

A special thank you to Joe for reading some of my book before I decided to have it published.

Sylvie Gallimore

THE SOUTHERLY CURSE
(BEFORE THE POET'S TRAP)

Austin Macauley Publishers™
LONDON • CAMBRIDGE • NEW YORK • SHARJAH

Copyright © Sylvie Gallimore (2019)

The right of Sylvie Gallimore to be identified as author of this work has been asserted by her in accordance with section 77 and 78 of the Copyright, Designs and Patents Act 1988.

All rights reserved. No part of this publication may be reproduced, stored in a retrieval system, or transmitted in any form or by any means, electronic, mechanical, photocopying, recording, or otherwise, without the prior permission of the publishers.

Any person who commits any unauthorised act in relation to this publication may be liable to criminal prosecution and civil claims for damages.

A CIP catalogue record for this title is available from the British Library.

ISBN 9781528925495 (Paperback)
ISBN 9781528964326 (ePub e-book)

www.austinmacauley.com

First Published (2019)
Austin Macauley Publishers Ltd
25 Canada Square
Canary Wharf
London
E14 5LQ

My first novel, *The Poet's Trap*, was received very well and several people, who enjoyed the book, asked me questions about how I had formed the characters. I read my book again and began to think that I could produce another book that led up to *The Poet's Trap*, explaining how the main characters came to be entwined. There has been a special interest in a young woman, originally called Agnes; and her wayward father, Adam Southerly, the Earl of Wetherley. This book *The Southerly Curse (Before the Poet's Trap)* is the prequel that led up to the original novel, *The Poet's Trap*. I hope this book is readable as a stand-alone, as well as a prequel to the original.

I need to thank a few special people who have given me so much encouragement, they have driven me on to write this latest novel and I thank them wholeheartedly. Obviously, a big thank you to my sons for their encouragement and also to David, my eldest grandson, who organised a Facebook page so I could promote *The Poet's Trap* in the first place and all his advice since. Steve Webster for help setting up a blog to promote myself as well. A big thank you to my friend Robin Rostron, whose opinion I greatly appreciate, he gave me my first review. Also, Pete Foxworthy, a great friend, who unfortunately passed away in July 2017 after a short visit with my family. I cannot say enough about him and his encouragement; if he had been my manager, I think I would have gone far, miss you always, Pete.

Also, Tracey Causer, whose brilliant review amazed me. Without you all, I probably might not have started another book.

I had a notion to try to write in the style of the period but decided that far cleverer people than I do that very well, so I decided to make it readable to the modern world.

I did intend it to be a separate novel about George, Adam and Agnes, but as their lives intertwine so thoroughly, I decided to combine the three to avoid too much repetition.

Sylvie Gallimore

The Prologue

The Southerly Curse (Before the Poet's Trap) is the second fictional novel by Sylvie Gallimore. The first novel, *The Poet's Trap*, set in 1850 England, told the story of Sir Henry Fitzroy, the son of a wealthy trader who was widowed when he lost his wife, Amy, in childbirth. He has a much loved 16-year-old daughter, Esme, and they live in Falford Hall, a building dating back to the 16th century near Bath. Esme's life is changed drastically when her cousin writes a scandalous, fictitious poem implicating her unfairly in an illicit romance.

When towards the end of The Poet's Trap, Esme's cousin Robert falls in love with an inferior young woman (Agnes), and Sir Henry sets about discovering her lineage, believing her to be of higher birth than she would have them believe. He discovers that her father, Lord Adam Southerly, the Earl of Wetherley, was the son of a very dangerous man. The Southerly connection is the subject of this latest novel.

The Southerly Curse (Before the Poet's Trap) first tells of the evil George Southerly, who spreads poison where ever he goes, walking over anyone who gets in his way and leaving a trail of misery. It is followed by his son, Adam Southerly's impossible task to try to right all his father's wrongs and finally weighed down by the task and realises that he is only a man after all and all men have their limitations. It tells of his fight to be proud of his family name that has been dragged into the gutter by his inhuman, lecherous, degenerate father, George Southerly.

It shows Lord Adam Southerly to be a good and kind man at heart and a man who gathers sympathetic people to him easily. He is not a worldly man like his father and cares too much at times, if this is possible, for other people's feelings. It tells of his fight to right all his father's wrongs. He is a man, like all men, he tries, sometimes he succeeds and sometimes he fails spectacularly. He puts a lot of his faith in people that his rank would not expect, marries unwisely and is haunted by what he considers to be the sins of his father. People around him believe strongly that blood will out and however hard he fights it, he will become his father. He tries desperately to prove them wrong.

Later in the book, it tells the story of the Countess of Southerly's life from the moment she meets and falls in love with Adam Southerly, the Earl of Wetherley, and all the twists and turns that life throws at her. Ending up with the life and trials of Seraphina (Agnes), Adam and Dorothia's daughter.

I hope the reader finds this book is readable as a stand-alone as well as a prequel to the original, The Poet's Trap.

Our story begins in the tiny village of Weston-Under-Wetherley round about 1803. It is a quaint village that nestles in a valley under the shadow of Wetherley Wood. According to the Doomsday Book, the village takes its name from the wet stone and the woodland to the north known as Wetherley Wood. Weston-Under-

Wetherley is on the right bank of the River Leam in the County of Warwick, just on the edge of the Valley of Avon.

There are approximately 30 small cottages, mainly just one bedroom abodes, not enough to house the amount of labourers needed to farm the land. Many labourers and skilled men come in from neighbouring villages, such as Cubbington and Hunningham, to work. The sandstone ashlar Hunningham Bridge over the River Leam is well used by shepherds, farmhands, foresters and people looking for work. It has been standing for around 100 years since about 1703 and consists of three semi-circular arches with cutwaters that span the river; while there are a further two semi-circular flood water arches on the west bank. The river is prone to flood.

Also, in the village you can find St Michael's Church, dating from the 13th century and well used by the local villagers. There is no school in Weston-Under-Wetherley so village children, those that bother to do so that is, go to Cubbington or Hunningham to learn if they can afford to do so, and their parents can spare them. There are always chores to be done and errands to run, this does not always allow enough time for learning.

There are three major properties in Weston-Under-Wetherley; one of them, Wethele Manor, (spelt in the original way), which is overlooked by St Michael's Church.

Many of the workers on this estate have been laid to rest in the churchyard. Wethele Manor was built in the 16th century and was originally a thatched house called New House Farm, and over 200 years, it has been added to and re-built in places and is now a large Georgian three-storey house of grand proportions.

The second large property that provides work for villagers is Weston Hall, a very grand looking building that stands on the left side of the road leading from Olney to Weston-Under-Wetherley. Weston Hall sits behind huge iron gates with elaborate stone pillars. There is a large portion of stabling and a granary crowned by a rather ornate cupola. There is a large inner courtyard that the villagers call the jail yard, it is surrounded by very tall imposing looking walls. Weston Hall stands on the site of what was once a large timber framed building that was demolished in the 1750s by the then owner, Lord Clifford of Chudleigh. It was re-built in its present state in a simple but impressive Georgian style and is lived in by William Umbers, a man of considerable means.

The third and final mentionable house is Weston Manor Lodge, built as a lodge house to accommodate friends and relatives of the Earl of Wetherley so he could make use of the hunting that Wetherley Wood provided. The Lodge was originally part of a larger estate, the main building, the stately home, was a huge, mainly timber and brick built, construction that had burnt down some 50 years previously. It was widely believed that one of the servants had accidentally knocked over a candle in the attic as that is where the fire began. They had managed to save a great many of the family heirlooms, wall hangings, silverware, furniture etc. before the fire took hold. Seven servants lost their lives, mainly ones who slept above stairs, others attempting to save the earl's possessions. Everyone involved in the saving of the contents of what was once Princethorpe Hall were rewarded admirably by the Earl, Adam Southerly, the present Earl of Wetherley and many of their descendants still work at the estate. The Lodge was renamed Weston Manor Lodge out of superstition, although it was a good, three miles outside of Weston-Upon-Wetherley on the road towards Princethorpe. It was always the intension to re-build the great house but as to date, this has never been attempted; all that remains is a footprint of the original building, the large stone steps that once took you to the front door remain but very little else. The interior of the building, being formed by wooden walls, did not help when fire took hold. The Lodge, however, has been extended many times over the past years and is now a most impressive looking building of stone construction. The enlargement of the lodge took away the necessity to re-build the original building. The present earl's family home is actually in Yorkshire and is a very large estate. He, however, likes to escape to Weston Manor Lodge as often as possible, especially in the winter, Yorkshire being a much colder county.

The earl owns several hundred acres of good arable land around the Lodge and employs a great many local men and women to harvest his crops. There are only a dozen cottages that belong to the Lodge, and they all are for the occupation of employees—gardeners, stable hands, gamekeepers, a wagoner, cooks, maids, general servants, the poultry keeper; the only servants house within the Lodge full time are the housekeeper and her husband, who acts as general repair man. There is also a cordwainer employed and living in one of the small cottages on his property for the sole purpose of making fine leather saddles, shoes and other goods from leather imported from Cordoba in Spain. This craftsman's eldest son acts as an assistant, learning the trade as he works. General crop hands, anyone needed to till or plant the crops, shepherds, fruit pickers etc., are all brought in from neighbouring villages. There are regular markets in the neighbouring villages where you can buy not only vegetables and animals but you can hire help as well.

The present earl, Adam Southerly, is a hardworking, honest employee, much admired by his work force.

Chapter 1

The book I should have written first. This is the story of George Southerly, a man of considerable wealth, charm when needed and influence who used his extreme good looks, which he inherited from his parents, and money to act as he saw fit and not how the law or human kindness dictated. He grew up feeling that he was above the law, and any actions he took were of no consequence. He answered to no man and behaved like the devil's advocate on earth.

George was the only son of the Adam Southerly, the Earl of Wetherley, and his wife, Lady Sophie Loveridge. The earl's money comes mainly from investment in the mill and cotton industry in Yorkshire, where the family home is situated. Southerly mill and weaving sheds are second only to the earl's rivals the Waud family. The family estate is in Keighley Manor, not far from Bradford; it is a very fine house in large grounds that include a fine hunting wood and a large lake that contains a great many fish that are caught and eaten in the manor, sometimes caught by the earl himself, who enjoys all manner of outdoor pursuits.

Adam Southerly, George's father, was born in Keighley in 1750 and undertook an arranged marriage with Lady Sophie Loveridge in 1774 when he was aged 24 and she was just 19. He had only met the young woman on two occasions before his engagement was announced. Sophie was extremely pleased with the match as she had been previously promised to an ungainly young baron, who she had taken an instant disliking to on being introduced the previous year. The young baron, not even 19 himself, had a preference for men and fortunately for Sophie, this information came to light before the marriage could take place. The young man had put a gun to his head ending any speculation that they might marry anyway.

Adam Southerly was definitely a lover of women and his extreme good looks and cat like green eyes attracted all the eligible women around. So Sophie considered herself fortunate that she had been chosen to be his life partner.

Lady Sophie was as fair as the earl and many commented that they looked like two angels bound together. Luckily, Adam was as taken with Sophie as she was with him, and although it was an arranged marriage, it was a happy choice for both of them.

Just over a year after their wedding, in 1775, Sophie gave birth to a healthy, full-term daughter who they called Verity. The child was a very beautiful and good-natured baby. When Sophie realised, just a year later, that she was expecting again, she was quite happy. Verity had been an easy birth and an easy, much loved child, and she had a strong desire to give the earl a son to carry on the family name.

In the autumn of 1777, Lady Sophie went into labour in the prepared room. Doctor Prouse, who delivered Verity, and a midwife as such were on hand but the birth was not straight forward; the umbilical cord had managed to get tied round the baby's neck and the doctor had to work very hard to deliver the baby in one piece.

Many years later, people wondered if it might have been God's way of telling everyone not to allow this baby to come into the world.

The baby was a good-sized boy, also fair but slightly grey in colour; Doctor Prouse guessed that it was because its airway had been restricted for a while trying to arrive in the world. Three days later, the boy, now called George after the King of England, was a good colour but, unfortunately, the same could not be said of his mother who had bled heavily during the birth. Adam had insisted on sitting with his wife and spoon feeding her broth to build up her strength, and although she survived never re-gained her strength. She was, from that day on, the shadow of the young woman that Adam had married, and although he always treated her well, he no longer treated her as a wife.

As Verity and George grew up, Lady Sophie over indulged them; all the love she had previously felt for Adam was passed onto the children. It created a great rivalry between them, each trying to vie for their frail mother's favour. The earl took a greater interest in the mill and spent a great deal of his time looking into the running of the buildings. He did have other financial interests abroad and from time to time, went out of the country with his valet to inspect these holdings.

When the earl was a boy, the market town of Bradford was being taken over by the wool and spinning industry so Keighley, being some 10 miles from Bradford, seemed an ideal place to settle. A very large property was purchased there by his father and building work had immediately started to make it into one of the finest stately homes for miles. This was considered to be the family home now, even though the family had owned property in Weston-Under-Wetherley for a lot longer. They all retreated to Weston-Under-Wetherley when the winter came in; the Yorkshire home being near the moor brought very poor weather so the trip down south was very much a ritual. The earl started to take a strong interest in Southerly Mills and running of them, which kept him out of the house a great deal.

Verity and George became unruly, ill-mannered and generally hard to handle, whilst their mother looked on with a kind of simple smile and bought them lavish gifts to calm them. By the time George was five-years-old, he was starting to show signs of a very unpleasant nature. He liked to trap birds in the garden and maim them so they could not fly away and then took a great deal of pleasure in watching the feral cats attack and kill them. By this time, Lady Sophie had slipped into a kind of twilight world; she did not seem to notice or care about anything that was going on around her.

Verity had learnt the art of looking pretty and making people believe that anyone who looked so charming, must in fact be angelic, which she was far from when in Georges' company. Both, her and George, took a great delight in unsettling their mother by bringing toads and frogs into the house, whilst dinner was being served. The children always ate their meals in the nursery and if their father was away, Sophie ate alone, and it was at these times that the frogs or toads would suddenly appear on the dinner table causing their mother to fall into a faint. She was very prone to fainting.

Chapter 2
Early Signs

Adam Southerly arrived home one afternoon to find his wife in a state of total confusion and demanded to know how long she had been like this and what had caused the problem. The butler explained that something had occurred at dinner the previous day that had sent the mistress into a deep faint and when she woke, she seemed confused. He said that he had called the doctor and he was told it was her nerves and she should be treated gently and quietly. Adam sat next to his wife, lifted her hand and asked her what was ailing her and all she could say was toads, which he did not understand.

Later that day, Adam went to fetch some presents that he had brought back from his travels for the children and Sophie. First, he lifted a beautiful feather fan from his case and showed it with pride to his wife. A slight quiver of a smile crossed her face as she took it from him and he was pleased. By now, the children were as close as they could be without actually getting into the case themselves, anxious to see what treasures were coming their way. Adam gently withdrew a hand mirror, it was beautifully engraved with a silver frame and handle. He handed it to Verity, who grabbed it without a word of thank you. Then Adam brought out a book, bound in the finest leather and printed exquisitely. It was a copy of Gulliver's Travels by Jonathan Swift. Adam was a keen reader and loved books, especially ones that were bound well. George did not share his father's interest in literature and when handed the book, he looked at it and threw it as far as he could across the room. Before anyone could stop him or even realise anything further was going to occur, George stormed over to his sister, snatched her present from her and slammed her hand mirror against the wall breaking the glass and followed this act up by snatching his mother's fan and snapping it in half. The room was in an uproar. Adam's mouth just fell open in shock, Verity was lying on the floor in hysterics and Sophie had once again fainted.

It took the joint strength of a footman and the butler to control George and hold him still, even this was a struggle as he kicked and screamed like a mad thing. The doctor was summonsed and Sophie, who had regained her senses, was taken to bed and the boy was given a sedative to calm him down.

The doctor told Adam that in his opinion, the boy had a severe mental problem and suggested that he should be confined to his room until further examinations and opinions could be gathered. Reluctantly, the earl agreed to this line of action and after a further week of doctor's visits, the child being bled to release the evil in him; after potions and opinions, it was decided to let the matter rest and allow George the benefit of the doubt; the earl did not want to believe that his son and heir was unstable and it was easier all round to suggest that the boy just had a bad-tempered moment.

Life went on. Verity avoided her brother where possible and spent more time sitting with her mother, at lessons with her governess, Hannah Yelland, or tending to the flower beds. George seemed to have got over this wild moment and Adam was happy that he had decided to leave things as they were.

Early one evening, George was roaming the halls, as he did quite often, when he heard a noise coming from the young governess's room, He crept up to the door and listened carefully. He could just make out his father's voice so he hid until the door opened and the earl stepped out of the room. George did not say a word and did not give himself away; he did, however, tap on Miss Yelland's door and when she opened the door, looking slightly dishevelled, expecting to see the earl, George simply looked at her from his hiding place, smiled and waited until she went back into her room, walked away, leaving her un-nerved, storing the information for another day.

No one seemed to notice that George was still acting strangely. When out of the sight of adults, he continued his practise of trapping wildlife and enjoyed torturing the poor, unsuspecting creatures. He had a tutor, a young man of 29 who had taken holy orders but had decided that his place was in the real world. His name was Benjamin Brown and he had only been with the family a few months when he began to worry about George and his erratic behaviour. The family dog produced a litter of pups that everyone admired and George became jealous of the attention the creature was getting. Brown watched the way George picked up the puppies and accidentally dropped them; he noticed that the height from which this occurred got higher and higher. He bravely went to speak to the earl about his worries. Adam listened carefully and decided that if maybe he allowed the children to choose a puppy each and take care of it, it would be good for both, George and Verity. The earl sent for his children and after they were sitting down, he asked them if maybe they would like a puppy of their own to train and take responsibility for. Verity was particularly keen on this idea and had already had it in her mind to ask her father if she could have one of the pups. She sprang to her feet and ran to her father, flung her arms around him and then without another word, rushed from the room. Adam and George went together to the stable where the pups and their mother were kept and discovered Verity already there with her chosen puppy in her arms. George's face turned the colour of thunder.

"How dare you pick a puppy before me?" he screamed at his sister. "I am the son and heir, I chose first and I want that one." With that, he snatched the pup from Verity's arms and was about to leave when his father stood in his way.

"There are seven puppies, George, give that one back to Verity and pick another," he said sternly.

"You cannot make me, I want this one," the child replied looking up at his father defiantly.

There was a look on the child's face that scared the earl, it was a look of pure hatred and evil. It quite left the earl wondering what to do next, after all, the child was only seven by this time. Adam looked round at Brown to see his reaction, but he too looked absolutely amazed and did not speak.

"Verity, would you like to pick another puppy, my dear?" The earl asked nervously. By this time, George looked triumphant and Verity was crying.

"No, Father," she said between sobs. "I have been coming here every day, hoping you would let me have a puppy of my own. I really want that one. George hasn't even looked at the rest."

"I don't need to," replied George. "If you want it, it must be the best and I want the best."

Verity stamped her feet and screamed hysterically. "Well, you can't, you can't," she cried.

"Right," said their father, now more annoyed than alarmed. "Neither of you will have a puppy. Put that creature back, George, and go to your rooms." No protest would change his mind so George almost threw the little bundle back at its mother and stomped off in a fury.

Both, Brown and Adam, stood and watched as the pair walked away into the grip of their governess.

"I do not know what to make of him, Brown," said the earl. "I fear he is disturbed."

"I fear you are right, Sir," was the reply. "Maybe a little stronger discipline might be called for or a boarding school."

"Seven does seem a little young to give up on the boy, don't you think, Brown?" replied the earl.

The next day, however, brought home the fact that George was no ordinary bad-tempered child. When Verity crept down to the stable to look at the puppies, she found they were all dead, each had its neck broken. She screamed and ran to find her father, who found it impossible to believe so he went to investigate for himself. The family bitch was whimpering, nudging the little bundles one by one and licking them, trying to bring her pups back to life. For a moment, he thought that he was going to be sick. He marched up to the nursery and dragged his son out of bed, marched the boy down to the stable closely followed by the governess and Brown. With his hand firmly gripping the back of the boy's neck, Adam forced the child to look at his handiwork, which he denied doing. Still with fury in his heart, Adam asked Brown to pass him the nearest spade and told his son to dig a hole, big enough to bury all of the puppies.

George did not protest, cry or object to the task; in fact, he marched out into the garden quite happily and managed to find a spot where he could dig up one of Verity's favourite plants. Despite her protest, Adam did not stop the boy. When the hole was considered deep enough, the boy put the pups into a box, took them to the hole and tipped them un-ceremoniously into it, covered the hole and strolled off with a huge grin on his face. Everyone just stood, mouths open, watching him go.

Within a week, the earl had made a decision, he felt as though he had no choice, George would go to a boarding school hoping that would calm the boy down and dispel a bit of discipline. The next few days were spent packing the trunks that George would need to live at the boarding school, only coming home for occasional visits. The earl had decided on a school run by monks, it was some 30 miles south from Keighley and the boarding school occupied a large portion of the original monastery. The monastery had somehow escaped complete destruction when Henry VIII cut himself off from the Catholic Church of Rome and declared himself Head of the Church of England in 1539 and the dissolution of the monasteries took place. A portion that was damaged was rebuilt and when Elizabeth, the first, came to the throne, it was re-occupied.

Some of the monastery was still in use but to help the upkeep, several rooms had been set aside as a school. Most the boys, that stayed there, slept in a dormitory but the earl felt that this might be a little too harsh for his spoilt son, so he paid extra to have him roomed in a single room of his own. It was not very comfortable as it had originally been a monk's cell. Adam sent a comfortable chair, a rug for the floor and extra bedding with the boy so he would feel more at home.

George could see that all the protests in the world would not change his father's mind so he left quietly, without a farewell to anyone, cursing his sister under his breath as he felt it was all her fault; if she had not made such a fuss about the puppy, he would have got his own way and he would not have had to be so spiteful.

A few months passed and it was decided that Adam, Sophie, Verity and a skeleton staff would go to their other property in Weston-Under-Wetherley. They often moved lock stock and barrel to Weston Manor Lodge for a couple of months, a year, and the children loved it there. There was a wood to roam in and other children of their age. Adam though that it might be good for Verity to have a change of scenery.

Chapter 3
The Devil's Return

Everyone was still in Weston Manor Lodge when it was decided that George could come home for a week or two. The fathers had reported that George had settled in well at the school and seemed very repentant of his bad behaviour and they thought this should be rewarded.

Weston-Under-Wetherley is quite a way from Keighley and although the boarding school was actually en route to Wetherley, it was still quite a journey for a young boy of eight coming up to nine. The idea did not phase George so everyone was ready and expecting him when he finally arrived at Weston Manor Lodge.

Keighley was now the family home but it wasn't originally so. Before the original manor House was burnt down near Weston-Under-Wetherley, having been a particularly fine, large building that had been in the family for many generations, the stately home in Keighley was just an occasional retreat. It was, however, from the North that the main family wealth came. After the fire, the family spent more and more time in West Yorkshire, only coming to Weston-Under-Wetherley to escape the very cold Yorkshire winters. Keighley is on the edge of Keighley Moor and, as such, open to inclement weather and high winds. In the summer, it is a fine area to hunt and ride.

The newly enlarged lodge was renamed 'Weston Manor Lodge' out of superstition and was originally just an off shoot of the large manor house, mainly used as a shooting lodge. The original building was a good, three miles outside of Weston-Upon-Wetherley on the road towards Princethorpe. It was always the intention to re-build the original great house but as to date, all that remains is a footprint of the original building, the large stone steps that once took you to the front door remain but very little else, all very overgrown now. The lodge, however, has been extended many times over the past years and is now a most impressive looking building of stone construction. The enlargement of the lodge took away the necessity to re-build the original building.

The earl owns several hundred acres of good arable land around the lodge and employs a great many local men and women to harvest his crops. There are only a dozen cottages that belong to the lodge and they all are for the occupation of employees, gardeners, stable hands, gamekeepers and such like. Anyone needed to till or plant the crops, shepherds, fruit pickers etc. are all brought in from neighbouring villages. There are regular markets in the neighbouring villages where you can buy not only vegetables and animals, but you can hire help as well.

George arrived in Weston-Under-Wetherley on a warm summer's day in June. It was quite unusual for the family to be South in the summer, they usually headed that way as the bad weather arrived in the North. Verity had improved in temperament and manners—a great deal since her brother had left—but he had only just stepped inside the door when there was a noticeable change in the young girl. It was as if George has some sort of control over her.

George was eager to re-acquaint himself with the local children. They had always been encouraged to mix with the country children as well as upper class children of friends. George was always leader of anything that was occurring in Wetherley. He had not been long away from the boarding school and just three days into his month trip back to join his family when disturbing thing started to happen in and around the village. Firstly, Reverend Barnett, the vicar of St Michael's Church in Weston-Under-Wetherley reported a break in. Someone had broken a window on the side of church and climbed in, throwing items about the place, scattering the flowers placed near the alter and leaving the church in disarray. Nothing had actually been stolen. The window was the size that would only have allowed entrance to a small child so Reverend Barnett realised immediately that it must be one of his young parishioners. He took the opportunity at morning service to speak about the incident and suggest that whoever was responsible, come and see him after afterwards to ask for forgiveness before the devil claimed their soul. Two very frightened children hung back after the service and waited for the vicar. The two were unlikely candidates, sons of hard working farming people and not known to cause trouble of any kind; their names were Tom Bishop and Samuel Guest. They both told the same story, George Southerly had made them do as he instructed with threats of using his power over his father to have their father's ruined. The vicar felt the stories ran true and later that day, walked up to Weston Manor Lodge to speak to Adam Southerly, the Earl of Wetherley. His heart was in his mouth by the time he reached the front gate, and he wondered seriously if he should just let the whole thing drop. Just as he had decided to head back home and forget everything he had been told that day, young George came running towards him, chasing a rather scruffy looking dog that had obviously strayed onto the property.

"Young, Sir," the vicar cried. "Could I just take a moment of your time?"

George stopped what he was doing and walked over to the vicar curious as to what the man could possibly want with him.

"I am sorry to take you away from whatever you were doing, young Sir."

"I was only chasing a mutt off of our land," replied George, standing a few feet from the vicar and looking him straight in the eye. "I was going to teach it a lesson, not to return here again."

There was something in the boy's eyes that un-nerved the vicar. He laughed nervously.

"What do you want?" asked George. "Do you want to speak to my father?"

"Well, my original purpose was to speak to the earl about you, but as I have your attention, I may as well speak directly to you."

"You wanted to speak about me!" replied George, looking rather annoyed. "What could my father possibly be interested in about me that you could tell him?"

"Two boys have told me how they entered the church on your instructions and did a little damage," replied the vicar nervously, feeling very foolish that a mere child could un-nerve him in this way.

George laughed and turned to walk away. He turned for a moment to reply to the vicar. "I think you forget who is the master here, you will be very sorry if you speak to my father and any boys that have spoken to you about me will be equally sorry." With that, George walked away swinging a crop that he was carrying from side to side as he went.

Reverend Barnett hurried back to his wife and children and immediately told his wife what had occurred.

Two days later, the vicar was told that Tom Bishop had met with a rather nasty accident out in the fields and as a result, had a badly broken leg. There were no details as how this had occurred but his friend, Sam Guest, had disappeared; ran away, it seemed, from home so maybe he could shed some light on what had happened. A shudder went through the vicar as he remembered and understood young George's threat. He went off quietly to pray, ashamed that he found himself afraid of a mere child.

A few days later, Verity found a cat with a kindle of kittens hiding in an outhouse at the manor. She had placed mother and babies into a box and taken them up to her room. Verity was nearly 11 and had just been allotted her own room away from the nursery. Just two days later, George wandered uninvited into Verity's room and heard a scratching noise coming from under her bed. A close inspection uncovered the little furry creatures, still in the box, their eyes not yet open. He just took one of the kittens.

When Verity returned to her room with a small amount of fish and meat for the mother cat, she realised that one of the babies was missing. She hunted high and low for the kitten and when she could not think of anywhere else to look, she gave up the search.

Two days later, George slipped into Verity's room and removed another tiny, helpless kitten. Verity once again hunted high and low for the baby. There had been originally seven kittens and now there were only five. She went to her governess, Hannah Yelland, and told her the story of the missing kittens. Hannah Yelland was a delicate-looking, young woman of about 23, she had been brought up in a nunnery and was very well read. They went together to Verity's room, brought out the box from under the bed. George, who had been watching, tapped gently on Verity's door and she bid him enter. He went over and looked at the kittens and told Verity loudly that the mother and babies all looked flee ridden and should maybe be bathed. Miss Yelland told George that the kittens were too young to be bathed. He burst into hysterical laughter. Miss Yelland and Verity looked at each other puzzled.

"I think you must be right, maybe that is why the ones I borrowed drowned so easily," he said.

Verity ran out of the room and down to her father's study, burst in through the door without knocking and told her father what George had said. Adam sprung to his feet. He had already heard the story of Tom and Sam, not from the vicar but from one of the servants and was worried that maybe his son, of not quite nine years of age, might be a monster. He ran up the stairs, two at a time, and found Miss Yelland in tears and George back in the nursery. On questioning Hannah, he realised that something was seriously amiss; the young governess refused to tell the earl anything and said that Verity must have misunderstood her brother who was obviously only joking. Adam felt that the young woman was under pressure to support George's actions, though he could not imagine what hold George could have over the governess. With trepidation, he entered the nursery to find that George had the box of kittens and was feeding the mother cat with scraps. The sight was quite delightful and Adam decided that maybe Miss Yelland was telling the truth and the boy had been joking.

"Why have you taken Verity's kittens?" asked Adam walking over towards his son.

"Because Verity ran off and the cat looked hungry," was the reply.

The earl spluttered and mumbled and just told George to return them as soon as possible.

A few minor incidents occurred in the next week before George was sent back to his boarding school and his father gasped with relief as he waved the boy off. A large grin had filled George's face as he waved out the window of the coach and the reason for this was soon understood when Verity discovered her remaining five kittens floating in a small fish pond at the rear of the manor House. A day or two later, the gardener found, after exploring a newly dug spot in his flower bed, the body of the mother cat.

Sam Guest had re-appeared at his family home looking very thin and bedraggled two weeks after George returned to boarding school. He would not explain where he had been or why. Tom Bishop's leg eventually healed but it left the lad with a permanent limp. Many stories resounded round the area but nothing was ever proven or spoken of in the earshot of the earl.

Christmas came and went, the earl declined to allow his son and heir to come home for a visit even when it was Georges' ninth birthday and then Easter. The boy had been separated from his family for over a year and a half and the earl had no desire to call the boy home.

They had stayed in Weston-Under-Wetherley for a lot longer than usual and had just returned to Keighley when Sophie showed signs of distress. Had Sophie, the boy's mother, not grown very unwell, George would have been left indefinitely boarding with the monks. Unfortunately, Sophie wanted to see her son before she left this earth and the earl could hardly prevent this from happening, so he sent for George.

George had grown considerably in the year he had been away, in confidence and stature. When he stepped from the coach, he looked more like a young man than a boy of nearly 10. Verity was now 12 years old and she had also changed a great deal. Without George's influence, she had managed to turn into a pleasant, quietly spoken young woman. George noticed immediately how much his father favoured Verity and frowned with disapproval.

Sophie seemed to brighten up considerably when she saw her son at the foot of her bed looking every bit a gentleman. However, just one week later and Countess Sophie was lying in the family crypt having been weakened by a cough that would not leave her day or night. Verity was heartbroken but George seemed un-moved.

Adam decided to allow his son to stay unless proved wrong to do so and let the past lay where it was, in the past, forgotten. George seemed improved in temperament and temper much to the earl's delight. Also, they were once again in Yorkshire, away from the trouble caused in Weston-Under-Wetherley, so it seemed an ideal time to allow the boy back into the fold.

Chapter 4
Danger Erupting

Benjamin Brown was sent for. He had gone to teach in a school nearby and although, at first, reluctant to return to Keighley Manor, an increase in wages settled the affair. George was none too pleased to see Brown as he felt that he had influenced the earl in the decision to send him away; he has, however, grown up enough to realise that if he can win Brown over, it will be to his advantage.

The following months went by without too many dramas. It was now 1787 and George was 10 years old, he had his 10th birthday in Yorkshire. The family had decided that as George was doing so well, it was best that they did not return to Weston-Under-Wetherley at this time. So the first winter and Christmas was spent in Yorkshire. It had snowed and the manor House had been almost unreachable. Adam liked to exercise his horses but the slippery weather had prevented this. He could not fish because the lake was frozen over and they had very few visitors. The earl was beginning to bore of Yorkshire. He had never been one for parties so rarely accepted invitations of any sort; he preferred outdoor pursuits and because of the restriction imposed on these because of the weather, life was starting to become very dull. In Weston-Under Wetherley, there was always hunting in Wetherley wood. The weather did not prevent this activity. Whenever the family transported themselves to Wetherley, Adam always took his best hunters, George and Verity's ponies and his favourite gig. There seemed to be a great deal to do in Wetherley and Adam was annoyed that his son had spoilt his overview of the village with his bad behaviour.

Christmas didn't turn out to be as bad as anticipated. The nearest large property with occupants on the earl's social level had also decided to stay in Yorkshire for the first time for many years. So the earl took the opportunity to hire extra kitchen staff and invite his neighbour—Baron Alfred Fisher and his wife, Baroness Anne Fisher, their daughter, the Honourable Miss Agnes, who was only two years old and son, John, who was just over five and the Baron's brother Sir Brian Fisher to spend Christmas and New Year at Keighley Manor. They would, of course, be bringing any staff they felt necessary with them, from nursery maid to valet. Baron Fisher's younger brother had recently lost his wife and so he had invaded the Baron's home, whilst he decided which way to go in his life. It seemed that Sir Brian had many mistresses and could not decide which one he was going to install in his home. He felt that he had to allow a certain amount of time to elapse to show due reverence to his late wife before doing anything. Baroness Anne did not approve of Sir Brian or his life style and was not anxious to allow him to influence her children by spending too much time in their company.

Sir Brian took an instant liking to George and spent a great amount of time talking to the child. A 10-years-old George found Sir Brian's stories of mistresses and adventures trying to outflank husbands extremely amusing. The earl was not aware of the conversation that were passing between the two, he just saw that his son seemed suitably occupied talking to this young man, who was after all only 20 and newly widowed. Sir Brian had married a young heiress just 18 months earlier. Had he not been caught in a compromising position with the young woman, it was doubtful that he would ever have been allowed to marry her? She had died in childbirth due to unforeseen complications after a short marriage.

The Baron himself came from a very wealthy family and he had already bestowed part of his fortune on his beloved son and daughter, determined that although his son would inherit the majority of the family wealth, his daughter would, in her own right, be a very rich woman.

The Christmas period and New Year went so well that by the time the Baron and Baroness returned to their own home, plans had been made to marry George to Agnes at a suitable time. Agnes being a great deal younger than George, it would give him time to sew his wild oats and settle down before marrying.

If George did not know about the birds and the bees before that Christmas, he certainly did after. Sir Brian was a debauched young man of dubious character and morals, and he took great delight in giving intimate details to his young protégée about his life style. A month after the Baron and his entourage returned to their family seat, the earl received a letter from Sir Brian asking if George could be allowed to visit him at his home on the outskirts of Bradford, there was a fine river to fish in and he felt the company might be good for both of them. He had told Adam how he had lost a son when his wife died and how much having George around would ease that pain. If Adam had asked a few questions, he would have discovered that it was a daughter that had been still born. Adam thought it over for a few days before speaking to George, who was so enthusiastic that he felt he had to say yes.

So George went to stay with Sir Brian Fisher for what turned out to be three months and reluctantly returned for his 11th birthday. During his stay in Bradford, George was introduced to alcohol for the first time. Actually that is not strictly true, he had been allowed a small glass of wine at the last Christmas gathering but this was different. It started with an odd glass of sherry and progressed during his stay with Sir Brian. He was also allowed to try his first pinch of snuff that had not been appreciated and not repeated; 10 years of age was a bit young, even for a depraved person like Sir Brian to want to corrupt a child.

As soon as George returned, the Southerly family packed up and went to Weston-Under-Wetherley for a few months.

George seemed quite subdued and seemed to seek out older boys to spend time with. He also occasionally hung around his father's desk, drinking from any decanter he happened to find. Not enough for anyone to notice but enough to excite the boy, especially when it happened to be whiskey. Verity, at 13, was becoming quite a beauty and George started to enjoy accompanying her to church and parties. Verity's friends were slightly older than George and he enjoyed this. Verity, being a good-looking, young woman, also made a lot of the older boys want to befriend him so they could meet her.

The earl had been without a female influence for a few years now and had not noticed the changes in his daughter or the attention she was receiving, encouraged by George. George spent a lot of his time watching people, mainly women, in fact he had turned into a bit of a voyeur. He did not enjoy fishing very much but often set out for the local river when it was warm to watch the young girls from the village cooling down in the water.

His father, however, had decided that the boy had grown out of his wickedness and was growing up. A mistake he would live to regret! Verity was starting to make a mark on the world, everyone wanted to meet her. At first, George found this funny and then it started to annoy him that people were trying to befriend him just to meet his sister; he was beginning to be very jealous of the attention she was getting.

Two more years passed and the family travelled to and from Wetherley to Yorkshire at different times of the year. The Baron and his wife and family often visited the Southerly's and Adam took a keen interest in Agnes, watching her grow. She was now five years old and it was quite apparent that she was not going to grow into a beauty like Verity; she was a mousey little thing, shy and quiet, still she was a very rich little lady and that would bode well with anyone. Amazing, how attractive a plain woman can become when she has money.

George also went at least twice a year to stay with Sir Brian in Bradford, having his education increased at every visit but not necessarily in the way his father had hoped. The last time this occurred, Sir Brian drove George home and encountered Verity; it was the first time that he had seen her properly since she was 11 and she was now 15—tall and slender with hair that hung like golden silk down her back. She had her father's green eyes as did George. George talked his father into inviting Sir Brian to stay a few days, and Brian immediately went about working his charm on Verity, who was quickly besotted by this handsome man of the world who could make her laugh. George realised that Verity was taking this friendship that he had nurtured away from him, and Sir Brian was also starting to use him to reach his sister. A tinderbox of emotions was beginning to engulf George; his sister had stepped into his private domain and he felt threatened.

George was only 13 and had not had any sexual encounters as yet, though he had watched Brian with enthusiasm through cracks in door with various mistresses whilst staying with him, so he knew a lot more than most boys of his age.

The day before Brian was due to return to his own home, George sent a note to Verity, pretending it was from Sir Brian, asking her to meet him in the herb garden by the fountain. He also sent a scribbled note to Sir Brian, supposedly from Verity, requesting the same meeting place. George had many letters from Brian and also knew his sister's handwriting so it was not too difficult to forge the letters he wanted. George had chosen the fountain as a meeting place because the grounds were extensive, and he wanted to be sure that the two would meet easily. The fountain is a very prominent feature, it is extremely large with an almost upright fish like creature in the centre, its mouth wide open. The water burst from the mouth into what looked like a huge shell. George strategically placed himself in a good position where he could see all he wanted to see and pounce when needs be. The pair met as arranged. Verity was very nervous as she had never met a young man alone since the age of 11 when she was told that it was no longer seemly to do so. 11 had been the day when her childhood stopped and training to be a wife began, and now she was 15. She had dressed very prettily in a pink muslin shift that touched the floor, tied tightly round the waist with a wide pink silk sash. Her hair was tied back slightly and she wore a woven wide brimmed hat. She was not dressed formally, just comfortably but she looked delightful all the same. George found himself looking at his sister in a manner he had not done so before.

Sir Brian was already in place when Verity arrived. He was leaning nonchalantly against the fountain, trying to look disinterested. She approached and he stepped forward to greet her, picking up her gloved hand and kissing it lightly. Close by was a stone seat and he guided her to this and sat down, signalling her to join him. George had anticipated this action and he was directly opposite the seat, carefully hidden behind a large shrub.

Brian had never been rejected by a woman and assumed that all females, however old or young, were unable to resist his charms. He tried to pick up her hand and remove her glove so he could kiss her flesh but she objected. She fidgeted uncomfortably, remarked that she should be going back inside. Verity was feeling uncomfortable and realised that she had made a mistake by agreeing to meet a much older man; she could see in his eyes that this was not a game. It did not take long before Brian started to get impatient and made a grab for Verity causing her to cry out. This then created a panic in Sir Brian who placed his hand firmly across her mouth to prevent any further noise. George could tell by his eyes that he did not know what to do next, there was pure panic therein. George decided that now was the time to pretend that he was simply passing and rescued his sister, holding her forever in his debt and Sir Brian, hopeful, as a slave to his demands. Both things appealed to George a great deal. All those fish he had caught, dangling from the hook trying to escape, look what he had caught now, he thought to himself. He darted across the path, Brian was already fumbling with Verity's bodice moving his hands about her body, whilst she tried to escape.

"You swine," George cried, trying not to laugh at the absurdity of the occurrence. "Unhand my sister."

Brian stuttered something about Verity inviting him to meet her, and George demanded proof to which Brian handed him the note. Verity, fighting for her breath and dignity, said it was a lie and he had summoned her, handing George her note.

"I think you should be gone, sir." George said simply. "Go before my father hears of this. My sister is a child and you have taken advantage of our hospitality."

Sir Brian did not need telling twice, he was off like a rabbit being chased by a fox, leaving Verity to throw herself into her brother's arms for protection.

"Come, sister, let's move a little way away from this spot in case the brute returns," said George as he led his sister towards the heavily flowered and well-covered pergolas on the far side of the herb garden.

All the activity had stirred up George's blood, and he found that he was unable to control his desire to take revenge on his sister for usurping his role as the important child in the family and punishing Sir Brian for preferring Verity to him.

As they walked closer to the pergolas, he could smell the jasmine and honeysuckle that hung and entwined about its structure; in the sunshine, it was a beautiful spot to sit, you could look across the rose garden and inhale all the wonderful aromas that encircled and engulf you. Verity was still shaking and holding tightly to her brother as they walked. He gently led her into the pergolas and sat her down on the bench that ran its whole length. She tried to control herself and dabbed her eyes with a delicate lace bordered handkerchief. George placed his arm across her shoulders in a protective way and she smiled at him; he suddenly felt a surge of adrenaline shoot through him, it was not planned, he just wanted to have these two people under his control. He was 13 and had never as much as kissed a girl. He remembered how he felt as he had watched Sir Brian with his array of women, it was strange sensation that shot through his body making him feel almost crazy but this was different; he felt an indescribable desire to ravish his sister. His sister was no longer his sister, she was a desirable woman sitting next to him. He realised that if anything happened, it would be the finish of him; this was something he would never be able to talk his way out of.

By early evening, the household was in a panic. Sir Brian had left, taken all his belongings and taken his leave saying an emergency had come up. Verity was nowhere to be seen. A search party had formed to look for the girl, she never missed meals and was always close to the house.

George approached his father. "You do not suppose that she has eloped with Sir Brian, do you?" he asked. "He did seem to take a liking to her."

Adam looked extremely alarmed at this suggestion.

"Do not worry, Father," continued George. "She is probably sitting somewhere nursing a broken heart because he has left without her. He did flirt disgracefully with her."

"George," replied the earl. "I believe you might be right. Verity is probably sulking in the stable, she did seem rather taken with Sir Brian." At that moment, he noticed a scratch down his son's face.

"You need to get that scratch attended to boy," he said lifting the boy's chin to examine the scratch.

"I walked into a rose bush whilst searching for Verity, it is nothing of concern, Father," was the reply.

The earl smiled at the boy and released him.

It started to get dark and every outbuilding, stable and barn had been searched without a trace of Verity. It was George's suggestion that they spread out into the gardens, Verity was fond of flowers. They had already looked in the nearby gardens that she loved to tend to.

Adam and George were standing on the steps of the manor when they heard a cry in the distance. They started towards the sound only to be met by a maid servant screaming and running towards them.

"What the devil has happened girls," the earl cried, catching the girl by her arm as she tried to run towards the shelter of the house.

"The devil has happened, Sir," she said, shook herself free and was gone.

Next to appear was Brown looking very weary and stooped. "Oh, Sir, this way, it is terrible." Brown turned as he spoke and walked towards the fountain in the distance.

They did not have to get too close when they saw Verity was lying on her back, half in and half out of the fountain. One arm hung over the edge of the creation, her head had been submerged when she was found but Brown had lifted her head onto the rim of the fountain. Both her legs were curled under her and under water, her skirt billowed about on the surface and the water in the fountain was red. The girl's stockings were torn, her sash on the floor, some way off, and she was generally in disarray. It was obvious at one quick look what had occurred here.

The earl hurried to his daughter and noticed a note clutched tightly in her dry left hand; he prised open her fingers and looked at the note, which he handed to George.

"Put that safely away, boy," Adam said to his son. Looking back at his daughter's lifeless body, he knelt on the wet floor and cried like a baby.

Everyone left the earl where he knelt until he had calmed himself, and the Brown offered to carry the girl back to the house. A maid was told to fetch the doctor and another message was sent to the Baron telling him that his presents was needed immediately.

Verity was taken up to her room and laid on her bed. She was dripping wet but this did not stop the earl wanting his daughter placed where he felt she belonged. He sat by her bed waiting for the doctor to arrive and dried her hair a little whilst there, sobbing quietly between gasps for breath. The earl was a very moderate man, he was always willing to give any man the benefit of the doubt. Although his mind was in turmoil and he was sure that a man who had been a guest in his house had committed this heinous crime, he was not prepared to rant, rage and pick up his shot gun to go and seek him out until his fears had been confirmed.

The doctor arrived within the hour looking very grave. He had been the family doctor for many years and had helped to bring Verity into the world. He passed George on the stairs and asked him how he was.

"I am fine, nothing has happened to me, why would I not be," was the cold reply. The doctor just carried on up the stairs thinking to himself that the boy might be in shock, though he had seemed very calm.

Doctor Prouse entered the room and was shocked to see this beautiful, young woman in the prime of life lying lifeless there on the bed. He asked everyone but Verity's personal maid to leave, whilst he examined the body. He needed the young woman to help him remove the girl's clothes for careful examination. Clara, the maid, was not keen to attend to her mistress in this state; she was too upset but understood that she was needed so stayed and did as asked.

The Baron had arrived with his man servant quite quickly after being summoned and had, at first, gone into the study with the earl. Adam showed his neighbour the note that he had prised from Verity's hand. The Baron was speechless.

"We will not jump to conclusions at this time, Alfred, let us wait until we have the doctor's opinion," said the earl.

"Could my brother have rejected the young woman and she drowned herself in sorrow?" asked the Baron hopefully.

"It did not look that way to me, Alfred," was the reply.

"Has your brother returned to your home?"

"It was all very strange. He had said that he would visit us when he brought George back but he has not appeared as yet; I assumed that he had stayed here with you for a few days so I was not surprised not to receive him," said the Baron.

An hour later, Doctor Prouse was shown into the sitting room where the earl, George and the Baron were now assembled waiting for him.

"I need to speak to you privately, Sir, the matter is very delicate," said the doctor.

"You can speak freely in front of us, Sir," the earl replied.

"I would rather not discuss my finding in front of the boy, Sir," was the reply.

George's face looked like thunder. "I am not a child. Verity is my sister, I demand to know what happened to her."

The earl turned to his son as he spoke. "No, George, the doctor is right," he said. "I will come and see you later and tell you everything I know. Go now, boy, and leave us alone for a while."

"You must promise to tell me everything, every details." said George strangely as he stomped out of the room.

The doctor watched George leave with a worried frown.

"Be seated, Doctor Prouse. This is my friend and neighbour, Baron Alfred Fisher. He has an interest in your findings," said the earl.

"Really, how so?" asked the doctor confused.

"I will explain that later, Doctor," replied the earl. "Now please tell us what you believe was the cause of my daughter's demise."

"She did not drown," he started. "Her neck has been expertly broken. I do not believe she suffered this injury from a fall, I believe someone broke her neck."

"Murder, oh my God!" exclaimed the Baron.

"Just so," continued the doctor. "But that is not all, the girl had been violently defiled. She was obviously a virgin and there was a considerable amount of blood on her petticoats, her undergarments are missing, her stockings torn, I am afraid the child was raped, there is no doubt about this."

The earl fell into loud wailing and sat with his head in his hands.

"Should I go on, Sir," said the doctor gently.

Between sobs, the earl managed to tell the doctor that he needed to hear every detail of his daughter's last few moments on this earth.

"I would say that she fought hard and the assailant will have scratches on his face or arms; there is skin and blood under her finger nails," continued the doctor. "I believe she was placed in the fountain after death to mislead us into thinking that the girl had fallen and drowned in the fountain. There are no head wounds to suggest that she struck her head, however."

"So some swine has defiled and murdered my daughter within sight of her home and safety," concluded the earl.

"That would be my opinion, Sir. We need to inform the authorities immediately," said the good doctor.

"No," replied the earl. "I do not want the world to know how my daughter died. I will handle this myself."

"It cannot be done, there is a murderer out there, someone else could fall prey to him," replied the doctor, alarmed.

"I am pretty sure who the perpetrator of this crime is, Doctor," answered the earl.

"You do not suspect your own son surely, Verity was his sister," said the doctor, not altogether surprised.

"How dare you, of course not man, George is a child," replied the earl loudly in protest.

"Then who?" the doctor asked confused.

The earl handed Doctor Prouse the crumbled note. "This was found in my daughter's hand."

The doctor read the note and shook his head. "So you think the writer of the note enticed Miss Verity to her death by arranging a meeting," he said looking doubtful. "Why did he not remove the evidence? He had taken a lot of trouble to place the girl in the water, why allow this note to stay dry and be found?"

"Maybe in a panic," replied the earl. "He was obviously not as thorough as he thought he was or as clever."

"I assume you know this man," said the doctor.

"I do," was the reply.

"And what do you intend to do about it?" the doctor asked concerned and slightly confused.

"I can promise you that he will never hurt another person on this earth," said the Baron with a stern face.

The doctor noticed that a tear was running down the Baron's face as he spoke.

"I am to assume that you do not want my findings widely known," said the doctor worried.

"I, we do not want them known at all," was the earl's reply. "I think I owe it to you to explain that the note was written by Baron Fisher's younger brother, he has verified the writing. He is slightly unstable and will be treated accordingly. I only wish that I had realised the extent of his mental problems before I allowed him into my home."

Baron Fisher hung his head in shame. "This is a hanging offence for sure. This will ruin me and my family, better we have Brian locked away from the world quietly. What good would it do exposing the man, it would not bring the girl back."

"Quite so but..." started the doctor.

"There are no buts," said the earl.

"No please, Doctor Prouse," said the Baron. "I am a very rich man, I can do you and the village, in general, a lot of good if I retain my wealth and standing. Just tell me what is needed, I will see that the funds are available to you."

"Good heavens man, what sort of doctor do you think I am to be bought and sold like this?" was the shocked reply.

"A good and honest doctor who if you sleep on it, will realise that I can do more good as a man looked up to than the brother of a deranged murderer."

"Let us all sleep on it," said the earl. "Come back, if you will tomorrow, we will all meet again and decide what is for the best."

"Surely you want justice for your daughter," said the doctor.

"Justice but not at any cost," was the reply.

The doctor left bewildered. He passed George in the hall and noticed the scratch on his face and a thought crossed his mind. The doctor had always suspected that George was a very unstable young man and had been from birth.

Meanwhile, the Baron and the earl sat down and hatched a plan to hide the circumstances of Verity's death and send Sir Brian abroad in exchange for Agnes marrying George at the appropriate time. It would be kept quiet for all their sakes.

The village church suddenly acquired a much needed new roof, the church yard was cleaned and tidied and benches set about in appropriate places, and Sir Brian, when faced with the evidence of the note, put a bullet in his own brain saving the Baron from the trouble of having to persuade him to leave the country. The man had left his brother a note swearing his innocence and telling him that he had received a note from Verity inviting him to meet her, but with no evidence of this, Alfred folded the note and placed it in a box intending to destroy it later.

Verity was buried alongside her mother in the family vault in Keighley, the earl was never the same after her passing; it seemed to suck out the strength from his body.

Verity's governess, Hannah Yelland, was reluctantly sent to another post with good references; Brown was kept on, though he found the task of guiding George an impossible one. Stories about Verity's demise ran riot all over the town, no one was ever privy to the actual fact besides the little group of conspirators, but there were enough servants that had seen or heard a little to fit together a likely scenario.

Doctor Prouse found it impossible to live with the knowledge he had, so he took ship for the Americas and didn't return to his home land for many years.

Chapter 5
The Devil Earl

Life went on, George and his father travelled to Weston-Under-Wetherley and back to Keighley at different times of the year. George no longer joined the village children in any form of entertainment, in fact when in Weston-Under-Wetherley, there was a distinct lack of young people to be seen. The young women, as they reach puberty, seemed to be sent to relatives and the boys kept far away from Weston Manor Lodge. George still had a few nobler born youngsters that sought his company, idle young men that did not wish to follow rules and because they had wealthy parents, did not have to. The earl noticed that George seemed to gather what he would call nature's undesirables to his side.

George grew to be a very handsome young man, he had his father's green eyes and fair complexion, strong jaw line and noble baring. His face was framed by angelic curls that masked the fact that this man was the spawn of the devil in disguise.

George has a sort of presence. When he enters a room, you can immediately see that he is a man of consequence; his bright eyes look right through you, like a cat. All of these God given gifts he uses to his best advantage. George is a lecher of the first order and like a lot of men with wealth and influence, thinks everything and anyone is there for the taking. All the female staff live in fear of his unwanted attentions and he would often take his belt off to men who cared to chance interfering. To keep a roof over their heads, employees had to either keep well out of George's way or do his bidding, whatever he so desired. Young girls born in cottages near the lodge were kept out of sight and dressed in dowdy clothes to escape the future earl's attention; when they start to reach maturity, they were quickly shipped off to relatives or nearby large houses to work. Such is George's reputation and one that will stay with him for the remainder of his debauched life. Only once had his father, the earl, questioned George's behaviour only to be told that George knew about him and Hannah Yelland. This shocked the earl as he thought that he had been very discrete. Unfortunately, as the earl grew older and tired, he took less interest in controlling his wayward son.

George did everything and anything that caught his fancy. He smoked and drank to excess and had women of low morals brought to his home for his friends and him to make use of. His father didn't seem to notice or care anymore. He held poker evenings where people could win and lose their lively hood on the turn of a card. Stories abounded of young, noble men who bet their whole inheritance on the turn of a card whilst under the influence of opium acquired at the Southerly home; some of which blew their brains out on returning to their own homes and realising what they had done.

At 23, George had taken a fancy to a young woman, the daughter of a friend of his father. The young woman was of good birth but the family were in debt and mortgaged up to their ears. The earl wanted a good pairing for his only son, one that brought in money to the family. The earl believed that George had only taken a fancy to Lord and Lady Denver's daughter, Bella, because a 'friend' of his has told him that he had fallen in love with her; George did not like anyone having something he did not have. The young woman in question was only 17, but dark and beautiful. Her skin was an almond colour, her mother having some foreign blood in her and her eyes were almost black. The contrast between the two, George and Bella, was quite striking. Bella had certainly fallen for the future earl's dubious charms, but her family were alarmed at the prospects of George Southerly being introduced into their family, however rich he might be.

It was the Baron's son, John Fisher, who had told George in confidence that he intended to ask for Bella's hand in marriage. Sir John had an abundance of wealth so he did not need to make a match based on finances. He had met the delectable Bella at a gathering on Easter and had been taken by her beauty and charm, she was certainly an elegant, young woman. John had nurtured this friendship over a couple of months and had asked her if he might approach her father and ask for her hand; she had seemed to be completely of the same mind as John and was willing to enter a marriage with him until George Southerly heard of this arrangement. Because George disliked anyone having anything he did not have, whether he wanted it or not, he used all his charm to win the young woman away from Sir John. Bella was surely the most beautiful young woman for many miles around, and although George had no real desire to marry at all, he did not want John to have something or someone that people might consider special. So he made himself, for a short while, into a charming and handsome suitor, lavished the young woman with gifts and won her heart. She had no idea that she was going to lose a good and kind man, Sir John Fisher, and gain a fiend of the first order, not seeing past his looks, carriage, power and status.

When George's father heard of his son's fancy, he confronted him telling him that it was not possible for him to marry anyone other than Agnes Fisher. George erupted like a volcano, all sorts of evil threats spilled from his mouth but for once, his father stood firm.

The earl rode over to Lord Denver's one Sunny afternoon to explain that any offer his son might have made towards their daughter was not possible as he was already betrothed to Agnes Fisher, a long standing arrangement that could not be broken. Lord Denver was extremely relieved as he could not imagine how hard it would have been for him to tell George that the match was not possible; he was as scared of the young man as anyone else. Quickly, plans were put into place to send Bella to relatives abroad.

George was furious that his father had dared to interfere in his marital plans, though he was not really that bothered about the loss of Bella, being assured that there were a great many other young women out there that he could lure, and he had already made up his mind that if Bella returned, he would make her one of his mistresses. However, he stomped about the manor and was as unpleasant as possible to everyone for a few weeks in protest.

After George had calmed down, the earl told his son that unless he wanted to be dis-inherited, he must fulfil the promise made on his behalf after his sister's death to marry Agnes Fisher, who was now coming up to 19.

"Verity, may she rot in hell," he shouted, "still she spoils my life and yet she if long gone."

The earl was visibly upset by this outrage but still he stood firm; George must marry Agnes Fisher, who had her own great personal fortune. Unfortunately, Agnes was timid, young woman, not particularly attractive to look at with a week chin, thin lips, small dull eyes and mousey coloured hair. She was not ugly by any stretch of the imagination but she was also not pretty or exciting. She was a very well read and intelligent young woman with many accomplishments. She could play the piano forte, sew with a delicate touch and produced very impressive water colour paintings.

Agnes, being the daughter of a Baron, no less should have been given a degree of respect. She had, however, not been George Southerly's, the Earl of Wetherley, choice of a wife, there was no attraction what so ever, even her money did not interest George. He wanted a wife that others would envy, a pearl he could show off, a woman with looks but no back bone as he did not want to have to continually argue, his word was law and he liked life that way. He disliked Agnes for her meekness and charitable ways and made up his mind only to speak to her when absolutely necessary and have a great many mistresses.

The wedding was a lavish affair, the Baron having known for a number of years that his daughter would eventually be a countess and would live a life of luxury and wealth because of the actions of her uncle Brian. The Baron never doubted that his brother was the perpetrator of the heinous crime, though others wondered. The fact that Baron Fisher actually believed that the Earl of Southerly had saved his family name made it necessary for him to allow his daughter to marry George, although he personally disliked the man as much as everyone else.

Not long after George's marriage to Agnes, his father, Adam Southerly, the Earl of Wetherley, died suddenly in his sleep, leaving George a vast fortune. Rumours abounded that Adam Southerly was fit and well the day before but somehow died in the night. George was known to roam the corridors of the manor at night and one of the maids, who was very quickly sent away, swore that she saw George going into the earl's room just before one in the morning. Whatever had occurred will never be truly known but the earl was buried alongside his wife and daughter and the new earl became a very powerful and wealthy man.

The earl 'visited' his wife once or twice a month, much to her dismay. He was a violent, uncaring man in all he did and 'love making' was no exception; he isn't one for conversation so most of the visits were very short. One such visit resulted in the Agnes realising that she was with child. The earl was thrilled, mainly because it meant that he could avoid his wife from then on providing she produced a son and heir.

Agnes' pregnancy marked the beginning of George's blatant pursuits of women. George was inclined to force himself upon any and every young woman employed in his household. Most of these young women considered it to be a hazard of the job and put up with it but occasionally, one might object and start to make a bit of noise about their situation. These women were almost always arrested at some point and taken by the runners to Warwick prison on Barrack Street accused of stealing and therefore, any suggestion that the earl has assaulted them was simply thought of as slander to get themselves out of trouble.

People can be hanged for stealing as little as five shillings worth of valuables, this was a sure way of ridding oneself of unwanted titter tatter. Amazingly, most of these unfortunate women were found to have a small trinket in a pocket when searched and although they swore that they had never seen it before, the case was always proved against them.

In 1804, after a long and difficult birth, the countess was told that she would not be able to carry any more children full term, so her husband considered her useless. Luckily, for her, she was delivered of a fine strong son, which they called Adam after his grandfather.

As soon as Agnes produced the much needed heir, the earl had no further use for her. She found her life a lot less challenging and could now keep her own council which suited her, she also had her charity work which she found very fulfilling. She was always interested in prison reform and education, everything the earl found totally uninteresting. Although the earl does not approve, he does not interfere with his wife's activities either, it keeps her amused and out of his way.

Agnes was a kindly soul and made a point of visiting every little cottage on the estate at least once a month to see that her workers are comfortable and then pestering the earl about things such as leaking roofs. He had no interest in the way his people live so long as they did their appointed jobs, so to keep his wife away from him, he set up a maintenance account that she had total control over. It was never increased, so she had to be careful to keep within the budget set and she enjoyed the challenge. Unlike her husband, Agnes was bothered by conditions that their workers might have to endure. He considers that having provided his workers with houses, however small and damp, he has done his duty as lord of the manor. His wife, however, is a different kind of person, she cares that the roof might leak and the bedding is damp and the stove might not work.

Chapter 6
Other Happenings to Ruin a Good Name

Life was always difficult in Weston Manor Lodge, more so than it was in Keighley. The majority of the outrageous incidents happened in Wetherley. It was almost as if the earl came to Yorkshire to rest from his behaviour and when bored, returned to start another chapter. That is not to say that he was not notorious in Keighley as well, he was. He had many mistresses, some were wives of his friends or acquaintances, unbeknown to them, of course, in several parts of England.

George went to Southerly Mill from time to time, just to see where his great wealth was coming from. He had no interest in the running of the mill or weaving sheds, just the income it brought him. He stayed away from any rival weavers and they were all happy that he did so; only appearing occasionally to strike fear into his employees. On one of his visits, he decided that his manager, who had worked happily under his father, was too familiar and lenient towards what he could see as slow workers. So he interviewed a number of would be candidates for the job and settled eventually, after a few false starts, on a unfeeling man called Matthew Morgan, who would run the work shop exactly as the earl intended. The earl did not want to have to enter the mill again unnecessarily and gave Morgan carte blanche to do whatever he needed to keep the mill running and the profits high and he was paid accordingly.

Back in Weston-Under-Wetherley, the Baron's son, John, had gone to Lord Denver and asked for Bella's hand in marriage as he had always intended only to be told that as he was now related—all be it by marriage—to George Southerly, it was out of the question. The Denver's did not want any stain on their line and would not consider a match with anyone, even tentatively, related to George Southerly, the Earl of Wetherley. John was heart-broken and swore never to marry, a promise he kept all his life. In fact, he became a recluse in the outskirts of the village and was rarely seen out in the open. He hoped that no one would remember that he was related to George Southerly in any way.

When George and Agnes had been married just over five years, Agnes arrived on her brother's doorstep begging to be allowed to stay. Marriage was, of course, sacrosanct and once you have promised to love honour and obey, you were trapped. Although Agnes showed John bruises that she had sustained on one of the rare occasions that George had decided that his wife was better than nothing and had sought her out at night, he refused to get involved between husband and wife.

The next day, John was surprised to receive a visit from his brother-in-law, George, the Earl of Wetherley. Reluctantly, the earl was allowed into the drawing room and John was sent for. John had to compose himself before he walked into the room to confront his sister's husband.

"This is an unexpected honour," said John.

"I doubt unexpected, brother-in-law," was the reply. "I believe my dear wife came to see you yesterday. No point in denying it."

"Why would I deny my sister coming to see me? It seems quite a normal thing to happen, we do after all live in fairly close proximity."

George laughed, "Do not take me for a fool, John. I know she came to cry on your shoulder and tell you how cruel I am to her."

"Are you?" was the reply.

"The woman only gets what she deserves," said the earl. "I am her husband and a red-blooded man. If I need or want my conjugal rights, I have the right to them at any time. Do you not agree, John?"

"I have never really considered such a question, as you know I have never married," John replied feeling very uncomfortable.

"Oh yes, of course, brother. The lovely Bella preferred to go abroad than marry you, didn't she?" George laughed as he spoke.

"Whatever you say, George," was the casual reply.

"I will tell you something else, John," continued the earl, "that beauty has married recently and found her husband lacking, I have had to step in and satisfy the woman on his behalf. Quite a chore."

Sir John just stood still, not quite sure how to react to such a blatant insult to the woman he once and still did love.

"You look a little flustered, brother, do not worry. I only came to tell you not to accept any visits from my wife unless I am with her, which is an unlikely scenario." George said smiling widely. "I do not believe she will visit you again but if she does, you have been warned."

"She is my sister, surely she has the right to come here and speak to me. I am her only relative since our parents passed on."

"She is your sister but my wife. What I say goes and she does not call here. Do you understand?"

John could do no more than nod. George Southerly swept out of the property without a backward glance. John called his butler to him. "Howard, I will not be at home to that man ever again, never allow him access to this house, please," to which, Howard replied that it would be pleasure to comply with Sir John's wishes. Feeling very troubled, Sir John poured himself a stiff whiskey and sat himself down near the fire.

Chapter 7
Maud Minford

Adam was born in 1804 and inherited his father's good looks, there the similarity ends. From the moment he first became mobile, he got used to feeling his father's wrath.

Although Agnes made a point of only employing slightly older plain women, occasionally, the earl found someone within his walls of interest to him for a while. It was usually the nanny/governess because they tended to be younger women.

From a very young age, Adam would be asleep in the nursery, and he would become aware of the nursery door opening and a shadowy figure entering long after dark. He would try to keep his eyes tight shut and not see what was happening. The figure would creep past Adam's cot bed and over to the far side of the room where the nanny slept in a single bed of her own, close by to keep an eye on the future earl.

Adam became quite used to the noises that emulated from the bed in the corner of the room. He was only very young but he already knew that something was not right about this nocturnal activity. After his father left the nursery, Adam would lay a while listening to the sobs of his nanny, wanting to speak but afraid to do so.

The very first time this happened, Adam had made the mistake of sitting up in bed and calling out, only to feel the sting of his father's belt across his back and a sense of feeling betrayed by his father as he was not old enough to understand why he had been beaten. However, he soon learnt that when the door creaked open, he should act as though he was fast asleep until it closed again behind the visitor.

His nanny had bathed his sore back and held Adam until he had cried himself to sleep that night. The child had no idea what he had done to deserve such cruel treatment. She also tried to explain to him that sometimes, it was better not to understand what is going on around you.

Adam also realised from an early age that the reason there was such a turn-over of nannies and governess's and several other servants was his father. They would stay as long as they could stomach and then flee in the night. One nanny, Maud Minford, lasted longer than most and Adam became very fond of her. She read to him and made him laugh. There was very little laughter when he was growing up. Adam's mother kept herself to herself, Adam realised as he grew older that this was self-preservation, but it also prevented him from feeling the love of a mother.

Early one morning, there was quite a commotion in the lower hall. It was loud enough to attract the attention of almost everyone living and working in the manor. Maud's voice rang out loud and clear.

"But my Lord, where shall I go if you will not give me a reference?" she cried in anguish.

The earl replied that he cared not where she went so long as it was away from his house.

"But, Sir, I carry your child, you promised me that if this happened, you would take care of me," she replied between sobs.

"You cannot prove the brat is mine," replied the earl. "I will not be blackmailed by the likes of you young woman. Go and rid yourself of this problem, then we can see what can be done."

"This is not a problem, Sir. It is a life, a life you have put inside me," Maud shouted for all to hear.

This was followed by a loud thud where the earl had struck the young woman causing her to fly across the room and knock over a small side table. The woman sat on the floor trembling and sobbing.

"Get up, woman," shouted the earl. "Pack your bag, take care, not to take anything that is not yours. Be gone before I lose my temper."

Maud struggled to her feet and ran from the hall, up the stairs towards the nursery. Adam quickly jumped back into the room and tried to look innocent. He watched his nanny throw her meagre possessions into a carpet bag as she sobs loudly.

"Maud," he said softly to her. "Please, don't leave me, everyone leaves me."

She stopped what she was doing and swept the boy up into her arms for a moment. "I can promise you little Sir that if I could stay, I would but I cannot."

Adam's mother chose that moment to come into the nursery, she took the boy from Maud's arms. "I am so sorry, it has come to this," she said.

"Oh, Madam, I am so sorry," replied the nanny. "It was not my desire to have this happen. I could not prevent it and live under this roof. I did not want to dishonour you, Madam."

"Believe me, girl, I understand perfectly," Lady Agnes replied, holding out her hand to the young woman and giving her a small broach. "I cannot give you money, I have none at my disposal. I am at his mercy as much as the next person. Take this and sell it. It will give you a roof over your head for a few nights at least. I can do no more."

"But, Madam..." Maud started.

"No buts, I will say I have lost it if anyone notices."

With that, Maud Minford left the manor house forever and Adam and his mother watched her walk down the path and out of sight, both had tears in their eyes.

"I do not understand, Mother," said Adam.

"Unfortunately, you will one day, Son," was the reply.

His mother had cried over the poor girl's fate, which annoyed his father even more.

Chapter 8
The Shadow of Evil

It was several years after the Maud Minford incident that a young laundry maid's husband was shot dead in the Wetherley woods so say on his way to speak to the earl about treatment of his new young wife. The story was that he was mistaken for a poacher, though not many people believed that.

Young Adam was growing up under the shadow of his evil father. Everyone was polite to Adam but he was clever enough to realise that it was fear of his father that made him popular and not his own personality. Adam could not have been less like his father if he tried, he was a kind, gentle caring young man. When an unwanted child was introduced to the family, as a whipping boy, he made up his mind never to cross his father in any way. Unlike his father, he did not relish the sight of someone being punished for some mishap he had generated. The boy, Martin and he grew to be extremely good friends. Adam was a very studious pupil and enjoyed feeding on any knowledge that came his way. He had a strong appetite to learn, history being his favourite subject. Martin usually sat alongside Adam and as a result, the two became inseparable. Luckily, George did not notice this friendship developing or out of spite, he would have sent Martin away.

In 1817, the Southerly moved once again up to Yorkshire to Keighley, Adam was by now 13 years old. Whilst in Keighley, George met a Parisian family called Clout, who had come to England to escape the dramas of France at the time. They were a well-to-do family, financially very well off with two young daughters. Camille was the youngest, just 13, and her older sister was Anastasia, who was 15. Unfortunately, Annie, as she was called, had a hair lip and the Earl of Wetherley found even the slightest deformity appalling to his eyes. The poor woman's default was hardly noticeable, she had an amazing figure and splendid thick silky hair but still, the earl could not look at her. Camille, on the other hand, was an extremely good-looking, young woman who he took an instant liking to. Camille, however, found the earl very unnerving but was easily under his control however hard she fought it. Unfortunately, for Camille, her mother, father and sister died very suddenly in a coach accident. She had intended to be on the same coach but had been persuaded by the earl to stay put because he wanted to ask her opinion of something. The mystery of how the coach overturned was never fully settled but it left Camille alone in a strange land. At first, the earl appeared to be kind and caring but as time passed, he started to dominate Camille. One day, he took her to a whore house in Keighley and deposited her there, telling the madam that the girl was there for his use only and paid her to keep the girl safe. As she had nowhere else to go, there seemed no point in fighting.

The earl first 'visited' Camille when she was just 15. Until that moment, she had not fully understood what her duties would be but the earl made the position quite clear to her; she was there for his pleasure whenever he was in town. Her job was to do whatever he asked of her. It is amazing what you will do if you are hungry enough, Camille thought to herself. On three occasions, Camille tried to escape, each time she was stopped by another woman within the whorehouse, usually someone she had trusted. The madam had beaten her severely with a willow cane but when the earl appeared and heard what had occurred, her fate was far worse. He was strong man and he enjoyed inflicting pain on a young woman; she was beaten with his strap until blood ran freely down her back and then he expected her to act lovingly towards him as she lay in agony and he took advantage of her weakened state. For close on six years, Camille allowed this to be the way her life ran.

Several years later, when Camille was not even 25 but no longer considered young and desirable by the earl, another delicate young woman was brought into the whore house and left there to be trained for the earl's amusement. This child, Kitty, of just 12 years of age had been bought by the earl alongside her eight-year-old brother, Robbie, from a man who no longer wanted to feed Robbie, who was starting to be too big to be a climbing boy. The earl had taken the children back to Keighley Manor and left the boy in the kitchen to do whatever chores needed doing but had taken the girl away, returning with her looking like a beautiful doll. The child was exquisite, delicate skin like porcelain, hair like falling golden waves crashing onto her shoulders, eyes bluer than the sky itself. Even the earl could feel that the girl was too young to be ruined but his mouth felt dry at the thought of being the one to deflower such a creature. Kitty was placed in the whorehouse with instructions that she should be kept safe until he deemed her old enough and then he would ask for her. No one else was allowed to touch her in any way, she was to remain as pure as new laid snow. These actions were typical of George Southerly, the Earl of Wetherley. Sometime before the purchase of Robbie and Kitty, the family returned once more to Weston-Under-Wetherley and Agnes slipped out of Weston Manor Lodge and hurried to her brother at the edge of the village, this time she had a maid with her. Howard rushed Agnes and her maid into the sitting room and shut the door quickly behind her, glancing nervously each way before he did so. John was pleased but surprised to see his sister.

"Agnes," he cried. "You take a big chance coming here sister. I assume George does not know your where about."

"My husband is like an evil presence who know everything, he knows if I cough, I do not understand how."

"I imagine he has paid spies, Agnes," replied her brother. "I believe he has forbidden you to come here, he came to see me and said as much."

"I need your help, Brother, I cannot live like this. This man is inhuman." With that, she took off her cloak and showed John bruises, even more dramatic that the once he had seen on her last visit. "He means to kill me one day, I am sure of this."

"I do not believe even he would do anything that drastic, Agnes," was the reply.

"He threatens harm to our son, Adam, if I run away, he means it John. I need to bring Adam to you and seek your protection," Agnes said with a tremor in her voice.

Ashamed as he was of himself, John refused her request and said that he would not interfere. After some persuasion, however, he promised to go to Weston Manor Lodge and try to speak to George about his behaviour. With that, Agnes and her maid left, never to enter John's house ever again. Two days after Agnes' visit, John had a few stiff whiskeys and built up the courage to go and confront his brother-in-law, George, however had been expecting the visit. When Agnes and Mary, her maid, returned to the lodge, the earl had cornered Mary and forced the girl to tell him word for word what had occurred at John Fisher's house.

John Fisher was shown into the study and within a matter of moment, he was seen hurrying off up the path away from Weston Manor Lodge with the threat of unbelievable cruelty to be inflicted on his sister and a bullet especially for him. George had also hinted that the maid, Mary, was probably at the bottom of the well if he cared to look. Whatever the truth of that statement was, the young woman was never seen again.

John was so ashamed of his cowardly behaviour that he decided that he would only ever leave his home after dark and only when necessary and that he would never marry. He did not want to be associated with such an evil man as his brother-in-law surely was. From that moment on, brother and sister were estranged.

Lady Agnes realised that she had to put up with her life and fight her own battles as no one could save her, her husband owned her lock stock and barrel. She started to devote her spare time to helping others and took a great interest in the work of women such as Elizabeth Fry.

Betsy Fry had visited Newgate Prison for the first time in 1816 and had been appalled by the conditions the women and children were kept in. The women's section was overcrowded with women and children, some of whom had not even gone to a trial. The prisoners did their own cooking and washing in the small cells in which they slept on straw. Although she wanted very badly to do something to improve the conditions in Newgate Prison, she needed her family backing to actually make any progress and it had taken her a few years to gain this. She used to go to the prison and read to the inmates but she wanted to do more than this. The more Agnes read about Elizabeth Fry, the more eager she was to do something worthwhile. She realised that although her husband rules her, she could still do good outside the home, and she dreamed of emulating such women as Betsy Fry, after all even she had needed her male relatives to assist her financially. However, Agnes could not imagine George offering to assist financially in any way, unless it was to his benefit. Having a wife who was interested in prison reform did make it easier for George to persuade those necessary into helping him deal with tiresome female servants. Agnes had no idea that George only allowed her 'do good meddling', as he called it, to flourish because it was of use to him.

When Betsy return to Newgate, she was able to fund a prison school for the children who were imprisoned with their mothers. Some children in prison actually became better educated than those on the outside. She helped form the *Association for the Reformation of the Female Prisoners in Newgate*. This association provided materials for women so that they could learn to sew and knit, and once they were out of prison, they could earn money for themselves.

Agnes was not a Quaker like Elizabeth Fry but she wanted very much to emulate the woman, knowing that any good she did would be limited by her dependence on her husband's better nature, which he did not have. It gave Agnes a sense of purpose. She visited local prisons, workhouses and insane asylums amazing herself with her sense of purpose and inner strength. Occasionally, Bathsheba Mountjoy, the vicar's wife would accompany Agnes, taking blankets and food parcels. Although the earl was hated and feared, nonetheless, his poor wife was thought highly of.

Chapter 9
Thomas Bishop

Whilst in Wetherley, the earl took a great delight in bullying a young farmer called Thomas Bishop. Thomas was the young man that years before had forced to climb into the vicarage and had broken his leg mysteriously after he told the vicar, who had put him up to the prank. Thomas was now a married man and George took a great delight in visiting his cottage when Thomas was out and keeping his rather plain wife company. He did not actually do anything, he just sat menacingly and watched her and told her things that he had decided to do to her one day when she was least expecting it. Thomas had been to see the new vicar, Phillip Mountjoy, who had taken over from Reverend Bennett when he had retired some time ago. Phillip was a married man with three daughters—Dorothia, Everline and Elizabeth—his wife, Bathsheba, and mother-in-law, Seraphina. He was an easily approachable man and Thomas had gone for advice. Thomas told the vicar what the earl did on a regular basis to un-nerve him and wondered what he should do about it.

"I assume this brute is not someone to converse with in a reasonable way," said the vicar.

"Far from it, Sir," replied Thomas. "When I was a youngster, George forced me and Sam Guest to break into this church and steal something. Neither Sam nor I could bring ourselves to steal from a house of God so we just threw a few flower about and left. During the next sermon, Reverend Barnett said that God would send the devil down to strike those responsible if they did not confess so Sam and I stayed after church and told him it was us."

"Just you and Sam, I assume, George did not add his weight to this confession?" replied Phillip.

"No, Sir," continued Thomas. "Quite the contrary. Reverend Barnett went to speak to George and he was furious that we had implicated him."

"That was rather ill done of the vicar," commented Phillip. "Do go on."

"The next thing I remember was lying with my leg in the cider press. I had been struck from behind and carried to the barn. The press clamped down on my leg and I have walked with this rather pronounced limp ever since. Sam ran away and hid or his fate would have been the same, I am sure."

"Thomas, my only advice to you would be to move far away if you can before the brute actually acts out any of his threats," said the vicar. "Do you have any family elsewhere?"

"I have an uncle in Chester but I am not sure that I could earn a living there," said Thomas. "I only do light duties because of my leg as it is but the small holding is mine; left to me by my father."

"I am not a rich man but I am comfortably off," said the vicar. "I will buy your small holding from you, no one needs to know at this time. You write to your uncle and see if maybe there is a similar property you could buy or rent nearer him."

Thomas was overwhelmed. "I did not come expecting this, Sir. I only wanted advice. Why would you want a small holding?"

"I assure you I do not but I will rent it out for a time and allow the next tenant the chance to buy it if he wishes to," said the vicar with a smile.

"I would like to spoil the evil earl's fun if I can. My wife has recently become acquainted with Lady Agnes and I have heard enough stories about the earl to believe that he is capable of any atrocity. I cannot imagine even he would threaten a man of the cloth."

Thomas went home, a very happy man to write to his uncle as suggested. Unfortunately, his rather foolish wife taunted the earl with the news when he arrived on one of his unexpected visits. When Thomas arrived back home from the market, he found his wife in a sorry state, her lip was cut and she was heavily bruised. Her clothes were torn and she was shaking uncontrollably, too scared to tell her husband anything at all. The village had a local potion maker and she called and gave the woman a sleeping draft. Thomas picked up his shot gun and marched up to Weston Manor Lodge, where the earl was waiting for him. Thomas was shot dead as he entered the grounds. An inquest found the earl to be in his rights to protect himself and the verdict was self-defence. No mention was made of Thomas's wife and what she had suffered.

Reverend Mountjoy was horrified and blamed himself, believing if he had just sent Thomas away, he would still be alive.

Not long after this event, one of the laundry maids, Freda Prout, found herself to be pregnant by the earl. When she told him, he told her to leave immediately and never mention it to anyone. Freda ran home and told her father, who had always suspected that the earl dealt badly with his daughter. He decided to go and face the earl. However, this did not happen as at some point in his journey, Bill managed to step on a man trap. Once again, talk was that somehow the earl had managed to plan the man's demise, though no one knew how.

Stories bounced about Keighley for many more years connected to the earl's behaviour. In 1826, when the earl was racing about the lanes near the lodge in his new sporting gig, he knocked down a young village boy called Arron Duggan. How it occurred, no one knows as there were no witnesses, there never are when the earl is involved. The boy could have stepped into the road by mistake or the gig could have mounted the verge, whatever the true story was, no one came forward to say but the earl did not stop and the boy lay there for some time before he was found and taken to his home where he passed away in great pain. Arron had only said that the earl had struck him and no more, which, of course, the earl denied.

Around the same time as the Duggan boy incident, the earl became aware that his son, who was now in his early 20s, had taken a shine to the vicar's eldest girl, Dorothia. The earl had not really noticed the vicar's brood but made a point of looking at them closely when next he was in church. The earl realised that Dorothia was a very striking beauty and wondered how he had managed to miss her. So he immediately made plans to marry Adam to an extremely plain heiress called Lady Petunia Pembrook, daughter of Lord Pembrook of Eathorpe.

George Southerly, the Earl of Wetherley, was having such a high time in Wetherley that he decided it was to be their permanent home, returning to Keighley only when necessary. He had already placed what he considered to be a suitable manager in Southerly Mills and did not feel he actually had to work in any way. He would be free to pursue his main interest, women, and intended to make Dorothia Mountjoy his latest conquest, willingly or not. The thought of snatching the young woman from under the nose of his son amused him greatly.

Chapter 10
Freda Prout

George Southerly, the Earl of Wetherley, was always a cold, violent, uncaring man. As soon as Agnes had delivered of a fine, strong son and heir, the earl had no further use for her. He had no interest in the way his people live so long as they did their appointed jobs. They could starve or grow fat, it was of no interest to him so long as it did not cost him anything extra, and he certainly was not bothered by conditions that they might have to endure. Needless to say, the workers and their families felt a warmth towards Lady Agnes and several have blessed their lucky stars that they do not have to live with the earl, regardless of the luxury inside the manor.

A great many stories are told about Lord George Southerly, the Earl of Wetherley. He was talked about as if he is the devil in the farming community. It is impossible to know how many of the stories are true as he is so disliked and how many are pure fantasy. Some believe that when female servants leave in the night, they have actually been accused of stealing and been taken by the runners to Warwick Prison on Barrack Street, and therefore, any suggestion that the earl has assaulted them is simply thought of as slander to get themselves out of trouble. People can be hanged for stealing as little as five shillings worth of valuables, this is a sure way of ridding oneself of unwanted titter tatter. Rumours are always bouncing around the area, none of which are ever proven. There was once a very largely believed story about a young laundry woman, Freda Prout, from Lillington who fled the lodge one day in a very distressed state. She was said to be with child and had confessed as such to her father who demanded to know the seducer. She had told him that it was the earl who had forced himself upon her, and she showed her father stripes on her back caused by his belt when she had fought for her honour. She confessed to her father that it was not the first time she had been attacked by her employer and that she had discovered she was pregnant and had told the earl, who said that he would beat the child out of her. She had ran as fast as she could for her life. The girl's father walked the almost eight miles in high dudgeon to confront the earl; however, this did not happen as at some point between Lillington and Weston Manor Lodge. He got his foot caught in a man trap, designed to catch poachers, they can break a leg at the very least and deter others. Bill was a very careful man and always kept to recognised paths so no one could understand how someone, as sure of himself, in the country could have made such a fatal error of judgement. Man traps are set well off the road in private land to prevent poachers, no one could remember anyone ever being caught in one for a great many years. However, Bill Prout managed to get himself trapped in a very large man trap and bled out before being found by his son, who had gone out in search of him with a few neighbours. Once again, talk was that somehow the earl had managed to plan the man's demise, though no one knew how. It was generally believed that this had been an orchestrated accident, though it was never made quite clear how or who set the trap. Nothing was ever discovered about the circumstances of this convenient accident, no one was ever brought to account for the incident. The story was that he had just wondered off the road into a notorious poachers' area and had paid the price of not sticking to the allotted path. People believed what they wanted to believe and that was that the devil earl had struck again.

The reputation of the earl was such that every crime of notoriety for miles around, someone would have put his name forward as the culprit. In May 1812, when Spencer Perceval, the Prime Minister, was walking into the lobby at the House of Commons about five in the afternoon from his house in Downing Street and was shot by a waiting assassin, some tried to suggest that Lord George Southerly might have had a hand in it—absolutely ridiculous but such was the dislike for the earl. Even after they hung the perpetrator, John Bellingham, a business man in his 40s with long felt grievances, rather foolish stories lingered.

Just the mention of the earl's name was enough to put the fear of God up most people. His poor long suffering wife found it very difficult, although she was liked by most despite her husband.

The earl insisted that the winter months were always spent in Weston Manor Lodge. The family home Keighley Manor in Yorkshire was a lot larger but although Yorkshire is a very beautiful county, it is always colder there. Adam had been born in Wetherley so he felt an affinity to the place and its inhabitants. He formed a strong friendship with Thomas Umbers, who was just a couple of years younger than him; Thomas' father, William Umbers, was the Squire of Weston Hall. The two boys used to hide in the woods, shoot rabbits and fish together. Thomas had an older brother called William, who was the apple of his father's eye. William, from a very early age, showed a strong interest in the running of Weston Hall and particularly, the livestock. Thomas, as the younger son, was allowed to run a little wild, knowing that he would not inherit the bulk of the family fortune or be expected to run the estate.

Adam was an only child and it was assumed that he would take over all his father's wealth and holdings eventually; unfortunately, along with the wealth, came the name. The name 'the Earl of Wetherley' brought fear into many a strong man's heart. Adam was, as yet, too young to realise the implications of having such a notorious father, but in time, he would be fully aware of what this would meant for him as he grew up.

Chapter 11
Growing Up

The Reverend Mountjoy had come to Wetherley from Birmingham wanting to allow his family the luxury of fresh air and open fields.

When Adam was 16, he first set eyes on the new vicar of St Michael's in Weston-Under-Wetherley's eldest daughter, Dorothia, and this brings us up to date with our story. The new vicar had replaced Rev. Barnett, who had served the parish well for over 40 years. Taking such a man's place is not easy in such a small community.

The new vicar of St Michael's at Weston-Under-Wetherley, Phillip Mountjoy, is of good birth. He was unfortunate enough to be the youngest son of Sir Peregrine Mountjoy and as such had been given the chance to take holy orders, which he found suited him very well, though he never took to life in Birmingham and was now very happy to be the vicar of St Michael's. There was a substantial church house that went with the job and he loves the surrounding countryside. Phillip Mountjoy had found his calling and was totally suited to the job, he had been almost forced into. It was common practice for younger sons of eminent people to go into the church or the army. One of Phillip's brothers had chosen the army but it was not for him.

Phillip lives with his wife, Bathsheba, three daughters—Dorothia, Everline and Elizabeth—and his wife's mother, Seraphina. He is a very pleasant man, totally surrounded by woman, so he takes a great pleasure in doing the rounds of the parish, just so he can escape the female chatter.

1820 was a very important year for Britain and Ireland as they had just lost their mentally unstable King George III at the age of 60, and he had been succeeded by the Prince Regent George IV, with all the pomp and tradition that accompany a new coronation. Church bells had tolled for the late king's passing and again for the popular Prince Regent as he was proclaimed king. Exciting time for people of wealth and importance and an excuse for people of lesser status to rally and celebrate.

Dorothia was only 12 when Adam first became aware of her. She had suddenly started to blossom and was now becoming a very presentable young lady. He always took the time to speak to her after Church services, and they had an easy relationship like that of brother and sister.

Over the years, Dorothia has developed into a very beautiful woman and when she reached the age of 17, many of the local boys started to show a strong interest in her. Adam only comes to Weston Manor Lodge twice a year, sometimes for three months at a time but the space between visits made Dorothia's transformation even more spectacular. He had no idea that Dorothia's heart had been lost to him at a very early age.

Adam started to take a great interest in the Church of St Michael's, he would visit the vicarage often and talk with Phillip about the scriptures and sometimes, they would look into the history of the church. Adam found himself becoming extremely interested in history in general, and this has started a life-long hunt for facts and details about where ever he went.

St Michael's stands on a bank in an enclosed churchyard. The church consists of chancel, north chapel, nave, north aisle, west tower, vestry and south porch. The vicar told Adam about the evidence of a 12th century church in the north and south walls of the chancel consisting of the eastern halves of two semi-circular-headed blocked windows, which they examined together. Early in the 13th century, the church had been almost entirely rebuilt; the tower was added early in the 14th century, the top stage being added later. A north chapel was built in the 16th century. Reverend Mountjoy took great delight in showing his young, enthusiastic friend around the church and pointing out any points of interest, insisting he called him Phillip. Adam was delighted to have an adult conversation with someone who knew so much about what was important to him. What started as a way to get to know the daughter turned out to be a much appreciated and valued friendship in the making. Phillip and Adam would often be seen wondering round the church yard, examining the graves and discussing the history of the area. It was clear that there had always been some sort of settlement in the shadow of Westerley Wood. Adam would often go to Warwick and look through historic files to find out about those that came before. The vicar had sparked a defining interest in history.

They talked about the late and new king and the ways of the world. These conversations were very stimulating and enjoyable for Adam.

Mrs Mountjoy, Bathsheba, was not so keen on the young lord. She had heard, from other women in the village, tales of his father, the Earl, and they did not rest easily on her mind. She was a God fearing, straight talking woman of simple tastes and ideas and was of a mind that blood will out and that Adam was his father's son. "It might not manifest itself for a few years yet, but it is as sure as night follows day, it will eventually," she would tell her husband, whilst warning her eldest daughter to keep far away from him. Bathsheba believed the earl to be in league with the devil himself, an opinion shared by a great many there-about.

Dorothia turned out to be her own woman and often joined her father and Adam in the graveyard, much against her mother's wishes. Adam always treated Dorothia with the greatest respect and tried to keep his gaze from her as much as possible. This was difficult because she had grown into a spectacular classical beauty.

And this is where the story really begins. It wasn't until Adam's friend, Thomas Umbers, mentioned that Adam's father had offered to take Dorothia under his wing now she was about to reach 18, that Adam realised that this was the woman he wanted to marry. He was, of course, also afraid for the poor young woman's safety having lived with scandal and insinuations about his father all his life.

That evening, Adam decided to inform his parents that he wanted to marry Dorothia, but this announcement was pre-empted by the arrival of one of the earl's cronies and his rather plain daughter. It seems that word of Adam's interest had reached the earl and as he had decided that Dorothia was to be his next mistress, his son had to be stopped in his tracks.

The unfortunate young woman, Miss Petunia Pembrook, is around 21 years of age, just a year younger than Adam and at an age when women are usually referred to as old maids if still single. She is, however, a great heiress and only a prolonged illness a few years previously had prevented her from being married off already. She had never officially come out into society because of this illness, so she had missed all the balls and occasions that bring you into direct contact with suitable partners. She also lacks any physical presence. She is tall, gangly, thin, her hair is dull and her eyes also. Although she is dressed in the very latest fashion, Regency style with high waist made of flimsy material, with a look of ancient Greece, she is not attractive. The fashion of the day makes her look even thinner than she is. Her hair is cut in the mode with curls that frame her face, a very pretty look if you have a pretty face; unfortunately, poor Petunia has not. Adam felt a pang of pity for the girl, she looked down trodden like his mother and timid like a bird. Whatever pity he felt for the young woman was counteracted by the fact that he did not desire to engage in any marriage outside one he chose.

Adam and Petunia were seated close together, whilst a light supper was served, and he tried very hard to make polite conversation. It was quite obvious to Adam that Petunia would have been willing to marry a one-legged ogre if it would get her off the shelf, she made that point quite clear. As Adam is rather an Adonis, she could not believe her luck. Her father had told her that she was to meet a possible husband, and she rather assumed that he would be a great deal older than her and not attractive. She had been brought up to realise that her father's choice would be the way her life would go, her own wishes would never be considered so she didn't waste her life even looking. Adam, however, did not want to sell himself short and tried to convince the young woman that there would be someone out there that suited her far better. He tried to get an insight into her interests but she was not very open. She had been told to look meek, mind her manners and only speak if spoken to. Adam was hoping for a wife that had a bit of spunk and an interest in all things so conversation would flow freely, he did not want a mouse to worry about. It was a very strained and awkward couple of hours that he could not wait to come to an end. However, the earl was adamant that Adam must marry Petunia and informed the girl's father, Lord Pembrook, before they left, that it was a match and an announcement would go in *The Times* as soon as possible. The young woman looked extremely pleased with the match and the deal was done and dusted all within two hours of the two young people being introduced.

Resistance put up by Adam to the arranged match was met with the threat of disinheritance. Even when he proclaimed his undying love for Dorothia, his father would not be moved. He simply said, "Show me a boy whose heart has not been broken and I will show you a disaster waiting to happen."

Adam went to his mother and begged her assistance in this matter, but her fear of her husband made her refuse.

"No one does what they want in our position, Son," she said. "Your father and I had no choice when we wed. That is the way of the world."

"Not my world," Adam replied. "I will not be sold like a stallion to the highest bidder and end up unhappy like you, were you and father ever happy together?"

"We are not put on earth to be happy, Son," was the sad reply. "We are here to keep our line going, only the poor are allowed the privilege of choice as they have nothing to lose."

"Mother, I will not marry Lord Pembrook's plain and boring daughter and no one will make me," Adam shouted.

Hearing the noise, the earl entered the room and without uttering a sound, struck his son about the face with such a force that Adam flew across the room. The young man staggered to his feet and seeing the rage in his father's eyes, declined to follow his instincts and strike back.

"You will marry where I tell you, boy," bellowed the earl. "You will marry and go to Yorkshire, away from the little miss that has turned your head."

"And if I refuse?" Adam asked in a shaky voice. His mother placed her hands over her face in alarm.

"You leave this house without a penny," was the reply. "See where your high ideals get you when you are hungry!"

Adam pulled himself up to his full height and started towards the door. His father caught his arm as he passed. "Do you think you are the first to have to marry a dull bit of skirt just to follow convention?" The earl pointed towards his wife as he spoke. "Do you think I would have chosen to marry that simpering creature? No, I too had an eye elsewhere."

"I have heard you have several eyes elsewhere, Father," came the brave reply.

The earl raised his hand as if to strike and then, instead, gave out a short laugh. "Who would begrudge me a pretty lass in my bed when my wife is barren and useless, no one I know."

"Then you know some very low individuals," came the reply.

The earl simply pushed his son and without further ado, turned to leave the room. He turned back to speak to his wife for a moment. "I do not want you putting any ideas into the boy's head, it is full of enough rubbish already. And woman, do not forget that tomorrow we take the carriage to Eathorpe for afternoon tea. It will be a bore but it must be done."

"Why do you want me on this visit?" asked Agnes.

"Because it is where Lord Pembrook abides and I promised him that you would meet his wife and this you will do, no questions asked," was the reply. "Try your hardest, woman, to look presentable, not like a dowdy mouse as usual."

"I hope you do not wish me to accompany you as well." said Adam, alarmed.

The earl placed his hand on his son's face and turned it towards him. There was a clear imprint of where his ring had cut the young man's cheek. "Not with that mark on your face, boy," the earl said. "I will take the Barouche if the day looks fine or better, still I will take the gig, no point in flaunting our money."

Agnes looked horror struck at the thought of travelling even the two miles to Eathorpe in the Tilbury with her husband driving, he always drove too fast and she always felt uneasy.

The earl looked at his wife's alarmed face and said, "Yes, I will take the gig. I would enjoy driving myself and the way is an easy ride."

"Surely the barouche would be more comfortable, husband," replied Countess Wetherley hopefully. "It would look much better if we were driven surely."

"No, woman," said the earl with a slight laugh in his voice as he knew the pain he was inflicting. "I would like to drive, the road is a good one and it is not far. It would be good to show that we are not wasters, we are careful money people. Don't want his lordship thinking that we squander money so making it necessary to take his rather ugly girl off his hands for his monies sake."

"But we are after his wealth, there can be no other reason to lumber me with Petunia," Adam replied, a comment his father chose to ignore.

The earl owns an uncommonly pretty tilbury gig, blue in colour with gold trim. It is particularly light in construction with two very large gold painted wheels, a small folding hood that does not offer much protection if it rained but acts as shade on a bright day. It has beautifully padded seating made from red leather and is always admired when he is out and about in it. Most gigs are quite plain and purely functionary, whereas this tilbury gig had been made to measure extra light, made for speed as well as looks. It had been built to race around the estate, a favourite past time of the earl. The earl always uses his fine chestnut-coloured carriage horse to pull it as the two looked splendid together.

He ordered his son to go and make arrangements for the Tilbury to be ready the next afternoon at 3. The earl had really enjoyed upsetting his family and was looking forward to enlarging on their discomfort the next day.

After the earl left the room, the countess rushed to her son's side to examine the now rather prominent bruise on his face.

"My beautiful boy, what did you or I ever do to have such a life?" she said with a tear in her eye. Adam put his arm gently across her shoulders reassuringly.

"When the Good Lord calls his name, Mother, he will pay. Of that, I am sure," Adam said gently.

Chapter 12
The Eathorpe Visit

The very next afternoon, the earl and countess were dressed in their finery and preparing to climb into the gig for the journey to Eathorpe to partake of tea with what the earl hoped to be new relations in the near future. The earl was in particularly high spirits and carrying his long whip for the journey. He had dressed in a vivid yellow pair of close fitting trousers and a high waist Regency style jacket with large reveres. The jacket, which is blue, is cut short in the front but the back comes to just above the back of his knees. He was also wearing a rather splendid, elaborate velvet waistcoat, which has red with blue dots. The outfit is finished off with a white silk shirt and extravagant bow round his neck and a top hat, which he was carrying. His high black, closely fitted Spanish leather boots are so highly polished, they shine.

Countess Agnes looked extremely dull next to her flamboyant husband, though she too is dressed in the very latest fashion. She is wearing a rather pretty printed high waist dress, cream with a pale blue swirl effect pattern. She wore on top a high waist coat with elaborate pleated shoulders, the sleeves getting tighter until they reached her wrists and then finishing with a lace cuff. The coat does not hide the dress, being designed to hang open with just a thin ribbon at the bust line that is tied in a bow. The coat was not created to allow the two front seams to touch, it was designed as a frame for the dress underneath and act as a shield against the weather, being made of a heavier material than the dress. The countess looked quite delightful and she was quite pleased with her appearance. She tied her large bonnet tightly on the side of her neck, wanting to make sure that she did not lose it during the ride.

The Gig looked splendid in the sunshine, the gold painted wheels glowed and Rory, the chestnut horse had been groomed with great care. The groomsman held the horses' head patiently waiting for the earl to climb aboard.

Adam came to the front door and told her mother how well she looked, the countess smiled at her son and started to climb into the gig. Adam sprung forward to give his mother a hand up.

"Don't fuss so, Adam, your mother is perfectly capable of getting into a gig on her own," said the earl, obviously enjoying watching his wife struggle.

"That would be the case, Sir, if the foot stool was available but it seems it is not," replied Adam.

"Not my concern, boy," replied the earl. "I do not need it."

Adam thought it best not to reply to his father's last remark.

Very soon, the earl and countess were aboard the gig and ready for the off. The groomsman handed the earl the reins and the gig pulled away without a backward glance from the occupants.

Adam stood and watched for a while as the gig picked up speed; he knew that his father would drive the horse hard just to unsettle his mother.

Chapter 13
The Warning

The Reverend Phillip Mountjoy was sitting in his study looking over some papers when he heard voices in the corridor outside. He stood and went over to the door, opened it to find his wife, Bathsheba, talking to the squire of Weston Hall, William Umbers. The squire was a regular church goer as were his two sons, Thomas and William, and they had spoken on many occasions, but Phillip would never have counted the squire as a friend and was surprised to see him in his hallway.

Squire Umbers, on seeing Phillip in the doorway, hurried over to him, hand outstretched, which the vicar readily shook.

"I am sorry to disturb your peace, Vicar," said the squire. "My son has passed on a piece of information to me that I felt I should immediately bring to your door."

The Reverend Mountjoy intrigued, invited Mr Umbers into his study and asked him to be seated.

"You sound in earnest, Umbers, how can I assist you?" asked the vicar signalling towards a decanter of sherry on his desk as he spoke, offering his visitor a glass which was declined.

"My son, Thomas, has come to me with a wild piece of information, which I felt should be immediately passed on to your good self," continued the squire. "He had already told George Southerly's son, Adam, and he was most concerned."

"I am really intrigued now. Adam has not rushed to me with any scandal or dramas," replied the vicar.

"I have probably got here ahead of him. I have no doubt that he will call later and tell you exactly what I am about to inform you of."

"Please, speak freely," said Phillip.

"It is a little delicate, reverend. Also, I do not know how well you are acquainted with George Southerly, the Earl of Wetherley," said the squire, in almost a whisper.

"I am not acquainted with him at all as such," was the reply. "And neither would I wish to be."

"I agree with you, Sir, neither would any sane man who has daughters hereabout," continued the squire.

"What has that devil done now that I have not already heard about?" the vicar asked concerned.

"It is not what he has done, it is what he intends to do," was the reply. "As you know there are endless tales that bounce about the village connected to this man, I am sure they cannot all be true. At least I hope they are not. Did you hear that it is suggested the man ran down little Arron Duggan and never even stopped to check how he was, the boy has since died."

"That I did but hoped it was an accident," replied the vicar. "Any accident is put at the earl's door, surely he cannot be responsible for them all."

"I have to agree but he is greatly feared," said Mr Umbers. "The villagers hide their daughters in sack clothes to escape the earl's attention, this should never be."

"I could not agree with you more, Umbers. I came from Birmingham to this village for the peace of the countryside, only to have to face the horrors of a lord of the manor, who makes the worst monsters in history look positively sainted."

"He believes himself to be above the law and uses his wealth and power to strike fear into everyone, including his own family," replied the squire. "The Lady Agnes is such a timid creature and his son, Adam, is a good friend of my Thomas; I didn't encourage the friendship at first but Adam has grown to be a good man, as embarrassed by his father as anyone."

"I am also fond of Adam, he has a keen interest in the structure of buildings and history which is something we have in common," replied the vicar. "What atrocity has the earl performed that has brought you to my door today, dare I ask?"

"At this moment, he has not fulfilled his latest scheme. I am here to prevent it having listened to my son," was the reply.

The vicar looked both, interested and worried. "Do go on."

"You have three good looking daughters, Mountjoy," the squire began.

"That I have."

"Well, it has come to my notice that the earl has singled your eldest daughter, Dorothia, out as being of particular interest to him."

"Good God man, what do you mean!" said the vicar, alarmed.

"We are all aware that George Southerly has many mistresses and even more conquests that did not go willingly to his bed," began the squire.

"What are you suggesting?" said Phillip, his face flushed.

"I am not suggesting anything, I am giving you fair warning," was the reply. "Thomas overheard a conversation that suggested that Southerly has a desire to add your eldest daughter to his list of damaged goods. He will come to you and suggest that he takes her under his wing, introducing her to the right people but really his plans are more sinister. He is a hard man to turn down, he can make people's lives very miserable."

"He could not make my life miserable enough to allow me to sacrifice my daughter's honour. What should I do?" asked the vicar, quite beside himself with worry.

"There is no doubting, Dorothia is a very comely young woman and I believe my son is correct. He has gone to warn Adam, who I believe has a softness towards the young woman himself," replied Mr Umbers. "I would suggest you think of a relative quite some miles away and send all of your daughters there post haste. That man moves fast once he has a mind to."

Phillip stood up and paced the floor for a few moment. "My mother-in-law has a very good friend in Brighton whose middle son married for a second time, a few years ago, into quite a fine family, the Fitzroy's of Somerset," he said. "The wife, Mary Fitzroy, that was now Lady Bradbury, is a few years older than Dorothia, possibly six or seven years. She has been in poor spirits having miscarried on three occasions but now happily almost full-term with child. Maybe the chatter of young women about the house might lift everyone's spirits, I believe the whole house-hold to be extremely worried about the possible outcome of this pregnancy, which is understandable. I will write and see if they would allow my daughters to visit for a while. It is about time they ventured out into the real world."

"That is an excellent idea, Mountjoy, do not hesitate. We are talking about the shadow of the devil here," added the squire. "We are worldly enough to outsmart the fox, unlike his previous victims who had no escape."

"It is terrible state of affairs when you fear being employed by the earl, I have heard such unbelievable tales."

"Believe them, man," replied the squire. "I have lived within this shadow all my life, anything you have heard is the tip of the iceberg. That man is evil personified. Adam himself told me how his father had thrown out a governess when she became pregnant with the earl's child. There have been an inordinate amount of young women, so say, caught stealing from Weston Manor Lodge and carted off to Warwick Jail."

"Good heavens, are you suggesting that the man has his way with these poor woman, and then makes it impossible for them to protest by sending them to prison on trumped up charges?"

"It is not a suggestion, it is a fact. The earl has many in his pocket, money is a powerful allies and can keep you out of the reach of consequences for actions."

"I must write to Brighton immediately and hope that this will be far enough away to keep my daughters safe," said the vicar, most distressed.

"I have done as I thought right and now, I have taken up enough of your valuable time," said William Umbers and with that, he left the vicar to put in motion his plans for his children.

Chapter 14
Changes

Adam decided to saddle his horse and ride over to the church and seek out Reverend Mountjoy, he felt the need to unburden himself. He intended to tell the vicar of his intensions towards Dorothia and the plans his father had made regarding Petunia Pembrook.

Adam tied his mount to a post and found Phillip in the nave of the church and on being noticed, was greeted like a long lost son.

"It is good to see you, my boy," said the vicar with a wide smile. He then noticed the mark on Adam's face. "How did this come about, might I ask?" he said waving his hand towards the injured area.

"I walked into something unexpected," Adam replied.

"Looks to me like it was someone unexpected, not something," came the reply. "That looks remarkable like the imprint of a ring on your face. Do you want to tell me about it, Son?"

"That was the purpose of my visit this afternoon," he replied. "I have a great many worries and I am hoping that talking them through with you will help clear my head."

"If you prefer and we can talk in my snug," was the reply.

Adam walked with the Reverend Mountjoy leading his horse behind him towards the vicarage. Adam thought to himself that how wonderful it would be to have a father like Phillip, who you could actually have a conversation with. The only talks Adam and his father ever had were confrontational and it was almost impossible to speak to his mother without the earl interrupting and putting the woman down. The thought that this was a normal family was very depressing for Adam.

Reverend Mountjoy and Adam soon reached the rectory. Adam tied his horse to the fence, they entered and then they settled themselves down in Phillip's snug. This was his escape hole, away from women and their idle chatter. The thought of idle chatter actually appealed to Adam, never having experienced it at home. Phillip called for tea, cake and sherry, he thought it best to organise everything at one swoop, and then they could settle down for as long as necessary.

"What is on your mind, my boy?" enquired the kindly vicar.

"My father has organised a very unfortunate pairing for me, Sir," replied Adam. "My mother and he have gone over to Eathorpe to take tea with Lord and Lady Pembrook, it is their unfortunate daughter that they wish me to marry."

"I am acquainted with the Pembrooks," replied the reverend. "They are an old and established family of considerable wealth I believe."

"Obviously, this is the reason I have been promised to their daughter," said Adam sadly. "I am sure she is a very worthy young woman but not for me."

"She is, in fact, quite an accomplished young lady I believe," was the reply. "I have met her on occasions. She is also very shy and studious."

"Studious, I do not mind at all," said Adam. "In fact, a lively mind is always an asset but I have my mind elsewhere. A much prettier young woman, who is much more to my liking."

Phillip smiled, knowing exactly who Adam was referring to.

"I was about to tell my father that I had it in my mind to ask for a young lady's hand when he sprung this trap to prevent it," continued Adam.

"Maybe he did not have a notion that your heart was lost elsewhere," said Phillip trying to speak kindly of someone it was very difficult to do so.

"I believe that you and I, Sir, know that my father knows everything that is going on within 50 miles of Wetherley, and it is one of his great delights, spoiling everyone's lives," Adam replied with a downcast face.

The look on the reverend's face showed that he agreed, but he did not reply.

"I believe, Sir, that you have known for some time where my heart lies," continued Adam.

"I have noticed a fondness developing between you and my daughter, I cannot deny that," was the reply. "I also have had it brought to my notice that your father, the earl, has taken a liking to Dorothia and has expressed a desire to take her under his wing."

"This is why I felt this was the time to act, after my friend, Thomas Umbers, warned me that my father had noticed Dorothia, I feared for her and your whole family," continued Adam. "I knew you would have the sense to send the girls away from my father's grasp but that would mean she was lost to me as well. It is a dilemma and one that could only be solved if I allow myself to be disinherited, but what use would I be to anyone least of all Dorothia if that happened?"

"None at all, boy," was the reply. "You are indeed in a cleft foot. I will set your mind at rest on one point though, Adam, my daughter thinks highly of you and if I had been asked about a match, I would have welcomed it. I cannot say the same for my good lady wife, she fears your father and actually believes, despite my earnest pleas, that blood will out."

"My goodness, Phillip, I am so sorry that she thinks so ill of me," was the reply.

"Time would have brought her round, my boy."

"It seems, however, that time is something I do not have," said Adam sadly. "I believe I will have to marry the Pembrook woman, much to my annoyance and my father will not see reason."

"I think that is the way your life will develop, my boy, and I, for one, am very sorry for that," replied Phillip, "My daughter will also be very unhappy but I do doubt that the earl would have agreed to the match anyway. I do not have the wealth of the Pembrooks."

"We do not need outsider's money, we are wealthy in our own right," replied Adam. "We both know that it is spite that has made my father choose such a plain and dull woman. He feels I should suffer as he has."

"Having spoken to your dear mother on very few occasions alone, I can only say what I have noticed and that is she is a kind and generous woman with a soft heart.

I have never been privy to her inner thoughts so I cannot vouch for her feelings about your father," said the vicar, choosing his words carefully.

"You are right, of course, Phillip," answered Adam. "I am very fond of my mother but wish she would show some back bone where my father is concerned. He treats her very badly and she never stands her ground."

"My dear boy," replied Phillip, "she is petrified of the bounder and who isn't? She is just a small and delicate being, her kindness to her tenants is boundless, she does at least stand up for them when needs be."

"That is true," agreed Adam with a smile. "Perhaps I do my mother a disservice. I have seen strong men buckle under my father's demands. I assume I will just be another cog in this unending wheel of misery orchestrated by my father."

"You may find your life, does not seem so bad once you get used to what must be," suggested Phillip.

"It will be bad and I will be glad when you send Dorothia a long way away, so I do not have to look at her and compare her to Petunia," was the reply. "You will send her away, won't you, Phillip? Please, for her own safety. Your wife is quite right about my father and his lecherous ways. I do not want to end up like him, driven to seek other women because I am unhappy with a wife I did not want. Please tell me, it will not happen to me."

"I believe in the marriage vows and if you do also, then you will stay true to your wife and maybe even grow to like her at least," replied Phillip. "As for my girls, I had already set the idea in motion of sending them to Brighton as soon as I was made aware of your father's interest in my eldest. My mother-in-law, bless her soul, has a dear friend in Brighton whose middle son married Mary Fitzroy, a lovely young woman who I felt might befriend Dorothia and show her the delights of Brighton. You can be assured that the earl will not get his grubby hands on her, over my dead body will that happen."

Adam smiled, "Then I am happy. Keep her safe and I will obey if needs be but will put the inevitable off as long as I possibly can. Though knowing my father, the notice is probably already in *The Times*."

Phillip laughed. "My guess is that you are right, my boy. He would want to conclude his mischief as quickly as possible."

"Brighton is a city that interests me," said Adam. "I have wanted to visit the Brighton Pavilion ever since it opened, nearly three years ago. I intended some time ago to go and see the Brighton Dome built for the king when he was Prince Regent. My man had reason to go to Brighton and he told me of its splendid appearance. I could not persuade my father to allow me to accompany him, although I tried. Did you know that the Prince Regent used to stable more than 40 horses in the circular stable with room for groomsmen on a balcony above? That has to be some interesting building."

"I have had occasion to visit and your man is quite right, it is an interesting piece of architecture," replied Phillip. "Did you know that the stable is based on the Halle aux blés, the corn exchange, in Paris?"

"At least your daughters will not be bored in Brighton, there is much to see as well as long walks along the Kingsway, the front on the beach," said Adam sadly.

"Royalty has taken an interest in Brighton for many years, the king's belief that the sea air is good for gout has drawn many wealthy families to the region," replied Phillip.

"In any case, I hope Dorothia meets someone suitable who will appreciate her fully. I believe I can be happy if I know she is. Goodness knows that I wish I could just run away to Brighton."

Phillip poured a glass of sherry for him and Adam; they then sat back in large leather heavily studded chairs in front of the fire in silence for a while. The cake was home made by Bathsheba, Phillip's wife, and was delicious; they both wondered if she would have sent her best cake, had she known who the visitor in the snug was?

Chapter 15
The Accident, 1826

Phillip and Adam were enjoying the peace and quiet with a glass of sherry and a warm inviting fire in the rectory snug when suddenly the peace was broken by loud shouting from outside. Phillip sprung to his feet, followed closely by Adam, and they went outside to see a group of ruddy faced individuals all talking at once in excited voices. The oldest of the group, a man of about 50, with the appearance of a farm-worker hurried over to them.

"What is the meaning of this noise?" demanded the vicar.

"There has been a terrible accident," came the reply.

"What sort of accident?" asked Adam alarmed.

"I am sorry to be the one to tell you, young Sir, but your father's gig, the wheel came lose, he was going too fast and it crashed," was the reply from the group's spokesperson. He held his cap in his hand as he spoke.

"Crashed, where?" demanded Adam.

"On the Eathorpe Road, about an hour since."

"What of my mother? Is she hurt?" asked Adam, by now looking rather anguished.

"She is gone, Sir, the doctor said that her neck snapped as she fell from the gig." The man put his arm out to steady the young Lord, who looked likely to faint. "They say it was quick and she would not have felt a thing."

"Only fear but she has always been used to that. And my father? Is he dead also?" Adam asked, not really caring about the answer and assuming it was so.

"Oh yes, young Sir," was the expected reply. "He is well gone, Sir, it did not go so easy for him, he was thrown from the gig and pinned underneath it. He was still alive when they were found by a passing shepherd and in great pain. He lived on for maybe a quarter of an hour before the pain became too great and he succumbed to his injuries."

"Really man," said the vicar, alarmed. "Do you have to give such graphic details, it is this young man's father after all."

Adam placed his hand on Phillip's arm. "It is fine, my friend, I needed to know and this man was kind enough to tell me everything."

The man was twisting his cap in his hand. "I am sorry to say, young Sir, that your father will not be missed."

"How dare you?" shouted Phillip.

Adam smiled. "It is good to speak to an honest fellow." He held his hand out to the carrier of news as he spoke and they shook hands, much to the farm worker's surprise.

"I do not want you to think that we did not do all we could, Sir," continued the spokesman. "I ran for the doctor myself and the law has been notified. They have taken the gig to make sure that it has not been tampered with."

"Tampered with?" repeated Adam. "Surely they do not suspect foul play, it was an accident for sure. My father is known to race about in a dangerous manner."

"He was also a very unpopular man, Sir, many will be happy to hear of his passing," was the reply. "They have already questioned the Duggan boy's father."

"Why would they do such a thing?" asked Phillip.

"Surely you know, Father," was the reply. "Little Arron Duggan was knocked down and killed by the earl only last week."

"That was never proven surely," asked Phillip, shocked.

"Of course, it wasn't proven, never would be even if 100 men witnessed it," came a voice from the distant crowd. "But we all know who did for the boy and drove on without checking if he was breathing his last or not."

"And what of all the fine bred men's wives who the earl had taken to his bed," the group laughed coarsely. "One of those could have paid a groom to loosen a nut here and there."

The group of ruddy-faced men came closer, feeling braver. Another one spoke, "And what of old Bill Prout, his foot snapped in a man trap and left to die all because he was on his way to confront the earl about his daughter, Freda."

"That was just rumour, the poor man could have wondered off the path and fallen into a trap," suggested the vicar.

This comment caused a ripple of laughter amongst the assembled group.

"And I suppose it was a coincidence that the poacher, his lordship, shot last month, was also the husband of the new laundry maid who he attacked the day before!" came one voice.

Adam looked about him in horror. "My God, is this all true?" he begged. "God knows my father is, or was, a man not to cross but do you really believe he would kill in cold blood?"

"I believe he would and he has and he would see it as his right of birth," was the reply.

"I would like to say that I doubt you all but I cannot," said the young sir with a heavy heart, he turned to Phillip as he continued to speak quietly. "No wonder your wife does not want me anywhere near her daughter. Take the girls to Brighton out of this mess."

Phillip nodded and placed his hand gently on Adam's shoulder.

A rider joined the group and almost leapt from his stead. It was Martin, Adam's man servant, who had been looking for his master to try to give him the bad news before it reached him by other means.

"Sir, I am so sorry," he began. "I see I am too late to give you the terrible news. No one thought to come to the lodge and inform us until not so long past."

"Martin, I am glad to see you," replied Adam. "I am not clear in my mind what to do but first, I would like to see my mother if it is possible. Could someone show me the way, please?"

"No need, Sir," replied Martin. "They took her up to Weston Manor Lodge, she is at your home waiting for a Christian burial, your Lordship."

"Oh no, I am not the earl yet," said Adam, shocked at being refer to so nobly, he looked at the ground for a while and then realised that he was, in fact, now Lord

Adam Southerly, Earl of Wetherley. "And Martin, my father...is he up at the lodge as well?"

"No, Sir," came the reply. "They have taken him to the coroner in Wessex to make sure that he was not killed illegally. If you will excuse me speaking plainly, my guess is that he was in his cups and driving like a madman and hit a stone."

"My thoughts exactly," replied the new earl. "I have no desire to view his body, so let them do as they will. I would like to go now, however, and see my mother."

With that, the young earl walked over to his horse, untied it and rode off with his man servant at his side towards Weston Manor Lodge looking as pale as death itself.

Chapter 16
The Funerals

Phillip Mountjoy went ahead with his plans to send his daughters to Brighton having already sent a letter off to Lady Mary Bradbury, who he was acquainted with through his mother-in-law, Seraphina. They had already taken the coach to Brighton before the funeral of Lord and Lady Southerly took place.

All the servants at Weston Manor Lodge were instructed to go into mourning, which meant that the new earl had to provide suitable clothing for them all. He, himself, went into deep mourning for his mother.

A few days after the accident, the body of the late earl was released but Adam found it a very difficult task to get any local undertaker to take charge of this father's remains. It was as if they believed the devil itself would transfer itself into them if they touch such an evil man. His mother caused no such a problem.

Lady Southerly was laid to rest first. It was a beautiful sunny day and the new earl was pleased to see quite a few of the local people attend the service. He had organised for his mother's remains to be carried in a glass carriage pulled by four beautiful black horses. The horses themselves shone in the sun and their mains and tails were laced with red ribbons, Agnes' favourite colour.

He did not notice at first a stranger in the crowd, a man of obvious quality and bearing. He was tall and fashionably dressed in what looked like expensive mourning attire, which suggested that he must be related or at the very least, a good friend of the late earl or his wife. He had dark hair and eyes and supported a thin moustache.

It was when Adam got up to do the reading that he noticed the gentleman, who had arrived very quietly and slipped into the back pew of the church. Adam spoke in a clear loud voice and finished his allotted reading by adding that he felt his mother would be at peace now at last. Everyone who had ever had dealings with his father knew exactly what he meant.

Adam sat back down and instructed Martin to try to ascertain who the gentleman at the back of the church was. As soon as the service concluded, Adam tried to find the strange man to discover his interest in the occasion, but he had disappeared as quickly as he had appeared. Martin was not in sight so Adam hoped that meant he had maybe followed the gentleman, which was exactly what had happened. He had not stayed to see Lady Southerly taken to the crypt, Adam and the vicar were the only people to follow the casket to its final resting place.

Later in the day, Martin sought his master out to tell him what he had discovered. It seems that he had followed the stranger as he left the church and watched him walk towards an awaiting coach, catching him up just before he could climb into it. The gentleman was at first alarmed assuming Martin to be a footpad. Once Martin explained who he was and his role as regarding the Earl of Wetherley, the gentleman relaxed. The gentleman was, in fact, Agnes', Lady Southerly's brother, Lord John Fisher, who had not seen his sister for many years due to a falling out with the late Earl George Southerly. His sister had ran to him on one occasion when the late earl had beaten her rather badly, and he had gone to confront the bully only to be threatened at gun point and told that if he interfered, Agnes would suffer. He had never entered any property owned or lived in by George Southerly ever again and was feeling very guilty that he had left his sister in the hands of such an evil tyrant. He had never met Adam but had realised at the service that the young earl was more like his mother than father but did not believe that he would have been very welcomed as a relative. He had read about the coming funeral in *The Times*, having read that the earl and his wife's funerals were to be held separately. He felt compelled to see his sister laid to rest with a heavy heart that he had not done anything to help her whilst she lived. He handed Martin his calling card and told him that if and when Adam felt able to contact him, he would be very pleased to make his acquaintance. Adam was not sure if he wanted to know a man who would knowingly leave a woman, as delicate as his mother, with a monster but he put the card safely away.

Adam had to send for a man from Warwick and pay him a goodly sum, well over the normal, to deal with the funeral of his father. No one attended beside Adam, Martin and the vicar. Even member's from his father's club and gentlemen who had been considered his friends stayed away. It had been fine whilst the man was alive to spend lively evenings in his company, hunt on his land or even share some of his more unsavoury interests, but they did not want to be seen as friends of him as now he had no influence. Once shared interests, mistresses and best forgotten habits were swept under the carpet. Adam thought it rather sad that someone could go through life without a single real friend.

The service was short and to the point followed by the casket being interned in the family crypt.

Obviously, both parents were placed in the family crypt and that again caused further problems for the new earl; he could not find a local mason to add the late earl's name to the inscriptions. No one wanted to speak his name, let alone carve it in stone. The problem was eventually overcome by allowing a new apprentice to practice his skills.

Adam's distress did not end there, evil derogatory slogans were written on the crypt entrance denouncing the late earl to be the devil's right-hand man. At first, Adam tried to make the crypt good and clean it, but he soon realised that he was wasting his time and decided to wait until everyone got bored of this practice. Martin had found his master one time in great distress in the church yard and had managed to persuade him to leave with a great amount of difficulty.

"My mother did not deserve this," Adam said as he left. "Let the devil take him but my mother was a good person."

Chapter 17
Brighton

Dorothia and her younger sisters, Everline and Elizabeth, arrived in Brighton to spend the summer with Sir Gerald Bradbury and his wife, Lady Mary, who was heavily pregnant with her long awaited near first full-term baby. Lady Mary was looking forward to having other women around her at this time. Sir Gerald and Lady Mary had been married for seven years and in that time, she had miscarried several times, much to her dismay. Sir Gerald is several years older than her and he was beginning to believe that he would never be a father when this miracle occurred and now Lady Mary was close to her delivery date.

Sir Gerald is not a well man and suffers from lumbago, probably caused by a fall from his horse a few years earlier; he is, as a result, in constant pain and keeps himself to himself, rarely travelling outside the confines of his own home.

Happily they live in a very smart part of Brighton in a very large Georgian property, fairly near the Esplanade, the sea and the new splendid Brighton Pavilion.

The hallway of the Bradbury residence was full of luggage of all sizes, there was a remarkable number of hat boxes and large trunks. Usually when Sir Gerald and Lady Mary have visitors, they come singularly or in couples and the servants are used to handling large amounts of luggage, but no one had prepared the household for the amount of luggage that three young women might bring with them.

Mary greeted the young women like long lost relatives, she was so pleased to have company for a while.

"You have just missed so much excitement here in Brighton," said Lady Mary. "That wonderful painter, John Constable, was here for two whole weeks with his family. You could watch him putting paint to canvas, everyone was so thrilled."

"I would have loved to have seen him work," said Dorothia, excited.

"He was here a couple of years ago and was captivated by the sea, the birds and the breakers so he returned to sketch more," said Mary. "Brighton was all a buzz. Of course, his dear wife, Marie, is here most of the time, she has been struck down by tuberculosis and everyone knows that the sea air is the best cure for most ailments."

"It is a terrible illness," said Dorothia sadly. "I have seen many taken by it myself."

"Now, now girls, you have not come to Brighton to be despondent, you are here for a break from country life, the sea air will bring a bloom to your cheeks," said Mary with a smile.

Once shown to their rooms, it did not take the girls long to settle in. Dorothia was given a room to herself and Everline and Elizabeth shared, as they did in Wetherley. They were too tired from their journey to argue when Mary suggested an early night after supper and an early start in the morning.

Mary was very heavy with child so she felt it best not to walk too far; she did, however, need a shift dress collected from Mrs Tattam, the dress maker, having grown a little large for her present clothes, even the ones she had allowed to be let out. After a light breakfast, Mary asked a couple of the servants to act as escorts and show the three young ladies the immediate vicinity and to pop into number four Charles Street to pick up the package that was waiting for collection. Dorothia was more than happy to stroll about Brighton and take in the sights, her sisters were not quite so enthusiastic but they intended to all leave together accompanied by two of the servants.

"It would not do to have you young country girls wandering alone in the little back streets of Brighton," said Mary with a serious expression on her face. "We do not have a lot of crime here about but we are all worldly town people and know how to take care of ourselves. After all, your father has sent you here for your safety so I must make sure that I comply with his wishes."

"My father probably told you that we have had a dangerous threat hanging over Weston-Under-Wetherley for a great many years," replied Dorothia. "It has gone now and we will all sleep the better for it."

"By it, I assume, you mean the late Lord George Southerly," answered Mary.

"That I do, Lady Mary," was the reply. "He was the reason father decided that my sisters and I needed to look beyond our little village."

"Your dear grandmother, Seraphina, has always kept my mother-in-law up to date with the coming and goings at the village," said Mary.

"What is her interest in the village, might I be so bold as to ask?" enquired Dorothia.

"Lady Bradbury, my mother-in-law, was born just outside your present home, she is actually a distant cousin of George Southerly," replied Mary.

"Really, I did not know that," said Dorothia.

"No reason why you should, child," was the reply. "Lady Bradbury keeps that information very much close to her chest and the more she heard about George Southerly, the quieter she became about the connection. Gerald's late father chose to ignore that side of the family, they are very distant cousins after all."

"Sometimes, it is useful to have distant cousins if they are distinguished," added Elizabeth in an innocent way.

"There is a difference between distinguished and notorious," replied Mary. They all nodded in agreement.

"That does not explain how you know my grandmother," continued Dorothia.

"Your grandmother, Seraphina, became friends with Lady Bradbury senior before she married and after she moved from Wetherley," Mary explained. "They were both quite young and living in Bath, both from good families. I met Gerald in Bath at an assembly ball. So you see, our families are intertwined."

Dorothia smiled and nodded.

"Lady Bradbury was also acquainted with Lord John Fisher in her youth," added Mary.

"I do not recognise that name, Lady Mary, who is he?" Dorothia asked.

"He is the brother of Lady Agnes, George Southerly's poor, now deceased, wife," continued Mary, "He was much taken with the daughter of a mutual friend of your grandmother's but when his sister married George Southerly, he was treated like a leper."

"Do you mean that the man was evil even before he married Adam's mother?" asked Dorothia.

"Some people, I believe, are born evil. Strange, because his father was a good, hard-working man, there was some story of lack of breath during his birth that cause damage to his brain," was the reply. "Lord John chose to cut himself off from his sister so as not to have his good name muddied by George Southerly; something he regretted later when the poor woman was treated so badly and called out for help."

"He knew that Lady Agnes was being ill-used then?" said Dorothia sadly.

"Everyone did but marriage vows are taken very seriously by aristocracy when convenient. It seems it is fine for a man to behave badly towards his wife, physically or mentally, but if she were to step out of line, that is a different matter," was the reply.

"Adam, the late earl's son, told me that his mother feared Lord Southerly very much, as did he," said Dorothia most distressed. "No one should have to live like that. I will be very careful when I marry."

"You will have a great many offers, Dorothia, a woman of your looks and baring; think yourself lucky that you do not have the standing in the world that some have and you might be able to choose your own path," replied Mary. "I too was lucky but I know of others that have followed orders from their parents and married very unhappily."

"The late Earl of Wetherley was just about to marry his son, Adam, to a young woman called Petunia Pembrook, Lord Pembrook of Warwickshire's daughter, purely for the money," said Dorothia.

"You seem uncommonly familiar with this young earl, young lady," replied Lady Mary. "Some might say that he is a touch above your station, now he is an earl."

"I suppose you are right, Madam, but we grew up together and he was always very level headed and almost ordinary," Dorothia replied thoughtfully.

"Not too ordinary I hope, after all, he is an earl. From what I have learnt from your grandmother, it was to stop any ideas the young man may have had to marry you," was Lady Mary's reply.

Dorothia blushed, "We have never had such a conversation but I had always hoped that we might marry one day. I can see that I might have overstepped the mark, now he is nobility, though my father is the youngest son of a low titled gentleman."

"I know of the Pembrooks, they are a very well-known family, very wealthy but with a very plain, sickly daughter. Lord Pembrook had approached a few families previously to speaking to George Southerly, everyone of consequence knows what is occurring all over the country," said Mary with a smile. "Unfortunately, because the young woman is not of a strong constitution and most high ranking families are interested in the continuation of the family line, poor Petunia has never been considered a very good catch despite the family wealth."

"Oh dear, I feel almost sorry for the poor woman. It is a very small world, is it not, Lady Mary?" replied Dorothia. "My father is of good birth but being the youngest, this did not help him financially."

"Money is good but breeding is better," replied Mary, nodding and smiling as she spoke. "Carry yourself well and speak clearly in a cultured manor and the world will open for you."

Lady Mary then spoke to the older of the two servants being sent on the exploring Brighton mission.

"Take very good care of my temporary wards, Rogers, show them about the lanes and the esplanade, we can save the pavilion and museums for another day," she said. "And if you could please call in at Mr Potter's, the fishmonger, a couple of doors away from Mrs Tattam and pick up the salmon I ordered for tomorrows supper. Thank you, off you all go, I am going to lie down for a while."

Lord Bradbury did not really approve of his wife wandering about Brighton, ordering such things as Salmon; he used to remind her that they employed a cook and other servants for such menial work. Mary enjoyed a walk and looking at stalls, she was a practical young woman who liked to know what was going on about her and the price of goods.

The group standing in the hall left on their first adventure in Brighton, the ladies all adjusted their bonnets and with broad smiles, said their goodbyes to Lady Mary.

Dorothia and her sisters could not believe the amount of traders, all resident in Charles Street—builders, greengrocers, tailors, dressmakers, plumbers, confectioners and more alongside lodging houses. You had to travel a far distant from Weston-Under-Wetherley to obtain the services of these trades and buy these goods. Dorothia was amazed to see everything you could need, all there in one street.

Rogers was very informed about the history of Brighton and took a great delight in telling Dorothia and her sisters that how Charles Street is still referred to as 'Little Laine' by old timers in Brighton, it is situated between the seafront road to Rottingdean and the Leakway. There are a great many lodging houses to accommodate better off families wishing to escape smoke-filled cities and take of the sea air.

Rogers pointed out that Charles Street consisted of 16 houses but there were other about to be built between Charles Street and Broad Street. The houses all have bow-fronted windows or three-sided, bay-fronted windows to give more light and a feeling of spaciousness inside and to afford a sea view. Every house is slightly different in appearance due to them each being built at separate times. Many of the houses are clad in mathematical tiles to create a look similar to brickwork but to avoid the brick tax. The black shiny, glazed tiles laid on the timber exterior have a rather majestic look.

Rogers made a point of showing his charges the newly constructed Royal Albion Hotel built in the very latest Regency style and opposite Brighton Pier. He had a great deal of pride in his voice as he described the interior.

"Brighton is a very fashionable place to live and visit," explained Rogers. "It became so back in 1783 when the Prince of Wales, now our good king, God bless him, embraced Brighton as his seaside residence." He took his cap off as he spoke and held it near his heart. "That and the healing powers of the sea brought Brighton to the public's attention."

"It certainly is a very exciting place to be, Rogers," said Elizabeth. "And street lighting!"

Rogers laughed, "Yes, we have had street lighting for many years, some streets longer than others; in the area around Charles Street, it did not appear until 1802."

"We still walk about in the dark in Wetherley, though I remember that we did have street lighting when we lived in Birmingham a few years ago," said Elizabeth.

They walked around the sea front and looked at the bathing area for ladies and the bathing huts.

"If my lady will permit me," said Rogers, "I would like to show you the Royal Pavilion later in your visit. It is a marvel to behold. Our king, when Prince of Wales took out a lease on Thomas Read Kemp's farmhouse, right where the Pavilion stands today. Between 1795 and 1802, while in partnership with John Nash, Humphry Repton carried out landscape work in the Pavilion grounds. The king, then Prince Regent, acquired the land where the Pavilion now stands."

"How do you know so much about Brighton Rogers? It is a wonder to hear you speak," enquired Dorothia.

"I have always had a healthy interest in history and since I learnt to read and write, an equal interest in books," was the reply. "We are lucky enough to have a wonderful library and meeting place ran by Mr Tuppen and situated between Manchester and Charles Street. There is a wonderful historic section with maps and sketches of Brighton. You would not believe how often I go there."

"You sound very much like a good friend of mine, Lord Adam Southerly, he loves architecture and history," said Dorothia smiling to herself.

"He would love the pavilion then," was the reply. "There is an amazing Indian influence, although the building was originally just to house His Majesties horses and a riding school; happily now, it is put to better use and the grounds are magnificent."

"I, for one, cannot wait to see the library and the pavilion," said Dorothia.

Rogers, his assistant and the ladies all arrived back at Lady Mary's place, very tired and hungry. Their first day in Brighton was the start of a very busy and exciting visit.

Dorothia received a letter from Adam Southerly telling her about his latest adventures, its arrival caused a considerable stir. She read it to herself first before reading it to her sisters. The first letter was rather depressing giving her details of his parents' demise, and he wrote of the trouble he had experienced getting a funeral director and stone mason to deal with his father's remains. He told Dorothia how much her father had been a great help to him using any influence he had to sort out some of his problems, and how many miles his man, Martin, had to go to find someone who would engrave the old earl's details on the family crypt.

Dorothy expressed how cruel she found this as it was not Adam's fault that his father has so hated. Her sisters, however, reminded her that they were in Brighton because of that man and what he may have had in store for her if they had stayed and he had lived. Dorothia shuddered at the thought.

A second letter followed shortly explaining how Adam was busy trying to right every wrong his father had ever done and it was not an easy task. He had only gone into deep mourning for a month, for his mother only, although it was expected that the Manor House should stay in mourning for at least six months. He added that it was hard to mourn someone when people were actually dancing with joy at his passing.

Three months after the girls arrived in Brighton, Lady Mary went into labour and delivered a healthy daughter, which was named Amy Mary; Amy was the name of a friend of hers young daughter who she had always been fond of. Mary was remarkably well after the birth and regained her strength very quickly with the help of Dorothia and Everline, who found that they enjoyed taking care of the new addition.

Mary received a letter from Dorothia's grandmother telling her that one of the great houses in Weston-Under-Wetherley, Weston Hall—the ancient mansion of the Throckmortons, which stood on the left side of the road leading from Olney to Weston, just outside the village—had been entirely demolished; she did not have the details of why. Dorothia was most alarmed thinking it was the home of the Umbers, but Mary pointed out that there was more than one Weston Hall, this was the Throckmortons Manor House.

Many young possible suitors called at Lady Mary's and many invitations were received for the sisters to take tea and attend dances. The arrival of three very comely, intelligent and rather handsome young women had caused a bit of a stir in Brighton. Dorothia showed no interest in any of the likely bows and spent the majority of her time exploring Brighton, horse riding or in the library. She was quite content but beginning to miss her old life.

Dorothia showed no interest in any of the likely bows that came calling, but Everline very soon became engaged to a young man of the cloth. Like her father, he was the youngest son of a minor noble and as such, the family fortune and title had passed him by. He was, however, very suited to his calling and embraced it willingly. They were to be married in what Dorothia considered to be indecent haste because the young vicar had been offered the post of a travelling vicar, filling in where there was sickness. This gave the young newly-weds a chance to travel the length of England and see more than their previous lives had allowed. Dorothia thought that her sister should have taken longer to get acquainted before accepting the young man's troth.

Because Brighton was the hub of fashion, it was easy for Lady Mary to organise fittings for the wedding and brides maids' dresses, something that would, have been much more difficult in a small village like Wetherley. She thoroughly enjoyed the experience herself and gave Everline some very fine lace to trim her gown. Dorothia did wonder if maybe her mother might be disappointed in missing out on this part of the wedding arrangements and suggested to her sisters that they wait until they return home to go to Wessex and look for a suitable head piece for the day with their mother.

Despite the excitement of Brighton, Dorothia had almost decided that it was time for her to return to the family home and hopefully, the Earl of Southerly. She made up her mind that she would only return after going back for her sister's wedding for a short time. She had missed Adam and was beginning to believe that he would spend the rest of his life looking for rights to wrong and would forget her if she was not careful. He had already said in one of his letters that he felt he could never ask for anyone's hand until he could make the name Southerly one to respect again.

Chapter 18
Life Drags On

Whilst the Miss Mountjoy's were still in Brighton, *The Times* ran a large and very graphic article on the late earl's demise and life; the piece was eclipsed in interest only by Robert Jenkinson, 2nd Earl of Liverpool's dramatic win for the Tories over the Whigs on June 19th.

Stories ran in *The Times* and gazette for several months, people came forward to make claims against the late earl's character. Martin kept careful notes of each accusation, whilst Adam was growing more and more embarrassed about the bloodline he had once been so proud of. Speculation went on for months over the possible reasons why the gig had capsized? It was the general opinion of the locals that someone with a grudge against the earl had loosened the wheel; the list of suspects was endless from scullery maids to Barons.

Although several lesser people could have been considered likely candidates for the killing, Adam was also considered a possibility. After all, the engagement to Petunia Pembrook was immediately cancelled and that was to his liking.

Most people were in agreement that Adam would not have harmed his mother and whoever did cause the crash if, in fact, it was not an accident after all, did everyone a favour. Unfortunately, mud does stick and Adam felt that his every move was now being watched.

The stories travelled as far as Brighton and Lady Mary was quite alarmed that the young women that she had cared for were in contact with someone of such notoriety, warranted or not.

There was an inquest and Adam returned to Wessex to attend it and was exonerated but rumours persist. The inquest was reported in full as it was of great interest to many. Stories about the late earl in *The Times* painted him as a vile lecher and bully which, of course, he was, so Adam, as the new earl, had his hands full trying to rebuild the reputation of the Southerlys. He put all thoughts of Dorothia from his head and concentrated on building up the trust of his employees. He started by following through with his mother's work. He paid regular visits to his workers cottages and tried to bring them up from the hovels they clearly were to habitable accommodation. The men continued to hide their women folk when they saw their lord of the manor approaching, something that Adam at first found insulting and annoying but he became used to.

One Sunday, the Reverend Mountjoy took it upon himself to speak out for his young friend, who he had watched struggling from afar. It was a very full church that day and the sun was shining through the ornate stain glass windows. He followed his usual service pattern and when it was time to make his sermon, he spoke about Adam instead of from the scriptures.

"I am happy to see such a good turn out today because I want to speak to you about something that affects us all," he began. All eyes were upon him, including Adam's. "We have amongst us today his Lordship, the young Earl of Wetherley, most of you work on his estate. I want to ask you all one thing, have your wages increased since the young earl took charge?"

People looked one to the other and nodded.

"And also, do your cottage roofs now keep out the rain?"

Once again, they all nodded.

"So I ask you all, have your lives improved since the demise of the old earl?"

There were cries of yes and aye.

"Then why do you continue to treat our young earl like a leper? He is not his father, he is his mother's son that is for sure; she tried to be kind and the new earl is trying to follow her lead. Can you not see into your hearts and help this young man? Do you not think that he too suffered under his father?" The reverend looked round the church as he spoke and could see that he had touched a nerve; many blushed, others muttered to those seated nearest to them.

The reverend finished the service in his usual way and waited outside to greet his parishioners as they left. As was the custom, Adam left the church ahead of the rabble and he grasped Phillip's hand warmly. "I thank you, my friend, for your support," he said with a smile.

"You deserve all the support I can give you and more."

The rest of the congregation slowly trailed out and a couple of the older men made a point of doffing their hats to the young earl as they passed. He felt that maybe at last, a great cloud may have started to lift.

Slowly, more and more young women remained at home when they reached puberty and were not rushed off to the safety of relatives that could hardly afford to house their own, let alone extra children. Adam watched as his workers became friendlier and easier to approach without the look of fear in their eyes. But he was always aware of them expecting him to fall into bad ways. It became obvious, however, that there were some that would never believe that anyone called Southerly was worth a second chance.

The Reverend Mountjoy wrote to his daughters in Brighton towards the end of their stay there and told them how he had spoken up for the young earl in church and hoped it would be a turning point for him as he was trying so hard. Dorothia took great delight in reading this missive out loud to all and sundry.

One piece of good news reached the young earl and that was the intended marriage of Petunia Pembrook to the eldest son of a Baron. He grimaced at the thought of that poor young man being possibly forced into marriage with the very plain Miss Pembrook, for all her money.

It was a few months after his father and mother's accident when Adam took all his courage and went up the rectory to approach Phillip and inquire after Dorothia. He had been careful not to mention her after church and had only spoken to Phillip in a casual way. He luckily saw Phillip in the garden and did not have to actually knock on the front door. He was still a little afraid that Phillip's wife might chase him off with a broom. Phillip looked up, smiled broadly and walked over to greet his visitor.

"I wondered how long it might be before you came to visit, I miss our talks," he said kindly.

"Not as much as I do, Phillip, of that I am sure," Adam replied. "I have been keeping a very low profile since the accident. As you know rumours are still rife, was it me? Was it an angry wronged husband? Or maybe, even a kitchen maid whose virtue had been stolen. I can tell you, Phillip, I am sick of it. I would if I could just retire to our family home in Keighley; it is a substantial property, well maintained by our interests in the weaving trade. I could lose myself there and hope that the rumours do not follow me."

"But they will, my boy, they will be there before you," replied the vicar. "Where exactly is Keighley?"

"It is a small town, not far from Bradford in Yorkshire," replied Adam, "I have never really liked it there but my father preferred it to Weston-Under-Wetherley; more life, I imagine, whereas it is quiet here and only the hunting and shooting pleased him and the weather, of course, which is better in this region. We, Southerly's, own a large manor house in Keighley, originally funded by a very broad-minded, a forward thinking grandfather of mine. The family have always had property thereabouts. My grandfather saw the coming of the cloth industry and settled where he could build a large place to house workers that would have otherwise been working from inside their cottages, wool spinning and weaving cloth. I hope I do not bore you, Phillip."

"On the contrary, my boy, I am always interested in how people have developed," he replied.

"My grandfather was a good man, I assure you of that, Sir. There has only been one such monster as my father as far as I know, and I am learning more about him every day unfortunately. Most day, I read in the library and look through old letters and documents. It is quite an eye opener," Adam said starting to get enthusiastic about this insight into his past. "I have learnt that my grandfather, who I was named after, was a great friend of a man called Daniel Salt; they were friendly rivals in the woollen business, each trying to poach the others' employees, enticing them with money and shorter hours. The Salts lived in manor farm in Crofton near Wakefield. My grandfather and Daniel tried to outdo each other in all things, each trying to build their manors larger than the others, if I am reading correctly, it was all done with humour."

"Life is always better with a little humour," interrupted Phillip with a laugh in his voice.

"Oh dear, I am so sorry, I am starting to bore you," said Adam.

"Not at all, my boy," was the reply. "It is good to hear you talking so enthusiastically about something again, you have been so down."

"I have found it all very interesting," replied Adam. "My father did not share anything with my mother or me. I know far more since his demise than I ever knew before. I know the Yorkshire enterprise runs well in the hands of managers and overseers and that my father was never hands on like his father before him."

"I think you might have guessed that Adam," said Phillip. "So long as the money rolled in."

"Quite," replied Adam. "I have it in my mind to go to Keighley and look in on the workplace. I am a little concerned that as my father did not care how his farm workers lived, maybe he felt the same way about his weavers' and spinners' working conditions."

"I have no doubt, Adam, that you will be most distressed when you visit the source of your income. I think your late father, and I hate to speak ill of the dead, cared very little for anyone or anything besides his own pleasures."

"You are right, Phillip, and I fear I must make it my mission to set right all the wrongs my father made," replied Adam.

"You have set yourself a mammoth task, boy," replied Phillip.

"I have a purpose, Sir," said Adam.

"Which is?" came the reply.

"To make my name one that people respect, so I can ask your daughter to share it."

"Ah! I wondered when we would come round to Dorothia," said the vicar smiling. "Before you ask, my boy. Yes, she is still in Brighton and no, she has not met a young buck there that has taken her fancy; I fear that despite being taken everywhere and being introduced to everyone, she spends most of her time with Lady Mary and apparently, bores the woman to death talking about you."

Adam almost clapped his hands but thought better of it, he just grinned widely.

"My wife is most displeased," continued Phillip. "She still thinks you are the devil's spawn and never misses a chance to tell the girl."

"That is not so good," said Adam.

"I will say lad though, Bathsheba was almost impressed when word reached her of the kindness you bestowed upon that young woman in Offchurch recently." Phillip said with a smile. "Do not look so coy, the young woman you took from almost slavery and brought to your doorstep. Of course, Bathsheba thought at first, it was your father all over again."

"You mean Sally," said Adam. "I was afraid that people might think that I had an alternative purpose for the young woman. She is, in fact, my half-sister."

"So I understand," replied Phillip. "Bathsheba took it into her head to discover all there was to know about the woman."

"I am happy for people to know who Sally is, I only wish I had thought about her sooner, not that I could have done anything until my father was out of the way." Adam continued. "Her mother was my governess, Miss Maud Minford, she was a good teacher, very patient and kind. My father threw her into the street when she became pregnant with his child. I remember it as if it were yesterday, my mother cried a river but our hands were tied. I came upon Sally quite by chance at the market. She looked so downtrodden and bruised and yet there was something familiar about her. I spoke to her, not knowing who she was, and she told me her story. I then could see that she had the look of her poor mother, I was so ashamed."

"Did you check the story or just take the woman's word?" asked Phillip concerned.

"I was tempted to take it on face value but Martin, my man, became insistent that he be allowed to look closely into the woman's past. He has taken a great weight off my shoulders since the passing of my father and has given me a lot of strength and good advice. I had checks made into her past just to be sure," replied Adam. "Her poor mother had become very ill and had sold Sally as a child to a man, who beat her and worked the girl half to death. He in turn sold her on like a piece of meat. I had to pay a large sum to free the girl and I am sure her owner thought that I had dubious reasons for buying her."

"People who do bad, think the worst in others," added Phillip.

"I only hope no one else thinks that I have bought her for a mistress," said Adam.

"I think, without sounding insensitive," said Phillip, "you would have chosen a more desirable young woman to seduce."

"She will look fine enough once she is well and dressed accordingly," was the reply.

"What are you intensions?" asked the vicar interested.

"I must admit that I acted on impulse, I did not really think through the implications of housing this half-sister. I am going to have her educated further so she can maybe teach in a village school; it is what she wishes and we could do with a local school," replied Adam, "She has a little knowledge and can read and write quite well, taught by her mother, of course. Her mother also, having worked in a fine house, taught her some of the niceties that went with good breeding. She speaks quite well and holds herself upright. I am settling her in the lodge with a chaperone, providing a tutor; it is her dream, and will make sure that she never wants for anything. She has had almost 20 very hard years, it stops now."

Adam and Phillip were so engrossed in conversation that they did not hear Bathsheba approach. She coughed to attract their attention and they both span round.

"I was listening to your tale, Sir, and very commendable it was as well. If I was you, I would not tell too many people of your blood link to the woman, Sally; she will attract unwanted suitors after your money," she said wisely and almost kindly.

"I believe you are right, Madam, but for proprieties sake, I need people to know why she lodges within the walls of my home," said the earl with a bow. "I thank you humbly for your advice though and feel you might be right about unwanted interest from young men."

"Had you also considered that the earl, if we are to believe half of what has been said about him, might have other halflings out there that might want to make your acquaintance when they hear of your kindness to this young woman?"

Adam looked shocked at the thought of this.

"You cannot right every wrong. Also, the woman has a cough that might need attending." Bathsheba continued, "I believe that she might have a touch of consumption."

"My goodness, I had not noticed," replied the earl genuinely concerned. "I will seek medical advice immediately, thank you for bringing this to my attention. I do not want to lose her so quickly after becoming acquainted. I doubt she had ever eaten well."

Bathsheba curtsied a quick dip and told her husband that she had only come out to tell him that his dinner was on the table.

"Time for me to go then," said Adam.

"It would seem so, boy," replied Phillip. "I am happy you stopped by, I am also happy my wife chose that moment to listen in; she will spread the news, you will be ascending into sainthood before the week is out."

Adam laughed for the first time in over a year. "I am glad I called too, Sir. Can I just ask one thing?"

"Ask away, boy," was the reply.

"If I gave you a missive for your daughter, would she receive it?" he asked. "I want to tell her about Sally."

"With my good wishes, boy," Phillip replied.

With that, Adam turned and walked towards his horse and headed back to the lodge.

On arriving home, the young earl's first job was to send one of his servants to fetch the local doctor. He was very annoyed with himself that he had not considered getting medical advice sooner.

His second job was to sit with pen and paper and compose a short letter to Dorothia telling her how his life had changed since the accident and telling her that he hoped she would receive him in Brighton sometime soon. He tried not to leave anything out, telling her about Sally and how he had found her and taken her in. He did not want Dorothia to hear any half-truths. He also told her of his fear that his promise to right all his father's wrongs might prove to be a very costly business.

Chapter 19
Sally

Doctor Gordan did not arrive at Weston Manor Lodge until the following day having been told that the matter was not urgent. Having been shown into the sitting room and offered a glass of Madeira, which he declined, he waited patiently for the earl to appear.

"So sorry, Doctor," said the earl, slightly out of breath, to the doctor. "I was just walking in the garden, I did not see you approach."

The doctor had not met the earl before and was quite taken aback by his informal approach. He bowed gracefully and asked how he could be of assistance.

"It is a delicate matter, Doctor," began the earl. "I have my half-sister staying here with me. She is not yet 20 years old and has a cough that seems to be more frequent and laboured than I believe to be healthy. Please sit down, Doctor, I will not take up too much of our valuable time but I need to explain a few points."

The doctor scanned the room for what looked like a comfortable seat and the earl sat himself close by. The doctor was by now intrigued and very keen to hear what the earl had to say.

"As I said, the young woman is my half-sister. I would assume that you have heard many stories about improprieties conducted by my father. This poor girl is, in fact, the result of one such despicable action involving him and what was once my governess," Adam explained a little embarrassed.

The doctor looked genuinely shocked but begged the earl to continue.

"I was three or four when my governess was thrown from the house and chased away like a stray dog because my father had violated her and the result was a child in the making."

"Oh my!" exclaimed the doctor, holding his handkerchief in his left hand and dabbing his forehead.

"It was a shocking point in the history of my family and one that I now wish to put right, having found the child locally and bought her from her owner," continued Adam.

"Did you say bought, Sir? I must have misheard you," said the doctor alarmed.

"Oh believe me, Doctor, I had to pay good money to get the monster to part with Sally. Would you credit that in this day and age, people actually sell other people for numerous reasons," said Adam, now in full flow. "I could not comprehend this myself at first but it is a terrible world when a mother is so hungry and ill that she actually believes that she is doing her child a favour, selling her to the highest bidder."

"And you in turn have now bought the girl!" exclaimed the doctor. "For what purpose?" He looked genuinely concerned.

"Good heavens, man. To free her, of course, what else could I be looking for?" exclaimed Adam, who suddenly realised that the doctor might believe that he had alternative motives. "I am not my father."

The doctor looked embarrassed that he had allowed dark thoughts about the young man to enter his head. "Do you wish me to examine the young woman to make sure that she does not carry diseases into your home?" he asked.

"Good heavens, no," began the reply. "Actually yes, I suppose so but not in the way your question implies. The girl is my sister and as such, will be treated with respect. However, it was pointed out to me that she has a cough, and I felt that maybe she has not been treating her body well, through no fault of her own and she may need a tonic at least. She is very thin. I am trying to get her to eat little and often to build up her strength and appearance."

The doctor looked very relieved. "Sir, I would be very pleased to act as your sister's doctor and as such, examine her and put your mind at rest as to her health," he said.

"That, Doctor Gordan, is exactly why I have sent for you."

Adam walked over to a bell-pull near the door as he spoke and gave it a hearty tug resulting in a young woman in a white starched apron and cap knocking and opening the door without command.

"Alice," requested the earl, "would you see if Miss Sally is dressed and receiving visitors please."

Alice gave a little curtsy and replied that she had just left her mistress' room and that she was in bed nursing a very sour head and was therefore, indisposed.

Adam turned to Doctor Gordan looking alarmed. "I think this would be a good time for you to become acquainted with your latest patient. Do you not agree?"

The doctor nodded and picked up his medical bag.

Adam turned to Alice who was still standing in the open doorway. "Please, Alice, go up to Miss Sally, see she is descent and tell her that I have sent for the doctor, who I would wish to examine her immediately."

Alice smiled, bobbed a quick curtsy and hurried up the stairs. Unlike his father, Adam was always polite to the servants, he never commanded them, he always asked them politely to do his bidding and in return, they always gave him the very best service they could.

Alice quickly re-appeared and led the doctor up to Sally's room.

A very concerned faced doctor reappeared in the sitting room after nearly a whole hour. Adam could see straight away that the verdict was not too wonderful.

"Sit down, Doctor, and give me your findings, please," said Adam.

The doctor did as he was bid and sat down by the fire. "The young woman has, in fact, the beginnings of consumption, Sir," said the very serious looking medic. "Had you not found her when you did, I fear it would have been a very short life for her."

"So we can make her well then, Doctor," asked Adam, looking very uncomfortable.

"It is possible with good nursing but I fear it could be too late."

"I cannot lose her now, Doctor, I have only just found her," replied Adam.

"It might have been better for you, Sir, if you had not," was the honest reply. "You have put your household in danger, the young woman needs to be isolated and nursed through day and night. She will get a lot worse before or maybe if she get better."

"My goodness me!" exclaimed Adam with concern. "Alice spends time with her and I recently employed a chaperone for her. How is it passed between people?"

"There are many trains of thought on that, Sir," replied the doctor. "Some believe it to be air borne but it does seem that poor diet is a factor. I believe it to be passed from person to person, direct contact. Fresh sea air sometimes helps. It is mystery, people of good birth so they eat well, still seem susceptible to this disease."

"She would certainly have been living on left-overs and scraps. I can understand that this would make you susceptible to illness," replied the earl. "I have a friend in Weston-Super-Mare who could take in my sister for a while, would that help her recovery?"

"Your friend might not wish to put his own household in danger. I have noted that as one falls foul to this white death, others quickly follow," said the doctor. "And it does not seem to stop at poor and wanting people, the wonderful Miss Jane Austen died just a few years past of this same disease, and I am sure she had all the care possible."

"I am not encouraged by that, Doctor, but I have a friend with a sanatorium, I believe he might assist me," suggested the earl. "You may have heard of Doctor Edward Lang Fox."

"I have, Sir, he is an eminent psychiatrist, operates from Brislington House near Bristol, I believe."

"He has asked me to help fund a sanatorium in Weston-Super-Mare in Somerset for the mentally ill and I am prepared to do this, so my guess is he must have good links to the area," was the reply.

"There are definitely sanatoriums in Weston-Super-Mare as there are in Brighton, where people go to recover, but I think we are drifting from the immediate problem, Sir," said the doctor. "I need first to make sure that everyone else in this house is safe. I must see the two women you mentioned immediately. I need to be sure they are well. Then I will go and discover a woman who will nurse your sister, one who has contracted the disease and survived. She will have to stay here and the rooms they use will have to be scrubbed and cleaned every day. No one other than the nurse I allot you must come in direct contact with the stricken woman. Do you understand?"

Adam nodded and immediately sent for Alice and the new chaperone, explained the situation to them. Alice was most fearful but offered to stay and help, an offer that was declined. The doctor examined the two women and found they were in good health. The chaperone, Mrs Braund, a widow, was of particularly strong constitution and she said that she had nursed people with measles, mumps and chicken pox but never tuberculosis but was willing to stay close and do all she could for her new charge. Adam was so impressed with this response that he felt it difficult to keep his emotions in check. He knew that this turn of events meant that he would once more not be in a position to seek out Dorothia and was beginning to think that the fates were against this union. Doctor Gordan was a very forward thinking doctor. He believed in cleanliness being a clue to preventing the passing on many diseases. He also was friendly with a great many of the country's most eminent doctors and researchers and read every new paper that was produced. He was a great believer in prevention rather than cure. He promised to provide the earl with a very worthy nun,

Sister Teresa, that he used from time to time; she had, as a young woman, nursed young mutineers through the white death during the Froberg Mutiny of 1807, only to see then hung when well. She had also been nursing through the Anglo-Nepalese War of 1814 to 16, nursing British soldiers and Gurka alike, trying to save lives amongst bloodshed. Having been appalled by what she considered man's inhumanity to man, quoting the poet Robert Burns, she joined a convent.

Adam finished his letter to Dorothia in Brighton telling her all about his half-sister, and how he was waiting to meet a possible nurse for her, and promised to write again later.

Dorothia had been pleased to receive the letter. He wrote and told her that he had found a half-sister, Sally Minford, her mother having been his governess when he was young and defiled by his father and then cast out when found to be with child by him. He told Dorothia how her mother, Bathsheba, had pointed out that Sally seemed to have a cough that might be a problem. This piece of information made Dorothia smile because she was fully aware that her mother thought Adam was the spawn of the devil and should be avoided at all times.

Adam went on to tell her that he had taken her mother's advice and purchased the assistance of a doctor who declared that Sally had tuberculosis. For this reason, and possible for decorum's sake as he should still be in mourning, he would not be visiting at Brighton in the foreseeable future, concentrating on finding a good nurse for his sister.

Soon the lodge was looking more like a sanatorium than a house. Sister Teresa was a very efficient organiser, the place ran like an army barracks. Adam tried to keep the rest of the house running smoothly and separately from the nursing rooms.

The cook was kept busy making chicken soup and potions recommended by the doctor as well as feeding the rest of the household. Unable to visit his sister, banned by the good nun because of cross infection, Adam felt trapped and bored. He wanted to go to Brighton and speak to Dorothia but did not want to chance carrying this white death to her.

Adam was now keen to learn all he could about this horrible disease and devoured every book on the subject he could encounter. He did not pretend to understand all the medical jargon but got the significance of most of the findings. He read from cover to cover an account of the 4000 Mozambique Army volunteers that Britain imported to form a new regiment in Ceylon, Sri Lanka, between 1803 and 1810. By 1820, over 90% of these brave men had died of tuberculosis.

He read about Laennec and his invention, the stethoscope, which was used to listen to the inner workings of the organs. Most of this great man's findings were discovered through autopsies on those thought to have died of tuberculosis.

It was during this century that tuberculosis was dubbed the 'White Plague'. It was seen as a 'romantic disease'. Suffering from tuberculosis was thought to bestow upon the sufferer heightened sensitivity. The slow progress of the disease allowed for a 'good death' as sufferers could arrange their affairs. The disease began to represent spiritual purity and temporal wealth, leading many young, upper-class women to purposefully pale their skin to achieve the consumptive appearance. British poet, Lord Byron wrote, "I should like to die from consumption," helping to popularise the disease as the disease of artists.

Adam was, however, more interested in the possible cures than the stories behind individual deaths. He wanted to save his new sister. At least then he could say that he had managed to do something worthwhile despite his father.

The doctor called at first daily, then weekly as the young woman improved. It was tiring times for everyone.

An old friend, Sir James Sheppard, came to visit one day unexpectedly and was shown into the drawing room. Sir James had a property in Weston-Under-Wetherley, not a very large one, it was just a retreat. His real home was in Weston Super Mare and he had come to offer Adam any assistance he could with Sally, once she had been cleared of the tuberculosis.

"I believe we are well on the way to seeing my sister on her feet again, James," said Adam, holding out his hand to his friend who shook it. "It has been a long haul and for a while, I thought we were not going to see this day."

"It is vile disease, my friend, and I am so glad to see that you have not been touched by it."

"No, it has been kept very carefully in check," replied Adam. "The doctor has taken over a portion of the lodge as a hospital, and we do not venture there, he is very strict about it. And the nurse he has provided, Sister Teresa, a nun, is not to be argued with. Sheets are changed every day much to my housekeeper's annoyance, she does not relish the extra washing. I will reward her well when the time is right."

"Sounds like all is in order then and maybe you do not need my help," said Sir James with a warm smile. "I wondered if maybe when your sister was well enough, you and she could come down to Weston-Super-Mare and take off the sea air. It is supposed to be very good for you."

"So I believe, James," was the reply. "I would like to take up this offer when the time is right."

Adam went to ring for the footman to order tea when the door knocked.

"Enter," Adam boomed, surprised.

The door opened and there stood Sister Teresa, she stepped into the drawing room and looked about. "I am sorry, my Lord, I thought you were alone."

"No, as you see, I have a visitor, my first for quite some time," he replied. "This is a friend of mine, Sir James Sheppard." Sister Teresa curtsied awkwardly, Adam turned to Sir James. "And, James, this is the wonderful nurse I told you of."

Sister Teresa blushed. "Sir, I have a surprise for you." she walked over to the door and led a young woman into the room. "May I present Miss Sally Minford, the doctor said it is all over and she is well enough to mix with everyone."

Sally stood there looking like a pale and delicate fawn.

She was a remarkably beautiful young woman. She had a look of her mother about her but her father's complexion, striking blue eyes and blonde hair. The two men just looked in amazement at her. She had transformed like a butterfly, from a chrysalis into a creature of delicate beauty.

"My goodness, Sister," said Adam, quite taken aback. "I would not have known you. You are a real beauty and this Miss Sally Minford stops now, you are a Southerly and as such will be addressed just so."

The woman looked as though she was going to faint and Sir James grabbed a chair and placed it close to her.

"I thank you, Sir," Sally said looking into Sir James' kind, warm brown eyes. "I cannot believe how things have changed for me, how kind my new brother has been. Everything is so new." she sat down on the chair provided.

Adam approached the nun, "Are you sure that Miss Southerly is quite well?"

He was told that the doctor had made it quite clear that the infection was gone and that the woman was now fit to travel.

"In that case, Adam," said Sir James, "you must allow me to take your extremely beautiful sister to my property in Weston-Super-Mare, and we can make her the healthiest young woman in the world in no time."

Sally looked very embarrassed by all the attention.

"Would you like to spend some time by the sea, Sally?" asked her brother.

She looked a little alarmed and spoke in a quiet shaky voice, "Do you want rid of me already? I cannot go anywhere with a strange man, however kind he may look. I am so sorry, Sir, that I have caused you so much bother and expense. I can work, I will work only, please do not send me away."

Both Adam and James had a look of horror on their faces. Sally looked like a captured sparrow, frightened and frail. Sister Teresa did not know what to say or do either.

It then occurred to Adam that Sally thought that he had made her well just so he could sell her on, this is how her life had always been 'till now'. "Good heavens, woman," he exclaimed, "you won't go without Mrs Braund to chaperone you and you won't go without a complete new wardrobe of fitting garments and a maid of your own. I believe I will come as well, fresh sea air would not do me any harm either."

Sally looked so happy and relieved, she jumped from her chair and flung her arms around her brother. "I cannot believe how my luck has changed, how could I possibly deserve such a wonderful brother. Oh, I am so sorry, I doubted you for a moment."

"Never doubt me again, Sally, I am your brother and as such, I will protect you and keep you safe."

She smiled the widest smile possible and her whole body relaxed.

Adam took Sister Teresa aside to thank her for her gentle care and assured her that the convent would receive a donation accordingly. The elderly nun looked most pleased.

"Sir, could I just speak to you about a very delicate matter that I feel I should clear up, in case there was any doubt," she said mysteriously.

Adam opened the door and called for Alice, who appeared almost immediately.

"Alice, I am sorry to take you from your duties but could you just stay in this room with my sister and Sir James for proprieties sake, whilst the good sister and I step into the corridor for a moment?" said Adam, not wanting to further alarm his sister by leaving her alone with a strange man.

"I am at your service, Sister," he said, once they were out of hearing from others.

"As I say, it is a delicate matter, one I would not normally discuss with a gentleman like yourself or any man for that matter," Sister Teresa said in a low voice.

"I am all ears, Madam, please speak freely. I feel you would not be standing in front of me in this way if you did not feel it was important."

"It is, Sir, though of no importance to me."

Adam looked confused but stood quietly, waiting to hear what ever revelation he was about to be handed.

"Whilst delirious Miss Sally told me a lot about her life as a near slave."

"Go on."

"I thought it only right to tell you that although she was bought and sold, she was never defiled," continued the nun. "It was not through lack of trying by some but she was kept safe by her own instincts, and the fact that the men who she lived with had wives that took charge of her, obviously aware of the consequences if they did not. Miss did not make it clear to me if it was through their Christian duty or whether she was worth more intact, so to speak."

"Good God, woman, excuse my blasphemy, do you mean there were plans to sell her on?" asked Adam alarmed.

"Exactly, Sir," was the reply. "It seems you saved her just in time."

"My goodness, and I paid a goodly sum for her, the monster must have thought that I wanted her for immoral purposes," said Adam, quite shocked. "No doubt, there will be people who knew who I was and thought I followed my father's lead."

"I have no doubt about that, Sir," was the gentle reply, "But your conscience is clear so evil minds can think what they wish and they will. I just thought I should speak up for the young lady just in case you wondered."

"To be honest, Sister, I rather assumed that Sally had faced ever horror imaginable in her short life."

"And yet you still took her into your home!" said the nun with a broad smile.

"She is my sister," was the reply. "Nothing could be her fault, she has had no say in her life's journey until now."

The elderly nun took the earl's hand and kissed it much to his surprise. "You are the very best of mankind, Sir, and I am honoured to have helped you. Most would have caste the child into a nunnery and forgotten her."

"I am no saint, I assure you but I know what is right, and I do strive to do it where I can."

"My dear, Sir, you do very well and I am almost sorry that I now have to go back to my previous life," Sister Teresa said with a broad smile. "I believe you have other missions to complete and if I can ever be of service to you, please contact me. I would have liked to have followed your adventures, my guess is there will be many."

"I do have quite a list of wrongs to right and I do believe that the list will get longer and maybe I will never see the end but I will try my best."

"I know you will, Sir," was the reply.

They returned to the drawing room to find Sir James and Sally in deep conversation about Weston-Super-Mare and outlying areas.

"Alice, now you are here, I would like to ask you something," said the earl to the little maid, who looked nervous.

"Would you like to come with us that is Sir James, Miss Sally, Mrs Braund, who come to think of it that I have not spoken to as yet, and I to Weston-Super-Mare by the sea and stay at Sir James' farm, whilst Miss Sally recuperates from her illness? My sister will need a maid of her own and I believe you like each other well enough."

"Like, I love my lady," Alice cried in quite a loud voice. "I have never been further than the market, can I really come?"

"We need you," replied the earl. "How else will Miss Sally manage without a maid."

Alice almost danced up and down with joy. "I must tell my mother, she will be so proud of me, a lady's maid."

"Good Heavens, child, I am offering you work, not a total holiday," Adam said with a chuckle, most amused. "I will order some new clothes to suit your new post if that is acceptable. You may have to walk out with Miss Sally so you will need suitable day dresses."

Alice started to cry uncontrollably. "Please Sir, say no more, I am quite overwhelmed as it is."

Sally looked astonished and everyone else amused.

"Off you go then, child. Go, ask your mother, is she willing to allow you to come with us." said Adam gently.

Before he could even finish the sentence, Alice was gone from the room, bobbing a quick tearful curtsy as she went.

"Strange things women," said Sir James, rather amused by the scene he had watched. "From quite a young age, they cry if happy and also if sad, how are we supposed to know what is in their minds?"

"When we can understand women, my friend, we will know the secrets of the universe," was Adam's reply.

Adam took the time to write a short letter to Dorothia, knowing that he would not see her again for several more months. He wrote to tell her that Sally, with the help of the wonderful Sister Teresa, had been declared fit to travel and was going to Weston-Super-Mare with Adam's good friend, Sir James Shepherd, a chaperone and little maid to see if the sea air would bring the colour back into his sister's cheeks. He also told her that he was going as well and that he would write again from Weston.

A few days later, the happy little group set out for Weston-Super-Mare; it was quite a journey of many stops and starts. For such a long journey and the length of the intended stay, it was necessary to bring several employees. Martin, of course, who also acts as his lordships valet, a groom and two sturdy stable hands to drive the town coach. Sir James intended to take his own carriage. Mrs Braund was happy to visit the seaside and they took little Alice, the maid, with her mother's blessing to attend to Miss Southerly's other needs such as her hair and wardrobe. It was the first time that Alice had ever been outside of Weston-Under-Wetherley, and she was like a child in a sweetshop. The earl had provided Alice with walking out dresses needed to be a proper lady's maid; this alone was enough to make her grin in a rather mad looking way all the time. It was the first time for Alice and Sally to be greeted in inns as though they were valued. Sally spoke as little as possible, her accent rather gave away her lack of refinement, but she was a sharp-eyed girl and she watched everyone and learnt from that. She soon got use to men staring at her, she had this before but it was not to admire her looks as was now. She worked hard on her carriage. Sister Teresa, who had now returned to the nunnery, had shown her how to walk upright and not stride out like a ruffian. Adam was not insensitive to the debt he owed that elderly nun and the sisterhood benefited greatly. He even sent one of his father's carriages to the convent along with suitable horses with the suggestion if they did not need it, maybe it could be sold.

Chapter 20
Weston-Super-Mare

Sir James Shephard has a small holding known as Bleadon Manor Farm in Bleadon, not far from Uphill at the edge of Weston-Super-Mare. It consisted of just 70 acres of farm land. He is not a farmer as such, maybe a gentleman farmer would be more correct. He enjoys owning a few sheep, he employs a number of the local farm workers to attend to his land and his other animals. He takes pride in his flock of geese and has a great number of chickens. A large portion of his land is set out with chicken coops and large hen houses. He grows vegetables, mainly for their own consumption, he has a very large, elongated green house where tomatoes, lettuce and cucumbers are grown amongst other things. He employs several gardeners and poultry keepers, he also prides himself on his herb garden. On his land, he also has a cluster of cottages for his workers; they are just small, thatched roof abodes but in good repair, each with a small garden forming a tiny village within the small holding. They look neatly tended.

There is a small stream that runs through his property fed by the River Axe where in the past, Sir James has spent many a quiet hour fishing with just his groom for company. His stable is first class and he has several carriages. He favours a cabriolet, a light, two-wheeled, hooded curricle which is intended for transporting one or two passenger; it had a running board for the groom, a folding top and large rigid apron with very large, bright yellow wheels. It had originally been a hansom cab and Sir James had bought it and restored it to a very high standard. It is beautifully painted and very noticeable. Being slightly flamboyant, Sir James liked to be noticed. Like most gentlemen, he also had a lightweight gig for taking himself about in. He has only had himself to worry about for a number of years. Like Lord Southerly, he has no brothers. He does, however, have two sisters who are married and live elsewhere. Bleadon Manor Farm is not a fine house like Weston Manor Lodge but it is a substantial and comfortable property. Sir James is a shrewd business man, not born into money like the earl; he had learnt how to earn his. He had been one of the first people to take advantage of the trend towards sea air for your constitution and bought property in the Weston-Super-Mare area to let out to rich town gentlemen. He has managed to get himself a very comfortable lifestyle, not totally genteel but of a high standard. His father has only recently died and his mother has been gone for several years, so he is quite alone but he does not really enjoy his own company very much. All the staff that run the house and land have been with his family for a number of years, and he is on an easy going level with them. The small property that Sir James held in Weston-Under-Wetherley had been bought many years ago at his mother's request. Sir James' father had sent a London agent out to buy a smallish property for his mother-in-law to stay in Weston. The agent had made a mistake and purchased a reasonably substantial property in Weston-Under-Wetherley instead of Weston-Super-Mare. Once they had recovered from the surprise, they viewed the property and Sir James' grandmother liked the village so much that she moved there and stayed there until her death. Since then, it has just been a hide-away for any member of the family who fancied a change of scenery.

The group arrived at Bleadon Manor Farm and were greeted by a great many of the staff, all smiling and obviously, very pleased to see Sir James back in residence.

"I think you keep a happy ship here, James," commented the earl. "Everyone seems pleased to see your return."

"And, Adam, I am equally pleased to be back home," was the reply. "Wait until I show you the fishing on the land. I do sometimes go to the River Axe where the fish are in abundance, but I prefer the privacy of my little patch of water."

"I have not fished for years," replied Adam. "My father was not one for such frivolities. If he wanted fish, he sent someone out to acquire some."

"I cannot image the late earl sitting by a river bank waiting for a fish to bite," said James with a smile. "More likely, he would scare the fish away."

The young earl laughed as he and Miss Southerly followed Sir James into the house, followed by servants carrying baggage. Just inside the doorway was standing Pernell, Sir James' housekeeper come butler and anything else asked of him.

"Sir, we are all very pleased to see your safe return," said Pernell with a bow.

"Ah, Pernell," replied Sir James. "This is my good friend, the Earl of Wetherley, and his sister, Miss Southerly." Pernell bowed very deeply. "I wish you to make their stay with us as comfortable as possible."

"Of course, my lord, it will be an honour," was the reply.

"Also, Purnell, let me introduce you to Martin who is his lordship's loyal man servant, Alice who is Miss Southerly's ladies maid and Mrs Braund who acts as chaperone."

"Equally honoured," was the reply, which made Alice giggle a little.

They were all shown to their rooms that had been prepared for them as soon as the command reached Purnell by courier. The groom and other attendants of the coach were given quarters in the grounds and the earl's man, Martin, was shown to a small room in the attic, which he found most acceptable. The household had been eager to see Sir James' new friends as it was not a regular occurrence having visitors at the farm.

Sally and Alice could not wait to look around the farmhouse. Sally found it absolutely delightful. She loved the fact that chickens wondered into the kitchen unannounced and were shooed out with a great deal of good humour. She liked the look of the rosy-cheeked cook, who had a permanent smile on her face, and the shoe black boy, who cleaned the shoes with such enthusiasm. Everyone seemed so happy, it gave her a warm glow.

The earl made a point of making sure that the men he had brought with him were comfortable, and he informed them that whilst they were at Bleadon, they were to work for Sir James in whatever capacity he found fitting. They were quite surprised to find themselves helping with milking and lambing as well as taking good care of the hired horses.

Their first meal in Bleadon Manor Farm was fit for a king and Adam found himself honour bound to go down to the kitchen later and thank the cook personally.

He smiled to himself wondering what his father would have thought of such an action.

As soon as Adam had a moment, he wrote to Brighton so a further letter written to Dorothia arrived in Brighton a couple of weeks later; she had not expected to hear directly from the young earl and was even more surprised to receive so much detailed information. The Southerly crest was clearly imbedded in the wax seal and it caused a flutter amongst the inhabitancies of Lord and Lady Bradbury's house.

Adam went on to tell Dorothia about how having taken her mother's advice and purchased the assistance of a doctor, who had provided a wonderful nurse for his sister in the form of a very hardy elderly Nun, Sister Teresa, he had been able to go to Weston-Super-Mare with the group. He told her about Alice and how excited she had been and how he had enjoyed helping her and Sally find suitable clothes to take with them. Dorothia smiled at that thought. He went on to tell her how he was going to have a rest from seeking Freda and another possible half-brother or sister and enjoy the sea air himself after all the worry of Sally's illness.

Dorothia read the letter to her sisters, who were beginning to regard Adam as a hero, though Lady Mary had pointed out the fact that she felt maybe he had taken a lot on his shoulders and sounded as though he had not finished. Dorothia was also worried that the young earl's new missions might take him away from her altogether. He had added that he would write again at a later date and sent his regards to everyone.

The first couple of week in Bleadon was full of walks in Weston Wood, which they all declared was on a par with Westerley Wood, if not better, walks along the front at Weston Sands, climbs up the steep sand dunes of Uphill, boat rides and fishing. Sundays, the group attended church at St Peter's in Bleadon along with the rest of the household and farm workers on the estate. Everyone was having the most relaxing time and the days flew by. The earl knew that he had work to do elsewhere and that he could not stay too much longer, but he was so happy being part of what seemed a proper family that he was reluctant to rush away.

The earl was happy to leave his sister in the care of Mrs Braund and Sir James one Tuesday morning and made his way into Weston-Super-Mare in the gig. He was keen to see the island that his friend Dr Lang Fox had told him about. Lang Fox was anxious to acquire Knightstone Island and used it as a sanatorium for his mental patients. They would be free of prying eyes and have the calming benefits of the sea air. Previously, John Howe of Bristol had bought the island for £200 with the help of a friend and financial partner, Charles Taylor, of Yatton. Mr Taylor had funded the happening through his interests in an umbrella and parasol factory in Dolphin Street in Bristol.

Howe's Baths had only opened in July 1820, so was still in its infancy. There were hot and cold salt water baths, tea and coffee, and reading rooms for visitors. There was also a two-storey house erected on the island to house invalids as they began their recovery. Anyone could make use of the baths. The price of a hot bath was 3 shillings and a cold bath 1 shilling. There was further work in process. A West facing turret has been added to the main house and at the side, nearest the mainland, another turret; this time facing east and known as Arthurs Tower was in the process of being built. Adam was very keen to go to the island and see for himself if this was a likely investment for him. He had heard that the island was likely to be put up for sale in the next year to 18 months.

Knightstone could only be reached on foot at low tide, it was very much an island when the tide was high. So Adam went to seek out the local boat owner called Aaron Fisher, who would ferry, for a price, anyone out to Knightstone Island.

He landed on the island a little after two in the afternoon and had booked a return trip with Aaron in an hour. He felt that was long enough to get a feel of the place. Whilst on the island, he learnt that whilst excavating stone to build, they had discovered a dark vein of limestone that they called Weston Marble and when polished, could be used to build fine fire places in large houses. On the pretence that he was interested in such a fire surround, Adam found out all he could about this small but lucrative industry. There seemed to be a lot of people now involved in Kingstone Island.

There was a great deal of work being done on the island. Two years earlier, Rev Thomas Pruen had started the building of a low causeway to make it easier for people to reach the island; they were also building an outside swimming pool replenished by the tides. Soon, Arron would not be necessary, though some people would always enjoy being rowed across.

Adam drove the gig slowly round Weston, taking everything in and wondering if he should contact Dr Lang Fox. Although the earl dressed very fashionably, he was never flamboyant. His father had always been the dandy in the family and he had no desire to emulate him in any way. He still looked fine enough to stand out in Weston, and he caused a little stir where-ever he went.

In London, a place that Adam disliked immensely he probably would have been frowned upon, where as his father would have been top of the ton, no less. Adam had no desire to waltz about the capital city looking like a peacock, he preferred to be what was known as titled country genteel. He was flush in the pocket, which is probably not the case with a lot of the young aristocrats in London who were only out to find themselves rich wives in exchange for the title they would bestow upon them. His father had always talked flash and worn a wig, something else Adam did not want to emulate. His hair was thick and well-kept so the thought of a wig that would most probably itch was abhorrent to him.

He arrived back at Bleadon Manor Farm just in time to wash and dress for dinner. He was very keen to tell Sir James about all he had discovered as he valued his business head and involvement in the area. He decided to wait for a more appropriate moment, seeing that everyone appeared to be very excited.

Sally was keen to tell her brother how she had been to the lambing and had watched the lambs being born. Sir James said that he had not seen anyone so thrilled in his life. And how she had actually helped deliver one youngster, which she immediately had named Rosebud and had rushed indoors to find a ribbon to tie about the poor creature's neck.

They all laughed and Sir James added that Sally had made him promise to keep extra care of Rosebud, because she was hers now as she had heard that if you save a life, you own that life.

"Helping with the birth does not mean you saved the lamb's life surely, young lady," Adam said in good spirits.

"Oh but it does, Adam," she insisted. "The lamb had the cord round its neck and could have died without my help, young Jake, the shepherd told me so."

"Did he indeed?" said James. "I might have a word with him."

"Oh, please do not, James," she said loudly. "I would not have him in trouble because of my loose tongue."

"I am only jesting, young lady," he replied. "Rosebud is yours to do as you will with."

"Can I take her back to Wetherley?" she asked innocently to which Adam and James answered as one, "No," and explained that the lamb needed its mother to nurse it or it really would die.

"I helped Jake hold a bottle to a new born lamb this very afternoon so I could look after it," she added, looking appealingly at the two men.

"Did Jake explain that this was because the mother had rejected the baby or was too sick to feed it?" asked James.

"He did say something like that being the usual reason to bottle feed a lamb, so I could feed the lamb, you must confess that much."

"The mother will soon want her baby back. Would you wish someone to take your baby from you?" asked James.

"Goodness, no," replied Sally. "I will have to have both the mother and the lamb that would be the right thing to do."

James and Adam just laughed. Adam wondered at the innocence of his new found sister.

Another two weeks went by and Adam felt it was time to return to the work that he had left undone in Weston-Under-Wetherley and hopefully, to Dorothia if he could arrange a visit to Brighton. He knew that he needed to go to visit the weavers in his employment before he did any further travelling. He spoke to Sir James about them leaving in a couple of days, and he was very reluctant to let the party go.

"I suppose I cannot keep you here any longer, more is the pity," Sir James said. "I have become unbelievably fond of all of you, including little Alice, and will be sorry to see you go."

"I too have had a wonderfully peaceful time here, James, and would like to think I might be able to return sometime."

"My door will always be open to you and your beautiful and delightful sister," replied James, "who I believe is in the field grooming Rosebud, whether it wants to be or not."

"I have unfinished business in Wetherley with regards to my father's resting place," explained Adam. "Obviously, he and my mother are in the family crypt but the trouble I had persuading a mason to add my father's name to the ancestral list would amaze you."

"Really! Do they fear him that much, even after he has departed?" said James.

"It happens that they do," continued Adam. "I had no trouble with my mother. In fact, in the end, I held a service for her separate from that of my father. It was quite well attended. I will tell you about that later because something very strange occurred. The very next day, we held a service, at the vicars' insistence I might add, for my father and only Martin and I attended besides the vicar, of course. We cut it rather short as I had no heart in being there either."

"What a dreadful state of affairs," said James. "I cannot imagine how you must have felt."

"James," added Adam, "I would like to discover how to buy into the marble business. At Knightstone Island, they are digging up black marble like stone that when polished, makes very fine fireplaces."

"There is a quarry here-about that digs and uses that very same stone," Sir James replied. "I will make enquiries for you."

At that moment, Sally came bouncing into the hallway. "Why do you look so serious?" she asked.

"I am sorry dear if you think we look serious, there is nothing that need ever touch you," replied Adam. "James was just telling me that you have been grooming your lamb."

Sally held out a piece of well-chewed ribbon. "Look at the thanks I get for trying to make her look special," she said. "Rosebud ate her ribbon."

Both men tried to suppress a laugh.

"It is alright though, you need not worry," she continued. "Jake has painted a ribbon on with dye for me so I can see her in a crowd."

"It seems to me that young man has been extremely helpful, I must thank him personally," said Sir James.

"Oh, I wish you would, he is such a darling," said Sally.

"I know we run a not too tight ship here but I hope you haven't told him that," said Sir James, alarmed.

"Oh no, of course, I haven't," she replied most indignantly. With that, the men sighed loudly. "But Alice has," she added.

James and Adam both looked at each other, not knowing quite what to say.

Adam chose that moment to tell his sister that he needed to go back to Wetherley. She was not at all pleased and told him that she could not possibly leave Rosebud, she was far too young.

Sir James suggested that the ladies stayed on a while, they would be safe with him. "Your sister has improved in health so much in the last four weeks, another month would make her strong again for sure."

So it was decided that Adam would go home and return in a month or five weeks to reclaim his sister and her ladies. Sally was so pleased that she jumped up and down, and Alice had the biggest smile anyone had ever seen.

"I fear my shepherd Jake has lost his heart to Miss Southerly's little maid," said Sir James quietly to Adam, "and by the look of that smile, it is not one sided."

"Right then, young lady," said Adam to his sister, "I will leave you here to nurture your lamb, and you must promise me not to be too much trouble and to stay away from the rum punch."

"Adam," Sally exclaimed, "I have not even had a full glass of such a thing in my life."

"A good thing," was the jolly reply. "Think how much more trouble you would be if you had."

The next day, Adam started on his long trip back to Wetherley, sure in his mind that his sister was in safe hands. He knew that Mrs Braund would see no harm befell her, so with the protection of Sir James and her love of Rosebud, he knew she would be happy, and he did have a lot of travelling to do once he got home. She would have had to spend a lot of time alone and he did not think this would suit her at all. He had also made up his mind not to allow his sister to become a school mistress; she was to live the life she had been excluded from for too long and anyway, he found her company very refreshing.

He intended to visit the family seat in Keighley and sort out affairs there and see for himself how the business was run so he was very happy not to have to worry about Sally, whilst he tackled this new endeavour. She had promised to write regularly and he found himself looking forward to her missives. He also thought how lucky it was that he found Sally after his father's demise, or she could have been ill-used, the thought made him shudder.

Chapter 21
Back to Weston-Under-Wetherley

The Earl of Wetherley was quite used to long journeys, though he had no great love of them.

His journey home, he estimated to be an uncomfortable 110 mile so he was pleased that he had thought to travel in his highly sprung town coach that bore his family crest on the door panel. His right-hand man, Martin, sat opposite the earl and they indulged in niceties about the scenery, which made the time pass quicker. He had changed horses several times on route to Weston-Super-Mare and intended to take the same journey back, reclaiming the horses he had left at each coaching inn as he went and returning them to their owners. The final stop planned at Stratford-Upon-Avon would reacquaint him with his own horses, three pairs of almost matching greys. He had paid the stables a goodly sum to take very good care of them until his return. He had never left his horses for so long in a strangers care. His groom had offered to stay with the horses, which would have meant the earl would have to have hired a groom to come and stay in Weston for a very long time. He much preferred to have familiar faces around him.

First stop, Bristol, they pulled up at the same fine looking inn that they had acquainted on route. The earl had been more than pleased with the cleanliness of the rooms and the food offered. He was used to Flemish soup and mutton, boiled tongue with turnips or game pies, the usual fare in such watering holes. He was not a fussy eater, so long as the food was hot and the ale cold, he was happy.

The next stop was Gloucester, then a small inn between Cheltenham and Stratford-Upon-Avon, lastly Stratford, where they discovered the earl's beautiful horses in fine fettle. He did not always change horses so often but it was early in the year when he left Westerley, and he did not want to chance his high breed sturdy steppers on possibly slippery ground. He had already decided that they would go all the way with him to Keighley when he went there. It was the usual way of things: good stopovers to attend to everyone's needs, human and equine alike.

From Stratford, it was short journey to Weston-Under-Wetherley and the end of this first venture for the earl. He settled himself into the study to read as much as he could on the running of the woollen industry in the north and read through his father's papers on their holdings. He did not want to appear a green boy when he reached Keighley.

Adam decided to give himself a week's rest before taking on his next task.

His first visitor was the Reverend Mountjoy baring the gift of a very fine cake baked by his good wife, much to Adam's amazement. Adam was so pleased to see Phillip and hurried him inside to tell him all what had occurred in Weston-Super-Mare.

Phillip has an easy way about him that Adam found refreshing. The earl told him how much improved Sally was and how he had left her behind in his friend's good care. He told him the story of the lamb and how she would take quite a bit of persuasion to come home without it. They spoke cheerfully for a while before Adam broached the subject of Dorothia.

"I wondered how long it would take you to ask about my daughter," Phillip said with a smile. "She is still in Brighton and seems quite happy there at the moment."

"Do you think she will wish to stay in Brighton?" asked the earl.

"I think that will depend on you, young man," was the reply. "She has not looked at another man, though I am reliably told that she has caught the eye of several."

"I would be very surprised if that was not the case, Sir," said Adam.

Phillip took a letter out of his cassock pocket and handed it to the earl. "I have carried this about my person for nearly four weeks. It is, I assume, a reply to your missive to her. If I had a forwarding address, I would have sent it on to you."

"Yes, I am sorry about that, Phillip," came the reply. "I got swept up in the moment. One minute my sister was languishing on her sick bed at death's door, the next her doctor had given her the all clear. My good friend, Sir James Sheppard, was visiting the Westerley farm house he owns, and we ended up going back to Weston-Super-Mare to try the sea air on our patient. I did not intend to stay as long as I did."

"You look a lot better for your trip, Adam," said the vicar. "It has brought the roses back into your cheeks as well. You have had a rough trot, my boy, and your own health was looking a little waned. You cannot care for anyone if you are in need of care yourself."

Adam had unfolded the letter and was starting to read the contents. It was quite a formal letter giving details of what she had been doing, places she had seen and parties she had attended. It was a very proper letter as had his been to her. Adam handed it to Phillip.

"It is not addressed to me, my boy," he said, waving the missive away.

"There is nothing I cannot share with you," was the disappointed reply. "I have written to Dorothia in Brighton. Obviously, she has sent this before she received my letters to her."

"Do not be despondent, my boy, she is not going to throw herself at your feet. She has no idea how your life is going," said Phillip reassuringly. "Even Bathsheba is coming about, mainly because of your handling of your newly discovered sister and the much needed boost of funds to the nunnery."

"Hence, the cake, Sir, I guess," replied Adam. "As for the nunnery, Sister Teresa risked her own life to tend my sister, it was a mere bagatelle. Where should I go from here, do you think my friend?"

"Firstly, we should try the cake," said Phillip with a wide smile.

"My goodness," said Adam, shocked himself. "I have made no offer of hospitality, I was so pleased to see you at my door." He stood and walked over to the bell pull. The door was soon opened by a short, red-haired, pretty young woman who looked no more than 14, in a starched white apron and bonnet. Adam was quite taken aback by a strange face in his sitting room.

"I do not believe I know you, young lady," he said to the timid looking girl, who had sunk into a deep curtsy. "Who pray are you?"

"Sir," she said rather prettily as she stood up. "I am Alice's sister and I am doing her work whilst she is away, I hope you think this is appropriate, Sir."

"You are an ideal replacement for Alice and now I look at you, I see you have the same look about you," he answered with a smile that brought on an even wider smile from the little maid. "Are you staying in Alice's room?"

"That I am, Sir, I will away as soon as she returns or if you are not happy with this arrangement," the girl said.

"I do not want to keep referring to you as Alice's sister, and I assume you have a name of your own, child," he continued.

She laughed as she spoke, "Of course, I do, my lord. I am Kate," and she curtsied again.

"Where have you been till now, Kate," the earl asked.

She answered in a real matter of fact way as if this was normal. "Hiding, Sir, like most young women near about."

The earl was quite taken aback by the young woman's honesty and realised how many very relieved parents there must be that the old tyrant has gone, and they can now be allowed to keep the company of their own daughters without fear.

"You will never have occasion to hide again, Kate," said the earl. "Not whilst I am lord of this manor. I am happy to make your acquaintance, young lady, and I would like you to please fetch the vicar and I some tea and bring a couple of plates so that we can taste the cake he has brought."

The young woman smiled up at the earl and asked if maybe she had better take the cake to the kitchen and get cook to slice it neatly for him.

"I think you are a wise young woman, Kate, and I think that is a very good idea. I thank you for thinking about crumbs on the carpet."

"I hope I was not too imprudent, Sir," Kate replied, a little nervous.

"I would say you were wise beyond your years," he pointed to the cake as he spoke. "Please take it and make sure you and cook get a slice each as well."

Kate giggled a little, took the cake and left.

"That was nicely done, Adam," said the vicar approvingly. "You have a lot of work to do to gain total trust here and little steps, little steps."

"I think I will be keeping Kate on," said Adam. "I believe Alice has lost her heart to a member of Sir James' staff; if I am right, she will be reluctant to return to Wetherley Manor Lodge."

"It doesn't seem to take long for one to lose their hearts these days," said Phillip.

"That fact I find worrying," replied Adam thinking of Dorothia.

The tea arrived along with the cake neatly arranged on a large plate. It was, as suspected, a delicious fruit cake.

Phillip left with a message of gratitude to his wife for the cake. The earl then took out the letter again and read it over and over hoping to find an encouraging word slipped between the lines but unfortunately, he could not. It was open and friendly enough but it could have been written sister to brother and he wanted more.

He sat down with pen and ink and wrote a long, detailed account of his time away, of his new sister and how her health is improving. He even told her about Kate and the hope that his workers would stop hiding their women folk adding that he had his eye set on only one woman. He hoped that might prompt a response that he wanted.

A few days later, Dorothia received the letter that Adam had written from Bleadon Farm to tell her that he had gone to Weston-Super-Mare with his good friend, Sir James Shepherd, taking a chaperone and little maid to see if the sea air would bring the colour back into his sister's cheeks. As he had gone as well, he could happily say that his sister was looking quite splendid. He told Dorothia how pretty Sally had turned out to be under all that grime, he also found himself telling her how Sister Teresa had assured him that the girl's virtue was intact despite the terrible life she had led. Dorothia did find it hard to imagine such a conversation between an earl and a nun. He also told her about Rosebud and how Sally had taken to the lamb so fiercely that he imagined he would have to include it in his menagerie and finally that he was off to Keighley to inspect the mills and see for himself how his workers are treated. Dorothia felt a quiver of worry, guessing that Adam would find many wrongs to right up in Yorkshire.

Adam finished the letter very formally but promised to keep her informed of his further activities. She read some of the letter to her sisters and Lady Mary but held some details back, folded the missive carefully and slipped it into her pocket.

Very soon, Adam was packing again, this time for the trip to Yorkshire. He dropped in on Phillip before he left and told him that he expected to be back within a month or maybe even sooner if all went well.

Chapter 22
Keighley, West Yorkshire and Robbie

The earl had spent the last few days, before he left for Keighley, reading and absorbing everything he could about the weaving and wool making industry. Keighley was the family home but it wasn't originally so. Before the original manor house was burnt down in Weston-Under-Wetherley, it having been a particularly fine large building that had been in the family for many generations, the stately home in Keighley was just an occasional retreat. It was, however, from the North that the main family wealth came. After the fire, the family spent more and more time in West Yorkshire, only coming to Weston-Under-Wetherley to escape the very cold Yorkshire winters. Keighley is on the edge of Keighley Moor and as such, open to inclement weather and high winds. In the summer, it is a fine area to hunt and ride. Adam always wished to spend longer in Weston Lodge than Keighley.

Adam had read all about how on 17 October 1305, Henry de Keighley, a Lancastrian knight, was granted a charter to hold a market in Keighley by King Edward 1st. This made this then insignificant town into a market town and that brought wealth to the area. Adam's forefathers had an interest in the market town of Bradford at the beginning of the 1800s and could see that the wool and spinning industry was beginning to take over a large portion of the work there about. Keighley, being some 10 miles from Bradford, seemed an ideal place to settle. A very large property was purchased there and building work was immediately started to make it into one of the finest stately homes for miles.

Adam's grandfather, although quite elderly by then, took an interest in the cottage industry that had sprung up in the Bradford area. He saw the merit in providing a workspace for weavers so they could work away from their own cottages. There were a few like-minded men around at the time and a lot of rivalry, usually good-natured. Adam had grown up alongside a young man called Titus Salt, who was born in Morley near Leeds. His father, Daniel Salt, was one of the first to make a large investment in the weaving industry and encouraged Adam's grandfather to do likewise. Daniel Salt, who lived in manor farm in Crofton Nr. Wakefield, soon built up a very lucrative woollen business and Adam's grandfather concentrated on the weaving side of cloth making.

Adam intended to visit the Salts whilst in Yorkshire but his main reason for going was to re-acquaint himself again with an old friend, Christopher Waud. Christopher was just two years older than Adam but he had ran his father's, Robert's, mills and weaving sheds for a number of years despite his youth, because his father was in ill health. Adam felt that as a novice in business in general, Christopher would be a good port of call. The Wauds own and run the Britannia Mills and weaving sheds in Bradford. Originally, Robert Waud had manufactured brushes from Bank

Street in Bradford but the pull of the weaving industry took him onto that path instead. Adam and Christopher had always got on very well so it was hoped that by looking round the highly successful Britannia Mills, it might give Adam ideas as to how he could improve the working of his own mills.

Having read a great deal about the mill industry, Adam had been made aware of the pit falls of the workers leaving their cottages to go to work. Most weavers had large families and if the wives had to stay home and look after children, it would mean just one wage coming into the house. Whereas when they worked from home, they could keep an eye on the children and both work. This, of course, led to children going to work in the mills alongside their parents, some as young as four years old. Adam had read about the dangers children were exposed to in this sort of environment and it worried him.

With Martin by his side, the earl set out for the long journey to Keighley. They took the Oxford Road to Warwick, then on to Leicester, Nottingham, Sheffield, Leeds and then Bradford West Yorkshire. They had rested at many a good inn for refreshments and sometimes for the night. From there, they went straight to Keighley and arrived just before dusk to be greeted by a timid looking household. It struck Adam straight away that how different his arrival was at Keighley to Sir James' welcome at Weston-Super-Mare. This was obviously the new earl's first visit since the demise of his father and the longest time the house had been without a visit from its lord.

Obviously, the young earl had sent word ahead of his forthcoming arrival so the pantry was well stocked, and it did not take very long before the covers were on and a very substantial meal was placed before him. He knew that his father had kept a good wine cellars, though he had never been permitted to view it. After he had his full of fricassée of rabbit, roast sirloin of beef, various vegetables and sauces, apple pie and pancakes, he felt tired but happy to be alone in the house with no feeling of friction. The housekeeper and butler were husband and wife, which worked very well. Mr Frost, the butler and his long serving wife were very eager to discover if the young master intended to make Keighley his home again, now his father and mother had gone. Adam decided that he would have an early night and in the morning call the household together and explain, as much as he knew himself, what his intentions were.

After a fitful night, Adam woke, got dressed and wondered down to the parlour. Laying there for his pleasure was cold meat, bread and cheese and a jug of wine. He had never been a big eater first thing in the morning and the cook knew what he liked, having known him from a small child. She, like the rest of the staff, had always liked Adam and his down trodden mother.

When he had finished eating, he called as many of the staff as was possible into the parlour to speak to them. Mr Frost bid them all be quiet and allow the young master to speak.

"I realise you all would have heard or even read about the accident that befell my parents," he began. "I want you all to know that I was exonerated of any possible involvement of the occurrence."

"I should hope so too, Sir," said Frost. "I think there are many that would be in front of the queue before you, Sir."

"I have learnt that over the past few months, Frost, myself. I am sorry to say that my father had the mark of the devil upon him."

"You should not say such a thing about your own father, Sir," said Mrs Frost rather shocked. "He must have had some good points surely."

"I would have liked to think so, Mrs Frost, but I have been hard pushed to hear anyone tell me any," the earl replied sadly. "It appears that the coroner ruled that the earl was driving erratically as was his way and the wheel loosened."

"That is the way we thought it would have been, Sir," said Frost.

"I have called you here today because I want to know if you wish to continue to work here with me at the helm. It has taken me several months to even start to gain the trust of my workers' families in Weston-Under-Wetherley, and I hope I will be able to try to do the same here," continued the earl.

"I, for one, do not believe that you are your father in any way," said Frost.

"I hope not and I hope to prove this fact," said the earl. "I intend to right as many wrongs as I possibly can but I fear they are numerous."

"It is not your place to put right what your father did wrong, he pays for these now, God willing," said Mrs Frost. "Your dear mother was a kindly soul and I, for one, think you favour her."

There was cry of aye, aye and hear, hear in the room.

Adam smiled widely and thanked everyone for their support.

"If you have anything you need to discuss with me privately, please wait behind, I would wish to make a fresh start," continued the earl. "I have a lot to learn, I have not even been in every room of this house myself and certainly, never the wine cellar. I know the stables very well and the kitchen, but I would like to be conducted round the rest at a convenient moment. Some rooms were always barred to me."

Mrs Frost asked if she might be allowed to show the young earl the books and then the house, which he said would be most acceptable.

"I will only be here a few days to make sure everyone is happy and to view the mills," Adam continued. "I wish to be sure in my own mind that the conditions our people work in are acceptable. Now if there is nothing else, please go about your business and remember that I am here to speak to you, so if you need to inform me of anything, just do so."

Mrs Frost cried out that she would call back in half an hour to start the tour

There was a small ripple of applause as everyone filed out leaving a small lad standing alone. He looked about eight or nine, had a mop of light brown curly hair, dirty nails, scruffy clothes and looked far too thin.

Adam turned to the boy and smiled, "Do you need to speak to me, boy?"

The boy took his cap from his head and bowed slightly. "If it pleases you, Sir, I do."

"Who are you?" asked Adam. "I do not believe that I have ever seen you before. What is your name and your purpose here in the house?"

"My name is Robbie and your father bought me around two years ago now, Sir, I am a chimney boy."

"A chimney boy, one who goes up chimneys to clean them?" asked Adam. "What do you mean bought you?"

"I used to belong to a sweep in Bradford, who bought me from my uncle when my mother died," said Robbie, matter of factually.

"And how old are you, Robbie?"

"Of that, I am not quite sure," was the reply. "I believe I am eight or nine years old."

"Good heavens child, eight or nine years old. What else do you do besides climb chimneys?"

"I clean the stables, peel potatoes, sweep the paths, anything I am told to do, Sir," was the reply. "I believe the master was about to let me go or sell me on because I am getting too big to climb the chimneys now. I was thinking I might go to Bradford, look for my sister and maybe be a whitewing for a while."

"What the devil is a whitewing, Robbie?" asked the earl feeling a little lost and unworldly.

"They sweep the crossings for fine gentlemen so their coats don't collect too much dust, Sir."

"Do they now? I feel I have a large piece missing from my education. Now you mentioned your sister, where would she be?"

"I do not know that, Sir, I have not seen her since the master took her away," was the reply.

Adam took the boy over to a chair, sat him down and pulled another up beside him. "What do you mean by took her away?"

"It was like this, Sir," began Robbie nervously. "The master bought my sister and me from this cove. She used to sell posies and matches, whatever she could find."

"Did she go up the chimneys as well?"

"Oh no, Sir, certainly not. She was coming up to 12 when I saw her last."

"And your sister, what was her name?" the earl asked kindly.

"Kitty, Sir."

"And what does she look like?"

"She looks like Kitty, she was turning into a pretty little thing, everyone said so, long fair curls, a bit lighter than mine."

"And what did my father do with Kitty? Did he set her to work?"

"I only saw her fleetingly the once. He had her washed and dressed and she looked like a real lady," the boy smiled as he spoke but Adam looked very worried.

"How will you find her if you do not know where she went?" Adam asked.

"The master said that he needed her for a while, then he would find her a job in one of his mills. Must be in Bradford, stands to reason, Sir."

Adam's head was full of horrified thoughts. "I feel you should stay and work for me, Robbie, I need an honest young lad in my pay. I will see if I can find Kitty when I go to inspect the mill."

Robbie looked delighted.

There was a quiet tap on the door and Mrs Frost entered, she looked surprised to see the earl and the young lad sitting close together deep in conversation.

"Robbie, I hope you are not bothering his lordship," she said concerned.

"On the contrary, Mrs Frost, Robbie was telling me how my father bought him and his young sister, and I have said that I will see if I can see her when I go to inspect the mill."

"That is very kind of you, Sir. I need to talk to you about young Robbie at some time, Sir, anyway," Mrs Frost said.

"Talk to me now, whilst we are all together."

"It is a bit delicate, Sir," she continued.

"In what way?" Adam asked.

"He was brought here as a sweeps boy but I fear he was already too big for the job," she said.

"And now you do not know what job he should do. Am I right, Mrs Frost," replied Adam, looking straight at her face.

"You are very astute, Sir," she answered.

"I have told Robbie here that I would like him to work for me, I think I could use a boy like him to run errands for me, maybe clean my boots, what do you think?" Adam asked Mrs Frost.

"Well, I don't know, Sir," she replied.

"Is the boy to be trusted?" asked Adam.

"As honest as the day is long, won't even take a biscuit unless pressed to do so."

"Then it is settled, the boy works for me. I want him scrubbed and dressed properly. I would like someone to take him to buy some clothes becoming of his new role. Nothing too fancy, a good pair of trousers, sturdy boots, a few shirts, warm coat, gloves, you know what a lad needs."

Robbie looked as though all his birthdays and Christmases had come at once and Mrs Frost just stood there with her mouth open in amazement.

"Don't look so shocked, Mrs Frost, the boy will be quite safe with me. I swear it on my mother's grave. You all will be."

Mrs Frost appeared to have a tear in her eye as she thanked the earl and told him that she believed they would be safe now.

Adam turned to Robbie and told him to run off and do whatever jobs he had left to do, because tomorrow he starts his new life.

Mrs Frost waited for the boy to leave the room before she spoke to the earl. "You cannot right all your father's wrongs, Sir. You will be pretty light in the pocket very quickly."

"I can try to right a few. Do you feel like I felt, did he buy the boy to get the girl?"

Mrs Frost threw her hands to her face. "I feared so, Sir," she said. "She was so young but so bonny and Robbie was too large for the chimneys. He would have been out on the street if your father had returned."

"My thoughts exactly. Do you think I will find Kitty in one of the mills?"

"Rumour has it, she is in the river, Sir," was the reply.

"Good God, woman, am I really the spawn of the devil?"

"It is not my place to say, Sir, but clearly he was an evil creature."

"I will look round the house if you will please, Madam," he said politely. "Tomorrow, would you please see that Robbie is clean and presentable? I intend to take good care of him, not a word to the boy of what we suspect."

"My lips are sealed, Sir, if only you knew the half of what I have seen."

"I want to know everything, every sordid story ever told, every mystery that involved my late father. I want no more surprises. I fear that I was too busy keeping my own person safe that I did not see what was obviously under my nose."

"You were very young, Sir, you still are," said the kindly housekeeper.

Chapter 23
Bradford and the Mill

Adam enjoyed his look round the house. He went into rooms that had previously been barred to him, rooms obviously laid aside to entertain. There was a room just for cards with a dozen or so well-covered card tables scattered about. Adam imagined the large gatherings of like-minded gamblers in this room, getting well-oiled on rum punch and port and exchanging bawdy stories, the thought made him cringe. Although the room had been well aired, the smell of stale tobacco still lingered on the drapes.

The wine cellar was even more extensive than he believed it would be—brick arched ceilings in room after room full of barrels, bottles, rack after rack. Adam had to duck in places where the ceiling was low. He could not imagine why anyone would need such an extensive supply of alcohol.

"The wine bill alone must have been crippling, I do not want any further supplies purchased until we have several racks free," said the earl.

The next day, he found Robbie scrubbed and dressed in borrowed clothes and waiting for his new master to come downstairs for his breakfast. After asking the boy if he had yet eaten, he made Robbie sit at the table whilst he ate so he could tell him what he expected from him. Adam pushed some of the cold meat and bread over towards the boy insisting that part of his duty was to taste the food put in front of him. As he watched the boy eat hungrily, he wondered how anyone could hurt such a trusting child and vowed to discover what had happened to Kitty, good or bad.

Adam had been in Keighley for five days, making sure Robbie had all he needed and checking on the livestock and outhouses. Then he took the boy with him when he visited the workers, who had tied cottages on his land, hoping that having a young lad with him might put everyone at their ease. Adam visited every cottage and made sure that every roof was sound. He ordered a thatcher to deal with any roof he was not happy with and also checked the general living conditions within. His people were generally nervous of him and untrusting. He tried very hard to convince everyone that he was not his father, and he would never act the way he would have. He had always believed himself to be popular amongst the staff, and now he realised that it was fear of his father that formed their views. Even having Robbie by his side seemed to throw a degree of suspicion his way. It was hard to believe that the son could be so different from the father, even everyone's love of Adam's mother did not shake the general opinion that bad blood will out.

Every time the young earl returned to his home, he felt a great disappointment that the staff in the fields could not accept him as readily as the house servants.

He had done all he could, so his next venture was to inspect the mills and see what working life was like there. However, he wanted to go and speak to Daniel,

Titus Salt and Christopher Waud before he went to his own mills and weaving sheds in Keighley. He wanted to compare the conditions in his friend's businesses and the one his father had run, fearing that he would have a lot to do to bring everything up to scratch. Adam thought that two nights in Bradford would be long enough for him to get a feel of the way things should be run, having only ever heard good reports about the Waud and Salt's mills. The next Monday morning, an excited Robbie, the earl and Martin, all climbed on board of the coach ready for the journey to Bradford.

They rattled along the 11 miles on the turnpike road to Bradford. Keighley was an intersection with other turnpikes, the Bradford to Keighley turnpike, Keighley to Halifax and the blue bell turnpike from Bradford to Calne. It was also a road that was notorious for pot holes and more worrying were the tales of odd robbers that could be found hiding amongst the bushes on the roads. Highwaymen, as such, were really a thing of the past but there was always the odd footpad, who tried his arm at holding up a coach or jumping a gentleman staying in a coaching inn.

Adam spent a great amount of the journey enlightening Robbie as to the dangers in the world.

"I will come to no harm in your care, Sir," was all he could say.

"I jolly well hope you are right, boy," was the reply. "But if you lose sight of me, do not wonder off with strangers, are you carrying two purses as I suggested?"

Robbie proudly produced the small leather pouches that he had tucked into his tunic.

"Now, boy," began Adam, "this is a trick that Martin and I use regularly, do we not, Martin?"

"That we do," replied Adam's valet, Martin, not having the vaguest idea what his master was talking about but trying to look as if he was in the picture.

Adam took out a pouch of his own and emptied a handful of copper and silver coins into his hand. He gave Robbie two farthings, two halfpennies, four pennies, a silver three penny bit and a sixpence. The boy's eyes were open wider than it seemed possible.

"All this blunt, Sir, I beg your pardon," exclaimed Robbie. "It cannot be for me."

"Why not, child, you work for me, do you not?" was the reply.

"I haven't earned a penny yet, Sir," said the boy.

"You are working now, you are looking out for footpads," Adam replied.

"Am I, Sir?" Robbie replied and turned his face to the window. "That I am, Sir."

"Now, Robbie," began Adam, "put a couple of coins in one purse and the rest in the other. Do not mix them up. In the unlikely event of a footpad or street robber accosting you in Bradford, hand over the lesser purse and run."

"Do you feel that we may come across such rum touches as would rob us in broad daylight, Sir, in Bradford?" the boy asked looking worried.

"No point in wrapping it in clean linen, boy, there are rum touches, as you call them, everywhere and we need to be prepared," Adam replied. "I think a youngster like you should be safe enough though."

The boy looked a little alarmed but did as instructed.

"I hope you do the same, Martin," said Adam.

"I do, Sir," he replied. "It was a trick that I was taught by my father many years ago." Martin then pulled on a thin strip of leather that was round his neck on which hung a George 3rd cartwheel penny, dated 1797.

"What the devil is that, Martin?" Adam asked.

"This, Sir, was given to me by my grandfather when I was very young. He had the blacksmith make the hole so I could wear it round my neck in case I was ever without a penny to my name," was the reply.

Martin placed the coin into Adam's hand so he could feel the weight. "I thought it looked heavier than maybe it should," the earl said.

"It is, Sir," was the reply. "It is known as a cartwheel penny because of its weight and size. I probably have kept it too long to spend as they do not make them this heavy anymore. Weighed down a gentleman's pocket, no doubt." He placed the lace back round his neck as he spoke. "I keep it for good luck."

"A good idea, Martin, we all need a bit of good luck," replied Adam with a smile.

Robbie took what seemed like an age deciding, which coin he would put in which pouch, much to Adam's amusement.

The rest of the journey was taken up with idle chatter.

Soon the coach was pulling into the Devonshire Arms Coaching Inn on the corner of Church Street and High Street, an inn recommended to the earl. The building had been completely rebuilt in 1788 in a classic style, the high fashion of the day with Tuscan columns. It was a fine looking building.

As they pulled to a halt, Adam reminded Martin that he had a task to complete in Bradford for him. "I need good sturdy walking boots for the boy if you please, Martin," he said. "Also, a few handkerchiefs, no more of this wiping noses on arms, boy." Adam smiled at Robbie as he spoke. Adam handed a roll of notes to Martin warning him to keep them and himself safe and to buy anything else that he thought a small boy might need.

Martin is a good-natured young man, just turned 27, quite tall, just a touch below six foot, slim, dark hair and eyes and with a pleasant open face. He was quite happy to take charge of the boy for a few hours, whilst the earl went about his business.

They entered the inn and caused a degree of confusion when they did so. The coach clearly showed the earl's crest, a sight not very welcoming in any inn in Bradford or anywhere else for that matter. The news of the earl's demise had reached far across Yorkshire but no one as yet knew what the new earl would bring with him. Adam stepped lightly down from the coach and offered a hand to Robbie, which in itself caused a stir. Martin leapt from the coach unaided and went in ahead to organise rooms for two nights stop.

They booked two bedrooms and the use of a side room to eat undisturbed. It was assumed that Robbie was maybe the earl's son or nephew and no one was given any explanation as to why the boy travelled with them. The earl told the inn keeper that he would pay him well if he saw to the needs of his groomsmen and horses.

"I wish them to be fed, watered and bedded in comfort, both groomsmen and livestock. My men will attend the horses, they will be no burden to you, my good man."

As soon as their baggage was in their rooms, they washed up after the journey and then met downstairs for something to eat. They were pleasantly surprised by the quality of the table set before them. Adam did feel that maybe it was half in fear that the cook had made such an effort.

Robbie was sharing a room with Martin, there was a small trestle bed in the room as well as a large comfortable looking one; the trestle was the sort that very often Martin slept on in the same room as his master when they were away from home. Robbie was more than pleased to have a bed of his own, having slept mainly in the barn or occasionally, on a cold night, in the corner of the kitchen in Keighley Manor when Mrs Frost felt sorry for him.

When the boy saw the food laid out in front of them, he could not believe his eyes—goose and turkey pies, boiled leg of lamb and spinach, roast pigeon, roasted chestnuts, oysters in batter, sauces and vegetables. It was an array of food, the like of which the boy had never seen.

"Surely, Sir, this cannot be for just us three," he said in innocent wonder.

When the landlord replied, looking confused himself by this response, that it most certainly was, Robbie was quite speechless.

"This is quite excellent, Landlord," the earl said politely. "If you would be so kind as to furnish us with some ratafia or a glass of wine and some fruit juice for the boy, I would be grateful."

The landlord hurried from the room as quickly as he could to report to his wife that the young gentleman, although he had given his name as Adam Southerly, the Earl of Wetherley, bore no similarity except facially to the old, not missed and greatly feared earl.

The three travellers sat and ate their full and talked non-stop. Adam was never one for airs and graces, he thought all men equal, only money and title made them stand out one from another but a good man was a good man, rich or poor. He could converse with anyone and enjoyed doing so. Something his father found quite unbecoming of the son of an earl, and something he came down heavily on his son about.

Adam had sent word ahead to his mill owner friends and had arranged to meet each one separately, which meant they would have to spend two nights at the inn.

"When you have run the errand I have given you, Martin, please take the boy and look around Bradford at your own pace. And you, young man," he said turning to Robbie, "mind what Mr Martin tells you, keep an eye on your purse, keep out of trouble and stay safe."

"I will not let you down, Sir," was the reply. "If I may speak, Sir," he added.

"Of course you can, boy, what is it that bothers you?" replied the earl.

"You said you would look for Kitty, but you do not know what she looks like, should I not come with you to the mills, Sir?" Robbie said, concerned.

"It will be alright, Robbie," the earl ruffled the boy's hair as he spoke. "I will speak directly to the mill owners and ask after a pretty girl brought in by my father. They will know of whom I speak, you can be sure of that. I think it more likely that Kitty is in Keighley in our own mill."

"Maybe we should have looked their first then," the boy replied matter of factually.

"You may be right, young man, but I hope a couple of days will not make too much difference, and I did want to check that she was not here in Bradford first," came the reply. "I need to speak to some gentlemen here and I fear you will become very bored with the conversation. I need to learn about the mill and how they run. I do not want to sound like a green boy when I speak to the overseer in my own mill."

Robbie looked quite content with this answer.

"I would say you have set yourself a heavy task, Sir," said Martin. "These mill owners have been in the business for many years, I cannot believe you will learn too much in just two days."

"I know you are right, Martin," was the reply. "But if I have a few basic facts, it will make me look less foolish. I have read a bit about the trade but there are so many factions, so many jobs."

"My cousin is a hand loom weaver, works here about, it is hard and noisy work," continued Martin. "She tells me that the girls wear ear plugs to keep out the noise and learn to use sign language so they can speak to each other."

"I had heard that the noise was terrible, I really feel I have missed a large piece from my education by never been taken to view the workings of a mill," replied the earl.

"I doubt your father ever set foot inside the mill either," said Martin. "Except maybe to do someone a disservice, I beg your pardon, Sir, that was quite out of order."

"But probably very true, Martin. I am beginning to believe that my father may have been a little queer in the attic; he certainly did not behave like a sane man." Adam replied with a sigh. "If you need time to contact your cousin and any other kin, please make it possible as you are so close by."

"That is exceedingly kind of you, Sir," replied Martin. "I do have an odd cousin and uncle but as I have not seen them for a great many years, I will stay with the odd missive, thank you for thinking of me. You are not your father, you never will be. Just look around, you are eating with a raggedy boy and a servant, your father would have said it was you who were the madman but he would be quite wrong."

"I am no raggedy boy," cried Robbie. "I was but just look at all this fine gear that I am wearing." He stood up and twirled round making Martin and Adam laugh.

"A fine looking young gentleman you are for sure," said Martin.

The boy looked fit to burst at this praise.

"I firmly believe, Martin," said the earl, "that my father did me a great service by being the man he was. He showed me exactly the person I did not want to emulate. I do not want to be in the same world as my father or his cronies. It is going to take me a long while to convince people that he and I never were or could be alike, I hope my actions will eventually make this believable. It is an uphill struggle."

"One you will achieve, Sir," said Martin with a smile.

Adam and Martin had always spoken in an easy way. Martin had been with his young master since he was a little younger than Robbie was now. He was not a foundling like Robbie, his father had worked for the family in Keighley and had passed on shortly after retiring. So Adam and Martin had practically grown up together and because of this, they spoke of many things that master and servant did not usually share an interest in. Martin had been allowed to sit in on a lot of Adam's lessons, so he was reasonably learned. Martin's task had been of whipping boy but Adam had never given any cause for that position to be tested, avoiding any confrontation with his father. Adam was always pleased with Martin's honest and open answers to everything and enjoyed his company, another thing his father disapproved off, 'fraternising with underlings' as he called it. Martin did, however, know where the lines were drawn and tried not to cross them.

"I, for one, am away to bed, I plan an early start," said the earl. "You rise when you wish, your time here is your own. I will meet up again with you for supper tomorrow night. I hope you are plump enough in the pocket for your day tomorrow; if not, just drop my name and I will settle up on the morrow."

Martin took out his roll of bank notes and said that he thought he had a year's pay in his hand, and if that was not enough, he could not imagine what he was doing.

Chapter 24
Learning About the Mills

The next morning was as the earl intended, he rose before 10, had his breakfast and took a hired carriage to Britannia Mills where he had arranged to meet Christopher Waud and hopefully, his father, Robert, depending on his state of health.

The mill was made up of enormous oblong grey stone and brick buildings, quite a formidable sight and far larger than Adam had envisaged. He asked his driver to take the carriage down Portland Street, past Portland Mills on his right, left into Queen's Cut and left again into Victoria Street at the cross roads with Cross Street. Waterloo foundry was on his right and the reservoir, he was trying to get an idea of the size of the mill and weaving shed. Adam had only ever been to Bradford before on a couple of occasions that he could recall and never to see a mill. The sheer size amazed him.

Christopher was very happy to see Adam, they had not crossed each other's paths for a few years. Christopher is just two years older than Adam but has run the Britannia Mill and the weaving shed from quite a young age due to his father's delicate health. It seems that his father, Robert, was not well enough to make this meeting, though Adam felt it was probably due to the fact that Robert was not very fond of the old earl and did not want to meet his son. This fact proved to be correct.

Christopher took Adam into an office that had a large window looking down on the mill and its workers. The noise was deafening. Adam could not take his eyes off the rows and rows of looms clacking away beneath him. Young men and women wearing cotton mop caps to keep their hair from getting entangled in any mechanism. Nimble fingers working ten to the dozen. He was quite amazed.

"I take it, Adam, that your father never took you into any of his mills," said Christopher.

"I doubt he ever went into them himself," was the reply. "My grandfather was the man behind the empire, my father was a spender of money and destroyer of reputations. I do not think, so long as the money rolled in, he would have cared how the mill worked."

"You sound like my father speaking," said Christopher, feeling sorry for his young friend. "My father says exactly that of your ancestry."

"My father's untimely death has been a real eye opener," continued the earl. "I had no idea how ill thought of my father was or why until he met with his accident. I know how badly he treated my mother and I but beyond that, I tried to at least hope that he was a better man."

"I did not believe the stories that came our way after your father's demise," said Christopher. "Not stories about your father, those we all knew to be true, but the one that you killed him."

Adam looked a little taken aback. "I am glad to hear it, Christopher, my dislike of any man would never have driven me to such an act, I can assure you."

"I know that, Adam," was the reply. "Though many would thought that you were justified."

"I need to touch on a delicate matter, Christopher, regarding my late father," said Adam.

"I am all ears, my friend, nothing will surprise me," was the reply.

"Everything surprises me," began Adam. "This more so than most. I will not beat about the bush. I am looking for a young woman, more a child to be honest. Maybe 12 years old, coming up 13, very pretty called Kitty."

"You intrigue me, what has she done?"

"The girl has done nothing, without pressure that is," Adam continued. "I will tell you the whole sorry story. I came across a boy, or more to tell the truth, he came across me. He asked me to find his sister, bought by my father." Adam saw the shocked look on Christopher's face. "Yes, you heard me right, bought by my father alongside the boy but separated from him. The boy was to be cast out, of that I am sure; he was a sweep boy but getting too plump for the job. I have promised to look for the girl. I am hoping she may be working in one of the mills. I believe my father bought the boy to get the girl and dread to think for what purpose. The boy is now in my care, in fact, I have brought him to Bradford with me."

"She would not be in one of our mills, my father would never take on one of your father's cast offs, of that I am sure," said Christopher, concerned. "But I will ask about, I know several mill owners. I will get word to you if I hear anything. Kitty you say, do you know what she looks like?"

"I only know that he dressed her up and according to her brother, Robbie, she is fine looking with long fair ringlets," replied Adam, embarrassed.

"I cannot picture such a girl but with cloth caps on and working, faces all become one, I am afraid," replied Christopher. "I will see what I can do. I do not envy you, Adam, but you are good man. I fear this may be the start of a list of undetected crimes that you might wish to try to solve. Take time for yourself as well."

Adam thanked his friend for his concern and told him about Sally, he was most intrigued.

"If that is the way of things, Adam," said Christopher, "the girl is probably closer to home. He may not have damaged her as yet, maybe waiting for the child to become a woman!"

"I think you might be right," was the reply. "It is hard to think in a way so alien to your own thinking."

Adam stayed with Christopher for the majority of the day travelling from the mill to the weaving shed. Adam had no idea how many mills there were thereabouts, he was quite amazed when he was given a figure of over 100 weaving connected businesses in the Bradford area alone.

There were makers of the machinery to run the mills, loom makers, spinners, those who dyed the wool, those who collected and transported the wool, weavers, bobbin makers, silk providers, dye makers, frame engineers, shuttle makers, cotton spinners, cotton providers from foreign lands, croppers, clothiers—to name but a few. Then there were the workers, the weavers, spinners, finishers, bleachers, cotton bailers, hand loom weavers, mill labourers, mill boys and girls, cleaners—Adam's head was spinning.

By the time Martin and Robbie arrived back at the inn, Adam was tired and had written up copious notes about his visit to Bradford and the mill.

Robbie bounded in full of life and went straight into the side room, where he expected to find Adam. He had, on a piece of string, a rather thin, long-haired, little dog of no defined parenthood.

"Look, what I bought!" he said cheerfully. "She will clean up well and won't be any trouble."

"I am sorry, Sir," said Martin. "I turned my back for just a moment and the boy was standing there with this scruffy mutt by his side. I told him that it would not be a good idea to bring the creature here, but Robbie assured me that as you had taken him in as a raggedy boy, you would not object to a poor, sad creature like the one he had acquired."

Adam laughed heartily. "Oh dear," he said, "I was warned that if I tried to be too nice, problems would come my way. At least it is a very little problem."

"Do you mean I can keep her?" said Robbie, almost jumping for joy.

"I think if she, if that is what it is, was a little cleaner, it might be a pretty little addition to the family. I think my sister would love it also," said Adam.

"I will take her outside and wash her down," said the boy. "You will see how pretty I can make her." With that, he hurried from the room towing the poor bewildered creature behind him.

"I assume everything else was accomplished regarding the boy, Martin," asked Adam with a smile.

"It was, Sir, good sturdy shoes, several handkerchiefs, a pair of woollen gloves, very apt considering I believe, Sir, he was most pleased," was the reply.

"I am pleased as well, Martin," Adam said. "The boy is like a breath of fresh air, Sally will love him. As we now have a dog, it will be part of his working day to keep it clean and out of trouble. I have had a very productive day myself. I had no idea how much industry there is in these parts. My education was sadly lacking when it comes to real life. These people, young and old, work so many hours for so little reward."

"They do at least have work, Sir," Martin replied. "This puts meat on their bones and a roof over their heads. I am sure that every one of them is grateful for every penny they earn, however hard the work may be."

"I hope you are right, Martin," Adam replied. "But the noise, so many looms in one space, so many people, the heat —not a place I would care to spend my days."

"Happily, Sir, you never will need to."

"That is true, Martin, but I do propose to make sure that my workers are properly attended to. There appears to be no medical facilities. A young woman fainted and she was merely taken to one side to recover and then later, I saw her back working."

"She would not have wanted to lose her livelihood," explained Martin. "Did you learn all you needed?"

"I learnt very little, there was far too much to take in on one visit, it would take me months," came the reply. "I learnt that the way the warp and filling threads interlace with each other is called the weave, and that there are three basic weaves —plain, satin and twill—I have no idea which is which."

"Sounds to me like you have made a good start, Sir," remarked Martin.

"A start is all it is. Weaving involves using a loom to interlace two sets of threads, one warp thread is called is an end and one weft thread is called a pick. I am planning to throw this knowledge into any conversation I have at my own woollen mill, even though I have no idea what I am talking about."

Martin laughed as he replied, "That is a good start, you sound most informed."

There was aloud tap on the door followed by the entrance of the inn keeper, who came into the side room and laid the cover on the table ready for supper. "If you are worried about your boy, Sir," said the man, "he is with my misses in the kitchen, feeding that scrawny mess of a dog and drying it off after its bath."

Adam looked alarmed. "I do hope that he is not bothering your good wife too much. Please tell her to send him to me as soon as she finds him too much trouble."

"He won't trouble her, Sir. She likes bairns, none of her own you see, nature didn't allow such a luxury," was the reply.

"I am sorry to hear that," replied Adam sincerely. "A woman needs a child to nurture. Do thank her for me."

The inn keeper smiled at the earl. He was surprised himself how he was drawn to the young man, even though he had made up his mind not to like him because of his father.

"Might I ask, Sir," he said, "is the boy a relative or a servant? He says that he is a foundling but I was not sure if he speaks the truth."

"Robbie always speaks the truth," was the reply. "He was a sweep boy, grown too large for the task. I came across him by chance and he is now in my care. He is a good-hearted lad."

"Strikes me, my Lord, that he has a kind-hearted benefactor," said the inn keeper as he turned to leave.

As soon as the door was closed behind the man, Martin turned to Adam and told him that he believed he had won yet another doubting Thomas to his cause. Adam just smiled.

The food was already on the table when Robbie and the little bitch reappeared in the side room. The little creature, although painfully thin, had a beautiful white fluffy coat and bright eyes. She looked quite a picture. Adam smiled to himself liking the dog to his sister; in the way she had turned into a rose when first thought to be a dandelion.

"What do you propose to call your new friend?" Adam asked Robbie.

"I thought to call her Daisy after the lady downstairs," was the reply. "I did ask her if it would be fine to do so and she cried, so I am not sure if I should call her this."

"Be assured, Robbie." said Adam forcefully. "The woman will be thrilled with the choice of name. You will learn when you get older about women and tears."

The boy looked confused but accepted the answer without question.

Soon the table was covered in an array of food, even better than the night before. There was a chicken broth to start with, fresh, home-baked bread, crimped cod, a goose pie, scallops, lightly cooked eggs, vegetables, apple pie and pancakes dripping with honey. There was a separate plate with bones and finely chopped meat for Daisy.

"I hope you will be satisfied with the meal, Sir," said the inn keeper as he placed the last dish on the table.

"My dear man," replied the earl, "I have never come across a finer cook than your wife. Even my own would come a close second to her skills. Please thank her for me and also for her care for the boy."

The man blushed slightly and nodded, he turned at the door and bowed to the earl.

The happy three sat and talked for a couple of hours in the light of the coal fire burning in the hearth. Robbie sat crossed legged with Daisy close by until his eyes could not stay open any longer.

"You have a dog now, boy," said Adam with a smile as he sent the boy to bed. "No more surprises, if you please, tomorrow young man."

The dog trotted up the stairs after its new master, as meek as a lamb.

"I hope Daisy does not cause any problems in the night for you, Martin," said Adam.

"If she does, I will deposit it down into the kitchen," was the reply. "Do you have any tasks for me tomorrow, Sir?"

"No, Martin," was the reply. "I would wish you to have as pleasant a day as possible, doing as you wish, with a small boy and even smaller dog in tow," Adam laughed as he spoke.

The next day, Adam was first down again and was fussed over like a long lost friend by the inn keeper. He took the time to go down into the kitchen and seek out the inn keeper's wife to thank her for her fine food and care of the boy. She was, as expected, a rosy-faced woman of large proportions and jolly manner. She curtsied so many times that it was hard for Adam to suppress a laugh. He asked if there was anything he could do for her, and she was so embarrassed that she could only stutter an incoherent reply. Adam went back up to the side room and wrote a short note for Martin expressing his desire for him to buy a small gift for the inn keeper's wife, nothing too fancy, just a trinket that would amuse her. Then he headed off to meet his old friend, Titus Salt, to learn a little more about the mill trade. Titus lived in manor farm in Crofton, Nr. Wakefield but was going to Bradford that day on business, so they had arranged to meet in a hostelry in town.

When Adam arrived back at the inn in the late afternoon, he was once again tired and trying to remember all he had been told. He was happy to see Titus, who was learning the trade from his father, Sir Daniel. They were hands-on mill owners, unlike his own father.

Adam's father had never approved of the friendship that Adam had struck up as a child with Titus. Sir Daniel Salt was a Baronet, born in Morley near Leeds and, as such, considered to be titled gentry and not deemed to be a member of the nobility. Such snobbery annoyed Adam intensely but it was quite usual for his father to belittle people for such things as rank.

Adam spent most of the day with Titus, being shown around Bradford and talking about the industries there about. He was surprised how different Bradford was to Keighley and even more so to Weston-Under-Wetherley. He watched the whitewings that Robbie had spoken of sweeping the dust from the road, where gentleman passed hoping for a penny for their trouble. He watched willow plaiters on the side of the road selling their baskets when finished. He got the general idea of wages across the different weaving skills and learnt a little more about the mills before taking a carriage back to the inn.

He washed his hand and went into the side room to write down what he had learnt that day. He heard Martin and Robbie as they entered the inn, the dog yapping at the boy's side. The boy almost crashed into the side room.

"Look what Martin bought, my Lord," said Robbie dragging Daisy over to the table, where Adam was writing notes. He had a long, thin piece of leather fixed to a collar. "Isn't it fine?"

Adam looked up and smiled.

"I am away to show Daisy downstairs what I have bought for her namesake and get my pup some food." With that, Robbie vanished as quickly as he entered.

Martin was almost knocked over by the excited boy as he left the side room.

"That boy is like a whirl wind, I hope he did not wear you out today. Did you manage that task I set you, Martin?" asked the earl.

"Oh yes, my Lord." Martin replied. "I thought long and hard about an appropriate gift for such a woman. My plan was at first to buy a thick woollen shawl to keep out the weather and draught, but I thought she would have several already, being a wool making town. I thought her not made for lace trimmed handkerchiefs or useless items. Then the boy brought this shop window to my notice."

Adam looked intrigued and a little apprehensive.

"The boy spotted this enamel clasp, the sort you pin to a shawl at the points to keep it around you once it is about your shoulders," Martin continued with pride. "It is a pretty piece, I thought long and hard about buying it, wondering if it might be too much for the woman to accept. Not wanting to embarrass her."

"Was it that expensive?" asked Adam. "Oh no, Sir, not unseemly so, a mere bagatelle, a trinket," Martin continued. "I had thought about a small pearl broach but thought that too extravagant but as I say, the boy spotted this."

Martin took out a small, velvet draw string pouch from his pocket and tipped the contents onto the table in front of the earl and a small enamel clasp rolled out. Adam picked it up and examined the item. It was indeed a pretty little piece. Martin pointed to the clasp. "Do you see, Sir, it has a daisy depicted upon it. What a clever boy was he to spot that!"

"A remarkable eye for detail," replied the earl, amused. "I believe the woman will like this very much. Thank you for your care in choosing such a gift, Martin."

After the three of them had eaten yet another splendid meal, Adam found his way down to the kitchen clutching the little pouch containing the enamel daisy. The inn keeper's wife was sitting at the large refectory table, flour on her face from pastry making. She jumped to her feet as she saw the earl approaching and fell into a most uncomfortable looking curtsy.

"Please, Madam, do not be so formal," said the earl with a smile, most amused by the woman's nervous attentions. "I have come to thank you for your efforts to please us with your culinary skills but more so for putting up with Robbie's enthusiasm."

She stood for a moment unable to speak and then stuttered out that the boy was a pleasure and a joy.

"I am glad you found him not too tiring, Madam," said Adam kindly. "I to find him a delight in this hard world."

"He has told me all about your kindness to him, a hero to him you are, Sir, and rightly so," said the woman, a little embarrassed, never having conversed with a man of rank before.

"A hero, I hope not, Madam, but I thank you anyway." He held out the pouch and placed it into the woman's hand. "Do not be embarrassed, I beg of you. This is just a trinket chosen by Robbie to thank you for your care."

The woman stared down at the pouch for what seemed like an age to Adam before she pulled open the draw string and gently removed the clasp. She looked wide eyed at the enamel daisy and burst into floods of tears, so loud did she sob that it brought her husband running to what he thought might be her aid.

"What is occurring here?" the inn keeper yelled in a very loud voice.

"I gave your good wife a small thank you gift and I am afraid the heavens have opened up," was the reply.

The inn keeper took the clasp from his sobbing wife's hand and looked at it closely before handing it back to her. "She is over whelmed, Sir," he said calmly as he placed an arm around his wife. "People are rarely so kind. She cries tears of happiness, a strange breed women."

"Yes, I believe so, in fact I was telling Robbie only the other day about women and their tears," replied Adam. "I must say that rarely have I seen such an out flowing of tears."

"She never does anything by halves, my misses," came the reply. "Cooks too many pies, the waste here is a crime."

Martin appeared at the door of the kitchen. "There is a messenger to see you, my Lord," he said.

The earl went upstairs to greet the messenger and take a missive from his hand from Christopher Waud. True to his word, he had spoken to several mill owners and one such person, the owner of Spring Mill in Bowling, Bradford, had taken on a young girl last year, sent to him by a gentleman's gentleman. It sounded possible that this could be the missing sister. Adam prayed that this would be the case, he did not relish the idea of having to tell Robbie that his sister was at the bottom of the river as suspected. It was becoming clear that they might have to extend their stay.

The earl scribbled a quick reply and sent it back to Christopher. He then informed Martin that they needed to go out for a while, spoke to the inn keeper's wife, who was by now eating out of his hand, and asked her to keep an eye on Robbie for a while. He told her exactly where he was going and why and explained that because he was by no means sure that the girl will turn out to be Kitty, he did not want Robbie's hopes up, so he would not tell him anything at this stage. She was more than happy to be included in this adventure and promised to show the boy the workings of the kitchen and keep him amused. Adam felt that he had left Robbie in good and safe hands.

Adam and Martin set off to Spring Mill in a carriage. On arrival, they were greeted by the manager, who had been appraised of the reason for the visitors. He had already sent for the young woman in question. Adam waited with trepidation for the girl to appear. He knew as soon as she stepped into the room that she was not the one he sought.

A delicate, timid child stood before him, probably no older than 10, although the manager assured Adam that she swore she was 13. The girl did not look cut out for the hard work that a mill offered. Adam sat the child down and asked her to tell him about herself.

Her name was Lizzie and she had been left orphaned by the white plague; all her family, mother, father, brother and sisters taken from her. Adam asked her where she lived and she replied that she slept wherever she could; having lost her home, it being a tied cottage connected to her father's work. She had not been allowed to stay even long enough to collect her clothes.

Adam was appalled by such callous behaviour.

Adam took the mill manager aside but having heard of Adam's father's reputation, he was reluctant to take up the offer to buy her off, so he could take her away and apply her to work that would better suit her constitution. The girl was frail, having been left after a bout of TB with a weakness and the manager admitted that her work was substandard. The manager did not think that the girl would ever make a good webster (female weaver) or even a woollen billy piecer as they called the workers who joined up pieces of broken yarn. After a deep conversation and promises of the girl's safety, Adam was allowed to take Lizzie away with him. At the inn keeper's insistence, Martin had brought a blanket which he wrapped around the girl as he led her out of the mill to the awaiting carriage. The girl looked very bewildered and frightened. She only stopped shaking when they alighted from the carriage at the inn, and she was put into the care of the inn keeper's wife. Daisy fussed and fretted over the girl and insisted on her sitting down to a bowl of freshly made chicken broth before anything further was said or done.

Lizzie was quite bewildered by all the attention.

Daisy took the earl aside. "What now, my Lord?" she asked.

"I do not know, Madam," he replied. "I only know that I could not leave the child there. She is a delicate one, she would not last a year in such conditions. She has no one, what could I do?"

Daisy smiled the widest smile the earl had ever seen. "You did right, Sir. Sorry I am that she was not the girl you sought, but I would be glad to take her on myself. I have no children and no one to pass my culinary skills on to. Could I maybe be permitted if she is willing to keep her here with me? She will get clean clothes, a warm bed and a full belly."

The earl was absolutely thrilled with this suggestion.

"I was going to ask to keep the boy, Sir," continued Daisy, "but I know for sure, he would never be parted from you."

"Nor I from him, Madam," replied Adam.

Robbie was disappointed that the earl had not as yet found Kitty but was happy that the young woman was safe now and knew that his saviour was looking for his sister as promised. Adam ruffled the boy's hair and promised to continue his search.

Needless to say, Lizzie was very happy to stay in the inn and be part of the family therein. The earl insisted on giving Daisy a roll of bills to pay for new clothes for the child, as well as paying over the odds for his stay at the inn.

As they were preparing to take their leave of Bradford and The Devonshire Inn, the landlord asked if he might have a private word with the earl, which was readily agreed to. The earl, already dressed in his heavy travelling coat, waited in the side room for the inn keeper's tap on the door.

"I wanted just a quiet word with your lordship before you disappear from our lives," began the man. "Firstly, my wife and I would like to apologise for any coldness that we expressed on your arrival, we now know that the father is not the son."

"Please, do not apologise. I face this every day and probably always will," was the reply.

"Not if my Daisy has anything to do with it, Sir," replied the man. "There will not be a man, woman or child in these parts who has not seen that clasp you gave her, and she will treasure Lizzie as her own—a dream come true for her. You will not stop her from excelling you to sainthood."

"Oh good heavens, man, I did not rescue Lizzie to gain adulation, I can assure you," replied Adam rather embarrassed.

"I know that, my Lord. It is the other that you seek for the boy's sake," continued the man.

"It is at that, though I think it will end in disaster and tears. I fear the child is lost," said the earl sadly.

"It is no fault of your, Sir, the fact you are trying to find Kitty is in itself a fine act."

"I do not need to hear flummery, it is matter of honour," the earl said.

"I see clearly that you are a man of honour, Sir, and everyone will see you in this light on even the slighted acquaintance. I wanted to make a suggestion about Kitty."

"You have a thought as to where my father might have placed her?"

"My wife suggested a nunnery but I thought maybe she would be too difficult to remove at any time," said the man.

"I had thought of that myself and I have written to a good nun, who nursed my sister to get her advice. Do you have any other thoughts?" the earl asked.

"I spoke to a friend and he suggested a cat house."

The young earl looked bewildered. "A cat house!"

"A whorehouse, Sir. She would stay safe there, be taught the trade, if you will excuse my bawdy talk, Sir," said the man, "The women there would treat her well, keep her safe and well fed. I doubt their kindness would have run to defying your father when he came to re-claim her though, and now he has passed, they may just bring her on as a woman to work there."

The earl looked shocked. "Oh my God, man, why did this not occur to me?" he exclaimed. "Now I must find her, she can only be 13 or 14, a mere child, before her lot is equally as bad as it would have been before my father's death."

"I did not mean to alarm you, Sir," said the man. "But it stands to reason, there are not many places to hide a young woman. I would say that she might live a lot longer where she is, if in fact that is where she is, than if your father had removed her."

"You are probably right, most people believe she is already at the bottom of the river. You are a good man," replied the earl. "I do not know where to start to look."

"I would not suggest you looked anywhere yourself, Sir," replied the man. "You must have men in your employ who could call in such a place and ask about. If your carriage turned up, the girl would magic out the back door faster than a rabbit down a hole. Do not forget, not everyone knows you are a different kettle of fish to the last earl."

"My good man, if I thought for one moment that people would judge me as being like him, I would join my mother underground. I would just like to hear one good word about the man, one thing I could be proud of."

"You can be proud of yourself, my Lord," was the kind reply. "You may be of his blood but I believe your mother's influence was stronger than his. I would suggest you too look closer to home, Sir, for the girl; she would have to be within easy reach."

The earl smiled and shook the inn keeper's hand. They walked together to the coach where Daisy was fussing over Robbie and the little dog. Lizzie stood nervously, pretty as a picture, smiling and guarding a very large picnic hamper that had been prepared for their journey. Martin placed the hamper in the centre of the inner seating in the coach and they climbed aboard.

"Do not forget all of you," said the earl as he climbed aboard.

"If you hear anything of the girl I seek, get word to me, and if you need anything yourselves, do likewise. Your kindness has touched me greatly."

Daisy burst into tear and buried her face in his apron.

Chapter 25
Back to Keighley and the Mill

They arrived back at Keighley. On the journey, the earl had only touched on the idea that Kitty might be in a brothel; he did not speak of it in front of the boy so it was only when he and Martin were alone that he could bring up the possibility. Martin thought it was indeed a possible hiding place but also added that he himself had no knowledge of such places in Keighley. Adam gave him the task of seeking out a couple of likely lads that could go to any cat houses that might exist and try to discover the girl's whereabouts. He wanted the greatest discretion to be used. He did not want tongues to wag and any suggestion that he might be interested in such places like his father.

Robbie had jumped from the coach and rushed down below stairs to show Mrs Frost his new friend. Daisy had been given a wide yellow ribbon and it was tied round its neck in a bow. The animal bounced around the kitchen causing a bit of an uproar as it chased the resident mouse catcher out of the door.

Mrs Frost is a good natured woman with a soft spot for children and animals; the cat was a foundling, abandoned by its mother, a little wild but a good mouser so she earned her keep.

She gave Robbie a slice of cake and listened to his tales of his visit to Bradford. Soon, she was informed of everything that the earl had done, she knew and approved greatly of how he had taken Lizzie and placed her in safety. She never thought in her wildest dreams that she would ever be proud to say that she was the housekeeper and cook for the Earl of Wetherley.

Two days later, Martin went to look for the earl with two, not too rough but unpolished, gentlemen in tow.

"Sir, this is Bill Glover and Sam Stoves, they have volunteered to help you in your endeavours to find Miss Kitty," said Martin. "They have heard the tale and are keen to help. They are good, honest working men, I have looked into their back grounds as much as time allowed."

The earl sprung to his feet and put out his hand to shake theirs, they were taken aback and bowed deeply. "I assume that my man has fully informed you of what I need from you two gentlemen?"

The men smiled at each other, they were not used to being referred to as gentlemen.

"There is no point in me wrapping the story in clean linen, my father's reputation would have gone before him."

The two men nodded.

"I have a young lad in my care and I seek his sister placed somewhere by my father. I am hoping you gentlemen might assist me to find her," continued the earl.

"I wish to return her to her brother and safety. I fear she may be in a brothel, the thought was placed in my mind by a very worthy gentleman, who wondered if this might be the only sure place to hide a young woman."

"Do I have permission to speak, my Lord," said Bill, a large, broad shouldered man with a large round face and hands like spades.

"Of course, man."

"I believe that if the girl is underage, she will probably be working in the laundry or acting as a maid until she reaches her prime, so to speak."

"I hope this proves to be true, Bill," replied the earl. "I would like to think that she has not been placed in danger at such a tender age. I think she may be touching on 12."

"Girls as young as that are made to look older and sometimes put to work early, I am afraid, my Lord," continued Bill. "We may be too late."

"I hope not," replied the earl. "I want her removed, tarnished or pure, it is not on her head that this has occurred, it is a wrong I must right. Can you do this for me, gentlemen?"

"We would be honoured to try, Sir," was the reply, "though there is no guarantee that we will find her in such a place."

"I am aware of this, gentlemen, but it is a start," replied the earl. "Do what you can, discover what you can and report back to me. If you can find the girl and manage to make good her escape, all the better; but if you find out that she is being protected, I will think again about how to release her."

Martin gave the men a roll of bank notes as requested and they left to begin their task.

"I assume they will not just run off with the bung we have given them," the earl said to Martin.

"That they will not, Sir," replied Martin. "I took great care to put in their minds that you had power and influence that you chose to use for good, but it could equally find anyone who double crossed you."

"Martin!" exclaimed the earl, "I do not think that the large one would be easily intimidated, he was built like an oxen. Do you think that they will make good their task?"

"I think they have as much chance as any, Sir," was the reply. "I am assured that luckily, there is only one brothel that actual gentlemen would be likely to acquaint in Keighley."

This latest mission underway, the earl sat down to continue a letter that he had started to Dorothia explaining his absence for such a long while. He decided to leave nothing from this letter. He told Dorothia how he had come across a young lad, Robbie, who had been bought by his late father, George Southerly, as a sweep boy when it was obvious that the boy was too large for the job. Alongside Robbie, George Southerly had bought the lad's very delicately beautiful young sister, Kitty.

He told her about Robbie and his little dog and how it had been suggested to him that Kitty might be in a bad place, and his plans to release her but fears that she was already in the river.

He wrote how he was trying to discover more about the running of mills and his meetings with Titus and Christopher. The kindness of Daisy and her husband and how his father's reputation followed him like a bad smell. He finished by telling her that he felt it would take a great many years for him to be accepted and not thought of as the possible spawn of the devil, and he understood if it would be too much to expect a young woman like her to face such a difficult task. He told her that he hoped she would find a young man of good standing, who would give her a comfortable life and wished it could have been him.

With a heavy heart, he sealed the letter with his signet ring bearing the family crest and placed it in a tray in the hallway to be posted on to Sir Gerald and Lady Bradbury's address, given to him by Dorothia's father, for eventual delivery into her hands.

Adam then wrote a shorter, cheerful letter to his sister, Sally, and one to Sir James telling them of his adventures. He said that he would join them in Weston-Super-Mare as soon as his latest quest was completed and promised to bring Robbie and the dog with him.

The earl settled into a few days of normality in Keighley whilst waiting to hear the results of his latest search for Kitty. He intended to read a little more about the weaving industry before going to visit Southerly Mill, the mill set up by his grandfather and now owned by Adam. His heart was not in the mill industry, he was too concerned about Robbie's young sister and others like her. Adam had just been reading in full the vagrancy act passed by the Parliament of the United Kingdom in 1824. Having met Lizzie and hearing how easy it was to lose your home, he was appalled to read that this act made it an offence to sleep rough or beg. Anyone in England or Wales who was found to be homeless and trying to cadge money from others could be arrested. Adam wondered how such children as Lizzie could possibly be criminalised, simply because their parents had died and they were forced to leave their homes.

Adam read of how the law had originally been enacted to deal with the numbers of homeless and poor in the country due to the conclusion of the Napoleonic Wars in 1815. He was appalled to read how the discharged military men, who had fought so bravely but returned to find there was no work for them, were treated; many had slept rough on the streets. At this time, there had also been a massive influx of migrant workers from Ireland and Scotland in search of work. Old laws were no longer affective to deal with all these homeless people, so Parliament had invoked this new, 1824 Vagrancy Act.

Punishments for vagrants and prostitutes could be up to a month's hard labour. Adam was amazed that such an act could blanket cover such a wide range of people and reasons for homelessness. He became very determined to find Kitty and save her from any laws that she may be on the verge of breaking. He was also starting to realise just what a privileged life he led.

The earl asked Martin to accompany him to Southerly Mill. They arrived in the middle of the next morning and went straight to the manager's office. Like the other mills he had visited, the office was high above the work force below, with a large window allowing the manager to view the workers. They passed other smaller rooms with clerks and scribes working away. Adam introduced himself to the manager, Matthew Morgan, who was very shocked to see him as he had only met the previous earl on two occasions and that was to lay down his frame work of rules. It was as Adam suspected, his father had never set foot in the place from that day forth.

The mill appeared to be dark and dusty and very noisy. As Adam looked down, he noticed small children clambering under large looms and reappearing with handfuls of what looked like dusty balls. He asked the manager what these children were doing and it was explained to him how these youngsters gathered the threads of wool that fell under the looms to keep the looms free of the dust that formed, so they did not jam up the mechanism. It seemed there was no age limit either way in the mills. Children as young as four or five dived under the looms and elderly ladies with still nimble fingers worked until they dropped. Children developed coughs through contact with the dust and there was another danger of moving parts. Adam also noticed floor walkers, formidable looking men, who made sure everyone was pulling their weight.

The earl decided to walk about the mill floor and look up close at the conditions his people worked under. He did not have to spend long on the floor to find himself distressed by what he saw. Men and women old before their time through sheer hard work and long hours. Fingers that were once nimble, now bent and twisted and obviously, painful.

Suddenly, there was a deafening scream from one end of the floor. Martin ran in the direction of the noise to find a young lad, of maybe 7 or 8, holding out his arm, dripping blood with two fingers missing at the second joint. He was, apparently, a boy employed to untangle threads before they snap whilst the loom still is working. He had caught his fingers in the mechanism, like many before him.

A woman rushed over and bound the boy's hand in a piece of cloth, only to be reprimanded by the manager for wasting material.

Adam was on the scene as quickly as he could and his blood was up. "What is wrong with you, man?" he shouted at Morgan.

Matthew Morgan was quite taken aback, no one ever argued with him in the mill. "The boy is no use to us now, my Lord, why waste good cloth on him?" he said matter of factually.

"This is a child, man," said Martin, equally annoyed and putting a protective arm about him.

"He'll not work here again," continued Morgan. "I'll pay him up to this morning, but he will not reappear tomorrow."

"Excuse me," said Adam. "Are you telling me that if someone is injured here, they are just cast out and not even treated for their injuries?"

"I only follow your father's orders, Sir," was the reply.

"Well, my father's orders no longer count in this mill, Morgan," replied Adam. "We need to sit down and re-write a few rules and do this straight away. First, I want the boy taken immediately to a doctor."

Martin was deep in conversation with the woman who had bound the boy's hand. "Might I be permitted to take him, Sir," he said. "And could I also take this good woman, who incidentally is his mother?"

"If she leaves her post now, she need not return," said Morgan.

"I think you have forgotten who the owner of this mill is, Morgan," replied Adam very annoyed by this time. "Please, Martin, take the boy quickly and this good lady. Take the carriage and return for me in two hours if possible. Mention my name, my money is good if not my name."

Martin swept the boy, who was now quite faint, up into his arms and he and the boy's mother hurried from the mill. It suddenly occurred to Adam that the whole shed was in silence, the looms had stopped. It was an eerie place—narrow windows allowed streaks of light to enter, candles burnt on the walls, you could see the dust dancing in the rays of light. Adam had only been there a short while and he already could feel the effects of the dust in the back of his throat. Looking round, he could see that most the workers had pieces of material round their mouths and noses. It looked like sea of highwaymen and women with their faces half covered.

One worker was busy cleaning the mess that the blood had made, he threw wood chippings over the splashes of bright red liquid and proudly produced the fingers that had been sliced asunder.

"How often do such accidents occur?" the earl asked Morgan.

"They are rare, my Lord," was the reply. "Maybe one a month, sometimes less."

"One a month! Children are maimed once a month!" repeated the earl, shocked beyond belief. "And what happens to these fingerless individuals?"

"How would I know?" was the reply.

"Do you not make inquiries into their wellbeing after such a happening?" asked the earl.

"Why would I, Sir?" was the simple reply.

Adam had a strong desire to strike the man but resisted the urge. After telling the workers to continue, he walked back to the steps leading to the office with Morgan and bid him to join him to consider new ideas for the working conditions. Morgan was one for an easy life so he didn't argue.

The next hour was spent going over the rules that his father had laid down about the workings of the mill. Adam was determined to make life easier for all concerned, starting with those that had been maimed in his employment. Adam demanded a list of all employees who had been injured enough to have been dismissed. Morgan said it would take him a couple of days to compile such a list so it was agreed that Adam would return to collect it at a later date.

Adam's grandfather had supplied water pumps in the court yard of the mills and the first rule Adam put forward was that every hour, workers stopped what they were doing and went outside to get a drink to cool them down and clear their throats. Morgan complained quite verbally about the working hours that would be lost but Adam suggested shift, one person taking over from another as they took this short break. Only time would tell if it was practical or not. He asked for an explanation of how the finances of the mill were run and who was in charge of which aspect.

Morgan took the earl into the small rooms off, one by one. There Adam met the accounts people who handled the buying and selling of raw materials and the sale of the finished product. There was a clerk that kept a record of employees and their wages.

"How are wages decided here, Morgan?" the earl asked.

"Your father gave me control over everything, who to hire and who to fire, how many hours each should work for how much pay, whether to increase or decrease pay," was the reply.

"I understand that experience would gain you more money, but what would make you decrease a persons' money?" the earl asked.

"We might have someone like old Annie," Morgan began to explain. "She was here afore me, Sir, but she is getting slow now, so I don't deal so kindly with her anymore."

"So the poor woman has given many years of loyal service but you have cut her pay because she is slowing up?"

"Stands to reason, my Lord, if everyone slowed down in their work, where would the profit go? Down, that's where they would go," replied Morgan. "No use to anyone. I was on the brink of giving her the shove."

"You will do no such thing, man." replied the earl adamantly.

"We cannot keep all drift wood, Sir," exclaimed Morgan. "Stands to reason, no profit in that."

"Then we will find a broom maker to make brooms with very long handles and women like Annie can sweep under the looms," said the earl. "We will find easier work for loyal workers at the end of their working lives."

"This liberal thinking will be your ruin, Sir, mark my words."

"You may be right, Morgan, but I would like to try to introduce ideas to make working in my mill at least safer," Adam replied. "Now, I want to see the books, I want to see what we pay these poor souls."

Morgan took the earl and introduced him to the wages clerk, who seemed most amused by the arrival of the owner, never having met the previous one.

Adam sat down and turned page after page, whilst the clerk explained the differences in responsibilities and how they acquainted to wages. It all seemed quite easy to follow. Pennies for the sweep boys rising to Morgan's own money.

"It is standard pay, my Lord," said Morgan. "Ask anyone, I don't do the workers down, I pay the average."

Martin returned within the allotted time and hurried up to his master, who stopped what he was doing to hear what Martin had to tell him.

"We got the boy to your own doctor, Sir, he cauterised the lads' fingers to stop the bleeding and seal the wound against infection. You would not believe how brave that wee lad was. It must have been agony," said Martin. "The good doctor gave the boy's mother instructions on how to care for the boy in case of the sweats breaking out and a fever taking hold. I told him that you would settle with him later."

"You did well, Martin," replied the earl. "And what of the mother, how was she bearing up when you left her?"

"Very tearful as you would imagine, Sir," replied Martin. "She is a widow woman and the boy helps in his small way to put food on the table. They live with the woman's brother in very cramp conditions but at least they have a bed."

Morgan just stood with his mouth open, unable to comprehend that why anyone as rich and powerful as the earl would be the least bit interested in the lives of such unimportant people.

"Morgan, I am going now but I will be back in two days, and I expect a full list of injuries that have occurred here in the past three years at least," said the earl sternly. "I think I would be expecting too much to go back further than that period. I would also like a list of the longest serving employees."

"For what purpose, Sir, might I ask?" said Morgan.

"No, you may not ask," was the brisk reply. "That is my business, yours is to follow instructions." The earl shot Morgan a warning look and added, "No one is expendable."

With that, Adam and Martin left the mill and headed back to the family home. They talked as they walked towards the awaiting carriage.

"More wrongs to right, my Lord, I guess," said Martin gently. "I spoke at length to the injured boy's mother and she explained to me why so many very young children work here."

"Go on."

"It seems that since weaving ceased to be a cottage industry, that is work done at their homes," continued Martin as asked. "Since workers were made to work in factories, women had to take their children with them as they could not keep an eye on them whilst working as they used to. Obviously, no one wanted young children running about willy-nilly so they were allotted jobs; simple jobs like gathering broken thread, all for a few pennies. The men could not earn enough on their own to cover all their expenses. Though I was also told that many of the men drink far too much and a lot of the wages go on such pleasure instead of food on the table, which is why so many women work."

"I understand," replied Adam. "So if we stop the children working, the women will have to stay home and they will all starve."

"It is as simple as that, Sir," replied Martin. "This is one thing you will not be able to sort out yourself."

"I can see that, Martin, thank you," replied the earl. "Nothing is as simple as it sounds. You can't save the children because you only bring them more hardship if you do. I will have to concentrate on righting my father's wrongs, not the countries."

"This task of yours will wear you out and quickly empty your purse, without taking on all the wrongs of the civilised world," said Martin with a smile

"I will not be foolish about things, Martin, but something must be done for people who are maimed for life surely at a young age," said the earl. "How many other fingerless children walk the streets or worse, still have died of blood poisoning or simply loss of blood?"

"I have a feeling that we shall be face to face with quite few, my Lord," was the reply. "Maybe, Sir, you could consider employing someone of a goodly disposition to follow through this work in your name. It should not really be expected that a man in your position should actually do all the leg work."

Adam stood silently for a moment and then thanked Martin for his brilliant suggestion, one he intended to make happen.

"Martin, if you can think of likely candidates, please introduce them to me," said the earl.

"Might I suggest, Sir, that we put an advertisement in *The Times* and interview likely people."

"Make it so, Martin," was the reply.

Chapter 26
Kitty, the Poor and Maimed

Two days later, the earl and Martin returned to Southerly Mill to collect the list of injured employees. It was longer than Adam hoped and he was quite taken aback by it. There were different degrees of injury. The one that stood out as being the most common was the loss of finger tips but the one that struck the earl the hardest was one where a child had received a whipping injury across his face from a loose thread. Adam was amazed to read that a boy of only six had lost one eye as the cotton slashed across his cheek. This was one child that he needed to find and make sure he was safe.

Clutching the list, Adam and Martin decided to call in on the young man who had started the whole procedure and his mother, who had not apparently returned to work as instructed by the mill manager.

The earl's carriage was a strange sight, winding its way through mud laden roads between sad looking cottages. They pulled to a halt outside what seemed like a fairly neat thatched cottage, the garden was neatly attended and there was clean washing on the line.

Martin stepped down from the carriage and tapped gently on the door, which swung open under the very slight pressure he had used. The mother, who he now knew to be widow, Sparkes, was busy kneading dough and she jumped to her feet in fright seeing Martin framed in her doorway.

"Do not be alarmed, Madam," said Martin. "My master has just come to enquire after your son, Tim's, health."

Widow Sparkes wiped her hands on her starched apron and looked most embarrassed. "He has fared better than I expected, Sir. All thanks to the earl and your kindness and the doctor's quick and thorough care," she said. "He has gone to the market with my brother this day. I have no idea how his life will progress, but he is a brave lad and he has not complained."

"He is a brave lad, I saw that and he will be safe," said Martin. "My master has sworn to this. He is also looking into other children injured in the mill to see how they have managed. Do you know anything of a young lad called Lawrence Hill, who lost the sight in one eye?"

"Everyone knew Larry, Sir," was the reply. "He walked under the hooves of the mail coach, turned his blind eye to the road. Some say that he did it to save his mother, the worry of him."

Martin was absolutely horrified. "My master had come to seek him out, he will be as saddened by this knowledge as I am, Madam."

"Rumour has it that the new earl does not follow the footsteps of the deceased one," she said. "I believe the story to be true. Thank your master for his concern."

"He is outside, Madam, if you wish to speak to him."

She shook the flour from her hair and walked to the door nervously. The earl alighted from the carriage to greet her warmly.

"I am glad to have the chance to thank you for helping my boy but you should not be here about, Sir," said the widow. "Your fine clothes will be spoilt."

"I came to ask after you, Madam, not be worried over," was the reply with a smile.

The widow curtsied in a deep and graceful manner.

"What will become of you now, Madam?" asked the earl.

"I believe I will take up the widower Brown's offer of marriage; he has asked me several times but now I fear that his protection is needed. So I will accept."

"Is this what you want, Madam?" Adam asked kindly.

"People like me very rarely get what they want, Sir. We settle for what is best for us and Mr Brown is a good, hard-working man."

"In that case, I wish you well," replied the earl. "I would like to give you a little something to tide you over; I fear you will find life harder now that your boy has lost some of his fingers. I would not like to see him picked up for vagrancy or begging."

"Nor would I, Sir," was the reply.

The earl climbed back into the carriage and Martin slipped a small roll of notes into the woman's apron pocket before jumping up alongside his master. The woman was left most confused and tearful standing in the dust thrown up by the earl's carriage. She hurried inside and took out the roll, it was more than a year's wages.

Martin suggested to the earl that the widow Sparkes was an uncommonly handsome woman, so he was not surprised that there would be men seeking to help her to which, the earl agreed and smiled.

"A pretty face can get you a long way in the world," he said.

"The wrong way sometimes, I am sure," replied Martin thoughtfully. "If the aroma from her kitchen matches the taste of her cooking, she will make the man a good wife."

"Maybe she should try to sell her wares before she commits to a marriage contract," suggested the earl. "Good cooks are much sought after."

In the carriage, the earl stared at the list; there were 15 serious injuries in the past three years, two could now be ticked off but 13 remained to be found and their circumstances checked. Adam was not sure what he was intending to do about each case but thought that maybe the man he found to oversee this work could see what degree of help was needed in each case, and then they could act accordingly when the full facts were in front of them.

Back in Keighley Manor, Adam was glad to spend a few hours with Robbie and Daisy. Such a simple life for a while and a much needed break from the stress of trying to work miracles.

Adam's peace was shattered by Martin knocking at the sitting room door with news brought by Bill Glover and Sam Stoves. Adam rang for Mrs Frost to take Robbie for a bath, not wanting the boy to hear anything these two men were likely to repeat.

Martin went to arrange refreshments and the earl and his new searchers sat by the fire. Bill began by saying that he and Sam had gone to the cat house two days running to make their selves known. Bill smiled a rather leery smile towards Sam.

"No way we would get any information as strangers," said Bill. "Those girls might have taken us for rozzers."

"I understand your thinking, men," said the earl.

By now, Martin had joined the group and was pouring out a glass of rum punch for everyone, which was accepted readily.

"The girl is there, we are sure," said Bill. "I spent an hour in the company of a very pretty, young girl who was barely of age, and when I questioned her birth, she said that there were others younger than her there waiting to be presented to the right customer."

"Oh my God," exclaimed Adam. "Can we not secure her release if it is indeed Kitty?"

"I am told, Sir, and believe me, I do not know this to be gospel but there are men out there that will pay a lot more for the privilege of laying with an unsullied maiden."

"Privilege, good heavens, man," said Adam quite distressed. "We must save the child."

"Both Sam and I are in agreement of that, Sir, but the problem is how?"

"I suppose I could go in and present myself as the devil of the first order and ask for the girl," said the earl.

"I do not think you would carry that off too well, Sir," said Martin. "You would surely end up paying to set every last woman within the bawdy house in the way of a new life. Worse still, you would be seen and the news would spread and you will be seen as your father all over."

"I do not want that, Martin," was the reply. "I think, Bill, I will ask you to return again to the brothel and offer to pay a goodly sum to see the girl at least. If you believe her to be Kitty, after you have had sight of her, then we will think again."

"I will surely do this for you, Sir, on the morrow," was the reply.

Martin gave the two men a roll of notes and they left, leaving the earl most distressed. "I assume the women in the brothel will not just hand the girl over to any cove," said the earl.

"I believe that if the price is right, they will part with Kitty, if indeed the girl is the one we seek," answered Martin.

"My guess is, Sir, that you will want the child saved, whoever she may be anyway."

"That was my thinking, Martin," was the reply.

The next evening brought Bill back alone to the manor.

"I believe the girl is the one you seek, Sir," he said. "I only caught a glimpse of her but her hair was as you described, blonde ringlets that fell about her shoulders, large blue eyes. Maybe touching 13 years of age."

"That must be her," replied the earl. "Your work for me is done now, my man and I thank you greatly." He handed the man a couple of notes and Bill looked well pleased. "If I ever need a likely helper again, I will seek you out."

The burley fellow bowed and left.

Later, Adam explained to Martin his plan to rescue the girl. "I am not going to beat about the bush, Martin," he began. "I intend to take Robbie with me and enter the brothel through the front door. I am going to tell the woman who runs the place all about Robbie and who I am and why I want the girl restored to her brother. She can believe what she wants of me, but I feel this direct approach will serve me better than sending people to creep about."

"I actually believe you are right, Sir," replied Martin. "The right amount of financial incentive has been known to work wonders."

"Tomorrow, I will put the plan into action."

"And, Sir, I will be by your side," said the loyal man servant.

The earl smiled warmly at Martin.

Later in the day, Adam went to seek out Mrs Frost and her husband. He decided to tell the couple of his plan and the fact that he intended to take Robbie with him.

"I do not intend to explain too much to the boy," the earl explained. "I am going to tell him that his sister is safely kept in what is a place of ill repute but only for her own protection. I have no doubt that she will delight in widening the boy's knowledge once we have her safely away."

Mr Frost asked if maybe the earl should consider sending someone in his place to broker the deal, but the earl thought that rumours would leak out and if he took the up-front approach, people might be more inclined to think that he had nothing to hide.

"If I hear a word against you, my Lord, I will put people right," said Mrs Frost wholeheartedly.

"I do not want to dampen any plans but your father would have just walked into the front door," added Mr Frost. "He would have relished the notoriety."

Adam looked a bit crest-fallen at the thought. "Dammed if you do, dammed if you don't," he said. "I am taking the boy, I hope evil-minded people do not think that I take him for any dubious reasons. Maybe I should leave Robbie out of it."

"No, Sir," replied Mrs Frost. "Take the boy, he will melt their hearts if they stand firm and want to keep the girl. Take the dog as well," she laughed as she spoke and soon the group were at ease with the plan of action.

"No word to the boy, I will tell him on the way."

The next day, the earl was dressed in his finest clothes and Robbie with Daisy in tow were equally adorned for a day out. Martin was looking very formal but equally impressive.

Adam knelt down in front of Robbie, who looked very excited. "Now, lad, we have a possible sighting of your sister but it is in a place I would not normally acquaint."

"You mean like a bawdy inn?" replied the boy, which made both Adam and Martin laugh.

"I wish that was the case, lad," Adam continued. "She is under the protection of women referred to as ladies of the night."

Robbie looked around and then simply said, "But it is daytime, Sir, are we too early?"

Adam looked towards Martin. "This is harder than I thought."

"The master means that Kitty, if in fact it really is Kitty, is in a place he would not wish her to linger too long," said Martin trying to help his friend and master out. "We need you to be charming and alert, keep your eyes out for your sister, we may require you to call her name."

"It sounds like an adventure," said the boy excited. "Are we rescuing her from a deep, dark dungeon guarded by vampires? They are night creatures."

"Oh my goodness me, Robbie," said the earl, alarmed. "Your imagination is wonderful, how do you know of such things?"

"When I was a sweeps boy, my owner told us, boys, that if we strayed, the vampires would get us."

Adam smiled widely and stood up. "No vampires to fight today but we may need to charm a few women, that will be your job."

They set off in the family coach with the crest plain to see and pulled up outside a normal looking house, larger than most but quite undistinguished looking.

"Are we sure this is the place, Martin?" Adam asked.

"As sure as I am that we are about to be embarrassed beyond compare, Sir. I got Bill to show me the place," was the reply.

The three of them, plus the dog, stepped down from the coach. Already there were faces at the windows.

"I have never felt so nervous about anything in my life, Martin, too late to pull back now," said the earl.

"Onwards and upwards, Sir,"

Martin banged loudly on the door, although it was obvious that their arrival had been monitored, the door was slow to open. It just opened very slightly and a heavily powdered face of a woman of about 40 filled the crack.

"We do not open until nightfall, Sir, come back," she said and attempted to close the door. Too late, Daisy had already squeezed through the slight opening in the door and Robbie had the foresight to let her slip her lead. In the confusion, the boy ran into the house only to be confronted by a group of strange looking woman in different states of undress. There was a lot of giggling.

"I am sorry, ladies, to barge in on you unannounced," said Martin as he pushed the door wide open to allow Adam to follow him into the brothel.

A very formidable looking older woman appeared looking very stern. She had Robbie by the scruff of the neck.

"I am Lord Southerly, the Earl of Wetherley, and I suggest you unhand my boy immediately," said the earl forcefully.

"The devil's spawn come to visit us, girls," she said loudly to the gathered group.

Martin stepped in front of his master feeling very affronted by that remark. "How dare you, Madam," he said.

"I dare now the devil has gone to meet his maker," said the woman. "Have you come, my Lord, to take up his mantle?"

"I am afraid, Madam, that I have no idea whatsoever you are talking about," was the reply. "I have come for the girl, hidden here by my father for whatever purpose his twisted mind had considered."

By now, Robbie had twisted free and ran off to search the building for his sister. From the distance, his voice could be heard calling her name.

"Why would I give you the girl?" asked the woman.

"Because I have a lot of powerful friends and I will close you down in a blink of an eye if you do not," was the reply.

"I was paid well to teach the girl the tricks of the trade and keep her safe until he came for her," she continued.

The earl could hardly contain his anger. "She is a child. Surely, woman, you must have some compassion for a child."

"Compassion don't put food on the table."

Martin once more stepped up. "Enough, we want the girl," he said. "No harm will come of her, the boy is her brother and they need to be re-united."

From behind the group of women, Martin caught sight of Robbie hand in hand with a young girl. She was so delicate, like a porcelain doll; he found himself realising how struck the old earl might have been by her looks. "Come to us, Robbie," Martin shouted.

The women parted to allow the pair to pass but the woman, who was obviously the madam, caught the girl by her shoulder and prevented her movement. "This girl will make me a pretty penny in a year," she said smiling to show a row of very yellow teeth.

"The girl will leave now with me," replied the earl. "You have been well paid by my father and I do not wish to spend any more time conversing with the likes of you. We leave now and no trouble will befall you. Prevent this and I will have the place raided this very nightfall."

The woman's hand fell to her side and the four of them left the building closely followed by Daisy. As soon as the group were seated in the carriage, the earl gave a very loud sigh.

Kitty sat shaking, not knowing what to expect, her brother had a protective arm about her shoulders. She was like a delicate flower. The earl was so relieved that they had managed to find her in time to save her from a fate worse than death.

Back at Keighley Manor, Mrs Frost fussed and bothered about the girl like a mother hen guarding her chicks. "What now, Sir?" she asked.

This was something that the earl had not considered. He had taken on the boy, more as a ward than a servant and now he had a young girl to consider.

"I suppose I will take Kitty and Robbie to Wetherley when I leave," he said, not terribly sure.

"Oh my, good Lord," said Mr Frost in alarm. "Excuse the language, Sir, but you cannot possibly do that."

Adam looked confused. "Why ever not?"

"Look at the child, Sir," continued Mr Frost. "Have you ever seen a more beautiful young creature? Can you imagine the mean-minded people, those that hated your father, will think you are like him and hate you, his cronies will think you have become him."

"Just because I bring a raggedy boy and homeless girl to the comfort of my home!"

"What was your thought when you heard the boy's story?" asked Frost gently.

"I see what you mean," replied the earl. "I thought my father bought the boy to get the girl, you fear people will accuse me of the same. No one objected to Sally coming into my life."

"Miss Southerly is blood, Sir, the child here is not," added Mr Frost. "Also, I have not seen your sister but doubt that she holds a candle to this child in the looks department."

The earl had to admit that though he found Sally a very pleasing looking young woman, Kitty took the lead on this.

"The girl is like a doll, she is so pretty and delicate, she will need protection from the world as she grows," added Mrs Frost.

"You are not suggesting a nunnery surely," asked the earl, alarmed.

"Nothing that drastic, Sir," Mrs Frost replied with a laugh. "But you will have to think seriously, Sir. After all, the pair of them have been bought and paid for."

"You are right," was the reply. "It does not sound too good, does it? I was not to know the girl would be such a creature."

"We know that, Sir," replied Mrs Frost. "We know that if she had been covered in warts and bent, you still would have hunted for her but others do not."

"So I have made myself a stick to beat myself with," Adam looked thoughtful. "I will think about this for a while."

Adam looked at the two youngsters, happily chatting as if they had never been parted. He smiled to himself and went to his study to think alone for a while about how best to resolve this issue. He had already made up his mind that he would have to stay a while longer in Keighley.

So once again, the young earl shut himself away to write a long letter to Dorothia explaining why he had chosen to stay in Yorkshire for the foreseeable future. The letter took a little while to reach Brighton and the contents amazed her.

Dorothia noticed the earl's crest on the seal of the letter laying on the tray just inside the main door. She carefully turned the letter over and seeing that it was addressed to her, she took possession of it immediately and hurried to her room to read it.

'Dear Miss Mountjoy,' the letter began. Dorothia had hoped for a less formal beginning to the missive. *'I have had the most interesting time, adventures that I would have thought only came about in fairy tales. I told you about Robbie, the chimney boy, who is now firmly under my care. My father had bought the boy, I believe, to gain his sister, though I hoped this would prove to be untrue. However, after strenuous enquiries and searching, the girl was discovered in a brothel in Wetherley. I hired two men that I would not normally have made the acquaintance to search for the child, having given them a rough description of the girl. I only knew her to be around 12 or 13, of delicate appearance with very blue eyes and a mop of golden ringlets. These ne'er do wells discovered the child and reported back to me. Robbie, Martin and I made a bold decision to go to the house and demand the girl's release or I would bring the law down around their ears. This worked and we left with Kitty. I cannot describe to you how beautiful this child is. My house keeper agreed and it is quite obvious that my greatest fears about the reasons why my father bought the child are all too plain.. Now, I am faced with another dilemma. I intended to bring Robbie to Weston-Under-Wetherley and then on to be re-united with my sister. Now Kitty has added to my burden and everything is not so clear.*

My housekeeper, Mrs Frost, a good and kind lady, pointed out that if I arrived in Weston-Under-Wetherley with a brother and sister that had been bought and the girl looking as she does, there would be those that would suspect that I had the same fate in store for Kitty as my father had. So now I am wondering what to do next. I do at times miss the good counselling of your father, he was always wise and gave good advice.

I will write again to you when I have decided what is to become of Miss Kitty. I may simply leave her with Mrs Frost, she has a tender for youngsters, and go back alone. I think Robbie will want to stay with his sister for a while having just been re-united. I do hope, however, that he might go with me as I am loathed to leave him behind, he is such good company.

I remain your loyal servant and friend.'

Dorothia could not decide whether to be proud of Adam or shocked at his antics. She showed the letter to Lady Mary who laughed.

"I do not think this young man will cause any boredom, Dorothia," she said. "I think you will have to say goodbye to the quiet life if you choose to settle down with such a man."

"I believe he writes more like a friend than a possible suitor," Dorothia replied. "Such outrageous things to tell a delicate-minded young woman. I will write back and tell him how shocking his revelations are to me."

"Do so, child, if you believe they are," said Lady Mary with a smile.

Dorothia set about sending a very formal reply stating although she commended his actions, she felt that maybe he should not have shared to many details with a lady. She also pointed out that as the children, Robbie and Kitty, were now safe, he could relinquished his responsibility for them and get back to his normal life.

Adam was quite disappointed with all the letters he received from Brighton, they had been so cold and formal. He felt that having told Dorothia everything, she might have felt a closeness to him, but it seemed that she was more interested in protocol than information. He wondered if maybe he had open up too much to this young woman without really being sure of her feelings towards him.

Chapter 27
Sorting the Mill and Helping the Maimed

The next couple of days were spent interviewing likely candidates for the overseeing of finding and helping the children and women maimed in Southerly Mills in the past three years.

Martin sat in with the earl, whilst he spoke to each man and tried to decide if he was right or wrong for the post. It was to be a short-lived but highly paid post that needed handling with care and understanding. Three of the candidates were dismissed almost instantly, having shown the lack of compassion that the earl was looking for. The two men were beginning to despair of finding a suitable person to oversee such a delicate operation.

On the third day, a young man, a lot younger than the earl imagined would apply, came for an interview at Keighley Manor. He was a tall, good looking young man, with green eyes and a wide smile. Adam liked him instantly, although he wondered if maybe he was a little young. Martin showed the young man to a seat and Adam studied him for a while. He introduced himself as Simon Gibbs and bowed as he spoke.

"Might I ask how old you are, Sir, before we begin?" said Adam.

"I am 18, Sir," was the reply.

"You are very young to apply for such a post, Mr Gibbs," answered the earl.

"I thought you might think so, Sir, but I have heard that the new earl is also young, so I allowed my mother to talk me into applying for this post to prove my worth," was the reply.

The earl then realised that he had not introduced himself, he had just assumed that the young man would guess who he was. He stood and held his hand out to Mr Gibbs. "I am Adam Southerly, the Earl of Wetherley," he said with a smile.

The young man was clearly taken aback. "Oh my Lord, I never imagined that I would be interviewed by the master of the house himself," and fell into a deep bow.

As he rose, Adam caught the young man's hand and shook it. The look of sheer amazement spread across the man's face.

"Sit yourself down, Simon Gibbs, and we will start again," said the earl kindly, putting him at his ease.

"Why do you feel you are right for the task I have set?" asked the earl. "Assuming you understand exactly what I need from you."

Martin interrupted and told the earl that he had spoken to each candidate individually and explained the nature of the job in detail. "One candidate gave such a negative reaction that he was dismissed without an interview," Martin said.

"Thank you, Martin," replied the earl, "I should have guessed that everyone would have been correctly briefed. So as you were saying, young Sir, your mother suggested you apply."

"My mother is a kindly hardworking woman, widowed some five years now, and she had heard talk that you, Sir, were trying to prove your worth against the background of the damage done to your good name by your father, " he said.

Adam liked his open manor and smiled as he listened.

"I too have much to prove but not for the same reasons."

"Had your father damaged your lives?" asked Martin.

"Definitely not, he was a hard-working man," Simon replied sounding quite indignant.

"So explain further," said Adam.

"My father was a simple candle maker, he died in a fire in the works, as I said five years past now." Adam and Martin listened in silence. "I was 13 at the time and already been working in the mills for a couple of years, then another accident occurred and my mother has struggled since. She said that I had the compassion and experience to understand what work injuries do to families."

"Who else was injured in your family?" asked Martin.

Simon pulled back his cuff, removed his glove and revealed and mangled hand with three missing fingers.

"Good grief, boy," exclaimed Adam. "I shook your hand, I never realised."

"I did tell you that my mother was a clever woman," he handed his right glove to the earl to examine. Down three of the finger holes were carefully carved wooden pieces that resembled the shape of the missing fingers.

"Ingenious," said Martin, examining the glove himself.

Simon smiled.

"I really do not believe I need to look any further for the man I need for this task," said the earl looking very pleased. "I will pay all your expenses, I have a long list of mainly small children who, like you, have lost fingers. I wish to know if their families have suffered through this and compensate them accordingly."

"Might I be permitted to ask you, Simon, how you fared after your loss?" said Martin.

"I was luckier than most. My uncle, my father's brother, is a blacksmith. When it happened and it seems like a lifetime gone now, he cauterised the injury and, I believe, saved my life."

"Was nothing done at the mill?" Martin asked.

"Oh no, there was no medical help there, just an angry manager not wanting blood on his cloth."

"Which mill was this, Simon?" Martin continued to probe.

"I am afraid it was yours, Sir," said Simon looking at the earl.

"I only went back three years on the list or I would have seen your name no doubt, maybe I should look deeper," replied the earl.

"No, Sir," was the reply. "I believe three years is about right. The injured would either have died or come to terms with their losses."

"How did you help keep your mother?" the earl asked.

"As I said, I was luckier than most, I know my letters which helps, I can write a fair hand taught by my mother, who had a little learning and helped on by books," was the reply. "My Uncle also has been a tower of strength to us, he is childless and lives in a cottage behind his smithy; he took my mother, my older sister and younger brother in when we were forced to move after my father's death."

"This homelessness is such a familiar theme to me now," said the earl with a frown. "That is one of the things I need to know, did the loss of the pennies earned by a maimed child cause the family hardship such as this?"

"It would have depended on if maybe the mother worked as well and was needed to tend to the child, she could lose her job as well," was Simon's reply. "I have thought long and hard for many years about what would have become of us had my uncle not have been the man he is."

"He does sound like a good man," was the earl's reply. "And your brother, does he work?"

"My mother would not allow Tom to go into the mill. He works for my uncle, he is 15 now and had muscles like you have never seen. My sister is married and away."

"I would like to meet your family, Simon. They are the salt of the earth," said the earl seriously.

Simon laughed, "My mother would probably faint on sight of you, Sir. My uncle provided me with this garb so I could come here today," said Simon looking at his clothes.

"I will provide you with a good coat, walking boots and anything else you feel you will need whilst you go about my business. Take a carriage to anywhere you need to be and bill my man here. Do not appear too wealthy in case people become suspicious of your intensions."

Simon laughed at that thought.

"How have you gone on since the finger loss?" asked Martin interested in the young man.

"As I said, I read and I have taken an interest in figures, helping my uncle with his financial affairs, he has been so good," began the young man. "I lost a few months to the fever, my mother thought I was a goner but her good food and care saved me. I have learnt to bail hay and I can do a great many things one handed. I cannot hold a hammer so cannot be of any major use to my uncle. I have taught myself to write left-handed, not so neatly."

"I believe you have been a credit to you mother and an example of getting on with life and not feeling sorry for yourself," said the earl impressed.

"I feel sorry for myself sometimes, you can be sure of that, Sir," replied Simon.

The young man was given the list, his wages organised and he began his very long and arduous task of hunting out people who had probably moved on. Both, the earl and Martin, considered that they had found a perfect person to carry out the work.

"Well, Martin," the earl said with a sigh, "that is one less task I need to worry about."

"Indeed not, Sir, now we can concentrate on Robbie and Kitty."

Adam looked worried for a moment. "Martin, I might ask you to go to the blacksmith and make yourself known to him. See that the man has everything that he needs and make sure that the widow Gibbs is well and not in need in any way.

"I rather expected you to make this suggestion, Sir," was the reply.

The earl decided that he would stay a further three months in Keighley to make sure that all he had organised was either finished with or well underway. He wrote immediately to Sir James in Weston-Super-Mare and explained, in full, everything that had happened and his future plans. Adam was very concerned that he had left his sister for twice the length of time planned already and hoped that James would be kind enough to continue his temporary guardianship of her. He need not have worried, Sally was as happy and contented as it was possible to be and Sir James was enjoying the company.

Once again, Adam wrote to Dorothia to tell her that he had been delayed in Keighley, and that he had hired a young man to seek out children that had been injured in Southerly Mill to see if they needed any help.

'Seeing up close the dangers to children and frail workers in the mill, I am constantly worried. A child no more than six years of age lost all but two of his fingers on his right hand, whilst I was in the mill. My man, Martin, took the boy swiftly to the doctor and his life was saved. Martin and I have been interviewing likely candidates for the job of seeking out other maimed children due to accidents in Southerly Mill and have found an excellent young man, who starts immediately on the task in hand. I will inform you more fully about that when I next write.'

Your servant as always.

She was worried that this obsession of his to right all wrongs could keep him away from her forever. It seemed that every time he sorted out one problem, another showed its face. Dorothia spoke to Lady Mary about Adam and read his latest letter to her. It told about the boy in the mill and the way Morgan had treated the mother and child, and how it had moved the young earl to try to discover how many other youngsters had fallen foul of the machines. Although Dorothia felt proud of Adam, she also wondered if this new crusade make sound the death knell of her hopes to marry him. Lady Mary warned Dorothia that how a man on a mission can put every other thought aside, and maybe she should look beyond this present crush and find a more suitable partner with no problems to solve beyond finding the right wife.

Two months to the day that Simon Gibbs had been appointed to help the earl, he arrived at Keighley Manor with a large amount of paperwork in hand. Adam was very pleased to see him and especially impressed by the fact that he had knuckled down to the job and not allowed it to be strung out to gain more money.

Simon was shown into the earl's study. "Sit yourself down, Simon," said the earl.

Simon Gibbs was happy to do as instructed and placed on a nearby table the papers he was carrying. There was a gentle tap on the door and it was Martin coming to join in the conversation.

"Ah good, Martin, just in time. Well, my man, how did it go?" the earl asked Simon eagerly.

"It did not prove too difficult a job, Sir. Everyone on the list seems acquainted with each other so that made light of the business," was the reply. "I would say that half of those we sought were in other employment of sorts. As they get older, they will find good employment harder to find. There is a shortage of work for men with all their working parts here about."

"That is encouraging at least, what sort of employment?" asked the earl genuinely interested.

"Mostly collecting and carrying. I found the odd way maker, which is a job working on the roads. I found one lad who had an adapted spade to dig with. Needs must, Sir, it is amazing how people can adapt."

"And financially, how do they fare?"

"The pittance they got in the mill was not hard to cover. As I said before, children get paid very little anyway but without those missing fingers, a man might not fare as well later in life. I did find two lads in the work house and another in prison."

"How did you deal with that?" asked the earl.

"I paid the bail to the warder to release the prisoner, Matthew Fowler, imprisoned for stealing an apple! The other two, I paid the going rate for them to leave the work house. All of the lads were not yet 10 years of age."

"And what of their lineage?" asked the earl.

"One, Jack Newman, picked up for vagrancy, appears to be alone in the world, his father having abandoned him. The other boy, William Hope, also in the work house was there with his mother and sister. The mother has poor eyesight and the sister a little simple," was the reply.

"Good grief man, how did you deal with that?"

"I have not done anything as yet, Sir, I am hoping to take advice from you. Matthew and Jack, who seems to be alone in the world, I have placed with my uncle; he says that they can work there and sleep in his barn for the time being," said Simon.

"Do we know where the errant fathers of the boys found in the work house have taken themselves?" asked the earl.

"General opinion is that Jack Newman's father has gone to sea," was the reply. "He just walked away and abandoned the boy. Very hard for the boy, his mother's whereabouts is also unknown. Common belief is that she took to prostitution, some say she is dead in a gutter somewhere. She did originally enter the work house with the boy but left soon after."

"No likelihood of us tracing either of them then," remarked Martin. "And the others?"

"William Hope's mother and sister have been in the work house since the accident. The father ran away when his wife started to lose her sight and was finding it difficult caring for the daughter who, as I said, is simple minded," continued Simon. "He drank heavily and the talk is that he has probably drunk himself into an early grave by now."

"A disgrace to mankind," said Martin, annoyed.

"Not everyone is strong enough to deal with life's problems in the way that Mr Gibb has," replied the earl smiling at Simon.

"Right, well first let us deal with our own needs. I am about to sit down to eat and would like you to join me, we can discuss this there and then." The earl walked over to the pull cord in the corner of the study and before long a servant appeared.

"We have one more for dinner, Clarkson," said the earl to the servant. "Mr Martin is to join us as well. Are the children around?"

"Master Robbie has gone fishing, my Lord, and I believe Miss Kitty to be in the kitchen helping Mrs Frost," Clarkson replied.

"Do not disturb the child unless she wishes to join us. Thank you, Clarkson, that is all. Tell Mrs Frost that we will be ready in half an hour," was the reply. "Please show Mr Gibbs where he can hang his coat and wash up for dinner, Clarkson."

Clarkson showed Simon to a small off room with pumped running water and a small stone sink. Having taken his top coat from him, he left him alone in the room saying that he would return to show him the dining room.

Simon was most amused by the care being taken of him and smiled to himself, thanking his good luck for having found the courage to apply for this post.

Soon, Simon, Adam and Martin were seated at an overly large dining table that was heavily laden with all types of delicious looking food.

"This would last us a week in our house," said Simon.

The earl was a little embarrassed by this information.

"Yes, I think my good lady cook does over indulge us all. What we leave feeds the rest of the household but do not hold back because of that."

Martin laughed and assured Simon that the earl was jesting.

"Martin, so, we have two boys found in the work house, one with his poorly sighted mother and simple-minded sister. Any ideas how to overcome this problem?" said the earl.

"Was the problem caused by the lad not being able to add to the finances?" Martin asked Simon.

"Not wholly, Sir," was the reply. "The problem was caused by the husband running off when the boy was hurt, not wanting to deal with any other problems."

"So indirectly, it was the injury in the mill!" said the earl adamantly. "And general opinion is that the missing fathers have both gone to sea, willingly or not is not known."

"So no likelihood of us tracing them then," remarked Martin.

"It seems not, so it is the children we have to concentrate on," replied Simon.

"You have handled your problem very well, Simon, if only everyone was as strong willed," said the earl smiling at Simon.

"I had help, Sir, a good family can be your saving grace," said Simon.

"Do we know anything of the last boy, Matthew?"

"Matthew Fowler's father is said to be in prison somewhere, a thoroughly bad lot and best left to his own devises," replied Simon.

"Do not waste time searching for such a man, maybe we can save the boy from a life of crime," replied Adam.

"Despite his father, Matthew appears to be a good lad, lost his mother very young, they say. Was a good worker until he lost his thumb and first finger of his right hand," added Simon. "I am told that he tried hard in the workhouse to keep up."

"Children should not be in this position, we have to help these boys. We must give them some sort of hope for their future," said the earl quite emotionally.

"It is a good job that you are not looking to help other children injured at work, you would soon be completely overwhelmed," said Simon. "I have learnt so much in the short time, I have done this work for you, Sir. Children down mines, dragging coal in trucks on their hands and knees, their back bent before they reach puberty. Young lads like Robbie up chimneys from almost as soon as they can walk. Growing too old or big for the job and getting stuck in chimneys or scratching themselves causing poison to rage their little bodies, dying in agony."

"Good God, man," said the earl, putting his knife and fork down and looking quite pale. "I did not realise we would discover such a disgraceful attitude to children. Thank God, I found Robbie when I did."

"There is a lot to be ashamed of on this little island of ours," said Martin matter-of-factly. "You are doing your bit to address any part your family have played in the misuse of children. You cannot do any more, Sir, not when the families need every penny they can get. If you stop child labour altogether, families starve; it is a problem without end. We must concentrate on the job in hand."

Martin could visualise his master going on a sort of crusade to save the children of Britain and Ireland and making himself very ill in the process. He was not prepared to stand by and see that happen.

"Let us think about William Hope and his poor mother and sister," said Martin trying to concentrate Adam's mind onto the job in hand.

"I cannot think of a way to help the woman except financially, of course, but I feel that she needs more than that. What do you think, Martin?"

"The boy you say is 10?" enquired Martin.

"That he is, Sir. Two fingers from one hand and a tip from another, all swallowed up by a loom," replied Simon.

"Can the boy hold a brush?" asked the earl.

"I believe so, Sir," was the reply.

"In that case, I have the solution. William Hope comes here and does menial stable work. I will write to my great friend, Sister Teresa, and see if the woman and girl could be accommodated within the nunnery." The earl sat back on his chair looking very pleased with himself.

"I believe that would deal very nicely with the situation, my Lord," said Simon smiling.

"As for Matthew and Jack, is your uncle happy to keep them?"

"He says he is, Sir, but begs me not to bring any more to his door."

"Rightly so, Simon, it is not his problem," remarked the earl.

"I did find that two other injured boys on the list could still hold a broom," said Simon. "I found one of them sweeping the roads, clearing a path for gentleman so their clothes did not soil on the ground."

"My boy Robbie told me of this trade, I thought him mad," replied Adam.

"A penny earned, however, it is done is appreciated," was the reply.

"We will finish our meal and then we can go over the costs of the work you have done. I am wondering if there is a way I could pay to have your uncle's home enlarged to house these extra mouths," the earl said.

"That would be amazing of course, Sir," replied Simon.

"You have done well, Simon, I am very pleased. I am also glad to have my eyes opened to the ways of the world. Robbie told me a little of the job of climbing boys, but I think he got off lightly compared to some," said the earl. "I would like you to enlighten me further about this practise if you would, Simon. I could take my place in the House of Lords and see what I could do to right some terrible wrongs."

"I think you will find that climbing boys are employed in the royal residencies, so our immediate world is not ready to become more humane," added Martin.

"Good heavens, Martin, I believe you are right."

"I, for one, have been grateful to be able to do this task for you, my Lord, I have learnt so much. I have spoken to families that have children in the mills and others sold to chimney sweeps as climbing boys," said Simon. "I never imagined that there was a life worse than that of a mill hand."

"At least we can improve the lot of our young workers," replied Adam.

"Did you know that boys as young as four climb hot flues that can be dangerously narrow," began Simon, pleased to unburden his knowledge on others. "Some get jammed in the flue, suffocate or burn to death. The boys sleep under soot sacks and rarely wash. Their lungs fill with soot and they have difficulty breathing or dirt gets into cuts, caused when they buffed it that is climbed in the nude to make it easier to get into tiny spaces, their elbows and knees scraped raw allowing dirt to enter and poison them. Master sweeps buy children and they are apprenticed to the sweep, they are lucky if they make old bones. The fingers lost in mills are nothing compared to these poor little ones. Did you know that master sweeps are paid by the parish to teach orphans or paupers the craft? They or their guardians have to sign papers of indenture and that binds them to the sweep, like slaves, until they are adults. It is the duty of the poor law guardians to apprentice as many children from the workhouse in their care as possible so as to reduce the costs to the parish. The men who run the workhouse, where I traced our fingerless mill boys, were more than happy to give me any information. They were proud of the workhouse, telling me that they are saving adults and children from starving on the streets. They also arrange for small boys to be handed over to sweeps if their parents request it."

"And what do these poor little souls get in exchange for a life of misery?" asked Martin, fascinated and appalled.

"They are apprentices so they learn a trade. It is the master sweep's duty to provide the apprentice with a second suite of clothes, to have him cleaned once a week and allow him to attend church and not to send him up chimneys that are lit. Once his seven-year long apprenticeship is completed, he usually becomes a journeyman's sweep and can work for a sweep of his choice. Soot is also bagged by the climbing boys and sold. There are eminent people who are working to help improve the lot of climbing boys so we will one day see the end of such a practice."

"The sooner, the better I would say," replied Martin. "I have seen men with their extended sweep brushes, but I guess they only can be used on straight chimneys."

"Just so," replied Simon. "They need to redesign chimneys."

Two days later after Martin had visited the blacksmith, he reported that the cottage they lived in was, in fact, attached to another on one side that was nearly derelict. This obviously injected an idea of having the two houses knocking into one, once they had discovered the ownership of the unused one. This did not prove to be too arduous a task. The owner wanted far more than the hovel was worth but an agreement was struck, and the earl went about employing a likely group of builders to make the house water proof and accessible to the existing cottage. To say the family were thrilled would be an understatement. Simon was still imagining that he was in a dream and about to wake up.

A reply from Sister Teresa made it necessary to organise transportation for Mrs Hope and her daughter. They seemed happy with their lot in life and with the promise that William would be well cared for happily left for pastures new.

Simon found it quite right that the family were called Hope, as the earl had given them some at last.

The blacksmith already owned the property he worked from and his little cottage, so the earl made him a gift of the newly acquired property so the family would be safe from debt.

The earl made a point of calling on Simon at home to thank his uncle himself for his kindness towards a couple of unwanted boys. The arrival of a fine coach and its owner caused quite a stir. Simon's mother was all a fluster and curtsied so many times that the earl's head was beginning to ache, only the arrival of Simon calmed the visit. When Simon's widowed mother saw on what easy terms he was with the lord of the manor, she looked as though she would burst with pride.

Injured children that could not be set to work were compensated with small payments of coins, and every child was dealt with, in some way or another, much to the earl's great delight.

Simon was nearing the end of his appointed task and Adam was trying to think of another job to set him.

"Sir, I know it is not my place to think of ways of spending your inheritance but could I make a suggestion?" said Martin to the earl.

"Your input is always welcome," was the reply.

"Simon maybe could have some sort of role in Southerly Mill," he said. "Maybe keeping an eye on proceedings and the safety of the work force. You were going to implement a great many new rules; maybe Simon could watch and learn and report to you, and between you, the mill could be a safer place."

Adam smiled widely at this suggestion. "I would like to see the man Morgan put in his place. This is a fine idea and we will speak to Simon to see if he would be willing to take on this role, now he has almost completed the previous one."

Martin looked very pleased with himself. Both, he and the earl, had developed a great fondness of Simon Gibb and his gentle, kind family. Simon had just had his 19th birthday and Adam felt that this new position would make a very fine gift to celebrate.

"Simon has been generous but not too liberal with my money so far and I trust the boy whole-heartedly," said the earl. "We will take him to the mill and introduce him to Morgan."

"I am glad you said we, Sir, that is a visit I would not want to miss," replied Martin.

Two days later, the earl presented himself at Southerly Mill quite unexpected. Morgan hurried down to greet him.

"You should have told me that you were coming, my Lord," said Morgan in a fluster.

"Really, Morgan," replied the earl haughtily. "I always believed that the mill was mine to visit as I wished."

"Of course, Sir," Morgan replied nervously. "I merely meant we would have been ready to receive you."

"And yet here I am and it seems you have received me with no forward plans made."

Morgan was not quite sure how to respond to this sarcastic note in the earl's voice.

"To what do we owe the honour, Sir?" enquired Morgan.

"Simple, my man," the earl replied, "I want to introduce you to Simon Gibbs, my right hand man in finances." The earl turned to Simon. "Simon, this is Morgan, he oversees the mill. Until now, he has had overall run of the place and the wages of all who work here."

"Until now," said Morgan in a loud voice. "Surely you do not mean to put a mere boy of no experience over me."

"Not exactly, though if it was what I intended, I would not have to explain myself to you, Sir," was the reply. "Mr Gibbs to you, Simon has been sorting out the list you gave me of injured children and making amend for their losses."

Morgan sniggered, "Has he been sewing their little fingers back on?"

"Watch your tongue, man," said Martin, very annoyed by the impudence of the man.

"If you wish to keep your position in the mill, I suggest you listen very carefully to what I am about to tell you," said the earl. "I will have no more hokey-pokey goings on here. You will remain as overseer so long as Simon, who is my eyes and ears, thinks you are worthy. You will treat him with the greatest of respect. He now holds the purse strings and all money transactions and wages are to be passed by him first for his approval."

"You cannot be serious," Morgan said. "Your father put his whole trust in me."

"But I do not, Sir," was the reply. "And I am now in control. Mr Gibb will look after the wellbeing of my workers, any injuries will be reported to him immediately, any increases in wages or decreases will also be reported to him. Do you agree to my new terms or do you wish to seek other employment?"

"Do my wages go unaltered?" was the only question Morgan asked.

"They do but they do not increase," was the reply.

"I took my place here in Southerly Mill not long after the Jennies and mules that drove the mill wheels were replaced by the Arkwright water frame spinning machines. I have overseen many changes," said Morgan in a loud voice.

"And if you play your cards right, you will be here when we finally take delivery of the new steam engines I have been reading about."

Morgan looked relieved.

"Mr Gibbs will not interfere with the running of the mill, he is here for the workers," explained the earl. "I noticed that the dust within the mill sticks to the back of your throat."

"That it does but there is no way to mend that," Morgan replied.

"Possibly not," continued the earl. "But Mr Gibb will organise regular medicals of my workers. When a steady worker becomes unable to keep up, you will find a menial job for them until they retire. Mr Gibb will advise you on this. Also, he has found two boys on the injured list I gave him that can still hold a broom, so they will start working here tomorrow."

"Will they indeed?" said Morgan looking quite disgruntled.

"I do not have time to dilly dally here, man, do you keep your job or do I look for a new manager?" demanded the earl.

"I believe you will be the ruin of this mill, if you don't mind me saying," said Morgan.

"I do mind, obviously, but if you are correct, I will apologise. Until proven foolish. I wish my orders to be carried out to the letter and as I said, Mr Gibb is my eyes and ears. I can find a new manager, Morgan, I do not wish to because I believe you can run this mill well, if not kindly."

"Of course, I can. I do and have done so for neigh on nine years," was the reply.

Reluctantly, Morgan shook Simon's hand and the deal was struck.

Chapter 28
The Circus

Lord Southerly, the Earl of Wetherley, was planning to return to Weston-Under-Wetherley as soon as possible but now he had the added worry of Kitty; he was not sure how he should progress. He had just written to both Sir James and his sister apologising for his long absence from Weston-Super-Mare and asking their advice on his latest problem. Robbie, he had intended to take with him but as Mrs Frost had pointed out, the girl could undo all the good he had done to revise the family name.

His head was spinning thinking about his latest dilemma when Robbie came bursting into the study like a boy on fire.

"The circus is here, the circus is here," he cried in an excited voice.

"Indeed, Robbie," the earl replied.

"It is setting up as we speak on Keighley moor, I have seen the lions and an elephant."

"Who told you of such animals?" the earl asked.

"Why? Mrs Frost, of course, she showed me pictures and I went up to the moor with Harry from the stables and Daisy and there were cages being drawn along and in them. I saw a real lion and an Elephant walking behind—huge, bigger than a mountain."

"Now I suppose, boy, you want me to take you to the circus and see more clearly these wonderful creatures," was the reply, the earl laughed as he spoke.

"Of course, my Lord, that is why I have told you about it," was the honest reply.

"Well, as luck would have it, Robbie, I have never seen a circus or such wild creatures myself either, so I would love to take you, Kitty, Mrs Frost and Martin to see this one if that is what you would like."

"Mrs Frost told me that one of your kind, Henry 8th, kept lions and tigers and wild things in his garden in the Tower of London," said Robbie. "Did you not see them then?"

"She is a very knowledgeable woman and she is correct," was the reply. "But believe me when I tell you, boy, that I am not that old. Also, I do not think I am quite on the level of kings, lad, I am a mere earl," he laughed at the thought.

The boy just jumped up and down and danced around like a boy possessed. He then ran off to tell everyone he could find that the earl had promised him a trip to the circus.

Adam sent for Martin, who had already been informed of the forthcoming excursion by Robbie.

"I hear we are away to the circus, my Lord," said Martin smiling widely.

"That boy will be the death of me, Martin," replied the earl.

"I have promised him and his sister a circus visit. I would like you to accompany us and I need a woman to chaperone Kitty, so I thought to ask Mrs Frost."

"Maybe you have one more employee to find, Sir, a chaperone."

"I believe you are right, Martin, I will look into that shortly; meanwhile, I need someone to acquire tickets for us all. I must say it is a welcome break from worrying about what my next move will be," continued the earl. "I cannot think clearly about what I should do for young Kitty. Mrs Frost has persuaded me that I cannot appear in Wetherley with her in tow because tongues will wag."

"God save us all from beautiful women and evil-minded people, my Lord," was the reply. "I am not sure who causes the most problems."

Three days later, the happy group were dressed and ready to travel the short distance to Keighley Moor and the circus. They passed many people, family groups and individuals making their way towards the big tent. Around the edges of the tent were large-wheeled cages with exotic animals from different parts of the world—tigers, lions and there were also magnificent elephants tethered to poles. You could see clowns and jugglers practising before they went to perform.

The earl was shown to a front row seat, they were the most expensive of course. Robbie perched himself next to the earl, sandwiched between Adam and Martin and then Mrs Frost; lastly, Kitty sat on the end of the group looking very shy. The big tent did not take long to fill and the atmosphere was electrifying. Children chattered excitedly and adults moved about trying to make themselves comfortable on the wooden bench seats.

The earl, ever curious, was fascinated by the structure of the big tent, the way guide ropes held it firm. The construction of such a massive arena pulled into place by sheer force of numbers amazed him.

The tent fell into silence as the ringmaster ran in. He wore a bright red coat, a black top hat and trousers, long black leather boots and carried a long whip, which he cracked to gain the attention the crowd. Behind him ran a group of clowns, rolling on the floor and chasing each other about with buckets that they pretended to be full of water. When they turned to throw the 'water' at the crowd, out came sawdust. Everyone laughed.

Then followed jugglers, all dressed in white with wide sleeved shirts tight at the wrist, wide red sashes round their waists, delicate shoes and their hair tied back from their faces. They threw large bottle-shaped wooden pins in the air and caught them, causing the crowd to clap loudly.

Then in rode gypsy girls on horses bare-backed. They each wore white embroidered low cut blouses, brightly decorated with beautifully worked flowers with short gathered sleeves, red skirts, dainty black shoes and had their long, black hair flowing wild and free across their shoulders. Their bronzed skin and dark eyes took the men's breath away. They rode on the most beautiful pure white pedigree Arabian looking horses that stepped in tune to music and seemed to dance. Both, Adam and Martin, were mesmerised.

In the middle of the big top was a large cage and the ring master entered it. A door inside was lifted and into the cage rushed three very large tigers. A crack of his whip made them each sit on individual raised platforms. They snarled and showed their immense yellow teeth. The ringmaster commanded each one individually to perform in some way and after what seemed like a death defying age, the door that had allowed them entrance was opened again and the creatures left the cage to a roar from the crowd.

A trapeze artist swung above the crowd's head to everyone's amazement and delight. Then rode the male gypsies on splendid black horses; they were all dressed in white button-less over shirts that had wide gathered sleeves tapered at the wrist and tight black trousers. They swung from side to side on the horses' backs and swooped down picking things off the floor as they galloped around the ring. The females gathered in the big tent, looked as disturbed by these dangerous looking, handsome young men as the men did by the gypsy women.

There were fire eaters and dwarfs dressed in blue and white striped trousers and bright blue shirts; little dogs wearing what looked like ballerina tutu's, walking on their hind legs and dancing round and round in circles. Robbie swore to teach Daisy to dance so he could join the circus and the earl laughed.

Kitty just sat opened-mouthed, amazed by everything. Mrs Frost kept a protective arm about her.

A line of men, all brightly clothed, came into the ring on stilts, they looked like giants. A bearded lady walked around the ring much to everyone's amusement, followed closely by a doll like dwarf, small and delicate. The earl thought to himself how every sort of misery could be covered up here in a circus ring. A deformity could become an asset. He wondered at their carefree lives, moving from town to town, making people happy as they went.

Then before the finish, which included the elephants, the gypsy girls returned; their white horses looking splendid besides the black high steppers ridden by the men.

One gypsy stood out amongst the crown. She was the most beautiful creature Adam had ever seen. She wasn't delicate like Kitty, Kitty did not disturb his mind, she was a child to protect but this young gypsy woman, probably only 14 at the most, had a strange effect on the earl. Her magnificent thick, wavy hair floated over her bare shoulders. Her lips were painted bright red as were her finger nails, and her eyes were the largest he had ever seen, framed by the most splendid long dark lashes. She looked young, but not vulnerable like Kitty. She did not need protection and he needed protection from her gaze. She smiled his way and he felt himself go weak at the knees. It was the most disturbing experience of his life and he was anxious to leave the tent and go back to the manor and the safety of his orderly busy life.

The crowd swarmed out of the big tent. The earl and his group were swept up amongst the hoi polloi, who seemed to be as one in a joyous state of euphoria. Robbie skipped and jumped and ran about so full of excitement. Little Kitty held tight to Mrs Frost hand and looked bemused by the whole thing. The earl looked at the girl and thought what a strange child she was, timid and nervous, whist her brother feared nothing.

"Can we go back tomorrow, can we, can we?" said Robbie looking about to burst with excitement.

"Not tomorrow, Robbie," was the reply. "I need to work tomorrow and we need to make plans to go to Wetherley, my sister has been deserted long enough."

Robbie looked crest fallen and Martin approached Adam. "He will win you over, Sir, mark my words."

"No, Martin, he will not but I will give him money to go by himself, and when we get back to the manor, I would like a quiet word with you if you please."

Martin nodded, "Of course, Sir."

It took what seemed like an age to get back to where the coach was waiting to transport them back to the manor. Once there, Robbie set about trying to get poor Daisy to stand on her back legs. Mrs Frost said that the boy would not sleep that night for sure and her prediction proved correct.

After he had removed his cloak, Martin went to seek Adam out in his study as requested. He found his master looking worried, sitting at his desk.

"Martin, I need a friend more than a servant right now," said the earl.

"I hope I can be relied on to be both, Sir," was the reply.

"I felt the spectre of my father enter my bones today, Martin, and I am afraid." was the strange reply. "I need to get back to Wetherley and ask Dorothia for her hand in marriage before I am a ruined man."

Martin looked very confused. "I do not understand, my Lord, what has happened?"

"Nothing but it is what could happen that I fear. I felt something I can only describe as lust when I saw a gypsy bareback rider today, a feeling I did not like but it was strong," was the reply. "My saving grace is that she is very young and never would I cross that boundary, but I would not like to chance a meeting with her just in case."

Martin looked genuinely shocked. "Surely, Sir, you cannot be serious."

"I have a great fear that I am, Martin," the earl replied looking flustered. "Do you think blood will out? Is Dorothia's mother right?"

"Only if you let it be so, Sir," was the reply. Martin could see the anguish in his master's face. "I would think that most men tonight were drawn to the gypsy women, they try to draw the audience, that is their task. They offer something that women of virtue and breeding do not, excitement."

"I know you are right, Martin, I probably imagined that her eyes singled me out."

"I expect other men in the crowd felt they had experienced the same attention. It is a trick of the trade," said Martin matter-of-factly.

"That is as may be, Martin, and I believe you may be correct, but it does not alter the feeling that overwhelmed me. It was most disturbing," continued Adam. "I look at Dorothia, who is a great beauty herself and I feel a warmth, a desire to spend time in her company, but I have never felt the urge to enfold her in my arms and to hell with the consequences."

"I should hope not, Sir," was the reply. "I believe, Sir, we must think of a solution to the housing of Kitty and we should make haste and return to Wetherley."

"And I believe you are right, Martin," was the reply.

The earl spent a very disturbed night, unable to rid his mind of the gypsy. In the morning, he was determined to shake free of this strange feeling that had overwhelmed him and go back to Wetherley post haste.

Chapter 29
The Artist

The next day was a strange one, Robbie was trying to juggle apples and do other tricks that he had seen the night before. Kitty seemed even more withdrawn than ever and the earl seemed lost in thought. Just when he thought nothing else could occur, a stranger came calling. Clarkson showed the man into the drawing room, whilst he looked for the earl.

It turned out that the man was an artist and he had spotted Kitty at the circus and wanted permission to paint the child. He had with him a portfolio of sketches to show the earl that he was, in fact, genuine. Over a glass of Madera, the earl flipped through the sketches admiring them as he went. The man was indeed a very fine artist.

The man was called Pierre Conte and was originally from Paris. He spoke excellent English and as the earl spoke a splattering of French, they could communicate very easily. Adam was fascinated by the man.

Adam's eyes alighted on one sketch that made him feel very vulnerable again in the way he had the night before. It was of the gypsy that had unnerved him.

"This is a gypsy from the circus," he said.

"Is she not a most splendid creature?" was the reply. "I wanted to paint her but she is superstitious and thinks that her soul will stay in the painting; the sketch was a prelude to one I hoped to paint. Alas, that will never be."

The earl just stared mesmerised by the sketch. "What do you know of her?"

"Nothing other than that she is of Romany blood, 13 or 14 years of age and has the most exquisite bone structure, her name is Jeanette," was the reply. "She is an artist's dream as is your daughter, Sir."

The earl was unable to take his eyes off the picture in front of him. "Kitty is not my daughter, she is a foundling that I have taken under my care."

"Would you permit me to paint the child, Sir?"

"I can see no problem with that if you came to the manor and Kitty would like to sit for you," was the reply.

"I will pay you, Sir."

"Not me, you won't be painting me. If you pay anyone, it will be the child." replied Adam. "What will you do with the sketch?"

"I would like to actually catch the girl's likeness on canvas, I am quite well known in Paris and I would like to paint the child and possibly exhibit the painting," said Pierre. "Now you tell me that the child is a foundling, another idea comes to mind."

"Such as?" asked the earl.

"I run a school in Paris for aspiring artists and if permitted to paint the girl here and now so to speak, I feel that she might be able to make a very good living sitting for others."

"You mean you would like to take her to France with you. I could not permit that, she is in my care," replied Adam, alarmed.

"Surely she has a chaperone who could accompany her, Sir," said the artist. "Do you intend to adopt the child or make her your ward, what is your plan for her future?"

"I have only just become acquainted with the girl, plans I do not have," replied Adam honestly and he went on to explain the circumstances that brought the girl into his care.

Pierre appeared genuinely distressed by the girl's background. "I can see that you would want to be careful where the child goes from here."

"The boy I would willingly keep, he is already like a son to me, but the girl is a strange one," said Adam. "I will get someone to fetch the child and you will see what I mean."

Adam walked over to the bell pull and very soon, there was a tap on the door, it was Clarkson.

"Ah," said the earl. "Would you be so good as to fetch Kitty for me, Clarkson? I want to introduce her to this gentleman."

Pierre was greatly amused by the polite way that the earl spoke to his servants and told him so.

"It is amazing how much more helpful people are if you smile and say please," said the earl. "Also, I saw enough of cowering servants when I was growing up. I like to run a happy ship."

Very quickly, Kitty appeared at the door. She curtsied in the most charming way and timidly walked over to the earl and his visitor.

"I am told you wanted to see me, Sir," she said in her quiet little voice.

"Look at these pictures, Kitty," requested the earl as he laid a few out on the table for her to see.

Kitty's eyes danced over the pictures and she smiled. "They are wonderful, Sir," she said. "Who could draw such beautiful people? They all look so real!"

"This, Kitty, is a new acquaintance, Mr Pierre Conte, he is the artist in question," replied the earl.

Kitty's eyes widened until they looked as though they would burst from her head. "Tu es Trés intelligent monsieur," she said in French to everyone's amazement, "I would love to be able to do such a thing. One of the ladies where I stayed used to draw, nothing compared to you, Mr Conte, of course, but I enjoyed watching her."

"So you appreciate art, child," said Pierre in his broken English.

"Je fais, Sir, beaucoup oui," was the amazing reply.

"You spoke French, how do you know French?" said the earl, his mouth open in amazement.

"Je parle un peu Français, I do not speak very well, I am sure, but the lady who drew was French and she taught me a few words."

"Good heavens above. Whatever next," said the earl. "A French prostitute who draws. This is too much."

"She said she was from a good family," explained Kitty.

"How came her to the brothel, do you know?" asked the earl.

"She said it was the same way that I had," replied Kitty innocently.

"You do not mean she was placed there by my father, surely."

"If you are to believe what she told me, and I believe it, yes Sir," was the reply. "She took a particular interest in me and promised to keep me safe. I think she would have tried but you came and rescued me so I will never know. I do think about her, she did not seem happy in that house."

"I doubt that she is child," replied the earl. "I have an idea to rescue her from her predicament. You need a chaperone and if you like the woman enough, why should it not be her."

"I would love that, Sir," said Kitty. "Her name is Camille and she is very dark and pretty, not quite 25 and has no family in England."

"You have become well acquainted with the woman," said the earl amused.

"Excuse me," said Pierre, "I realise this is of no concern of mine but you have to agree that it is quite amusing that you are considering a prostitute as a chaperone of your young charge."

"It is another wrong I can right, Pierre. The list has become quite long and at least this I can do easily."

"How will you get to rescue the woman?" Pierre asked. "They will surely not allow you inside the property again."

"That is a thought," Adam replied.

"Can we, for a moment, come back to the reason for my visit?" asked Pierre. "Then I would like to offer an answer to your latest adventure."

"I am sorry, Sir," said Adam. "With all this French speaking and talk of rescuing young woman, I had clean forgotten. Kitty," the earl caught hold of the girl's hands as he spoke. "Would you allow Mr Pierre to paint you?"

Kitty looked up at the portraits hanging on the wall of the drawing room. "Do you mean like those hanging here?"

"Not so formal, maybe sitting with a cat or flowers," Pierre suggested.

"I would like that a lot, Sir," was the reply. "Merci beaucoup."

The earl had actually, until this moment, thought that the girl might be a little simple as she seemed so shy and timid and quiet. He suddenly realised that she was listening and not speaking for the sake of it.

"It is decided then," said Mr Conte. "I will pay a visit to the house of ill repute and ask this Camille to walk with me for a fee, you will be waiting outside and we will whisk her away. Such Japes. Easily done."

"It sounds easy," replied the earl as he walked over to the pull bell again. This time when Clarkson appeared, he asked for Martin to be brought to join him.

As soon as Martin entered the room, he was swamped with details of his master's latest plan. "I would ask you to be the one outside waiting for Camille. If you would rather not do this task, I understand," said Adam.

Martin was as amused as Pierre by the whole scenario. "I hope there are not too many other young persons in need of rescuing to appease your conscience, Sir, or we will never get back to Wetherley."

"How right you are, Martin."

Adam persuaded the artist to part with the sketch of Jeanette, the gypsy girl. He rolled it up carefully and placed it in a locked draw.

Two days later, Pierre Conte returned to the manor. He sat down to dine with the earl and then left on his mission with Martin, who pretended to be his footman accompanying his master and waiting outside for him. They took an unmarked carriage hired locally. Everything went according to plan. Pierre went into the whorehouse pretending that he only spoke French so it was obvious that he would be offered a French speaking woman. Camille was thrilled to have a fellow countryman to speak to in her native tongue. Pierre was able to acquaint her with the plan in French, so no one else could understand so it was a fairly easy rescue. Camille was obviously amazed that a gentleman would actually want to employ her knowing her history.

The carriage pulled up outside the manor house just under two hours from when it left. Camille, Pierre and Martin hurried inside and the carriage was returned. Mrs Frost had not been too keen on the inclusion of a woman of the night into the household, but she was beginning to understand that her new master was not one for convention.

The next day saw Kitty united with Camille and the first sitting for the painting. The young woman had been removed from her previous home at such speed that she had not had time to take any of her personal property with her. She stood where she was, wearing all she possessed. The next couple of days saw a procession of milliners, dress makers, glove, coat, shawl sellers bring their wares for Camille's approval.

Martin was quick to point out to his master the cost of such a venture. "We cannot have the woman dressed as a slut if she is to be Kitty's chaperone," the earl explained.

"Have you considered that people will talk?" said Martin, concerned. "You must admit it is a very odd arrangement."

"Do you know, Martin, I have come to the conclusion that I will be talked about whatever I do," was the reply. "I was rather hoping that as we removed Camille during the hours of darkness, we might have been unnoticed."

"I am sure someone would have noticed but they will not know from where the young woman had been brought," replied Martin.

"My thoughts exactly, they will think it is just a woman coming to be chaperone to Miss Kitty, her history will be a complete mystery, I hope."

"Have you now decided, Sir, that we are to stay in Keighley or do we return to Westerley as you said previously?" Martin asked.

"We will away to Westerley," replied the earl. "I have just told Robbie of my plans. I need to go to Weston-Super-Mare and see my sister. I left her in my good friend, Sir James' care nearly five months ago saying that I would return shortly. She will think I have deserted her."

"I guess you have told her of all the things you have done here. She will excuse your absence for sure," said Martin with a smile.

"I fear she will think me quite mad," was the reply. "Mrs Frost certainly does. I do not believe that she fully approves of Kitty sitting for an artist; she thinks it will make the child's head swell, let alone my choice of chaperone for the girl."

Martin just laughed. "Life is certainly full of surprises, Sir."

There was a tap on the door and it opened to find Miss Camille standing there, now dressed every inch like a lady. She entered the room and curtsied. "Sir," she said with a French tang to her voice, "I do not know how to thank you for bringing me here. I believed my life to be over and did not care what happened to me. Then Miss Kitty happened into my life and you rescued her and I felt a possibility that maybe one day, I too would be free. Here I am, it is like a dream." With that, she burst into tears, sobbing uncontrollably. "Merci beaucoup, merci beaucoup."

Martin and Adam looked at each other, not knowing how to deal with the present situation. The girl just stood and sobbed. Eventually, Martin could not stand it any longer and he went over to her and took her into his arms. She cried so much that his shoulder was getting quite wet. Martin looked at Adam with pleading eyes, looking for help. Eventually, the woman managed to calm herself and she stepped back out of the embrace that she had been held in for a good five minutes.

"I am so sorry, Sir," she said with eyes red from crying. "I am so scared that this is a dream and I will wake up."

"Oh dear," said Adam. "Please have no fear of this not being true. You are under our protection now. I am considering allowing Kitty to accompany Mr Conte to Paris but only if you go with him to protect the child."

Camille's mouth fell open, then she let out a short excited scream. "You would help me to go home?"

"If that is what you want," was the reply.

"Want?" she exclaimed. "I have thought of nothing else since I landed on these shores. I came here with my parents as a young woman. Paris was not always a safe place. We stayed with relatives, who have since passed on, and then my parents and sister died in a coaching accident, so they too were gone. The earl, your father, knew my uncle and he was kind to me for a while. As soon as I was alone, his attitude changed; he sent me to the whorehouse in the care of the madam there to be kept safely for him when he was in Keighley. He did not come very often, thank goodness, but I hated him. I am so sorry to say this, Sir, but the devil was in him."

"I have learnt this, Camille, do not be afraid to speak as you find," said the earl, shocked but not surprised by the young woman's story. "Please continue."

"I was only 14 when the late earl took me to the whorehouse," she continued with a tear in her eye at the memory. "I was kept just for his pleasure and no other man was allowed near me. I believe the madam was paid very well. I tried to escape a few times but each time, I was beaten quite furiously; I have scars on my back to prove my story."

"Who dared to do such a thing to you?" asked Martin.

"The madam, when she caught me, and then again by the earl when he was informed," was the reply. "The earl seemed to take a great deal of delight in beating a woman with a strap."

"I can imagine, I faced the same punishment several times when young," Adam replied.

"When Kitty came to us, I knew my time was up. He had a new bird to tame and I feared for her. To be honest, Sir, I also feared for myself as I knew that he would not want me alive to tell tales," Camille continued. "Kitty was such a dainty little thing, so pretty, I could see why he wanted her. But even he knew that she was too young. Thank heavens, he died before, before, well you know, Sir."

"Unfortunately, I do know," replied the earl. "I guess Kitty would have been a working girl eventually."

"I heard talk of it being soon, Sir. I was so afraid and could not see any way out," replied Camille. "You came just in time. Like a knight in armour rescuing the fair damsel from a fate worse than death."

Martin looked at the earl and they both fell into uncontrolled laughter at the picture before them. Soon, Camille joined in their mirth.

Before long, another letter arrived in Brighton from Lord Adam Southerly addressed to Dorothia to tell her how the circus had been at Keighley Moor, and he had gone with Robbie, Kitty, his housekeeper—Mrs Frost, and man servant, Martin, and how exciting it had been.

'Dear Miss Mountjoy,
I have so much to tell you. You will find it hard to believe the excitement that has come into my life of late. I told you about Robbie's sister and how Martin and I had rescued her with Robbie's help from the house of ill repute, where she was placed by my father. The purpose of this acquisition only became clear when we found her in a brothel and rescued her. You would never have seen such an exquisite creature, she is beyond beautiful—so delicate and so young. I shudder to think of her life if we had not found her. The circus came to Keighley moor and as you can imagine, Robbie, Martin, Kitty, my housekeeper and I, all went to watch them all perform. It was so exciting, Robbie is anxious to return tomorrow but I fear that he will be disappointed.

I made a new acquaintance a few days ago. A French artist called Pierre Conte. Such an artist, absolutely brilliant. He brought a portfolio that did him proud and requested that I allow Kitty to sit for, which I am going to allow. Kitty has quite amazed us all by showing us that she can speak a degree of French taught to her by a woman called Camille who she met in the brothel. Who would have thought it! Martin and my new friend, Mr Conte, returned to the brothel and rescued Camille. I am wondering where it will all end. She is a charming, young French woman of some breeding.'

Dorothia laughed, but was a little shocked at all she had read.

'My man, Martin, has said that he feel I am in danger of rescuing every lost soul in Christendom, and I fear that he might be right so I intended to return to Weston-Under-Wetherley very soon. I also feel that I have left Sally far longer than I had intended and believe I have imposed on the kindness of my good friend, Sir James, long enough. I intend to go down to Bleadon, on the edge of Weston-Super-Mare, where Sir James lives, and bring my sister home after I have rested in Wetherley for a few days. Having done so well and even enjoying the excitement, my next project is to search for Freda, the laundry maid, who I understand was defiled by my father and left with child and see how she fairs.'

Dorothia's sister, Elizabeth, was starting to see the young earl as a bit of a hero—a knight on a white stallion in shining armour, riding off to right wrongs and rescue maidens in distress. Everyone was most amused and Dorothia could not wait to write a letter to Adam and tell him of his exalted position. She was herself a little alarmed at the thought of all these waifs and strays being gathered. She was also hoping to tell Adam about her sister's forthcoming wedding with the hope that he might be in Wetherley to attend.

Chapter 30
Time to Decide

Yet another week passed and the earl was still in Keighley. Robbie had taken himself off to the circus in the company of one of the stable lads on a few occasion, unable despite pleading eyes to persuade the earl to return.

Adam had received a letter from Sally that put his mind at rest in that direction at least. She sounded full of the joys of spring. The simple country life suited her disposition and she was at peace with the world. Because she was a terrible romantic, Sally found all the stories of rescue and circuses very exciting. It was obvious from her writing that someone had helped her to compose her missive to him. Although her mother had been a governess and was reasonably educated, the hard life the woman led after her dismissal from Westerley-Manor-Lodge would have made teaching her daughter a difficult task. Adam was very grateful that she had taken the time to try.

Sir James also wrote and told Adam how much pleasure having Sally and her cheerful, innocent humour around gave him. He told of the romance that was blossoming between Alice and Jake, which he encouraged unlike a lot of property owners. James was a lot like Adam, he wanted everyone to be happy. It seemed that everyone was pleased with what Adam had done so far and were keen on him getting his house straight before worrying about them. James made Adam smile when he told him of how Sally had taken Rosebud up to her room, only to realise that sheep are not the cleanest of animals. She imagined the creature to stay like the little helpless creature she had first encountered and was quite disappointed to see how quickly it grew.

Adam decided that he would not tell Dorothia about his latest idea to make Camille chaperone to young Kitty, the rescue of Camille had probably shocked her enough. He thought it all might be a bit too much for her refined upbringing.

Adam received a letter written in her usual formal manor from Dorothia to tell him of Everline's friendship and intended marriage to a young man of the cloth, Allun Parton. Like her father, he was the youngest son of a minor noble and as such the family fortune and title had passed him by. He had been pushed towards the life of a vicar and he was very suited to his calling and embraced it willingly. This meant, of course, that Dorothia and her sisters would soon be returning to the rectory at Weston-Under-Wetherley for the wedding.

Adam also received a short letter from his mill owning friend, Christopher Waud, to tell him that his father, Robert, had passed away. It was expected as the man had been unwell for a few years; as a result, Christopher had taken over the mantle of mill owner at a young age and had carried out this task very well.

Adam went to the funeral of his father's old adversary and was amazed at the difference between his own father's funeral and its total lack of congregation and that of Christopher's father. Robert had been a hard-working, honest and popular man. The church was full. It made Adam feel a little sad and made him wonder which way people would react if he was to meet a sudden end like his father.

The earl spent most evenings in the company of his new friend, Pierre Conte. Pierre liked to work until the light became difficult and Kitty was a very patient sitter. Her calm disposition made it possible for her to sit quietly in one place for as long as was necessary. The madam had told her to stay as quiet and unassuming as possible so none of the 'gentlemen' would notice her and this had stayed in her mind. Pierre tried not to tire the child and use a great many of his preliminary sketches to cut down the actual time spent in sitting for the painting.

Adam found Pierre a lively supper guest and looked forward to his evening spent with him. Sometimes, Adam and Pierre ate alone and others, Martin, joined them. Adam had never liked eating alone. Obviously, most gentlemen did not share their meals with servants of any kind but Adam was not like most gentlemen.

For convenience, the artist was staying at the manor, so many hours were spent sitting by the fire, smoking and drinking rum punch and learning about France and its history. Adam had a keen interest in history and liked to gather facts. Pierre had an amusing way of describing even the worst events.

"The French like to fight, mainly the English," Pierre said with a chuckle. "When they do not have the English to fight, they fight each other, that is why they have so many revolutions."

"I have never been outside of England, another missing chapter from my education," said the earl.

"It is a great pity not to have seen the architecture of other countries. I have travelled to Italy, Spain and obviously, Britain, the differences are spectacular," was the reply.

"I wanted to go to Brighton and see the Brighton Dome. I was reliably informed that it was based on the Halle au Ble in Paris. I have heard that Paris is the home to many magnificent buildings so I am not surprised that we would wish to emulate some of them. I am told that it is a splendid building built to house the Prince Regents horses. Would this be correct Pierre?" asked Adam.

"If it is built along the lines of our Corn Exchange, it will indeed be a building worth visiting," replied the artist, "The Halle aux blés in Paris was built in 1782. It has a central cupola, several feet in diameter and nearly as tall in height, making the dome shape."

"That is how the Brighton Dome was described to me," explained the earl. "Apparently, in the centre of the room, there is a very large lotus shaped fountain used to water the horses. How splendid that must look."

"Splendid indeed," replied Pierre.

"It was thought when the scaffolding was removed that the glass roof covering the room would collapse. It did not, of course," Adam said with a smile.

"It was a very ambitious piece of construction as was the building in Paris," explained Pierre. "This style of building is called the Indo-Saracenis style, with a vast glass dome covering the room. We live in exciting time architecturally."

"It is wonderful to be able to talk to someone as informed as you, Pierre, about every aspect of the arts," said Adam keenly.

"I have never heard of Indo-Saracenis style of architecture."

"It is just the combination of Indian, Islamic, Gothic revival and Neo-Classical styles, the best of each," said Pierre knowledgeably.

. "You are a remarkable man, Pierre. I suppose if one paints, you have to understand all things of structure."

"Building shapes interest me as well as the human and animal form," replied Pierre.

Relaxed in peaceful conversation with his new friend, Adam was beginning to believe that there was a light at the end of the tunnel and maybe the horrors of new discoveries about his despicable father might actually come to an end. Until now, every revelation had brought an even greater challenge to be resolved.

Pierre sat at peace with the world, smoking the most elaborate pipe that the earl had ever seen. The bowl was a carved enactment of Paris in the 1700s; it featured figures and the guillotine, it was a work of art. Pierre told Adam how he had lost many ancestors to Madam Guillotine.

"I do not come from as great a family as yours, Adam, but I am, what we in France call, gentlehomme des 4 lignes, which means that I am a son and grandson of a nobleman," he explained. "I have counts and castellans in my lineage."

"Believe me, Pierre, when I tell you that having a grand heritage is not always a good thing, when positions have been used for evil," Adam replied. "I lay awake some nights wondering what horrors the morrow will bring. Just when I believe that I have heard all the base things possible in regards to my late father's morals, another horror rises up."

"Martin is right, Adam, when he tells you that you cannot be expected to carry the burden of all your father's faults."

"I could not, believe me," Adam replied. "I would be laid so low, I would not be able to move. I have found inheriting the name Lord Southerly, Earl of Wetherley, a mill stone round my neck."

"It must have gotten you out of a few tight spots surely from time to time," exclaimed Pierre.

"That it has, I must admit that I have used the power it gives me to enter places that might have been forbidden to me," replied Adam. "I still have a laundry girl to seek in Wetherley, who was cast out when discovered to be with child of my father's making. The rumour has it that my father arranged for the poor woman's father to be caught in a man trap whilst on his way to confront him. Can you believe such a story?"

"Unfortunately, having heard myself some tales, I can, though I cannot conceive how he could have organised that atrocity," Pierre replied. "Martin told me how hard you have worked to try to improve the mills and of the other things you have done to improve your standing in the community. You are a good man, sit back and let your father's ills go."

"I wish I could, Pierre, but they are there in my face every day," the earl said with a sad voice. "Just look at Robbie and Kitty."

"Yes, I do look at them every day, Sir, and wonder at what a miracle you have performed, taking two waifs and strays and making such delightful people out of them."

Adam smiled at that. "Do you believe in bad blood, Pierre?"

"Inherited evil, do you mean, Adam?" was the reply.

"Yes, in Wetherley, there is a woman I was intending to ask to marry me but her mother tells her that blood will out."

"Then the woman is a fool, my boy," replied Pierre. "Anyone can see that you are not your father and never could be."

"There have been moments, fleeting ones, when I started to doubt myself," said the earl thoughtfully.

"We all suffer from self-doubts, we would not be human otherwise," was the reply. "Not giving into temptation, violent acts or unkind actions is what sets us apart from men like your father."

"God willing I will always follow that path," said the earl.

"What are your plans if you find your laundry woman?" asked Pierre, changing the subject swiftly.

"Plans, I don't make plans, life jumps up and bites you when you are busy making plans."

"Will you add her child if it is alive to your family tree as you have Miss Sally?" Pierre asked. "My guess is that the woman would have paid someone to rid her of her burden."

"Don't say that, Pierre," replied Adam horror-struck. "Another innocent life on my conscience."

"And if it lives?"

"I fear any child of this other woman will be a different kettle of fish to Sally. Sally was bought to sell goods for her keep, clean, keep house, mind the children and run errands. Luckily, she was spared any possible evil intent by the man who bought her; his wife did, however, beat her mercilessly and kept the child underfed," was the reply.

"Why did she not simply run away?" asked Pierre, amazed.

"I asked her the very same question. Sally has a strange sense of loyalty, having been sold by her mother to the man, she felt that she had a sense of honour and duty to stay."

"Sounds to me like she has a bit of you in her, Adam," replied Pierre. "Maybe you will be as lucky with any new kin you inherit in your searches. Maybe the laundry woman's offspring will enchant you as easily as Sally has."

"Sally has a certain degree of education and understanding, I dread to imagine where I might find this new lost soul."

"But you will look?"

"Oh yes, have no doubt about that. I will look, firstly for Freda, then how many others will I find?"

"Do not look too deep, Adam," Pierre replied. "Just scratch the surface or you will make yourself ill. Also, you may find children who claim to be related that are, in fact, just trying to take advantage of your better nature. Always keep an eye open for a trickster."

"I believe you are right there, Pierre. I need to get back to Westerley and sort my own life out as well. I have neglected the woman I intend to ask to marry me and wonder if I have left it too long now. Also, I wonder if marriage is the way forward for me."

"Every man needs a mate, Adam, believe me," replied Pierre.

"You have never married?" exclaimed Adam.

"No, I have never found the time or the inclination, or more to the point, the woman," was the reply. "I have had a few dalliances, nothing too serious, and now I find that I have reached the age of 38 and wonder if I might rather be alone. Then some days, I look at the likes of Robbie and Kitty and wonder what it would be like to have a family."

"To have a son would be my dream," said Adam. "I do feel a tenderness towards Robbie similar to that of a son, but I am aware that he is not mine and if he chooses to go elsewhere, I have no claims upon him."

Pierre reminded Adam that he had actually bought the boy so he did have a claim upon him and laughed.

"The boy is a free man as is his sister," replied Adam. "It is hard to imagine being owned by another person. It is an obscenity against nature. I find that I do not have the same feelings about the girl, is this wrong of me? Even my father wanted a son and was happy to see my safe arrival, not that he ever showed any sign that he held me in any regard."

"Most men long for a son to pass their wisdom onto and their skills if they have any," replied Pierre. "Not that women cannot fish, hunt or do other useful things. Mrs Frost wanted a girl to pass her cookery skills onto, you want to ride and shoot with a son. I dread to think what plans your father had for your later education."

"At least I will never know, though he did tend to ignore me most of the time. He also wanted to marry me off to a very dull, plain young woman with money; my guess being because it was the way his life had gone and he did not want anyone to be happy," said the earl. "One day, maybe, I will have a boy of my own, fishing could be a possibility but I have lost my taste for hunting since my father's death, enough blood has been spilt."

"Robbie tells me that he goes often up to the moor and peeps in through the tent cracks at the circus performers," said Pierre. "Now there is a group of free spirits. I cannot imagine anyone owning one of them without a fight."

Adam found his mind wondering towards the moor and Jeanette, quickly snapping himself back into the real world.

"I agree with you there, Pierre," said Adam. "The gypsy women certainly know how to make the blood pump through your veins."

"English women are very pretty with their rosy cheeks and light complexions, hair tied neatly, no hair out of place, neat little bonnets," said Pierre thoughtfully. "They tend to plump out a little as they grow older but that does not take away their homely appeal."

"Do you mean you would favour an English rose if one took your fancy, Pierre?" replied Adam.

"No, it does not," Pierre replied. "Homely does not appeal to me, I like excitement, a little spirit in a woman. French women are very different from English ones."

"I do know what you mean, not about French women of course, I have only ever met Camille. But I do not want to live a domesticated dull life. I have been wondering if maybe I have been a little hasty looking for a wife," said the earl. "I fell for Dorothia's regal style beauty, she is intelligent and thoughtful and will make a good wife. She is also organised and capable."

"Goodness me, boy, she sounds dull," replied Pierre, which made Adam laugh loudly. "I think you need someone with a little more spunk, remember the fun you have had rescuing maidens from houses of ill repute, sorting out the mill and now you want to hurry back to a humdrum life."

"You do the lady a disservice, Pierre, she is a fine woman. She will make a very worthy wife," replied Adam. "Maybe I should run away and join the circus, the women there would never be considered dull."

"I do not think you need to take things that far, Adam," said Pierre with a chuckle. "You would be a brave man to take on one of those Romanies, they are fiery creatures. Best left to their own kind to deal with."

"But never dull," said Adam cheerfully. "But you are right, I have not sorted my father's dramas out to make more of my own. Any way, it is expected now that I ask for Dorothia's hand."

"But not written in stone," replied Pierre.

"You are a breath of fresh air, Pierre, maybe a little immoral in your encouragement of me to disappoint. Dorothia's father is a good friend, who stood by me when I was at a very low point in my life," Adam added.

"No reason to marry his daughter though," replied Pierre.

"Good heavens, no," said Adam. "The choice is entirely mine. I noticed her when she was quite young and would have married her sooner if my father had not died, not that he would have made that easy for me, he wanted her for himself."

"So you were trying to save maidens that your father had wronged or wanted to wrong quite a few years ago. It is not a new hobby."

"You are outrageous, it is not a hobby but an attempt to make good a very old and once honoured name, damaged by my father's lecherous ways. Dorothia is different, she is of good breeding and has impeccable manners."

"But is she for you, Adam?" was the reply. "I feel you are more French than British."

"What do you mean?" Adam asked.

"We French seek passion and excitement, whilst the English settle for romance and comfort and impeccable manners."

Although Adam laughed heartily at this exchange of words, he wondered if there was not just a little truth in Pierre's words. Pierre had a way with words, both verbal and written, he had a way of saying just what a person might be secretly thinking.

After a long talk with Mrs Frost, it was decided that Kitty would stay in Keighley to complete the painting and the earl, Martin and Robbie would return to Westerley to tie up a few loose ends there before returning once again, this time with Miss Sally. Adam explained to Mrs Frost that everything depended on a young woman in Weston-Under-Wetherley that he had loosely promised himself to. She smiled at the thought of her young master maybe finding himself a wife.

Robbie, Martin and Adam were sharing a breakfast repast when the earl approached the subject of going to Wetherley. Martin was prepared for this announcement but Robbie was not.

"Could I maybe stay here with my sister and wait for your return, Sir?" he asked.

"If that is what you really want to do, Robbie, of course you may," was the reply. "I will be sorry that you chose not to come with us, but you must decide for yourself what you want out of life."

"I will stay then, Sir, and look after my sister," was Robbie's reply.

"I think she has plenty of people looking after her, lad," was Adam's reply. "She also has Camille now."

"So I am not needed?" replied the boy.

"On the contrary, Rob, you will always be needed, it just means you have space to do something for yourself."

Meanwhile in Brighton, the girls went out of the front door of Lady Mary's house; Everline, obviously, for the last time as she was getting married and thanked her for her kindness to them. Elizabeth had decided that she had seen enough of the outside world and wanted to return home for good, but Dorothia promised to return for at least another season. She was hoping that if she was away a little longer, maybe Adam would have completed all his missions and miss her enough to want to settle down. She could tell by his letters that he was not ready to assume a steady married life at that moment in time. She did wonder if maybe she should go home and offer assistance and talked it over with Lady Mary, who advised her to allow the man to get it all out of his system in his own time.

Dorothia and Elizabeth returned to Weston-Under-Wetherley with Everline for the wedding ceremony, which was to be performed by their father in St Michael's in Weston-Under-Wetherley in a few weeks. They arrived home with the wedding apparel, all folded and boxed neatly, but there was still much to do—flowers to arrange, invitations to help with and the food had to be decided and planned. All far too much to expect Bathsheba to do alone. Everline's husband to be, Allun Parton, and his family were to come to Weston-Under-Wetherley for the wedding, so there were arrangements to be made for their accommodation. Both, Dorothia and her father, hoped that the young earl might be in Wetherley in time for the wedding, Bathsheba did not share their hopes.

Chapter 31
The Runaway

The next couple of days saw the household preparing whatever was necessary for their lord's departure to Weston-Under-Wetherley. Adam felt at ease knowing that he had made a decision and was about to put a few miles between himself and the young gypsy woman, who now haunted his dreams. He believed that once back in Wetherley, he would be able to concentrate on pursuing Dorothia and all would be as he had previously planned.

The hall had a pile of trunks and boxes in the corner waiting to be loaded into the coach for the long journey to Wetherley. The earl had taken the time and trouble to thank and say goodbye to every one of his staff. Pierre promised that the painting would be complete before his return to Keighley. Adam spoke to Kitty and told her to obey Camille and not to go out without her as she was now her chaperone; be good for Mr Conte and that he would be back soon.

Robbie was conspicuous by his absence. Clarkson and Martin had been out looking for the boy but returned empty handed. Then one of the maids rushed into the hall in a bit of a state. She bobbed up and down in front of the earl, trying to get his total attention.

"What is the matter, girl?" the earl asked.

"It is Master Robbie, Sir," she said looking nervous.

"What about him, child?" answered the earl looking about him. "Do you know where he is?"

"No, Sir," she said holding out a note to the earl. "I cannot read, Sir, but I guess this might tell you where he is. His clothes are gone from his room," with that, the girl burst into tears.

"Good heavens, girl," Adam took the missive from her hand as he spoke. "Don't blub, let us see what the young scamp has to say first."

"He has taken the dog," said the young woman, hammering the last nail in the coffin if there was any doubt that the boy had run away.

Adam unfolded the note and started to read it out loud, then he stopped suddenly and read it to himself. "It seems that we should have given a chaperone to Robbie and not Kitty; the boy has run off to join the circus. He says as he is not needed and I said he should seek his own path, he is doing just that."

"Oh dear," said Martin. "It seems we are delayed again, my Lord."

"It would seem so, Martin," was the reply and with no further ado, Adam ordered his horse be saddled and brought to the front. "Martin, if you would be so good as to accompany me, I would be grateful."

Within 20 minutes, the pair were sitting astride their mounts and were on their way to search out Robbie at the circus site. When they arrived, the circus was being packed up to move onto pastures new. The big top was already down and being loaded onto huge carriages. Martin and Adam got down from their horses and led them around the busy workers looking for the boy.

"Do not leave your horse unattended, Sir," said Martin. "Rumour has it that gypsies are horse thieves."

"Not all surely," replied the earl. "Let's hope we are amongst the exception. Maybe if you go in one direction and I in another, we will find the boy quicker."

"And if we find him?" asked Martin. "Do we take him back to Keighley Manor through force?"

"One bridge at a time, Martin, let's find the runaway first."

Adam walked through the hustle and bustle of a circus about to move, guiding his horse carefully over obstacles on the floor and under those overhead. In the distance, he spotted Robbie deep in conversation with a young gypsy lad of a similar age. He was so engrossed that he did not hear the earl approach, even though he was leading his mare. The first realisation that he had been discovered came when he felt an arm upon his shoulder.

Robbie span round to confront the earl. "Sir, I thought you would be away by now," he said simply.

"Did you really think I would leave before seeking you out to explain your actions?"

"Yes, my Lord, I did," he said matter-of-factly. "I wrote you a letter to explain where I was going."

"That you did, boy, and a well-written letter it was as well," was the reply.

The boy looked puzzled. "You said I could stay and do what I wanted, Sir."

"Possible I could have worded that better, I did not mean to include running across the country with strangers," replied the earl.

"But I can work with the circus, I need not be a burden to you anymore."

"I do not know why you would even consider that I find you a burden, child," said the earl with a smile. "I thought you worked for me and liked doing so."

"I did, I do," said the boy a little embarrassed. "But Kitty does not need me and you are about to marry or so Mrs Frost says, so I will possibly not be needed any more at all."

"Being needed and wanted are two different things, Robbie," replied the earl. "Of course life will go on without you but I would want rather you were in our lives."

Robbie smiled a wide toothy grin. "You have been good to me, my Lord."

"And I assume there is a but to that comment."

"Yes, Sir," replied Robbie. "The circus, I would love to join the circus. It is so exciting and they travel all over the country."

"What exactly would you be doing in the circus, Rob? Have you spoken to anyone about this?" asked the earl.

At that moment, Jeanette stepped from the shadows and walked over to the earl and his young companion. She curtsied before she spoke. "Sir, I was listening to you, I hope you do not mind."

Adam found himself unable to reply, lost in her large dark eyes. Adam had always found the strength to make a quick reply, even whilst confronted by his father, but this young woman seemed to confuse his mind.

"I have spoken to my father and he says that the boy can stay." She continued, "Father says that the boy can start by cleaning out the animals, like most newcomers do, and we will see as time goes on what he can do."

"I have brought Daisy with me, Sir," said Robbie.

"So I was told, boy."

"I am going to teach her to dance on her back legs," Robbie said proudly.

Adam laughed at that comment. "I hope she does not let you down."

Robbie suddenly looked distressed. "Oh Sir, have I let you down?" he asked.

"Certainly not, boy," was the reply. "I need to speak to this young lady's father," Jeanette giggled at the fact that she was referred to as a young lady. Her laughter sounded like the tinkling of a bell and Adam smiled her way, absolutely under her spell. "I need to know if he will take good care of you, and then if you wish to stay, I will put up no obstacles, I have no hold over you."

The gypsy girl caught the earl by the hand and led him round behind the caravan they were standing beside. Adam felt as though he was under some sort of spell and unable to resist, he walked silently with the girl. The feel of her hand in his was like a bolt of lightning; he had never felt so vulnerable in his life, not even when hiding from his father's wrath. She could have led him to the edge of hell and he would have followed her willingly. They walked up to a very large painted caravan and Jeanette tapped gently on the door. It was opened by a large man in his mid-fifties, he wore a handkerchief knotted around his head, a white wide-sleeved shirt and black trousers, round his waist was a wide red sash. When he opened his mouth, the sun reflected off a gold tooth. Adam was quite taken by the man's appearance.

"I am Lord Southerly, the Earl of Wetherley, Sir, and you are?" He held his hand out to the man as he spoke.

The patriarch of the circus looked confused but took the earl's hand and shook it.

"I am the owner of this circus and the girl's father. My name is Georgiou."

"Your daughter tells me that you are willing to take my boy with you on your travels," said the earl.

"Your boy!"

"I should explain, he is not actually blood kin. I found he had been purchased by my father as a sweep boy and when my father died, he passed to me so to speak," explained the earl.

"Surely you do not mean you own the boy?" asked the man.

"No, definitely not," replied the earl. "At the moment of my father's death, both, the boy and his sister, became free, as should everyone be."

Jeanette stepped up to her father and whispered in his ear. Adam was standing on the caravan steps. "Please come in, Sir, take some tea with us. I would like to know the circumstances of the boy being 'bought' by your father if it pleases you."

"If someone would kindly look after my horse and look for my man, who is searching the grounds for Robbie, I would like to tell you everything so you will be clear in your mind," said the earl. With that, Adam, Jeanette and her father climbed up into the caravan, his horse was tied up outside. Adam was amazed by the inside of this barrel shaped home on wheels. At one end, there was a curtained off area that he was told was the sleeping compartment and there was a painted table and seats, all brightly covered. On the walls hung beautiful woven cloth. It was a rainbow of colour. Adam looked around in amazement and admiration.

Jeanette laughed her contagious laugh again and offered the earl a seat. "I see you have never looked inside a gypsy caravan before, Sir."

"No, Miss," he replied. "I have never had cause to do so before but it is very beautiful."

She smiled and a warm glow entered Adam's soul. He was, both, frightened and fascinated by the young woman. "I watched you a few nights ago," he said. "You were magnificent." He suddenly realised that maybe he had over stated his appreciation of her talent.

"Everyone is drawn to my daughter," said Georgiou. "Who would not be? She looks like her mother, an angel."

"You are a very lucky man to have landed such a wonderful catch if the girl's mother is even half as beautiful."

Jeanette looked quite embarrassed. "My mother was better on the eye than I am, Sir, believe me," she said.

"I would think that would be impossible, Jeanette," was the reply.

"How do you know my name?" she asked.

"An artist friend of mine, Pierre Conte, told me," Adam explained.

"The man who made sketches of us all, he is very clever," she replied. "What is he to you?"

"He is newly in my acquaintance, he spotted Robbie's sister and asked if he might paint her and with her agreement, I said he could," Adam replied. "He showed me a sketch of you, very good it was as well and said that you would not allow him to paint you because you would lose your soul or some such reason."

Jeanette laughed. "It was an excuse, I said something that would make it impossible for him to argue. I do not like to sit still too long so would not like to be painted."

"That is a loss to the world," said Adam. "My young ward, Kitty, on the other hand, can sit quietly for many hours, I often wonder what she is thinking."

"Best not to know too much about the workings of young women's minds, Sir," said Jeanette's father.

Once again, the response was a laugh from Jeanette.

"You said your mother was better on the eye, am I to understand she has passed on?" enquired Adam.

"Some 12 years since, my Lord," replied Georgiou. "Jeanette was but a babe of three when she was taken."

A quick calculation in the earl's head brought him to the realisation that Jeanette was at least 15, a little older than he had imagined. He had told Martin that he believed her to be about 14, but he actually feared she might be younger. He felt a slight relief in his mind. The thought of such feeling that he had for a mere child distressed him greatly, to learn she was possibly 15 or even 16 lightened his mood.

Martin was discovered in the grounds and the earl sent him back to the manor house to inform everyone that Robbie was safe and that he was negotiating with the circus owner. Martin was not keen to leave his master alone with what he considered to be riff raff. Adam swore to return before long and told Martin that they would only delay their departure to Wetherley by an extra day.

The earl then settled to take tea with Georgiou and told him everything there was to know about the boy. He found Georgiou a good listener and was soon telling him all about his father and wrongs he had been trying to right. The time went quickly and soon, Adam realised that he had been sitting talking for well over an hour. Jeanette had been fascinated, she asked a lot of questions and listened carefully to all the answers. When Georgiou went to look for Robbie, the girl spoke freely.

"I saw you and what I thought to be your family at the circus," she said. "I am glad to know that it was not how it looked."

His heart leapt at the thought that she really had noticed him, he had not dared to imagine it.

Just as Adam was about to make a fool of himself by describing the effect Jeanette had upon him, Georgiou returned with the boy.

After further discussion, it was agreed that Robbie could stay with the circus; it returned every two or three years to the same place, so they would meet again. Robbie agreed to say goodbye properly to his sister and Adam reluctantly looked into the beautiful gypsy's face for what he imagined would be the last time, and he rode back to the manor with a promise from Robbie that if he felt he had made a mistake, he would contact the earl who would organise his safe return.

Adam returned to the manor to find Martin waiting anxiously for him. "I was not happy to leave you alone in that den of thieves, Sir. Anything could have happened, they could have kidnapped you," he said in earnest.

"And yet here I am, safe and sound," was the reply. "I believe you misjudge these people, Martin, they are free spirits, not thieves."

"Everyone knows that gypsies rob and steal and put a curse on you if you do not buy from them," replied Martin.

Adam laughed. "I think you are mistaken, Martin. Circus people are a different breed, they train to entertain and work hard. They are not a travelling rag tag of people, they are a community on the move. Do you think I would leave Robbie in their care if I had the slightest qualms about his safety?"

"So the boy stays with them!" said Martin amazed.

"Robbie is a free spirit like the gypsies, I think it will do him no harm to stay a while with them," replied the earl. "I have told him to come back at any time if he has made the wrong choice."

"So long as he does not grow to be a pickpocket or other sort of scoundrel."

"You must strike these ideas from your mind, Martin," replied the earl. "We all know that we are inclined to put our trust in the wrong people; sometime the people who let you down are not always the ones you expect."

"And the girl, did you see the girl?" asked Martin.

"I did and for that very reason, we go tomorrow, no more delays," was the reply. "She is about 15 years of age, not as young as I at first believed but still a child. Happily, I am not old enough to be her father."

Adam smiled but Martin looked concerned. "You did not leave the boy there so you had a reason to return?" he asked boldly.

"I do not believe I did, my friend, but my mind is not clear so I could not promise thus," was the honest reply.

"Then I will make sure we leave tomorrow, Sir."

Chapter 32
The Wedding and the Workhouse

Dorothia, Elizabeth and Everline all travelled to Weston-Under-Wetherley for Everline's wedding, which was to be performed by their father, Phillip Mountjoy, in the parish church. Allun Parton was a newly ordained travelling vicar, he did not have a parish of his own at this time but stood in for sick and absent vicars in any part of the country if needed. Sometimes, he stayed for just days and other times, several months in one place. He had quite a few tales to tell about his travels. He had met Everline Mountjoy at a dinner party during one of his short and infrequent visits to his family in Hove. They had found it easy to converse as Everline's father is a vicar and of a similar background to the young Reverend Parton; both being the youngest sons of minor dignitaries. There were so many similarities between the two families that conversation flowed like an endless stream. Allun's oldest brother had been taught the running of the family business, his second brother had acquired a commission in the British Army, two of his three sisters had married well and his third brother, who was just a year older than Allun, was quite a scholar and had gone to Cambridge.

Allun found that the life chosen for him suited him very well; by moving from parish to parish, he did not have time to tire of any one place and also had the privilege of seeing a little of England.

No one was surprised when Allun came to Lady Mary and asked her advice on if she considered it was with indecent haste that he wanted to ask for Everline's hand in marriage. Lady Mary could see, as soon as the couple were introduced, that there was a spark between them and volunteered to write immediately to the Mountjoys on Allun's behalf. There was not a lot of time to waste as Allen had already been given the news that he was to go to Hampshire for a longer than usual placement. The present vicar of St Andrew's in Hamble-le-Rice, a very small fishing village on the Solent, had a young son who had a serious accident whilst riding a horse. The vicar and his wife planned to take the child on some sort of pilgrimage to try to regain the use of his legs. This could take some time or if the child succumbed to any problems relating to his accident, a short time, it was unclear. Allun had said that he would go to Hamble as soon as had married and take his new wife with him, and everyone was willing to wait a few of weeks for this to fall into place.

Everline's parents were more than happy that at least one of their daughters had found a good match, something they had hoped for when sending the sister's to Brighton. There was just time to read the banns before the wedding. The girls returned to Weston-Under-Wetherley as soon as was possible, they had already organised the bride's and bridesmaid dresses so there was just the veil to obtain. Their mother, Bathsheba, was very pleased that she had at least a small part to play in dressing her daughter for her wedding. Sir Gerald and Lady Mary Bradbury had already explained that because of Sir Gerald's immobility and the new baby, it would be too difficult for either of them to attend the wedding, but the dresses Everline had brought home with her were the wedding present from the Bradbury's. The reverend and Mrs Mountjoy were quite relieved that they did not have to find suitable accommodation for such high bred persons as the Bradburys, much as they would have liked to thank them for their kindness to their daughters by having them attend. Bathsheba set about writing a thank you letter immediately.

There was much excitement in the rectory when the parcel of dresses was opened and examined.

"Everline, the material is exquisite, the lace trim, this must have cost a king's ransom," said Bathsheba, quite alarmed. "How can we ever repay Lady Bradbury or thank her enough?"

"Lady Mary enjoyed the whole progress of choosing cloth and seeing the dresses made up. I believe she would probably want to thank you for allowing her to do it," said Dorothia putting a calming arm around her mother's shoulders.

Phillip added that he felt Dorothia was probably right and that they should not all feel embarrassed by the generosity shown.

"It isn't as if they can't afford it after all," said Elizabeth with a giggle. "You should see the way she dresses her little baby, like a doll."

"Amy is a doll, a beautiful baby, so good, it was fun to help with her," said Dorothia.

"Lizzie, we are not paupers, we are not charity cases," replied Bathsheba loudly.

"I wasn't suggesting we were," Elizabeth replied. "But I was just saying, they have a lot of money, these dresses are probably a mere bagatelle to them."

"That is as may be....." Bathsheba was about to continue the argument.

"Enough," said Phillip quite firmly. "The dresses are here, they are a gift, extravagant as they may be. We should just be gracious and thank our benefactor."

"Quite right, Father," said Dorothia. "I hope someone is as generous if I ever marry. Everline will look like a princess."

"I think you are right, Sister," replied Elizabeth. "Maybe we could take the dress apart and reassemble it slightly differently for you, Dorothia, no one would know."

They all laughed.

Bathsheba had a great interest in the workhouses in and around Warwick and was very happy to have Dorothia back for a short time to assist her there. She mainly took blankets and warm clothes to the inmates as they were fed, not well but sufficient to keep them alive, but the cold in these buildings got into your bones. Bathsheba used to collect, wash and mend old blankets and when she had a fair amount, take them to one of the workhouses. Sorting out such items had been one of Dorothia's duties when she was in Wetherley. Mending and sending them on to the workhouse was one of the pastimes that Adam's mother, Lady Agnes, had always encouraged. Bathsheba did not know it but as Dorothia had it in her mind that one day, she would be the lady of the manor; she felt it was fitting that she should help her mother in this task.

"It is only right that we should spare a day from our arrangements to go to the workhouse," said Bathsheba to her eldest daughter. "Goodness knows when I will have time to go again."

Dorothia nodded in agreement.

"I am hoping, Daughter, to take a large bundle of darned woollen socks and blankets to the workhouse tomorrow and would appreciate your assistance," continued Bathsheba. "We will get one of the men to drive the pony and trap for us."

Dorothia had never actually been inside the workhouse and when she did step inside, she was horrified. The place seemed to be badly managed so not a lot of work was actually profitable. The place smelt as did the inmates, who looked cold and underfed. The managers were happy to explain to Dorothia the way the place ran, there was a daily workhouse schedule: rise at 6, 6.30 to 7.00 breakfast, 7.00 to 12.00 work, 12.00 to 1.00, lunch, 1.00 to 6.00 work, 6.00 to 7.00 supper and then they all had to be in bed by 8.00. Dorothia asked to be shown where the women and children slept. She was shown a large airless room, furnished with rags and straw on the floor and a bucket in the middle for sanitation. Most of the inmates had their own little spot where they kept anything and everything they owned close by, not that anyone had anything worth mentioning, such things would have been sold to gain extra food. She was told that fights regularly broke out amongst the paupers. There was not a lot of concessions made for sick or elderly, everyone had to do their share of work, though Dorothia was assured that in this particular workhouse, frail and elderly were set to keeping the place clean or chop wood. If someone was lucky enough to be able to cook well, they may be able to help organise the food rations, which were meagre to say the least. Breakfast was bread and a weak gruel, dinner was on a rotor system so as to vary the food a little—it could be cooked scrag-end of mutton, pickled pork or bacon with vegetables, always potatoes, yeast dumplings, soup and suet or rice pudding. All organised to fill the stomachs. Supper was always bread and broth, sometimes cheese and potatoes. People of worth came occasionally to inspect the workhouses and see they were run properly.

Food was served in the dining room, in the workhouse that Dorothia and her mother were visiting this day; there were separate dining rooms for male and female inmates as men and women were kept separate, even if married. Some of the other workhouse fed their inmates at different times as there was only one dining room. Those that ran the workhouse were fed the same as the inmates, only a larger portion, sometimes six times the amount given to a pauper. The main overseer of this workhouse was very proud of the way it was run and was more than happy to answer any questions that Dorothia or her mother raised. Dorothia, on the other hand, was appalled by the conditions that women and children had to endure.

People with even a little education always fared better in the workhouses because they could be set tasks such as teaching or even nursing, which stopped them having to do manual work. Most pauper apprentices were required to be able to sign their own indenture papers so there was a great call for people who could teach someone their letters. Most of the jobs performed by inmates were menial and pointless, such as breaking up stones or crushing bones to make fertiliser. There could be an occasional lace maker, who had come across hard times and her skills were immediately used for the benefit of the workhouse. Workhouses were starting to consider training children in skills that might help them, maybe to work in the mills or in the fields but it was not a general rule.

Dorothia was shown the punishment book, discipline was strictly enforced; minor offences such as swearing or feigning illness to get out of work usually meant they would have their diet restricted for up to 48 hours. Violent behaviour was dealt with severely, girls were punished in the same way as adults, and boys under the age of 14 could be beaten with the rod or other instrument approved by the guardians. Everything was written in the punishment book and it was inspected regularly by the guardians. Dorothia intended to ask Adam if he would become a guardian so improvements could be made. She did not relish the thought of having to make regular visits herself and felt that many of the people there were at fault, a view her mother did not agree with.

"You have had a privileged upbringing, my girl, not everyone is so lucky," she told her daughter.

The workhouses had been pushed to the limits by the improvements in agriculture that had put many farm hands out of work and the effects of the end of the Napoleonic Wars at the beginning of the 1800s were still being felt, so many men had returned home to no work or prospects of any, some with missing limbs that made working even more difficult.

As Bathsheba passed amongst the inmates deciding who she should give her blankets to, she sent Dorothia to speak to the women with small children; most of whom were unmarried and had been deserted by their lovers or cast out by their families. Dorothia believed that fallen women had made their own choices in life and had to be encouraged by her mother to do as asked and speak to them.

Dorothia walked over to a group of toothless hags and thought better of speaking to them and turned away.

She very soon found herself speaking to a rosy-cheeked young woman, who looked familiar to her. She was in fact Freda Prout, one of the laundry women who used to work at the manor, the one that George Southerly had deflowered and cast out. Freda recognised Dorothia as being the vicar's daughter and felt at ease talking to her. Sitting, dirty and thin, beside her was the child that the late earl had fathered.

"This is George," said Freda introducing her young son to Dorothia. "Stand up and bow politely, George."

The boy did as instructed.

"You called the child, George!" replied Dorothia. "I am amazed."

"What else should I have called him?" Freda replied. "The name makes me feel sick but now my precious son hold the same name, it does not appal me anymore."

Dorothia saw the logic in this. "What of the rest of your family, your brother?" asked Dorothia, concerned.

"My brother stepped quite neatly into my father's shoes, he takes any jobs he can and works hard but he has a family of his own to look after," was the reply. "So George and I came here, I do not want to be a burden to anyone. We will not be here forever," Freda smiled a feeble smile.

"I very much hope not," replied Dorothia. "I guess you heard how the earl met his end last year."

"I did, Miss, and I know it is not Christian to say so but I rejoiced on hearing the details of his final moments," the young woman said honestly. "My father died because of that monster, a more horrible death than the earl. Did you know that he bled out in a man trap of all things?" Dorothia nodded and Freda continued, "None of us could understand how father got caught in such a trap as he was very careful, always to keep to the path; everyone knows that man traps are laid on private land to catch poachers, my father was not a poacher, he was an honest man." Freda began to cry and little George came to her and put a thin arm round her shoulder.

"Please, do not make my mother cry, Lady," he said to Dorothia looking up at her with large green eyes, very much like the late earl's.

Dorothia gently wrapped one of the blankets she was carrying round Freda's shoulders before she replied. "I am very sorry, George, your mother is very lucky to have such a brave young man to help her."

Freda regained her composure. "It is OK, George, it is not this lady's fault, the fault is all mine; had I just gone away and not told my father, he would not have gone to speak to the earl and met such a tragic end. Poor papa."

The child looked very confused and the two women decided that enough had been said.

"I will leave another blanket for the boy and see if I can get your rations increased so we can put some flesh on the little lad's body."

Freda was so grateful that she picked up Dorothia's hand and kissed it. Dorothia was in a bit of a daze when she heard her mother calling her from across the room.

"We have kept these people from their chores long enough, Daughter, we must leave now," Bathsheba said.

Dorothia left with a promise that she would return and seek Freda out again. Mother and daughter could not get out of the workhouse fast enough.

"To whom were you speaking?" Bathsheba asked her daughter on the way back to the rectory.

"Just a woman with a sad tale to tell," was the reply. Dorothia did not tell Bathsheba that Freda was one of the young woman abandoned by the late earl as her mother's opinion of that family was well documented and she did not want to hear how evil the Southerly's were again.

"They all have sad tales to tell, Daughter, do not get too involved with anyone you meet there."

Dorothia and Elizabeth stood as bridesmaids to their sister, Everline, and regardless of the short notice, the wedding was well attended and beautifully done. St Michael's Church was full of spring flowers and Reverend Phillip Mountjoy took great delight in marrying his daughter to the young man of her choice. As was expected, Everline looked beautiful in her wedding dress and every woman there admired the workmanship. Dorothia and Elizabeth were equally pleased with the dresses they had to wear. Dorothia was already planning to do exactly what Elizabeth had suggested and alter it so she could wear it again.

Everline hardly had time to get used to being a married woman when she and her new husband packed to go to Hamble Le Rice.

Before Dorothia and her sisters had left Brighton, another letter had arrived from Lord Adam Southerly. He obviously had no knowledge of the forthcoming wedding, their letters must have crossed. He told Dorothia that Robbie had gone to join the circus and how unhappy he was about it but felt it was not his place to prevent the boy doing as he wished. He further told her of his intention to return to Weston-Under-Wetherley very soon to rest and then go and bring his sister back Bleadon. He did add that he hoped that he and Dorothia might manage to be in the same place at the same time in the near future and repeated his commitment to searching for Freda.

Dorothia decided there and then that she had to stop all this searching for George Southerly's fallen women or she would never get to marry Adam.

As soon as Dorothia returned from the workhouse, she re-read Adam's last letter with added enthusiasm and interest.

After Everline's wedding, Dorothia went back to the workhouse and took some money intended for the parish poor and gave it to the manager of the place, making it clear that it was to allow for an increase in food for Freda and George and that she would return shortly and make sure that her instructions had been carried out. He did look at the young woman strangely but did not argue.

It was time for Dorothia to return to Brighton and Lady Mary as she had promised. Her sister, Elizabeth, felt no obligation to keep any promise to return and she stayed in Weston-Under-Wetherley with her parents.

Lady Mary was thrilled to hear about the wedding and Dorothia felt that she genuinely regretted not being able to attend. She was, however, feeling fully recovered after the birth of her daughter, Amy, and was happy to be out and about in Brighton with her new friend.

After a very short time back in Brighton, Dorothia decided that it was time for her to return to the family home and thought that hopefully, Adam would have returned to the manor and then gone down to Weston-Super-Mare giving her time to carry out her plans to magic Freda and her son away once and for all.

Dorothia had missed Adam and was beginning to believe that he would spend the rest of his life looking for wrongs to right and would forget her if she was not careful. He had already said in one of his letters that he felt he could never ask for anyone's hand until he could make the name Southerly one to respect again.

Dorothia went out of the front door of Lady Mary's house in Brighton for the last time and thanked her host for her kindness to her and her sisters. Dorothia had decided that she had seen enough of the outside world, although she had found Brighton most stimulating, she wanted to return to Weston-Under-Wetherley and see how it fared now the threat of George Southerly had abated. The fact that Dorothia now knew where the laundry girl Freda was, she had it in her power to put aside another obstacle to her marrying Adam by informing him where he could find her, she was not sure if she wanted to part with this information just yet.

Chapter 33
Sending Freda Away

Dorothia arrived back in Weston-Under-Wetherley before the young earl and she decided that it was time she put pen to paper and inform him of Freda's whereabouts. She started the letter several times but could not manage to complete it. The thought that Adam might release Freda and little George from the workhouse and bring them to the manor did not sit well with her. Adam had already taken on a half-sister, would he claim George as kin as well? The likely hood seemed pretty strong. Would that mean that this ragamuffin might take preference over any wife Adam might take, that also seemed a possibility. Adam did seem prone to gathering ragamuffins to his bosom, he had already almost made a son out of Robbie, the young chimney sweep boy bought by his father. Did she want to marry Adam and spend her days in the company of ruffians and ill-bred children? She thought not and decided to keep the information that she knew of Freda's whereabouts to herself. Furthermore, she decided to do something about making it more difficult for Adam to trace them. It was an idea she had already formulated but was not sure if she would have the courage to put into practice.

Dorothia wrote to her newly married sister in Hamble and asked her help. Very soon, she received a reply to her missive telling her that Everline had found a position for Freda in a large house nearby where she herself lived, and if Dorothia could find some way of getting Freda to her, she would take the young woman to meet her new employer herself. A small room went with the job and George could also be found odd jobs to do about the place. Most of the working people in this part of Hampshire were involved with fishing or ferrying others about, so there was always a call for hardworking women, especially ones with laundry experience. Because Everline was the vicar's wife and had vouched for Freda, finding employment had not been too difficult.

Dorothia had not told her sister the whole truth, she had made out that Freda was an old friend of hers that had been led astray, she did not want anyone, not even her sister, to share her secret.

Bathsheba was particularly thrilled when Dorothia asked if maybe she could go to the workhouse in her place.

"It is wonderful, child, that you are showing such an interest in the poor of the land," she said smiling proudly at her daughter.

The next time Dorothia returned to the workhouse, it was to buy Freda and George's freedom and send them on their way to Hamble-Le-Rice.

As usual, Dorothia turned up with a bundle of warm blankets to distribute amongst the inmates. She was extremely anxious to get in and out of the building as quickly as possible and took a very short time locating Freda and George.

Freda jumped to her feet as she saw her protector come towards her, little George was already looking a lot healthier and was starting to fill out.

"Oh, Miss, I cannot thank you enough," Freda said grabbing at Dorothia's hand to kiss it.

Dorothia felt a slight touch of guilt about the whole operation, but she soon told herself that she was helping the woman and that this was her Christian duty. She had made up a parcel of clean clothes for the pair and told them to change quickly as they were leaving with her. Freda did not know how to reply, she just looked at Dorothia with astonishment and took the parcel that had been thrust into her arms. Whilst the couple changed out of their rags, Dorothia passed out the blankets that she had brought with her.

As soon as the mother and son were dressed, Dorothia hurried them from the building into the waiting carriage outside. Freda followed Dorothia like a faithful dog would its owner, she did not ask any questions. George, now dressed in slightly oversized trousers and shirt, looked at Dorothia as if she was an angel; the adoration rather embarrassed the young woman.

"Are we going home with you, Miss?" asked the boy in his childlike way. He actually spoke very clearly for a boy of not much more than three years old.

"I have arranged for you and your mother to start a new life some way off," Dorothia explained. "I believe you will both be happy where you are going."

"You are not sending us over the sea like convicts, are you, Miss?" said Freda alarmed.

"Of course not," said Dorothia. "I have come to set you free. I have a wonderful sister in Hampshire, near the sea, she has found you a place with a God fearing family."

"I have never heard of Hampshire," said Freda a little nervously. "What will be expected of us there?"

"I believe it to be a splendid part of England, lots of trees and open spaces," explained Dorothia. "You will actually be in a small fishing village called Netley, there is a large house there that needs a laundry maid and I have recommended you for the job. A room goes with the job and George can stay with you there."

Freda looked absolutely amazed. "Do they know my history, Miss?" she asked.

"They know all they need to know," replied Dorothia. "They believe you to be a young widow and I do not intend for them to know any more than that. I have vouched for your honesty and hard work and they can expect no more from you than a good day's work for your board and lodging."

Freda could not think of anything to say, she was struck dumb. Eventually, after a long silence, she asked how she would get to Netley and Dorothia told her that she had organised a place for her and George on a coach bound for Southampton and that her sister would meet her there and take her the rest of the way.

There was no more to be said, except that there was an overnight place for Freda and the boy in a local inn, and they would leave for Hampshire the following day if they had no objections. Dorothia had another parcel of clothes wrapped in brown paper for the pair. "You cannot arrive with just what you stand up in," she said. "I have put in the parcel a couple of my old day dress, gloves, a shawl and some slipper shoes. You have stout walking shoes on and a bonnet. My sister is organising clothes for George and she will have them with her when she meets you in Southampton."

"It is like a magic adventure," Freda said smiling. "It is all so exciting and you are an angel, Miss. I knew someone with such a beautiful face must be an angel."

Dorothia blushed and smiled. "Just drop me a short missive when you are settled to tell me that you are safe and well and I will be content."

"I do not write in a very learned way, Miss, but I will do my best." It was all the young woman could do to stop herself flinging her arms round, who she considered to be her saviour.

"You are an angel sent from heaven, Miss," Freda said. "I will never again think ill of people who live well on the hog. After my trials at Western-Manor-Lodge, I thought it not possible to trust anyone, and then you came like the sunshine after the winter and have changed our lives."

"I hope you will both be very safe and happy in your new lives," said Dorothia, truthfully praying to herself that Freda would never find a reason to return to Weston-Under-Wetherley.

Mother and son were dropped off at the inn to enjoy a good supper and the first sleep in a proper bed for years, ready to take the coach the next day for their new lives in Hampshire. Dorothia was very pleased with herself, it had cost her all the pauper money given to her father by Adam to distribute on his behalf, but she felt it was worth every penny.

Chapter 34
Wetherley, Dorothia and Changes

Having explained to the household that Robbie had chosen to follow a different path but would be calling to say goodbye, the earl made ready to return to Wetherley.

Pierre was to stay on at the manor and complete his master piece as promised. Camille seemed settled and Adam felt that he could leave everyone for a while.

Soon, the earl was on his way to Wetherley and the circus too had moved on, the ground was now empty. The grass had turned brown by lack of light when shaded by the big top and you could see clearly where each tent and caravan had stood.

It was a dusty and tiring trip back to Weston-Under-Wetherley and after two stops en-route, they finally reached their destination.

They hardly had time to unpack when visitors started to call. First was Phillip with news of his girls in Brighton. Everline had met a young man and was now married, the vicar expressed his regret that the earl had missed the wedding by a very few weeks.

"It was all arranged with the greatest of haste," Phillip explained. "Not because of any impropriety of course, but because my new son-in-law had a position to take up as soon as possible."

"I did not think it would have been for any other reason," replied Adam with a smile.

"The wedding was well attended, weddings in Wetherley always are. Everyone loves a wedding," Phillip continued. "The parish hall was crammed with people I had not seen for quite some time."

"Amazing, how a goodly selection of cakes, pastries and sandwiches can attract the hordes," Adam said good humouredly.

"Never a truer word spoken, young Sir," was the reply.

"I was sorry I could not reach you to offer you an invitation, Adam," added Phillip.

"I think it would have been wrong of me to attend and I am glad I did not have to make that decision," said Adam seriously. "I am still not a welcome face locally and I would not have blighted Everline's wedding for anything."

"You are probably right, my boy, much as I hate to think it is true."

Phillip went on to describe how beautiful Everline's sisters had looked, dressed as bridesmaids for the occasion, whilst Adam tried to look interested.

"Elizabeth decided not to return to Brighton, she was homesick," continued Phillip. "Elizabeth told me that even though Brighton was blessed with many wonderful shops, she had found herself being dragged to museums, art galleries and libraries by Dorothia, so she felt she would rather come home."

"It sounds as though Dorothia is enjoying Brighton," said Adam in a sort of enquiring manner.

"I believe she finds Brighton most stimulating," was the reply. "She was certainly quick to return."

Adam found himself feeling rather relieved, thinking that if Brighton held Dorothia's interest, it might give him more time to decide where his future lay.

So Adam had just missed meeting Dorothia in Weston-Under-Wetherley by a short time. He still had his mind full of Jeanette and was not sure what he wanted in life anymore. He had planned to leave Keighley with a clear idea for his future and that meant marrying Dorothia; unfortunately, he had seen the gypsy again whilst looking for Robbie and now he was not so sure.

A further week passed and Adam was just settling back into life at Wetherley, knowing he should really be making plans to go to Bleadon Manor Farm and fetch his sister home, when he received a message from Sir James to inform him that he was coming to Wetherley and bringing Sally himself. To say Adam was pleased was an understatement, he did not relish the journey down south so soon after returning to Wetherley. Sure enough, two days later brought this happy group to Wetherley Manor Lodge.

Sally looked extremely well thanks to the sea air and good food she had experienced in Bleadon. They embraced and Adam was so very happy to see his sister again. He pretended to look about. "You have not brought Rosebud with you," he exclaimed. "I felt sure she would be travelling this way."

Sally laughed, "I left her with her mother where she belongs as well you knew I would, Adam," she said lightly.

Sir James added that Sally had taken some persuasion to part with the lamb but the thought of a sheep in a carriage for two days was not an option.

"We have come with news, Adam," said Sally smiling. "Alice wants to marry Jake and James says that she has to ask you as she works for you, not him."

"I wondered when she was not with you that this might be the case," replied Adam. "Her sister, Kate, told me that one of Alice's letters to her had revealed a strong desire to stay in the Weston-Super-Mare district, I guessed there was a young man involved."

"You cannot refuse, Adam, she is so much in love," added Sally.

"Why would I stand in the way of anyone's happiness, dear sister?" Adam replied with a broad smile.

"In that case, Adam," said James in earnest, "I know we have hardly stepped over your front door step but can I ask you a very important question?"

Sally moved over to James' side and slid her hand through his arm. Adam smiled. "So that is the way the wind has blown."

"Yes, my friend," replied James. "I would like your permission to marry Miss Southerly and take her back to Weston with me. The country life suits her very well."

"Yes, James, I am not blind, I can see that," was the reply.

"I feel I have hardly had time to get used to having a sister when she is off but have no fear, with my blessing. I wish you both well."

James and Adam shook hands vigorously and Sally threw her arms round the pair of them.

"I assume you are staying a few days at least," asked Adam. "Do you intend to marry here or in Bleadon?"

"I have already spoken to the vicar of St Peter's and would like us to marry there, Adam," said Sir James. "It is my family home and I would have to make everyone travel a great distance if we married here. I assume you will come and give your sister away."

"I would be honoured." Adam rang for help to have James and his party directed to rooms that had already been allocated to them. "Will you be staying here, James?"

"Not me, Adam, I am going to stay in my own house. I want to give you and Miss Southerly a little time alone before I steal her away," said James. "Besides now we are officially engaged, it might look a little forward."

"That is thoughtful of you, James, but there is no need, but if you insist, at least I expect you back for supper."

Sally clapped her hands and then took James and Adam's hands in hers. "My two favourite men will be brothers, wonderful, isn't it!" she said.

"I suppose we will, sort of," replied Adam. "I always wanted a brother and a sister, of course."

Adam went to find Katie, Alice's sister, to give her the news of the impending wedding. James had brought a rough scribbled note from Alice to her sister insisting that she comes to be her bridesmaid. Katie skipped around with glee and Adam left her alone, much amused by the days happenings.

Before supper could be served, there was yet another visitor. Adam had retreated to his study to write to Dorothia to tell her of the latest news. Martin appeared at the door to tell him that the lady was here, accompanied by a young maid.

"Is Dorothia here?" he exclaimed. "I was led to believe that she was still in Brighton."

"Well, Sir," replied Martin with a smile, "unless your visitor has an amazing likeness to Miss Mountjoy, I believe it is her."

"Good heavens, this is a day for surprises," said Adam getting to his feet. "Show her into the sitting room if you will please, Martin, I will be there shortly."

Adam smarted himself up and went to the sitting room; he entered to see Dorothia standing there looking as beautiful as ever. Her dark hair was piled on her head and covered by a very pretty bonnet. His mind rushed back to Pierre's description of English woman. He stood and stared at her for a moment imagining her hair loose and falling about her shoulders like his gypsy. She was a very elegant looking woman—neat, tidy, tall and slim. He had to shake the image of Jeanette and her wild exciting look. Dorothia was his destiny, Jeanette was a dream and if he allowed it to be, his downfall.

"Such a coincidence, I had just started writing you a letter," he said. "Your father led me to believe that you were still in Brighton."

"I have not long returned to Wetherley," she answered. "My maid, Maud, and I have walked from the rectory and we cannot stay long."

Dorothia dismissed her maid, who curtsied a short bob and hurried from the room and then she turned to Adam.

Dorothia had taken a great deal of trouble over her appearance, she is always being told that she is a very elegant and beautiful young woman; she just hoped that the young earl saw her in this light. She had put her dark brown hair into a sort of bun and covered it with a new bonnet purchased in Brighton, her skin pale and fine, her cheeks rouged lightly for effect, a quick glance in the mirror at her reflection before she left the vicarage had made her smiled confidently to herself.

"I have come without my mother's permission so I cannot linger. I brought Maud with me for proprieties sake," she said. She went on to explain that how she had read Adam's letters many times and although she did not understand why some of the occurrences had been necessary, and some she felt were down right unrespectable for a man in his position, but she understood his desire to make good the Southerly name.

Every time Adam tried to speak, she hushed him saying that she had rehearsed her speech and needed to finish. She went on to tell Adam that if he wished to speak to her father, she would be more than happy to share his name.

Adam was rather taken aback by Dorothia's boldness and could not think of an immediate reply. He had already started to wonder if maybe he was not ready to marry, but now he felt that he had committed himself to Dorothia and this was the way he must go.

"Dorothia," he said with a slight quiver in his voice, "this has been a day for surprises."

"Not unwanted ones, I hope," was the reply.

"On the contrary, my friend James is to marry my sister and my little maid, Alice, is to marry a shepherd, I am quite overwhelmed," he said. "And now you come to me as I have always hoped."

Dorothia looked relieved and smiled broadly.

He started to tell her how he had unfinished business that he needed to clear up before he could commit to marriage but was cut short in mid-sentence.

"I have been looking into matters that concern you, Adam, matters that I know you would be following up on before you settle down. The laundry woman that carried your father's child."

Adam looked quite bemused by the thought of Dorothia looking for Freda on his behalf.

"Have you found her?" he asked with an excited smile.

"Yes, I suppose I have, at least I have found out what happened to her which amounts to the same thing," she said strangely.

"And the child, does it live?"

"No, that is one brother or sister you will not inherit, both the girl and the child are no more," was the sad reply.

"Tell me everything you know, how did this come about?" asked Adam anxiously.

"They say it was the shock of her father's grisly end. He bled out in a man trap, her brother found him," was the reply.

Dorothia went on to tell Adam what she had discovered or at least, the version she intended to give to the young earl.

"You remember, of course, that Freda's father found himself caught in a man trap, some say, whilst on his way to speak to your father," she began. "Most people believe it was a trap set by the earl, though I would hope that no man, however depraved, would do such a thing."

"I do indeed remember and agree," was the reply.

"Well, it seems that the shock brought on an early delivery of the child and it was still-born, never uttered a sound," she continued. "Freda, sad and left in poor health after the birth, followed her child in death quite quickly afterwards. Some say of a broken heart." Dorothia looked moved by this information.

"I am very sorry to hear this and also grateful to you for being the one to bring me the news. I do have one sister and a delight she is as well, my father would be shocked to see how she and I have bonded," Adam said.

She had practiced this speech many times and tried not to sound too matter-of-fact about the happening, not wanting to appear cold or unfeeling. Dorothia had formulated a lie to tell Adam and repeated it word for word knowing that Adam would have felt the necessity to seek Freda before he would settle down if he did not believe the woman was dead. The true story was far from the one she told Adam at this time and one she hoped she would be able to take to her grave.

Adam had appeared to be quite upset to hear the news that Dorothia had brought him, she felt as though he actually relished the idea of another sibling to care for and protect. This made her sure that she had done the right thing. The new sister, Sally, would soon be married and out of the manor house and the boy, Robbie, was no longer a threat, she was feeling quite confident.

Adam told Dorothia how he had sent out people to seek Freda of no avail and was surprised to find that she had managed to trace the woman when he had not.

"Maybe you should have asked for my father's help with your task as I did, Adam," said Dorothia. "He has the ear of most of the parish."

Adam nodded in agreement. Although Adam was sorry to hear the tale, he found himself relieved that he did not need to continue the search for Freda, a task he thought would take up a great deal of his time and lead to more problems that he would have to resolve. Adam went on to ask Dorothia if she knew how the rest of Freda's family had managed without their father, another question that Dorothia had anticipated.

"I felt sure you would ask," said Dorothia. "They survived. Freda's brother stepped into his father's shoes quite adequately to his credit."

Adam's suggestion that money be sent to the remaining members of the family was not encouraged by Dorothia, who explained that such an action could start a tidal wave of claims against his awful father that could leave the young earl very short of cash.

"I must send some monetary recompense to that poor family surely," said Adam.

"No, I must insist you do not," said Dorothia forcefully. "At least not in an obvious way. Your father was hated by a lot of people and some would still wish to see you brought down because of him and nothing you will ever do will be enough for these people. Do not put yourself up as agreeing that your father was to blame or you will find every single person with a grievance against the Southerly's, knocking at your door with their hand out. And believe me when I say there will be a great many. There are even some who still believe you had a part in your parents' demise, ridiculous as that is."

"And yet, you would still share my name?"

Dorothia laughed, "I know the son, my liking for your father was the same as most in these parts. But I know that the son is not the father."

"I thank you for that," replied Adam. "I just need to convince the rest of the world. A task I dread."

"It is difficult here, it is a small community and everyone knows everyone else; they feel each other's pain and each other's loss. I fear you will never be truly accepted here, Adam."

"Would it be too much to expect you to come to Keighley as my wife if your father will permit the union, if things become uncomfortable here?" asked Adam. "I seemed to have fared a lot better in the North."

"It is something I had already considered as a possibility," was Dorothia's answer. "I would like to see how the wind blows here for a while first. Also, Adam, I feel you must rein in your desire to save the world. Taking on a whore as a chaperone for a young woman was really the last straw."

"A whore she may have been but it was not her choice, this was of my father's doing," was the reply.

"That does not alter the facts. You are an earl and as such should be looked up to," added Dorothia.

"Also, she took care of Kitty and Kitty loves her. She has actually taken a great weight from my shoulders by her desire to look after Robbie's sister. I had no idea which way to turn regarding that young woman," replied the earl.

"But, Adam, she was not and is not your concern," said Dorothia rather coldly. "You made her such and placed the burden upon your own shoulders. You cannot seek out all who have been treated badly and take their woes on yourself."

"I do realise that, Dorothia, and I hope I have come to the end of my father's secrets, but if I have not, I will not step back; I will take responsibility, however tight the claims are on my soul and purse strings." He was a little disappointed by her lack of empathy with him on this.

Adam knew deep down that Dorothia was not the one for him, he had always thought she was but there was no longer that spark between them. He had lived an exciting couple of years and had grown up, but he could not find it in himself to go against convention and walk away to leave Dorothia in the embarrassing position of being rejected and jilted. He was not his father!

"You are a good man, Adam Southerly, no one can doubt that," said Dorothia with a smile. "You think the best of everyone."

"After all, Adam," she said very sensibly, "you cannot help anyone if you put yourself in the poor house. I would willingly help you sort genuine cases from fraudulent ones but it would not be an easy task."

She could tell by the way Adam stayed quiet that she had put forward a good argument to be frugal.

"Adam, I hope I am not speaking out of turn but I feel if we are to become one, I should say that I believe you should rein in your desire to save the world," Dorothia said. "One man should not expect to do so much."

Adam explained that he had only been trying to right a few of the wrongs caused by his father's choices in life. "It is just that once I started down a certain road, one thing seemed to lead to another. There was always another obstacle to overcome. It is impossible to suddenly stop once you are heading in a certain direction."

"I do not pretend to understand exactly what you are speaking of, Adam," continued Dorothia in a serious tone. "But I do feel that when you took it upon yourself to bring a whore into your home, where there were young people and even make her into a chaperone for the vulnerable young woman, you had hunted for and found, that was beyond my understanding and that of any decent-minded person."

Adam was quite taken aback at the thought of having to explain himself again to someone he thought would have understood. "A whore she may have been but my father had taken her when her parents died and used his power to keep her in that awful place for his own amusement, for pity's sake woman, what would you have had me do, leave her there?"

"You could have released her or sent her back to her homeland, you did not have to take her to your home."

"You could be right but it seemed the correct thing to do at the time. When Martin and Pierre brought her in after the rescue, she was like a timid little mouse, scared that she had walked into a worse trap than the one laid by my father years before," Adam replied, walking up and down as he spoke.

"That does not alter the facts, you are an earl and as such should be looked up to," added Dorothia, sounding quite annoyed. "If your servant and Pierre, whoever he might be, rescued the woman, surely it was their place to house her, not yours. I can only imagine what people must have thought."

"The abduction was carried out at my request. I could not leave Camille where she was once Kitty had made her circumstances known to me. She is an educated woman, speaks French and English, paints rather well and has a pleasant disposition," explained the earl.

"None of Camille virtues interested me," said Dorothia adamantly. "There are probably hundreds of fallen women in such places, there not by their own wishes but by necessity, do you intend to save them all? Your desire to save every fallen creature is beyond ridiculous and demeaning. I am willing to make you a proper Godly and honest wife but I am not prepared to share my life with prostitutes and ne're do wells."

Dorothia could see that a look of pure shock had crossed Adam's face and she wondered if she had maybe said too much.

He stood quietly still for a moment before he answered her tirade. "I believe I will make my own mind up as to who is welcome in my home, Madam!" he said angrily.

"I assume you do not intend to fill your home with prostitutes and vagabonds or acquaint whore houses," she replied equally annoyed. "As a refined and properly brought up young woman, no man could expect that of a wife."

"I do not intend to ever enter a whore house again in my life, it was something that happened out of necessity," Adam said in a calmer voice but still annoyed. "I sent Pierre and Martin to make the second visit, not wanting to bring attention to myself. I do not understand how word had reached this far giving details of my adventures."

"Adventures, do you call such actions adventures?" Dorothia said astonished. "What Martin or this Pierre do is of no consequence to me, they do not affect my life, but visits to whore houses for whatever noble reason by a future husband do not settle well on my mind."

"I would not call our intervention at the whore house a visit," replied Adam. "We went before it was open and barged in with the boy and a dog to seek out a child held there against her will. It was an adventure in a way."

"Who are the 'we' you speak of?"

"Martin and I, of course," Adam replied. "We took Robbie as it was his sister we were seeking and Martin and I had no idea what she looked like."

"What a good job! You took Robbie or you might have left with every underage girl you found there and then what would you have done?" Dorothia said with a degree of sarcasm in her voice.

"Luckily, this did not occur," Adam replied, "and if it had, we would have found a solution."

"You could have made each girl into a scullery maid or cook's assistant, the whole house could have been full of women of the night," added Dorothia. "What a fine place to take a vicar's daughter!"

Adam suddenly saw the ridiculousness of the conversation and burst into laughter.

"This is nothing to laugh about, Adam," Dorothia said, smiling herself. "I know you meant well and what you did was probably very noble, but if you take on all the cares of the world, you will just be making a rod for your own back."

Adam asked Dorothia how she had come to hear that he had taken Camille into his house as a chaperone; he did not feel it was common knowledge and he was sure that he had not mentioned it in any of his letters to her.

"Someone always knows someone who can pass on news, good or bad," Dorothia replied. "It is hard to keep secrets when servants travel forward and back and write home occasionally. It is the curse of education."

"The positive and negative side to everything it seems. You probably know everything else about my life in Yorkshire, I will have no other adventures to relate to you," Adam said.

"I only have the bare bones, I know about the chimney boy and your search for his sister but little else. These things you have told me of yourself. Scandal is only scandal if it is juicy," she said with a smile.

Adam went on to tell Dorothia about Robbie's decision to join the circus and how he had wanted to bring the boy to Weston-Under-Wetherley, telling her how fond he was of the little chimney climber.

"I became firmly attached to that boy, almost from the moment he made himself known to me. I am sorry you cannot meet Robbie for if you did, I feel you would understand why he has taken an important place in my heart," said the earl. "I wanted Robbie and Daisy to come to Weston and meet Sally, she would have found them both enchanting."

"Daisy? Is there another foundling?" said Dorothia loudly.

"In a way. Robbie found her, she is a very pretty, little mongrel dog," was the reply.

"Thank goodness for that, I am sure they are all truly delightful," replied Dorothia sarcastically. She wanted to be kind but found herself sinking under the sea of what she considered to be inferior hangers on. "If the boy has joined the circus, at least you have one less mouth to feed, you are free of one more burden."

"One I did not wish to be free of," Adam said with a sigh. Dorothia could see that this was one argument she would not win.

"My man, Martin, thought me foolish allowing the boy to wander around the countryside with what he considered to be a band of thieves," continued Adam. "But what could I do, he is not of my blood, I have no hold over him. Pierre did point out that as my father had bought the boy, he was mine by rights and I could have prevented him from leaving."

"I do find myself agreeing with your man servant, though I do wonder that he is allowed to criticise you to your face; I do not see why the opinion of a mere servant would be worth taking into account."

"I do not consider Martin to be a mere servant as you refer to him. He is a friend also and a loyal one at that," Adam replied.

"You do not pay friends, you pay servants," she said in reply.

"Some so called friends cost you more than mere servants, they borrow and do not repay, they expect more than you want to give. I have always found my servants behave beyond the call of duty when asked," said Adam. "Martin did not want to go anywhere near the whorehouse but when it happened that we needed to return for Camille, he would not allow me to go and risk being seen, so he and Pierre went. That is a friend, whatever you might think."

"And Pierre?" asked Dorothia.

"He is an artist. I have written to you about him, he painted some of the circus people and wanted to paint Kitty. He is French, of course, and a fine fellow," replied Adam. "His opinions on almost every topic are most enlightening and fascinating."

"And where is this paragon now?" Dorothia asked sarcastically.

"I left him in Keighley to finish his painting of Kitty," was the reply. "And as for the circus people, they are hard-working, honest folks. I would not have encouraged Robbie to go with them if I thought any different."

"I cannot understand fully why the choice this chimney boy has made affects you so deeply, but I can see it does, so we will say no more about it," Dorothia replied in a lot quieter tone. "You are a good man, Adam Southerly. There can be no one who could doubt that, except maybe my mother."

"I try to think kindly towards anyone unless they show me a reason not to," he replied. "I would only wish that others did me the same service. Pre-judgement is a harsh way to go."

"It is indeed," replied Dorothia, not too convincingly.

"Enough of this talk, Dorothia, please come with me and meet my beautiful sister and her betrothed, I think you will find them both delightful," said Adam, holding out his hand for her to place hers in his. She looked at the outstretch hand and touched it lightly with her lace gloved one but did not allow it to linger. Adam thought back to when he had gripped Jeanette's hand and had allowed her to lead him anywhere she had wanted to go, whereas Dorothia felt no compulsion to fold her fingers round his, she had touched his hand so lightly as if she would be thrown into Dante's inferno if her hand lingered any longer. Once again, Adam's mind returned to his conversation with Pierre and worried that he was being rushed into a marriage that was not for him.

Dorothia had no desire at all to meet Sally, knowing that the young woman was the illegitimate daughter of a fallen woman. Her Christian beliefs do not run to sharing intimate moment with the lower classes. She was, however, very surprised by the young woman, who stood before her in the next room.

Sally is the prettiest and most charming creature, she has an air of childlike innocence and sweetness. Dorothia was also surprised to discover that Sally is not altogether uneducated, her mother had taught her well. Much to Dorothia's amazement, she felt drawn to Sally like a moth to a flame, and like everyone who ever met Sir James, she liked him instantly.

Soon, the two women were talking like long lost friends and Adam took the opportunity to tell Martin that he had somehow managed to get himself engaged and told him of the circumstances.

Martin smiled. "Probably for the best, Sir, she will make a fine wife for you." Adam looked doubtful but smiled back. He went on to tell Martin that they had one less task to attend to as Dorothia had discovered what had happened to Freda Prout, the next person on the list to hunt out.

"Do we have another foundling to introduce into the family?" Martin asked.

Adam explained the circumstance surrounding Freda and how Dorothia had advised him against making any sudden generous gesture.

"You seem to have found a wise woman to be your wife, Sir," Martin felt that maybe his master had met his match.

"Yes, Martin, I could do worse, could I not?" he smiled fondly towards his wife to be, who was sitting, laughing with Sally like long lost friends. "Though I fear her heart is not as light as I would wish."

Martin was slightly puzzled and worried about that last remark.

Sally and Dorothia immediately became friends, Sally has a very contagious personality and manages to befriend everyone.

"Adam," called Sally to her brother, "I am to call Dorothia 'Dory', I feel her name is too long and formal."

"Sally, really, do you have the lady's permission for such a change?" he replied.

"She does," replied Dory. "I always found my name too long and I welcome a change."

"Miss Dory it is then, actually I rather like that myself," said Adam.

Everyone seemed quite pleased with this shortened name, it had a less formal feeling about it.

Sir James stayed in his own country house nearby for just a week, and then he returned to Bleadon to make his and Sally's marriage arrangements. All there was for Adam to do was take Alice's sister, Kate, and Sally to choose material; Kate for the bridesmaid dress she would wear for her sister's wedding and Sally for her own wedding dress. Dory was more than happy to take over the dress finding duties and Adam was more than happy to let her.

"I cannot believe the buzz of excitement weddings bring," said Adam to Martin one day. "Every female member of staff is equally all of a flutter about the forthcoming event. Goodness knows what it will be like here when I marry."

"I believe you will not be as interesting as the dress for Miss Sally, Sir," replied Martin.

"I actually hope and believe you are right. Slipping away somewhere quietly would suit me fine."

"I cannot see you to be able to get away with that as Miss Dory's father is the vicar," said Martin with a slight chuckle.

"It might not happen yet, Martin," replied the earl. "Bathsheba Mountjoy might not agree to the match."

"What!" exclaimed Martin in reply. "A vicar's daughter to an earl, I can't see her objecting to that; after all, you could ask any woman and she would willingly marry you."

"Because I am an earl I suppose, even though my father is still hated so much."

"It would surprise me if all memories of your father did not go out the window, if the gain was an earl in the family, Sir," replied Martin.

"I would prefer someone to want to marry me, not my title."

"I believe Miss Dory might be that person," Martin added with a smile.

Chapter 35
The Weddings

Days and weeks passed, the dresses were ready for the final fittings and Sally looked absolutely dazzling. The dress was white lace over pink organza, simple, Sally is so pretty that she does not need extra fussy ribbons and bows to make her look perfect. The dress was made exactly how she planned it. Adam was conscious that maybe his dear sister had kept the design plain to save him money, which he was very happy to spend on her. Kate's dress was a green taffeta creation, full skirt with daisies sewn into the neckline. Her beautiful red hair, full of curls, fell onto and around her shoulders and she looked as though she could have been the bride herself, even though it was quite a simple style. Adam did wonder if maybe he had over indulged the child and she might outshine her sister on her wedding day, which would be very wrong. He need not have worried because Sally had left instructions with Purnell, Sir James' housekeeper, butler and anything else asked of him to commission a local seamstress to make Alice look beautiful and not to worry about the cost. The seamstress, aware that the bride was after all only a lady's maid, kept the dress fairly simple; she smiled to herself as she created the dress and wondering at the kindness of the girl's employer.

Adam, Martin, Sally, Mrs Braund, little Kate, her parents—Mr and Mrs Able Bishop—and enough luggage to sink a ship made the trip down to Weston-Super-Mare. Alice was to marry her Jake two days before Sir James and Sally; the idea being to have a day to recover from the festivities of the first wedding before taking part in the second.

Alice and Jake married in St Peter's in Bleadon at 11.00 in the morning and Sir James had organised a wedding breakfast in the main barn, which had a large table formed out of old planks and supports, covered in several table clothes and with an amazing array of food laid upon it—pies, cakes, pastries, cold meat, bread and butter, cheese, fruit, tomatoes, ham, boiled eggs, assorted sweets and jelly. A barrel of beer was placed near the foot of the table and several large bottle of home-made cider were strategically placed about the barn. There were long bench seats either side of the table, enough to seat all of the invited guests and many that had just drifted in regardless.

Sally had made sure that there was plenty of colour by arranging wild flowers herself in vases on the wedding table.

Alice's wedding was a jolly affair, her father looked the proudest man in all of England and her mother, much as she had disliked the journey to Weston-Super-Mare, never having ventured so far from home before, had a permanent smile on her face. Everyone was decked out in their Sunday, best from the lowest of the low to the earl, Sir James and Miss Sally. Able Bishop had been quite overwhelmed by the fact that the earl had included him and his wife in the plans to attend the wedding. He had rather assumed that he would have to wave his daughter, Kate, off and wait for her return to hear the details of his eldest daughter's wedding. Sally was not about to allow this to happen. Having come up through the ranks herself, she did not want to see anyone left out; she still felt herself to be unworthy of the attention she received every day. Adam did not move in London circles, he could of course being an earl; he wasn't even a member of any gentlemen's clubs, although he had received several requests asking him to join them. So he did not have the usual gossip and back biting to contend with regarding his sister. Undoubtedly, there were plenty of people who were happy to talk about the situation and occasional items in newspapers, but Adam chose to ignore anything and everything that he felt intruded on his happy life style.

Before the wedding breakfast but after the actual wedding, Sir James, Sally and Adam crept away to allow the Bishop family to enjoy the day fully without those considered to be almost royalty cramping their style.

It had been a lovely day, the sun shone and the birds sang and everyone was very happy. Jake looked very handsome and Alice delightful. Kate won a few hearts that day as well.

"If our wedding is half as jolly, I will be thrilled," said Sally to James.

"I agree with you, dear wife to be," he replied with a wide grin.

Two days later, Miss Sally Southerly married Sir James Shepherd with as much pomp and circumstances that a small village church could endure. The whole of Bleadon village turned out to watch the squire marry such a pretty, young woman. Adam was so proud to walk arm in arm down the aisle with his delightful sister and place her in the care of his friend. Kate, once more, wore the dress designed for her sister's wedding and acted as flower girl for Sally, the poor child was fit to burst with pride. Kate held a pink satin ribbon in her hand, which acted as a lead for Rosebud who trotted quite unperturbed down the aisle with her. Adam smiled at Martin and commented that the cost of the dress was worthwhile after all. It had taken a little bribery—the promise of funds to restore part of the church knave, to persuade the vicar to allow Rosebud to be part of the service.

The couple came out of the church and walked under wicker arches that had been entwined with wild flowers. The front of the church was full of smiling happy faces and Sally seemed to be smiling the widest. James looked at her and wondered how he could have found such a wonderful creature to share his life with. They had looked back and saw that Rosebud had started to eat some of the flower displays, which made everyone laugh loudly.

A feast was laid on in Bleadon Manor Farm in the afternoon and every villager, servant and farm hand was invited to join in the festivities, some still recovering from the previous wedding. There was dancing and singing until dark, allowing Sir James and his new wife to slip away un-noticed to a coaching inn in Weston-Super-Mare for their first night as husband and wife. They had made no plans for a honeymoon as Sally felt that there was nowhere she would rather be than in Bleadon Manor Farm with all the animals.

Before he left for his sister's wedding, Adam spoke to Dory's father about their possible wedding, which he agreed to instantly. His wife took a little more time to agree but by the time James had completed the plans for his wedding to Sally, Adam and Dorothia were engaged; though in his heart of hearts, he really hoped that Bathsheba would put up more of a fight and the engagement would not stand.

They married the following month with the minimum of fuss and with none of the happy style that Adam had experienced in Bleadon, by Dorothia's father. Bathsheba looked as though a bee had got inside her mouth and stung her instead of watching her eldest daughter marry an earl.

It was small affair. The wedding breakfast was, however, quite lavish and set out in Weston Manor Lodge's main hall. Thomas Umbers, his brother—and squire William Umbers—attended the wedding at short notice and Sir James and Lady Sally Shepherd came up from Weston-Super-Mare, James to be best man and Sally matron of honour. The happy couple made a promise to visit Sally and James as often as was possible.

Martin found a moment to congratulate his friend and master.

"It has been a splendid day, Martin," said Adam whilst shaking Martin's hand. "If convention had allowed it, I would have had you at my side today."

Martin smiled and felt quite overwhelmed by this statement made by the earl. "I feel there will be a lot of changes, Sir," he said.

Adam looked about him and replied that he hoped not too many and also expressed the worry that everything might have been rushed. A thought that had occurred to Martin as well.

Adam and Dory set off to London for their honeymoon. Adam would have liked to have gone to Brighton but as Dory had only just returned from there, it was not a welcome choice.

Chapter 36
Married Life Begins

A month after the wedding, Adam took Dory up to Keighley to see the family home there and meet the staff, all of whom she had heard a great deal. He had to argue with Dorothia about the inclusion of Martin in the group to go to Keighley as she felt that Martin was all too familiar with the earl and now he had her ear, he should not need him so much. Adam explaining that Martin had family to visit in Bradford made it easier to appease his new wife, although he obviously knew that Martin had very little interest in his northern roots, adding that Martin also acted as a valet and he did not want to replace him. Adam did not want to lose his friend and accomplice in so many adventures and felt that his wife had a stronger, more dominant personality than he had at first realised. He was no longer allowed to include Martin at supper, though they did manage on occasions to have breakfast together before Dorothia rose. Adam had always been aware that some people thought him too familiar with what others considered as mere servants, but he appreciated loyalty and the honest opinions of everyone about him. Pierre had told him to look towards the mother before choosing a wife, they do tend to grow alike. Adam shuddered at the thought and was beginning to realise how worldly his French friend was.

A great deal of fuss was made of the earl and his new wife. Adam was keen to show Dory his Yorkshire home for her to meet the staff, and also, Adam had promised Dory that he would show her how the family money was appropriated. She was pleased that as the new lady of the manor, she would be given some responsibility regarding the running of the household and needed to know how the family money was made. Adam was very unlike his father, who thought women should be seen and not heard; he wanted a wife that helped with household affairs and Dory was not the type of woman to sit back and watch, she needed to be involved.

Mrs Frost, the cook, made a great fuss of Dory, asking about her favourite meal etc. and as a result, Dory liked the manor house and all the servants very much. She did not intend to take over the organising of each day's menu, though she did feel that she might like to add a few ideas here and there.

This was the first time that Dory became acquainted with Pierre Conte, Camille and little Kitty. They lined up to be introduced to the new lady of the manor; Kitty had the widest smile of them all and fidgeted in a way that was most unlike her. As soon as everyone had either bowed or curtsied, she broke from the line and flung her arms around the earl. They had all staying in Keighley Manor so Pierre could finish the painting of Kitty as arranged. Kitty was so excited that Adam was home and that she would at last see the painting that had been carefully kept from her view to be ready for the great unveiling. Although Adam was quite bemused to find that Pierre had taken up residents in Keighley Manor, even though he had completed the task of painting Kitty quite some time ago, Dory was not of the same mind.

"Are they not the most delightful group of people?" said Adam smiling at his new wife.

"I am sure they are most entertaining, Adam," she replied. "I am wondering though why everyone you seem to meet feels that they have a claim on you and stay under your care instead of making their own way in the world." This comment was directed towards Pierre and Adam realised this.

"He could not leave before he had shown me the portrait, surely you would not expect that?"

Pierre was, in fact, anxious to show Adam the portrait, which was covered in a white cloth in the sitting room waiting his arrival.

Pierre made a great theatrical event out of uncovering the painting but to say that the earl was, both, thrilled and amazed by the painting is an understatement. Kitty practically jumped out from the canvas, the likeness was so vivid. When the child stood next to the masterpiece, it was difficult to tell real from fantasy.

Dorothia had not seen Kitty before that day, although she had heard about the child. "I can see why you wanted to paint the child," she said. "She is like a delicate bud about to burst into the most amazing flower imaginable."

"That is exactly how I saw the child," agreed Pierre. "She is the prettiest creature I have ever seen. I beg your pardon, Madam, you are yourself a beauty, a rose that has blossomed, Kitty has the promise of more to give. I cannot explain it."

"You do not need to, Sir," replied Dory with a smile. "That was most poetic and I understand exactly."

Kitty stood next to the painting. "Is it not amazing, my Lord?" she said, most pleased. "It is like there are two of me. C'est Merveilleux."

Dory was equally impressed by the painting of Kitty. She could see immediately why an artist would find the child captivating. Kitty is, as he said, like a delicate flower and she has a quiet serenity about her.

Pierre was very careful to praise Dorothia for her more mature beauty, though she was not impressed or taken in by his Parisian charm. Dory wanted her husband to herself, she wanted these people, who she considered part of Adam's previous life, gone but was careful to be charming to everyone so Adam did not suspect.

"I don't suppose you have heard from Robbie," the earl asked Kitty.

"Indeed, I have, my Lord," she replied. "He sends me a letter from each place that the circus performs in. He does not write very well but he seems very happy with his new life and Daisy is part of the dancing dog act. Tres bon."

"I am happy Kitty that I made the right decision and let Robbie go," Adam said smiling down at the little girl. "It is wonderful to hear all his news and hear how happy he is."

Dory put her arm through the earl's and smiled at him, "I know you worry about the boy but you did all you could for him and you allowed him to make his own choice in life. It was the right thing to do."

"I know it was but I miss that boy every day," Adam said sadly. "To have a son like him would be a dream come true, so full of fun and mischief. I wish you could meet him."

"I will one day, when the circus comes back to Keighley," she replied. "And one day, also we will have a son of our own."

Pierre asked if he might be permitted to speak to Adam alone. Adam was intrigued. Dorothia decided to slip down to the kitchen and discover the details of what was likely to be their first meal in Yorkshire, whilst Adam and Pierre went into the office.

"First, I wanted to congratulate you on making a fine marriage, a very English one, of course," he said.

"Just so," was the reply.

"I too wish to marry, Sir, I never dreamed that I would but I do," revealed Pierre.

Adam was absolutely shocked. "Not Kitty surely?" he said.

"Don't be absurd," replied Pierre insulted by the suggestion. "She is a child."

Adam suddenly realised that he had assumed that Pierre had feeling for Kitty like he had for Jeanette and was ashamed to have make the comparison. "I am sorry, Pierre, of course it is absurd, who pray is the lucky lady?"

"Camille and I have decided that we could deal rather well with each other. We would like to return to Paris and if possible, take Kitty with us," was the answer.

"Good heavens, everything is happening. How does Kitty feel about this move?" Adam asked.

"I have not broached the subject before speaking to you, Sir. After all, she is your ward."

"Actually the child is nothing legally to me. My father bought her and that is where the story ends; she is s free person to go and do as she wishes."

"We would like to make it legal, maybe adopt the girl," said Pierre hopefully. "Camille loves her like a daughter and she is really taking to her French lessons like a duck to water."

"If Kitty is in agreement, I am happy, Pierre," was the reply.

"One more thing, Adam, as a wedding present, I would like to paint a miniature of you and your good lady if you would permit me to."

"Personally, I would be honoured and thrilled to accept your offer. I will, however, speak to Dory first."

Adam went to find his wife, who was down in the kitchen drinking a cup of hot mead and eating a slice of cake that the widow Sparkes had sent to welcome the earl back to Keighley.

Mrs Frost had exclaimed regarding how marvellous the cake was and that was coming from the lips of a renowned cake maker, a compliment indeed.

"Sir," said Mrs Frost in her usual jolly way. "Mr Martin appeared with this splendid cake sent by the widow Sparkes to celebrate your return. Having tasted it, I understand why Mrs Sparkes is well thought of in these parts for her cooking. She sells pies and cakes to all the best inns hereabout, did you know?"

"I did not know but I am very pleased to receive this information, because it means the woman is thriving despite what happened to her son," replied Adam, who turned to his wife to explain. "Her son lost fingers in my looms and she was to marry to keep the wolf from the door, but Martin told me that this did not occur after all. It is good to hear that she has used her own skills to feed herself."

He cut himself a small piece of the cake and ate it, nodding his head in agreement with Mrs Frost's verdict. "No wonder, the widower wanted to marry Mrs Sparkes, she is a fine looking woman and also a wonderful cook. What more could a man want."

Dory looked quite taken aback. "I hope a lot more, Mr Southerly," she said. "For I am relying on Mrs Frost to feed us and would not consider stepping on her feet in the kitchen."

Realising he had spoken a bit freely, Adam replied, "I was talking of the lower orders, Mrs Southerly. I only expect you to look decorative for my delight." He did not actually believe what he had said but felt the need to say it.

"My dear," he continued to his wife with a smile, "because you are indeed decorative, Pierre has asked if he might be allowed to paint a miniature of us as a wedding present."

"How wonderful!" was the reply.

"And, Mrs Frost, did you know of Mr Conte's intensions towards Miss Kitty's chaperone, Camille?" asked the earl knowing nothing got past Mrs Frost.

Mrs Frost laughed loudly and as she laughed, her whole body shook like a jelly in rhythm. "I guessed as much. They both being foreign and all and teaching young Kitty to speak French."

"Pierre has asked if he can marry Camille and take Kitty to Paris with them," Adam said to the two ladies.

Mrs Frost looked a little concerned by this latest revelation. "First, Robbie runs away to the circus and now little Kitty might go across the sea, whatever next."

"Nothing more I hope, enough surprises for me at least," replied Adam.

"It is good news, Adam," said Dory. "We can start our new life together without the worry of others."

"As they also want to take Kitty with them, the place will be quite empty. They will not, however, leave until after the miniature is completed, but Pierre is eager to return to Paris with Camille and hopefully, little Kitty as well," added Adam. "We would be able to visit Paris, maybe next spring and see them all."

Dory smiled, she was most enthusiastic about this venture. She felt it was three less incumbencies in their marriage, all gone in one stroke of a brush and she had plenty of time to put Adam off of a trip to Paris.

Pierre was thrilled that Adam did not take a lot of persuasion to allow the little group to go to Paris and Dory was practically singing with joy.

"Pierre's decision to take Camille and Kitty to Paris seems to have pleased you," Adam said.

Dory was careful not to let Adam see that she wanted rid of as much of his past as possible. "Oh, Adam, it is just that I love a happy ending and what could be better than Pierre marrying Camille and taking her back to Paris where she belongs and making a home for Kitty into the bargain. It is like a fairy tale."

"He is a fine fellow, Dory, and I am so happy that he and Camille have found each other," replied Adam. "As for Kitty, as beautiful a child as she is, I have never felt drawn to her in the way I was to her brother. Saying goodbye to Robbie was the hardest thing I have ever done."

"When we have a fine son of our own, you will feel the loss a lot less, Husband," said Dory. "You will probably not worry if the boy never returns."

"That I doubt, Dory," replied Adam.

"He is just a child, he has made his choices in life. It is wonderful that you take your responsibilities so seriously."

She did not say what she really thought and wondered how she could put some space between a few more of what she considered to be hangers on or unnecessary additions to the house hold. She was desperate to put a wedge between Adam and Martin, feeling that they were far too intimate. She had insisted that Adam and she ate alone, although Adam had often eaten with Martin if there were important issues to discuss.

"I realise that your man Martin and you have things to discuss and I am happy to see you occasionally in a huddle doing just that," she said. "But now we are husband and wife, meal times are for us alone, unless we have particular guests. It is the way things are done, Adam, it is a not a slight on your man servant. I would also hope that you allow me to be a sounding board for your ideas more and allow Martin to carry out his own duties. You do put a lot of pressure on him."

Adam understood that Dory was right but he was not happy to have to explain to Martin about the changes brought with marriage, though Martin said that he expected a lot more changes besides and took it well.

Dory wrote home to her mother and told her how she was slowly trying to undermine the influence Martin had, just a little comment here and a suggestion there. All very subtle moves taught to her by her mother. She found that she actually quite liked Martin but she did not like the intimacy or the history that she was not part of that he shared with her husband.

The next couple of weeks were taken up with Adam and Dory sitting for sketches for the miniatures. Kitty had been asking about Paris and she was so excited that she looked like she was going to burst.

Pierre and Camille married quietly by special licence with just Adam and Martin as witnesses, and the earl set his solicitor about looking into ways in which Pierre could adopt Kitty. It was decided that the child would travel with the newly-weds regardless of the outcome.

Although, both, Dory and Adam liked Keighley Manor very much, they had now decided that the majority of their life would be spent in Weston-Under-Wetherley instead; Adam had put up a strong argument to stay in Yorkshire but Dory wanted to be near her family and also felt that the earl was far too at ease amongst the servants in Keighley. So they decided to give Weston-Under-Wetherley a try and return to Yorkshire if they found it uncomfortable to be there. The locals down South were still not comfortable with the new Earl of Southerly, his father having been such an evil man, they were always looking for signs that Adam might follow suit.

As soon as possible, Adam and Dory returned to Weston-Under-Wetherley and Pierre, Camille and Kitty set off for France and a new life. Adam felt it was another problem lifted from his shoulders; he had wondered what would become of the girl but he also realised how much he would miss his new friends and was already wondering about the possibility of visiting them all in Paris at a later date.

Chapter 37
A New King, 1830

The first year and a half of marriage went by blissfully happily for James and Sally and Adam and Dory, they spent a lot of time together in either Weston or Wetherley. Sally and Dory were like sisters and Adam felt content with his lot in life. His original doubts about his choice were swept away in domestic normality.

In 1830, the unpopular, flamboyant King George 1V died after a long illness brought on by his own excesses, leaving the rule of Great Britain to his younger brother, William. King George had lost his only legitimate child, Princess Charlotte, when she was just 21, taken in childbirth having delivered a still-born son. There had been a great public outcry of grief at Charlotte's death as she was the promise of a better Britain; she would have been queen on her father's demise after years of rule by what was considered to be a mad-man.

As Prince Regent, George 1V had proved to be a wastrel, the nation hoped that after her father became king and then passed on, Princess Charlotte would revise Britain's fortunes. But it was not to be, she had died just three years before her father; with no other legitimate off spring to call on, the crown fell to his younger brother, William 1V. William had never expected to be king as he was the youngest of three male heirs and already 64 years of age. He had chosen a life in the navy and was immediately named 'The Sailor King'. Sadly, there was no outcry of grief for the lost king.

Adam, as usual, was fascinated by all the facts and problems the new era could bring. He tried to discuss the merits of the new king with his wife, but her interests did not stretch anywhere beyond the boundaries of the Wetherley property. Adam was, therefore, happy to still have Martin to talk about the ever changing world. They both agreed that the new king showed a degree of promise having abolished the cat o' nine tails whilst acting as admiral of the fleet. He had already promised to look into the poor law and child labour and try to abolish slavery within the British Empire, all things very close to, both, Adam and Martin's hearts.

Adam and Dory went to Weston to enjoy the street parties that were held in honour of the new king. Sally was so excited by all the bunting and happy faces, enjoying an excuse to be dancing in the streets.

Dory decided to give a little insight to Sally about the new king. Dory being appalled to think that a man of, what she considered, such loose morals could be king at all.

"Living with an actress for 20 years unmarried and producing 10 children, it is a disgrace," Dory would say.

She would not be dissuaded from her opinion, even after Adam explained that William had always taken care of the children and loved them and had been persuaded to marry Princess Adelaide of Saxe-Meiningen, who was half his age, for the sake of getting an heir. He had not strayed from his wedding vows for 20 years now and his first love, the actress, Mrs Dorothea Jordan, had been dead some four years having gone to France with her daughters. Dory was not convinced.

Sally, however, was swept up in the romance of it all and knowing what it is like to be an illegitimate child was pleased with the way the new king had conducted himself.

"What do they call the children, Adam?" she asked innocently.

"Besides bastards," whispered Dorothia under her breath, audible only to Martin who shot her a look that could have melted wax. She blushed and realised what she had said within possible ear-shot of Sally.

"I cannot remember their individual names, dear Sister, but they have FitzClarence as their surnames," Adam replied. "You always know if someone is the illegitimate offspring of royalty, they have Fitz in front of their surnames."

"I am not sure if I would want the world to know I was illegitimate regardless of my parenthood, it isn't very pleasant and I should know," replied Sally thoughtfully. "Should I really be FitzSoutherly?"

"I don't think so, Sally, I am not of royal blood," replied Adam laughing. "Anyway, you are my sister, that is all that matters. I hope no one has ever told you otherwise."

"No, they haven't actually, everyone has always been most courteous to me," replied Sally. "I am not sure why."

"Because you are a delight to know," added Sir James. "It certainly made no difference to my feelings for you, my dear wife."

Sally smiled up at her husband and squeezed his hand lovingly. Adam watched them and wished his wife was more tactile but knew it was not in her nature.

"I promise it is not be like a commoner having children out of wed-lock," continued Adam.

"Like my poor mother, you mean?" said Sally alarmed.

"No, not like Maud, your mother was taken advantage of by someone with power," replied Adam concerned that he has disturbed his sister's train of thought. "The king's mistresses chose to be so. All offspring would be honoured and treated well. It is somewhat of an honour to have royal blood flowing through your veins, however it got there, if the father accepts you as his. These offspring usually end up with titles. Affairs amongst royalty are not usually swept under the carpet, they are quite open about them and the mistresses treated honourable by most."

"One law for the higher classes and another for us, humble beings," added Dory sarcastically.

"I would not class us as humble beings," replied Sir James. "I can trace my lineage back to the Vikings almost and I guarantee that Adam has a family tree that anyone would be proud of."

"Until recently, I would agree with you, James," said Adam. "And my children will take pride again in their heritage, I hope."

"They will," agreed Dory.

"So you see, you need not feel sorry for any of the new king's children, they will always be treated well," concluded Adam smiling at his sister.

"Not as well as you have treated me, Brother, I am sure of that," said Sally with a wide smile that warmed Adam's heart.

As soon as Dory could get Adam alone, she tried to discover if Martin had told his friend and master what she had unthinkingly muttered; he did not appear to understand what she wanted to know so she left it, heaving a deep sigh of gratitude. She just whispered "Thank you" to Martin when she saw him next. He did not reply.

Dory was very fond of Sally and she had forgotten for that moment that her husband's sister was illegitimate and therefore, the term bastard could easily be laid on her. She would not like to have been the reason Sally was upset in any way. She also knew that Adam would have been furious if he had heard her comment; his continued defence of the innocent made him feel protective of people whose lives had been affected by the behaviour of so called upper classes.

They returned to Westerley again and life continued as usual. Then one day, everything changed with the announcement that Sally was with child. Although Adam was thrilled for both, his friend and his sister, he felt that this would mean a change in all their lives. Sally was not of a very strong constitution so she would not be able to travel to Wetherley easily; both Dory and Adam loved visiting the farm at Bleadon so it was not a chore for them to travel south every couple of months, but there was work to do at home and wondering about the country was not always convenient or possible.

Six months into Sally's pregnancy, Dory discovered that she too was expecting a baby. "The son you dream of, I hope," she told Adam.

Dory was very happy when she went to her family home to see her mother and to tell her the good news. At last, she felt that she was in charge, she was having Adam's baby, they would be a family, he would lean more towards her and she would be the lady of the manor.

"I will have a fine son and Adam will forget all about ragamuffins," she told her mother happily.

When the date came close for Sally to give birth, Adam told Dory that he intended to go to Sir James and offer support. Dory was not pleased. "And what if I need support, Adam?" she asked. "This is my first baby too, you know, what if I am unwell?"

"Your parents are nearby and I could leave Martin if you needed a man about the manor," was the reply.

"I would not dream of separating you from your precious man servant," she said icily.

"I do not understand the animosity you show towards Martin, he has always been a tower of strength to me," replied Adam rather desperately. "I have done everything you have asked, we no longer eat together, that privilege is for you and I alone. I do not understand. He has never been disrespectful to you."

"You and he share secrets," Dory said honestly. "He knows you better than you know yourself. I believe you would tell him far more than you would ever tell me."

"Any secrets I kept from you, dear wife, would be only to protect you," Adam replied.

"I do not want to be protected, I want to be the most important person in your life."

"That you are, dear heart," said Adam, "and as you do not need protection, I will be going to Bleadon in a couple of days to see James, it is very near Sally's time, he will need me."

Dory could see the determined look in Adam's face and decided not to pursue the conversation any longer.

"Take Martin with you, I will call one of the other servants if I need assistance," she added, trying to remind Adam that in her mind, Martin was merely a servant and nothing more.

As Sally drew close to her given date, Adam travelled with Martin to visit his sister and friend leaving Dorothia in the care of her mother and sister.

As James had no family close by and his sisters had their hands full with their own offspring, Adam went to offer moral support to his friend in Weston-Super-Mare.

Chapter 38
The Sins of the Father

Adam realised, as soon as he and Martin stepped down from the coach, that all is not well at Bleadon Farm. Alice, Sally's maid, was sitting outside and had obviously been crying a great deal. Pernell came out to greet the arrivals and rushed them into the hallway. Adam had noticed a barouche tethered outside and wondered who the visitor might be.

James rushed towards Adam, he looked panic stricken. "The child is breach, the doctor is here but he cannot turn it."

Adam was not that au fait with medical jargon regarding child-birth, so he did not grasp the seriousness of the statement. He looked for help to Martin, who looked equally uncertain.

Before Adam could ask any further questions, the doctor appeared looking very serious.

"Doctor Hague," said James, "this is my wife's brother, the Earl of Southerly. You may speak openly in front of him."

"I will keep it plain and simple, Sirs," began the doctor. "The child is ready to be delivered but he or she is breach, instead of the head being engaged ready, the feet are where the head should be."

"Surely, this is just like lambing," said James in response to this information. "I have delivered more than one such lamb, it makes it harder but both, ewe and lamb, have been fine after a few hours."

"That is probably true, my Lord, but sheep are tougher creatures than your delicate little wife."

"Do you mean she is in danger?" replied James, almost hysterically.

"I do, Sir, very much so. It may come to a choice between the child or the mother," the doctor replied.

"There is no choice, Sally comes first every time," James said in earnest.

"Your wife says otherwise, Sir."

"My wife is delirious, I say she comes first."

"I will do my best to save both, Sir James, but it is too late now for a caesarean, which is what she needs."

"A caesarean, aren't they dangerous?" asked Adam alarmed.

"The process is in its infancy, I agree, but I have successfully performed such a procedure fairly recently," replied the doctor. "It is not a course I would set upon lightly. The lady is too far into giving birth to use this process anyway, unless it was just to save the child when there is no hope."

"Good heavens, this must not happen, not to my beautiful sister," cried Adam.

"Do your best, man, I will pay you anything," said James in despair.

"Money is not the issue here, Sir James, it is the weakness in your wife's heart left by the TB."

"My God, I would never have allowed her to be with child had I known," said Sir James turning to Adam. "Believe me, Adam."

James fell weeping into his friend's arms.

"Had it been a straightforward birth, the weakness would not have mattered," added the doctor. "No one could have predicted a breach birth." The doctor felt a surge of pity for the new father to be.

"I must warn you also, Sir, that the child is a little early so it might need extra care," said the doctor. "It, being early, will make it smaller which may help your wife. I would like it to have waited another couple of weeks at least and possibly, it might have turned, but as you know the waters have broken that could bring infection and the baby has decided that it is ready, even if we are not."

With that statement, the doctor turned and went back to his patient.

Purnell, who had been standing a short distance away, asked if there was anything he could do for his master.

Martin, ever practical, suggested that maybe a wet nurse be found as he thought that maybe Sally would be a little too weak to be relied on in the first couple of days.

This broke Adam out of what could only be described as a trance. "Of course. We must find such a person."

Martin went out to ask Alice and Jake if they could make a suggestion. The young couple, who had no notion whatsoever beyond the thought that they could maybe bottle feed the child as they do with abandoned lambs, went off into town to make enquiries.

Four hours passed and Adam, James and Martin were firmly established in the drawing room. The brandy bottle was now half empty and all three of them looked drained of all colour.

"I wish Dory was here," said the earl. A comment echoed by everyone.

Alice and Jake returned with a woman in tow. Her name was Mrs Rosamond White, a newly widowed woman who had lost her husband and the baby, she was carrying, in a carriage accident. The carriage had left the road killing her husband instantly, she herself had been thrown from the carriage and escaped with only scratches but the tumble resulted in her losing her unborn child. She was heavy with milk as it was very close to her time. It was hard to tell how old she was as she looked as though she was carrying the worries of the world on her shoulders. Alice said that she had very little trouble persuading the woman to help, and everyone felt very sorry for the unfortunate widow as well as grateful.

Yet another hour passed and suddenly, everyone was alerted to the sound of a baby crying. James was unable to move, he was rooted to the spot. Adam looked pleadingly towards Martin, who slipped out of the room, followed by Rosamond. They had a short conversation outside the room and the young widow went to discover what had occurred. She went into the room that had been made into a delivery room and was back out in what Martin felt was an obscene haste. The woman looked so very pale and about to faint. Martin rushed to her and held her upright. "I am sorry, Sir," the woman said just before she fainted. Purnell and Alice took care of the woman and Martin entered the delivery room, coming out almost as fast as Mrs White. He could not speak for a moment. He just said, "So much blood," and hurried away to be physically sick.

Before too long, Adam and James had regained their senses and joined the group now gathered outside the room. The door opened and a woman, who had been acting as a nurse, came out with a tiny bundle wrapped in a once white towel, now a little messy. She handed the child to Adam who, in turn, passed the bundle on to James. Everything seemed to be happening in slow motion and in silence, which was broken only by the baby starting to cry. James opened the towel to reveal the tiny face inside and smiled down at what eventually was revealed to be his new son. Meanwhile, Rosamond had recovered enough to join the group and took the baby from its father. A quick look assured her that it had all its limbs and fingers and toes and was also a bonny boy. The baby was very well formed for an early birth. She asked if she should clean the child and maybe give it a feed, this shook everyone back into the present. James reluctantly allowed Rosamond to take the child out of his sight, and he walked towards the door to discover how his wife had faired. Martin arrived at the same time and barred his way into the room.

"I think the doctor need to examine your wife and make her look more presentable before you enter, Sir," he said.

Adam realised immediately that Martin was protecting the new father from whatever horror he would have encountered behind that door. "Let us sit back down, James, drink a toast to your new son and give the good doctor a chance to call us when he is ready." With that, he led Sir James back into the sitting room, poured him out and handed him a brandy, which he took without any sign that he knew what was happening at all.

Adam stepped out of the sitting room to speak to Martin, who indeed confirmed his worse fears that Sally had died delivering her son. Adam's face crumbled with sure distress and he sobbed like he had never done before, even as a child.

"I loved that woman," he said. "The sins of the father."

"Everyone loved Sally, my Lord," said Martin. "I do not believe it is God repaying a debt, you cannot think that."

"But I do, Martin."

The doctor finally came into the hall to confirm what by now everyone but Sir James was aware of; loss of blood had taken Sally and there was nothing that could have been done to prevent it. Her weak heart had just given out. The doctor offered to tell Sir James but Adam chose to do so himself. The anguished cry that echoed round the farm was felt by everyone who had ever been in contact with Lady Shepherd.

Adam stayed a further three weeks, not wanting to leave his friend until he was sure he could cope. The widow White, Rosamond, turned out to be a God send. She moved into the farm and took total care of the new baby. Sir James, at first, found it difficult to look upon the child, it looked so much like his beloved wife.

For reasons unknown to him, Sally had favoured the name Jasper if it was a boy, so the baby was christened Jasper James Shepherd.

Adam sent a messenger home to Wetherley to inform Dory of the terrible circumstances that were making it necessary for him to stay a little longer. James was in no state of mind to deal with any legal ramifications in connection to his wife's death. Adam, with Martin's help, dealt with the funeral arrangements.

Sally was carried in an oblong glass funeral coach pulled by two beautiful black horses. James had tied Rosebud to the back of the hearse and smiled for a moment remembering how foolish she was regarding that sheep.

The funeral was as moving as it was possible to be. The church was full of wild flowers, Sally was herself like a wild flower and loved nature. The vicar had never seen the church so full. It seemed that everyone for miles around had been touched by Sally's simple, gentle ways.

James had written a poem that he wanted to read at Sally's funeral but was too overwhelmed to do so. Adam suggested that he read it for him and at an appropriate moment in the service, he got to his feet and walked up to the pulpit. Martin could see clearly that his master and friend was too emotional himself to cope, so he walked up behind Adam and when he reached the pulpit steps, gently took the sheet of paper from him and climbed up the steps himself. Adam smiled a weak but thankful smile at Martin and returned to his seat. Adam thought back for a moment about the comment his wife had made a few years previously about Martin being a servant, because he paid him, and not a friend. He thought that even she would see the foolishness in that statement if she had been here today.

Martin took a moment to glance at the sheet, apologised to all and sundry saying that he would not read the poem as well as the writer but promised to do his best. He spoke in a clear, loud voice that echoed round the church.

Goodbye, my love, words so hard to say,
I will miss you all my live long day.
Why did the Lord snatch you from my bed?
Better He had taken me instead.

I needed you much more than He,
Why could He not have just let us be?
He took a gentle, harmless creature,
Too far, so I could no longer reach her.

I still feel your presence all around,
In the fields, the house and the ground.
The plants you nurtured, now in bloom,
I still place some daily in your room.

Did I hear your laughter on the breeze?
Your soft breath blowing through the trees?
Did I hear your footsteps in the lane?
No, I look, but you have gone again.

I laughed when you danced out in the rain,
How I wish I could see you dance again.
You loved all creatures, large and small,
And wanted to mother them one and all.

I remember how your eyes did shine,
Every time that they looked into mine.
I loved the child like way you looked at life,
I was so proud to call you my wife.

There was not a dry eye in the church as Martin walked back to his seat. He found it very difficult himself not too dissolve into tears as he read James' poem.

Sally was buried in St Peter's Churchyard next to James' parents.

James was beside himself with grief and Adam worried for his friend's health. Without the new baby to think about, it was generally thought that he might have been a danger to himself.

Adam ended up staying nearly three months, unable to make himself leave his distraught friend. Never had he seen a man so low. He thought to himself that this must be what true love is all about.

Adam reluctantly left Bleadon Farm and returned to his own pregnant wife; he felt that he could not leave her any longer as she was in the last three months of her pregnancy and needed his presence. Dory was still so distressed that Adam feared for her health but the pregnancy continued without complication. Adam had convinced himself that the sins of the father were now a curse he carried and did not expect his own child to be born healthy.

Dory had cried herself to sleep for several nights after hearing the news of Sally's demise. Some of the tears were for Sally as she loved her but most were for herself as she feared the same fate.

"I am fearful, Adam," Dory said one evening. "I am older than Sally and surely, if God can take such a young woman, he could just as easily take me."

"You are healthy, Dory, you have been well cared for all your life, you have good bones," Adam replied trying to sooth her fears. "Sally had a rough life when young, she had nearly died of the white plague when I found her, this weakened her. You have nothing to fear."

Common sense did not calm Dory's mind. Every night, she knelt in silent prayer begging God to help her and bring her a healthy son. Adam watched her, worried for her health and state of mind.

"I need this Lord, help me," she would say over and over.

Alone, she prayed for a son so it would never be necessary for her to have another child, she was so afraid. "Give me this one thing, Lord, a son. I will be a loving mother and will never ask for anything from you again."

Chapter 39
Seraphina, 1831

Two weeks before the predicted birth of the new baby, Sir James with Rosamond and Jasper arrived to be at Adam's side for the new arrival. Jasper was now a bonny looking lad with rosy cheeks and fair curls. The widow woman had been retained as a full-time nurse, nanny and possible governess to the child. Everyone could see now that she was a lovely young woman, only 22 years of age herself. Helping Sir James had helped her to get over her own loss. Dory took to her straight away. Rosamond was tidy, practical, spoke clearly and was a sensible young woman. Although Dory had loved Sally, she wasn't usually drawn to what she referred to as silly unworldly women. Rosamond was a well-educated young woman of a good family, not wealthy but comfortably off. She had an elder brother, Richard, who had taken a commission in the army at a very young age and had never returned to the family home from that day. Her parents had died during a visit to him in India where he was posted. It was only by chance that Rosamond had not accompanied them. She had come down with measles, which was very contagious, and the doctor thought it a good time for her parents to make the trip to India that they had planned and be away from the disease. They had not long stepped foot on Indian soil when, first her father and then her mother developed signs of vomiting, diarrhoea and sweating, which was put down to the change in diet. They both died within hours of each other and it was confirmed that it was in fact cholera. The family estate all passed to Rosamond's brother and she was literally homeless when he immediately put the place up to rent, which prompted her to accept a marriage proposal from the first man who offered for her. He was a gentleman farmer called Bradford White, several years older than her but of good health and reasonably educated. His very elderly parents lived with him and relied upon him, the farm being originally theirs. Rosamond enjoyed reading and conversation and would not have accepted Bradford if he had not proved to be quite literate, regardless of her position in life. Her father had left her a small allowance which Bradford insisted she kept for her own emergencies. Bradford was himself reasonably well off, his farm proved to be quite lucrative, and Rosamond's knowledge of figures allowed her to help a great deal with book keeping and generally running the household bills. These skills had also proved to be useful to Sir James. However, the elderly parents treated Rosamond as if she were their personal slave and her life had not been easy.

Dory was busy readying herself for the fast approaching event, whist Adam was still dealing with his own demons. She was very glad to have a sensible pair of hands to help in the form of Rosamond White. Her mother and sister were also on hand but Adam was never really totally comfortable around Bathsheba.

It was three and a half months after the loss of Sally that Dory gave birth to a healthy full-term daughter. The earl was thrilled with his child and did not comment on the fact that it was a girl and not a son. Dory was devastated. She had no desire to even look at the child. "Lord, how could you treat me so badly, I have always been your loyal servant," she said quietly under her breath.

The doctor had arrived in good time for the birth as had Dory's mother, Bathsheba, who assisted. After what seemed like a remarkable short time, the doctor came out of the birthing room and announced the arrival of, what sounded like by the noise coming from the room behind him, a very healthy child.

"It was an easy birth," the doctor said. He was a very forward thinking doctor, he did not believe in women lying in bed for too long after giving birth if all was well. He had seen the results of this medical care and did not approve. "She will be well very quickly, do not let her lay about for too long, short walks around the room will improve her circulation." With that, he picked up his hat and left.

Adam was too anxious to see his new daughter to accompany the doctor to the door, the doctor didn't seem to be perturbed by this, he just smiled as he passed the new father and left. Bathsheba was fussing about the room, making Dory comfortable, organising a change of clothes for her eldest daughter and telling the maid to bring a jug of warm water so she could wash the baby in the bowl that had been placed in readiness in the bedroom.

"She is a big, healthy, beautiful baby, Dorothia," Bathsheba said. "Not a tiny, little sprat like your sister, Everline, produced last year."

"The babe was a boy, sprat or no, and he is well and fit now, no doubt," replied Dory.

"A babe is a babe, girl," Bathsheba said angrily. "Do you think I did not want a son, of course I did, but I was content with the three girls that God chose to give me, and your father even more so. Stop this foolish nonsense, you will bring on the mind sickness that I have seen women get."

Once Bathsheba had done all she could to prepare the baby and make Dory look respectable, she left Weston Manor Lodge to go tell her husband that he was a grandfather again.

Adam entered the room, bent to kiss his wife who turned her face away. "I have failed you, Adam," was all she could say.

"You have given me a child, how can that be a failure?" he said kindly.

"She will not replace Robbie in your heart, I wanted a boy so much," was the tearful reply.

"The child is mine, ours, flesh and blood, it matters not that she is a girl. Do not be foolish woman, you have given me a fine child." With that, he picked up the little bundle. With his daughter safely in his arms, he proudly took her down to the servants telling them that she was the bonniest child even born. Everyone fussed over the tiny baby and agreed wholeheartedly with Adam's appraisal of the child.

The only one who did not look or sound thrilled with the addition to the family was Dory herself, who kept apologising because it was not a male child. As the minutes turned into hours and she was still crying pitifully and talking of her failure as a wife, Adam began to lose his patience.

"It is a healthy child, Dory, it is our child," said Adam reassuringly. "It makes not matter to me if it be a boy or a girl, you are well and so is the babe, I am a happy man."

"I know you are only saying that to make me feel better but I have failed," replied Dory.

"How could you consider this beautiful baby to be a failure? She is perfect," replied her husband sadly.

Dory cried and cried and no amount of gentle speeches or kind words could stop her. "I believe God had punished us," she said between sobs.

Sir James stepped towards the bed where Dory lay. "I would have given anything for Sally to have had a daughter and lived," he said.

"But you would have been happier if Sally had had a son and lived, deny that if you can," replied Dory coldly.

James sat on the edge of the bed, not knowing quite how to reply. "I am proud to have a son," he said, "I will not deny you that but I was proud to be married to Sally more so. I loved her beyond words and God took her away. You are here, you are well and you have a healthy daughter, be happy, Adam is."

"So he says but who knows what thoughts lay inside his head," she replied. "His head hold a great many secrets from me, I am sure, one more would not be hard to keep."

"Enough, Dory," cried Adam from the back of the room, still holding his daughter who was crying with hunger. "The child needs you, I need you, pull yourself together and do your duty by the baby, stop all this foolish pity. A healthy girl today, who knows, God willing, a healthy boy next."

"A boy next, so you admit the girl would never be enough for you."

Rosamond took the baby from Adam and took it over to Dory. "Be gone you, gentlemen, I will attend to Lady Southerly and help her with the bairn, it isn't easy with eyes watching off, you go."

"Thank you, Rosamond, I am most grateful to you," said Adam. "James and I will take Jasper into the garden for a while."

Not unexpectedly, the birth was followed by a bout of depression brought on, as the doctor thought, by the fear of death after Sally's demise and the fact that she did not give the earl a much wanted son.

Dory was not privy to a great many of the adventures that Adam and his man servant, Martin, accomplished before he married her, but she had heard enough about Robbie, who was now with the circus to know that Adam wanted a son badly.

Adam received a letter from Keighley just after the birth of his child, which they called Seraphina. Dory could not even bring herself to take an interest in the naming of the child. Adam settled on the name Seraphina after Dorothia's grandmother and Agnes, after his own mother. Dory had wanted to call her Bathsheba but her mother's distrust of the earl made that impossible.

The receipt of the letter meant that Adam needed to go to Southerly Mill and sort out a dispute between Morgan, the man who ran the mill, and Simon Gibbs, a young man he had originally employed to trace any children maimed in Southerly Mill or weaving sheds and who now kept an eye on the safety of employees at the mill. Simon Gibbs and Morgan did not see eye to eye. Simon understood the dangers of the mill's machinery, having lost fingers himself as a boy working there and Morgan only cared about profit.

James persuaded Adam that it might be a good idea for him and Rosamond to take Dory and the baby back with them to Bleadon, suggesting that the proximity to Weston-Super-Mare might do her good. It was the kindly Rosamond that thought of a solution to the present problem. She suggested to Sir James that maybe they could take Dory with them to Weston for the sea air for a few weeks, whilst the earl rode up to Keighley. She could keep little Seraphina safe and maybe the country life might appeal to Dory and bring her back to life.

Adam looked sadly at his beautiful wife, who had been full of such fun and wisdom. She looked as though the cares of the world were upon her and took only a passing interest in their baby, doing what was necessary and no more. So it was agreed, Dory and baby went with Sir James to Bleadon Manor Farm and Adam and Martin set off for Keighley.

Chapter 40
The Circus Returns

Once back in Keighley, it did not take long for Adam to resolve the issues at the mill. Simon had grown in stature and confidence and Morgan, who resented his presence greatly, challenged every action he took. Once Adam made the lines clear, Morgan promised not to step over them for fear of the loss of his job.

Accidents were almost a thing of the past and the workforce seemed to be a lot happier. Profits were very slightly down as predicted but not enough to cause concern. Adam was pleased.

"I am going to stay a while here, Martin. I need some time on my own for a while, so much has happened," said the earl.

"Do you wish me to return to Wetherley?" asked Martin.

"Of course not, man," was the reply. "I greatly miss our time spent together before I married. I did not realise how restricting marriage can be."

"It is only to be expected that a wife would wish to dominate her husband's time," Martin replied.

Adam Southerly's, the Earl of Wetherley, appearance at Keighley coincided with the return of the circus, whether this was by design or accident, only the earl would know for sure. However, once the problem, which turned out to be very minor was resolved at the mill, Adam did not hurry back to Weston-Under-Wetherley, he chose to spend time with Robbie.

It was near on three years since Robbie had left with the troupe and Adam wondered at the coincidence. It seemed like fate had stepped in to maybe lighten his heart. He immediately organised for the whole household to go to the circus and enjoy the delights and excitement that the big top had to offer and to see Robbie.

Mrs Frost was so excited at the thought of seeing the boy again, she walked about singing.

"It seems I was not the only one to be sorry that I let the boy go," said the earl to Martin.

"We all miss the little imp, Sir," was the reply.

"Kitty writes regularly and loves her new life, her writing is beautiful and I feel she is receiving a proper education. I am not so sure about Robbie."

"I am sure he has learnt a lot about hard work and life in general, Sir," said Martin with a smile.

"Do you think if Dory had delivered a son, she would have coped better?" Adam said thoughtfully. "She knew I wanted one badly."

"It might have helped but I think it was Lady Shepherd's passing that caused the depression, it brought us all down."

Adam just nodded.

The next day, Adam went alone to the circus to locate Robbie and see how he was faring in his chosen life. He walked about the grounds watching the men and women attending to their various tasks. They seemed, to Adam, to resemble a swarm of bees all buzzing about with one common purpose, to erect the big top and surrounding smaller tents as quickly as possible. It had been raining for the past couple of days so the ground was muddy, which made the task more hazardous.

Adam looked very out of place in his stylist clothes and highly polished riding boots, crop in hand, stepping over obstacles and through muddy puddles, leading a very fine black mare. He spotted Daisy first and close by Robbie. The boy had grown so much taller in three years, he was not positive it was actually him. He called his name and the boy turned towards him, his face so obviously delighted to see his old master that it lighted Adam's heart. Robbie ran to him and into his open arms like a long lost son.

"You will not believe how much I have missed you, boy," said the earl, his arm entwined around this lad, who was now a good six inches taller than when they last met. Adam held the boy at arm's length and looked at him closely.

"You have grown muscles, Rob, as well as height," he said.

Robbie was struck silent by the appearance of the earl and it took him a moment to speak.

"I have missed you too, Sir, and Mrs Frost," Robbie said at last.

"Do they treat you well here?" Adam asked

"They treat me like a man, I do men's work for a man's pay," was the reply.

"That was not what I asked," said Adam. "Do they treat you well, I can see you are well fed, they do not beat you or anything like that?"

Robbie just laughed. "Beat me, I would have run back to Keighley Manor as fast as my legs would carry me. No, they treat me well. I share a caravan, come let me show you."

With that, Robbie dragged the earl over to a small, brightly coloured caravan; he banged on the door, no one was inside, so he opened the door to show Adam where he lived. It looked like a smaller copy of the one he had entered nearly three years previously.

"There are four bunks, I am on the top to the right," the boy said proudly. "I stayed with Jeanette and her father for the first six months and then when they considered I was ready, I was given this spot to sleep."

Adam nodded his approval before being taken on an inspection of the grounds. "I cannot stay away from my job long, Sir, we each have to pull our weight, it is only fair," said Robbie. Adam smiled approvingly.

They rounded a group of tent erectors and walked straight into a group of young gypsy women; amongst them, standing out like a shining star was Jeanette. Adam had to catch his breath and realised that the feeling he had all those years ago were stronger now, the child had become a woman. He seemed to be drawn to her eyes. He took a moment to compose himself before he ventured over to thank her for her care of Robbie. She stepped from the group and smiled such a smile that made Adam's legs feel that they could no longer support his body. He was struck by the moral danger he was in, just by looking at this glorious creature, now touching 18.

The three of them sat down on one of the benches intended for the crowd in the big tent. She sweetly asked him how he had been, and he told her of the passing of his sister but added nothing further about his life. He asked her how Robbie had behaved, and she told him he was a hard worker and seemed to love the life they led. Robbie added that he did, very much.

Before long, a rather robust looking man came looking for Robbie. "I must go about my work, my Lord, I will come to the manor if it pleases you to visit when I have a day off." With that, he disappeared leaving Adam and Jeanette alone. It was quite apparent that there was a chemistry there. The girl aroused feeling that Adam felt quite unseemly for a gentleman of rank, and the girl looked at him with such soulful eyes that suggested his feelings were returned, making Adam even more anxious.

They talked quietly for a few moments before her father joined them. Adam sprung to his feet like a naughty school boy caught with his fingers in a cookie jar.

"Sir, I hoped to see you, Georgiou," said Adam. "I need to thank you for your care of my once ward, Robbie. I see he has grown in confidence and stature in your care."

"He is a good boy and welcome amongst us," was the reply.

Adam and Georgiou walked off to the main caravan leaving Jeanette sitting alone, Adam turned to say goodbye and her eyes appeared to plead with him to stay. He knew that he had to get back to Keighley Manor as soon as possible and never come here alone again if he was to save his soul.

Over a glass of Madeira, Georgiou told Adam of Robbie's progress with the circus, they laughed about the work the boy had put in trying to get Daisy to dance. The little dog was allowed to enter the ring with the others because she was a particularly pretty dog and the children loved her, not for her talent.

"The boy has been a welcome addition to the circus. Many of our troop have been formed from people without real homes, travellers," said Georgiou. "There are only a few of us that are really of Romany blood and we try to marry amongst ourselves."

Adam wondered if this was a veiled warning.

"Will Robbie still be welcome when he is of age?" enquired Adam concerned.

"He is one of us now, adopted into the clan so to speak. I doubt he will marry a gypsy but he will be welcome to bring a woman into the circus when he is ready," was the reply. "Romany's usually marry young."

"But Jeanette, she is not married, I believe," said the earl trying not to sound too interested.

"No, the girl has ideas of her own, she has rejected every offer of marriage so far," was Georgiou's frustrated reply. "Soon, she will be too old and the offers will cease."

"Surely, she is still only a child," replied Adam.

"I was married at 17," said Georgiou matter-of-factly.

"17!" said Adam in amazement. "You would not know your own mind at 17, surely!"

"It was not my choice, my parents put forward the woman I was to marry and I followed where they led."

"So you are not much different from me then, Georgiou, and I thought you were all free spirits," replied Adam astonished by this information. "My parents chose my wife to be. Fortunately, for me, my father died before the engagement could be announced so I was free to look elsewhere."

Georgiou laughed, "Maybe my daughter is hoping this will happen to me."

"I do not think so, Sir," said Adam. "She seems very fond of you."

"I believe she is. Her sisters have all married in the circus, she has no brothers," continued Georgiou.

"Did they all marry happily?" asked Adam rather naïvely.

Georgiou laughed again, "Happily, what has that to do with marriage. They have given me grandchildren and are fit and well, so life is good for them."

"Are they still travelling with the circus?" asked Adam.

"They are, my good Sir," was the reply. "One is married to a trapezes artist and she too is one of the act. The other has been married less than two years and has just had a baby girl. Her man is a bareback rider like her."

"So who did you have in mind for Jeanette?" Adam asked casually.

"Several ideas, she is a stubborn one that one, she will not budge," was the reply. "She is, however, so beautiful that I can leave it another couple of years before she loses her shine."

"I do not believe that she ever will, Georgiou, she is bewitching."

Georgiou smiled at the earl. "Ah, I see she has you under her spell."

"How could anyone not be," was the reply.

Adam felt himself wanting to prevent Jeanette from being promised to another when he had no right to do so and was himself a married man. He said nothing further on the subject.

The earl had insisted that Georgiou take a small amount of bills to cover any expense Robbie had caused before he started paying his way, and then he hurried away, confused and a little ashamed that he had not told the girl or her father about his wife.

As he led his horse back through the hustle and bustle that was circus life, Jeanette ran and caught him just as he was about to mount and ride away; he had already made up his mind not to ever come to this place again.

She stood a few feet from him, her long, wild tangled hair blowing gently around her bare shoulders. She said that she had come to say goodbye but her eyes said stay. She walked towards him and touched his arm very gently but to Adam, it was a hammer blow. His desire just to sweep her up and ride off with her was strong, and he could tell that she would not have objected. He closed his eyes, shook his head and then looked into her eyes. The girl was fully aware of the affect she had on men and had used this over the years to bring crowds into the circus. It was obvious that she wanted more from Adam than a customer on a seat.

"It cannot be Jeanette," he simply said. "God, I wish it could. We live too different lives." With that, he mounted his horse and rode away as fast as he could.

When the earl arrived back at the manor, Martin was waiting and could tell straight away that his master was agitated.

"My guess is you saw the girl again, Sir," he said.

"I did, Martin."

"And?"

"And nothing, I walked away. God, it was hard but I did," replied Adam. "I will make my excuses not to go to the circus when we all go."

"That will look very strange, Sir," replied Martin. "Surely, watching will be safe enough if you stay with the group. She cannot have that strong hold on your heart."

"I fear she has, Martin," was the reply.

"You have a wife, My Lord," Martin said simply. "I do not believe you will emulate your father, you have taken too much of your time mopping up the mess he left to add to it. I do not believe you will let your wife and child down."

"I hope you are right but I am afraid, Martin, that I have to repeat what I said to you some time ago. Sometimes, the people who let you down are not the ones you expect."

Chapter 41
Blood Will Out

Robbie arrived at Keighley Manor at around 4.00 in the evening of the following day. The boy, who now looked every bit a young man, though still only 13, hurried down to Mrs Frost on arrival. She could not believe the transformation. He rushed up to her and swung her round.

"You are a man," she said, almost sounding disappointed.

"Look at you, so handsome, so tall. I cannot believe it is you."

Robbie laughed and released his hold on the woman. "I have missed your wonderful cakes."

"Not too much looking at the size of you," was the reply.

They sat and chatted for a while and Robbie told Mrs Frost about all the jobs he had done and how Daisy was not the best dancer but the prettiest of the dog troop; how close he had stood to a lion and all about the elephants. He was so full of his new adventures that she was soon quite content that the earl had made the right decision when he let the boy go.

The boy stayed a couple of hours, eating with Adam and Martin and telling them all about the letters he had received from Kitty.

"She says we should all go to Paris sometime, would that not be famous!" the boy said.

"I, for one, would very much like to seek Pierre out one day, maybe when Dory recovers, we will all go on such an adventure," replied the earl.

When Robbie left, Adam promised faithfully that he would be there in a couple of days to see him in the ring and cheer him on. He looked at Martin as he spoke and smiled.

Two days later, true to his word, the earl and a group from the manor set out to the circus. They had front row seats and the big top was absolutely heaving with people, there was not a space to be had for any more customers.

The ringmaster ran into the ring, huge whip in hand, top hat on his head, red cut away long coat, white trousers and long black boots. He looked most impressive.

Horses and riders followed, then the dancing dogs, Daisy trotting behind, looking very pretty and enjoying the attention of the crowd. When Robbie came into the ring with the jugglers and clowns, the earl and his party shouted themselves hoarse. The boy was thrilled to see his old family there to cheer him. Then into the ring was wheeled a very large cage containing three huge stools. A wire tunnel that disappeared beyond the tent was fitted to an opening. Into the cage went the ringmaster, still clutching his whip. Silence fell on the tent and a door was opened at the beginning of the tunnel. A few moment later, much to the amazement of the crowd, a tiger strolled nonchalantly down the tunnel and into the cage. The ringmaster cracked his whip and the massive muscular creature jumped up onto one of the stools. It snarled and bared its massive yellow teeth. This magnificent creature was soon followed by two more, who at the sound of the whip also jumped onto the stools provided.

The ringmaster walked about the cage circling the tigers, each one bared its teeth as he drew near and raising enormous paws, showing clearly long, dangerous claws. The crowd squealed with delight and fear. Two of the tigers jumped down from their stools and approached the ringmaster; the closer they got to him, the louder the crowd roared. He cracked his whip and they sat on their haunches, then the whip cracked again and they lay down. What looked like the largest tiger was still sitting alone on its stool. Another crack of the whip, the two tigers jumped to their feet and walked towards the tunnel, then they just left one by one using the tunnel provided to allow them in. The last, the largest of the three, looked as though he was not willing to go, it was part of the act but it made it exciting. The ringmaster asked for silence and went up close to the tiger, its mighty head was twice the size of the man's. The ringmaster placed his whip on a hard wood ladder backed chair and stood in front of the tiger. He then used both hands to prize the animal's jaws open and allowed his own head to slip into the tiger's mouth for just a moment, he then removed it and released his hold on the tiger. The crowd went absolutely wild.

Martin leant over towards Adam so he could be heard above the roar of the audience. "I believe the animal has been fed a potion to make it docile."

The earl nodded in agreement, "Still a daring act, Martin, don't you think?"

Martin did not make any attempt to reply.

The ringmaster picked up the chair that he had placed his whip on and, holding it in front of him with the legs towards the tiger, used it to guide the big cat out of the cage; it turned and took a couple of swipes with its mighty paws at the chair before doing as asked. Everyone clapped and cheered.

In rode the bareback riders, men on black mounts and the gypsy girls on white ones. Adam scanned the group to find Jeanette, who was not immediately visible. After everyone had ridden round the rings couple of times, she entered. She rode in bareback and then started to perform all sorts of tricks. She swung from side to side and stood on the horses back at one point. Her exotic beauty had a mesmerising effect on the majority of the men in the tent, none more than Adam. Martin watched his master and realised that the gypsy had singled him out for her particular attention. He could see immediately that the earl was in danger of compromising his marriage vows. When the earl said he would walk home to clear his head after the performance, Martin offered to accompany him, an offer which was declined.

"Sir," said Martin, "that which we spoke of, please do not do this, come home now."

"I wish I could, Martin," was the reply. "But I need to speak to Jeanette, I need to tell her about Dory. There is a dark stain on my heart, I have not been honest with the girl and I feel that if I am, she will walk away and free me from this hold she has over me."

"What if she does not?" replied Martin.

"I cannot say, who knows," said Adam. "I would say that I would risk my very soul for one night in her arms. I know it would be wrong and nothing could come of such an encounter, but I might spend my whole life wondering what it would have been like if it did not happen."

"It must not happen, Sir," pleaded Martin.

"I know," was the reply.

Martin left with the group, a very disappointed man.

Martin did not see the earl again until early afternoon of the following day. Just one look at his master was enough to tell him that he had compromised himself. He had the look of a man that still carried that dark stain on his heart and soul. If he had been mistaken by the look, he was soon convinced when the earl announced that they were to leave for Weston-Under-Wetherley in the next couple of days, without fail.

Not a single word passed between them about what may or may not have occurred the night before.

The sudden necessity by the earl to return to Weston-Under-Wetherley with indecent haste and go down to Bleadon to retrieve his wife and daughter, weighed heavily on Martin's mind.

Chapter 42
Back to Family Life

Once back in Wetherley preparations were undertaken to travel to Bleadon Manor Farm and collect Dory and Seraphina. Martin was relieved and wanted to ask the earl what had occurred but he did not have the courage to do so. He and his master had an amazing relationship but he felt that this would have been a step too far.

Adam had some business to tie up in Weston with an old friend and eminent doctor, Edward Lang Fox, so this was an ideal time for him to do this. A few years previously, Lang Fox had asked Adam to help him to purchase Knightstone Island in Weston to open it as a spar for the mentally ill as they recover. In 1830, although nearly 70-years-old Dr Lang Fox gave up the running of Brislington House, an asylum near Bristol which was founded by him in 1804 in favour of putting all his money and interests into Knightstone Island. Fox was a prominent Quaker physician in Bristol and a pioneer of humane treatment of the insane. He wanted a place where people could exercise in peace and introduced fresh and salt water, hot and cold showers. He believed in sulphur baths and the use of sauna baths to drive out ailments. Lang Fox was very interested in the workings of the mind and Adam had consulted him in a letter when Dory had, what appeared to be, a mental breakdown after the birth of their daughter. The earl had taken an interest in the workings of the mind himself, having spent many a sleepless night worrying about the wrongs his father had undertaken, and he did think that it was possible that the late earl was actually insane, leading to the question, could this be carried on through the blood line?

In exchange for whatever assistance Adam gave the progressive physician, Lang Fox was to organise a trust fund for Seraphina, the details to be decided at a later date.

Adam managed to sort out everything of interest to him quite quickly so he took Dory and the baby home. She eventually, after a few months, recovered enough to start being involved with life again. Seraphina was a delightful baby and Adam found that he was very fond of her from the moment he first held the little bundle. He put all thoughts of his gypsy from his mind and settled down to being the perfect husband. The family travelled to Weston-Super-Mare regularly and soon, Rosamond had replaced Sally in everyone's affections including James, who announced his intentions of marrying the woman. It was perfect solution to his problems and she was a natural farmer's wife. Jasper had known no other mother, so he too was content with his father's choice. Sally would never be forgotten, the boy was the image of her; he too had the look of a delicate being, he had an ethereal quality as if he wasn't really of this world. He also had an easy smile and sweet, forgiving nature like she had. Seraphina called Rosamond Aunt and Dory referred to her as her cousin. It was a wonderful solution to Rosamond's personal dilemma. Before she had been hired by Sir James as a wet nurse, she had been living with her late husband's parents, a situation that was perfect whilst her husband was alive but quite uncomfortable in the circumstances. They had told her when she lost the child, their future grandchild, that she was no longer welcome; they had not actually asked her to leave but she knew that they were no longer wealthy people and one less mouth to feed would be a God sent. Bradford had managed the running of the farm for quite a few years prior to his marrying, so it was obvious that without him, the farm would soon become a burden so selling was the obvious answer. Because the farm was still in Mr White Senior's name and Bradford had not made any provisions for his wife, she felt that she would have to leave. Also, she had taken an instant liking to Sir James, it was impossible not to, had loved Jasper from the first and had grown more fond of everything about her life at Bleadon Farm that she could ever have imagined. Both her parents having died shortly before her marriage and her only brothers many hundreds of miles away, she really was alone in the world. Sir James offered her stability and she knew it would be easy to love him.

For a while, Adam was beginning to believe that maybe the curse had lifted and he was free of his father at last, that did not last.

The bout of depression that had claimed Dory's sanity for a while was starting to lift. She was starting to cope and felt a lot better and she and Adam settled back into married life.

Meanwhile, Sir James married Rosamond and everyone thought it was a very unexpected but appropriate union. Rosamond had been a tower of strength to James when his wife died and had nurtured Sally's boy as if he was her own.

When Seraphina was coming up to two years old, Dory was with child again and this time, she felt sure it would be a boy. They always intended to call their son Adam and she was happily busying herself ready for his arrival. Seraphina spent a great deal of her time with a young governess, Olive Hall, who appeared to find the child a delight. Daily, she would bring the girl to her mother and tell her of all the clever things she had done that day. Slowly, Dory was beginning to warm to the child, it was difficult not to when she was such an easy little girl, always smiling with lovely rosy cheeks and bright, intelligent eyes. Adam adored her. Months moved on and Dory still blossomed.

Dory was finishing off some needlework when she felt a stabbing pain in her stomach, strong enough to make her cry out. She stood up, tried to straighten her body but could not. Her maid, Kate, was first at her side.

"I am sorry to make such a fuss," said Dory, obviously in a lot of discomfort. "It is probably only the pickled eels that we had for tea, I may have over indulged."

Kate looked concerned as she helped her mistress onto the couch and put a stool under her feet, carefully folding the sewing that Dory had been working on. "Shall I call the master?" she asked, trying to sound unconcerned.

Dory placed her hand on her swollen belly and smiled, "I can feel him moving, so, Kate, it must be the eels. I will sit here for a while and see how I feel later. Do not disturb the master. Do you know where he is?"

"I believe he is in the rose garden with Miss Seraphina and Olive Madam," she replied. "I saw them heading that way earlier and have not seen or heard them return."

"He is not far away then, that is good," was the reply. "Run along and fetch me a warm drink, Kate, a little hot lemon and sugar should suffice, I have quite a thirst."

Kate was hardly out of the door when she heard Dory cry out again and rushed back in to find her mistress doubled over in pain.

"I am going for the master," she said taking charge. "And I am sending one of the boys for the doctor."

"Please do not alarm everyone, I am sure it is nothing," Dory replied, not very convincingly.

Kate ran to the pull cord in the corner of the room and very shortly, a stout young man of about 14 was standing in the door way.

"Thom, away with you to the rose garden, tell the master to hurry, then you run on to the doctor's, tell him that I believe the mistress is having trouble and there is two month to go before the baby is due." Kate was very calm and the boy did not argue, he just hurried off as commanded.

10 minutes later, Adam rushed into the sitting room, took one look at his wife's anguished face and called to Kate to send for the doctor.

"Already done, Sir," was her reply. "Thom has gone to fetch him."

Even in the midst of the drama, the earl took the time to smile at the little maid and thank her for her actions.

It seemed like an age before the doctor arrived and by this time, it was obvious that something was amiss. Strong arms had helped Dory up to the room that would be used for the delivery of the baby, and she was already lying on the bed waiting to discover her fate. Dressed in a white nightdress, the appearance of a red stain made it obvious that the baby was not prepared to wait for its' due date.

The doctor came up the stairs two at a time, he was the same young doctor who had delivered Seraphina, so everyone felt immediately at ease. Doctor Phillips hurried everyone from the room but encouraged Kate to stay in case she was needed. She was more than happy to oblige. The doctor calculated that the baby was not due for another six to eight weeks and wanted Dory to lie still to see if maybe he would stay where he was, nice and safe for a little longer; unfortunately, the little mite had other ideas.

It was short and almost painless delivery but the child, and it was in fact a much wanted boy, did not take a breath and nothing the doctor could do would induce him to. The perfectly formed little bundle was taken away and Dory and Adam were absolutely distraught.

Once again, a dark cloud enveloped Dory and she became withdrawn and depressed, even Seraphina's cheerful chatter could not make her smile. Olive tried each day to take Seraphina into her mother's room for a while, but it was obvious that the company was not welcomed. Adam tried to cheer his wife up, despite his own disappointment, but she was never quite the same after the tragedy, blaming herself for disappointing him again. Once more, Adam considered that maybe the sins of the father had come back to haunt him and now his wife firmly believed it as well. They both felt that Weston-Under-Wetherley was an unhappy place for them. They discussed the possibilities of moving back to Yorkshire for a short time, feeling that the change of scenery might lift the gloom hanging over the family.

It was the general gossip that Dorothia had not managed to deliver a live son because the old earl had cursed any union. Although most of the villagers were godly, there was an undercurrent of old-fashioned superstition and a great many sensible people thought foolishly that as the old earl had been the devil incarnate, forces were at work to prevent any male descendants from taking up where George Southerly left off. Dory's father, as the vicar of the parish, found himself continually trying to talk sense into older villagers. Adam found the gossip very hard to manage and as he firmly believed that the sins of his father had cursed him, he was most uncomfortable in Weston-Under-Wetherley as was Dorothia, despite the convenience of having her family close by. Most villagers could see that Adam was trying hard to right his father's wrongs but they also thought that the line should end there and so, stopping any chance of such an evil person moving amongst them ever again. Dory's mother was once one of the most outspoken about the old earl and had always maintained that blood will out; she has not been so vocal since her daughter married the devil's spawn as they call Adam. Older people who remembered all the details of George Southerly's evil doings felt that Dorothia's loss was in fact a blessing, a view that Dorothia did not share. She could often be heard praying out loud. One evening, Kate was walking along the upper corridor when she stopped at the main bedroom door, hearing her mistress' voice; she at first thought that she was in trouble but soon realised that her mistress was in fact talking to herself in an almost manic way.

"I tricked him, I was wrong, I am paying the price!" Dory said over and over again, only stopping when Kate knocked gently on the door to ask if all was well.

Kate had listened to her mistress' ramblings before and was beginning to wonder if losing the baby had cost Lady Southerly her sanity. Kate had one time gone to the master and repeated a few of the things she had heard, not in a tell-tale manner but out of fear that her mistress was going slowly mad, and she did not want to carry the burden of being the only one to realise this.

Adam had asked what sort of things his wife had muttered and were over heard by Kate.

"Please, Sir," the young maid said wringing her hands as she spoke. "I do not want to be disloyal, Sir, but the mistress worries me so. She talks out loud to herself in an anguished manner and her eyes look so wild. I felt that I had to speak to you."

The poor, little maid hung her head and stared at her feet wondering if she should continue.

"Tell me everything, child, I will not tell your mistress that I have any knowledge of her strange behaviour, though others have mentioned that they have concerns for her mental health," the earl said kindly, smiling at the girl to put her at ease.

"She talks about someone called Freda and a secret that God is punishing her for," said Kate in a quiet voice. "I do not know of whom she speaks and if I knock on the door, she just says that she had a bad dream."

Adam immediately thought that what she had told him that had happened to Freda, the loss of her child and then the woman's own life, had affected Dory more than he had thought. He wondered if Dory thought that God was punishing the whole family for George Southerly's part in Freda's demise.

"I will speak to the doctor, child," said Adam after a few moments. "Do not concern yourself, report to me if you think things are getting worse. I believe my wife will regain her senses shortly. She greatly mourns her loss, we both do."

Nothing more to be said, Kate curtsied and left the earl to his own thoughts.

Not long after the earl had returned to Wetherley Manor Lodge with his family, things started to get uncomfortable for him again. There was still an undercurrent of distrust, which the young earl found very difficult to live with. The men no longer hid their daughters or young wives but they seemed to stiffen and take on a protective air if he was about. Adam realised that the damage his father had done to the family name was irreversible. Dory had always understood that she might have to leave her family and move to Yorkshire if she married Adam and the situation stayed unmanageable. She had not been keen to move but they had always said that this would be the plan of action if necessary. The pregnancy had taken the thought of moving back to Yorkshire from their minds for a while, but now, as things had not completely settle down in Wetherley as well as the near full-term miscarriage of a boy, Dory believed that their lives in Weston-Under-Wetherley were cursed. Dory and Adam decided reluctantly that they should move to Keighley where they were more readily accepted. Adam was aware that his wife was suffering from depression after the loss of their would be son and that she was acting strangely distant from their daughter Seraphina, things that had been observed by members of staff and reported to him, things he had in turn discussed with the doctor. Everyone firmly believed that a complete change would help his wife to recover; she would have so much to think about and plan in Yorkshire, this might take her mind away from her sadness and disappointment. His dear little daughter had been the subject of innuendoes and comments that while she was too small to understand did bother her parents. People wished the child to remain barren so as not to continue the Southerly line. Adam could not comprehend how anyone could wish anything but happiness on a small child like Seraphina, and as she grew, he wished to protect her from any idol talk she might hear. It seems that the dislike of the old earl was so deep that it was about to destroy the life of Lord and Lady Southerly and their precious daughter. They only seemed perfectly at ease in Bleadon Manor Farm and Weston-Super-Mare, where they were accepted and the old earl was unknown. Adam's father had centred his worst behaviour round the Wetherley area, which made it harder for them to live there.

After a long discussion, Adam and Dory decided that they would make Keighley their main home for a while and discuss the situation once they had been in Yorkshire for a few months.

Bathsheba and Phillip, Dorothia's parents, had begged them not to leave but for peace of mind, it was decided that at least for the foreseeable future, the family would move up north where they were more readily accepted and hopefully, Dory would get better and think less about the lost baby. Bathsheba was fully aware that she had played a big part in up-rooting her daughter with her idle talk before the marriage, something she now regretted, memories are long when they want to be.

They all decided to wait until after Seraphina's third birthday before packing up to move up to Yorkshire. Dory's parents and sister made a great fuss of the child, so much so that Adam had to remind everyone that they would be back, they were not disappearing forever. Bathsheba was also worried about her daughter's fragile health and had wished that she could have stayed closer so she could keep an eye on her. Yorkshire to the Mountjoys was a foreign country or might as well be, it seemed so far away. They had all lived in Birmingham before going to Weston-Under-Wetherley and that was as far up country as they ever desired to be. Bathsheba herself had been born near Bath and her mother had originated near to Wetherley, which was why they had all migrated back there. Going to Brighton had been quite an adventure for the Mountjoy girls but happily for their mother Brighton is in the South East of the country and although not easy to reach, she considered it civilised.

Regardless of all objections, the house was closed up and the family and a few of the valued servants moved to Yorkshire.

Chapter 43
Robbie

In Keighley, Mr and Mrs Frost were very thrilled with the earl's choice and went about making the family very comfortable. Nine months past and Dory was beginning to feel at home, although she missed her mother, father and sisters greatly. She seemed to have accepted the fact that she had lost the baby but life was not over, and she had a healthy daughter that she should be concentrating on. It did make the family sad that it was very much more difficult to go down to Weston-Super-Mare, the distance being long and arduous. Dory and Seraphina missed their visits to the beach and Weston Wood, where they had enjoyed many picnics with James, Rosamond and Jasper. They did occasionally go to the coast around their present home, which was, in some places, quite beautiful but the weather was not so inviting.

Seraphina celebrated her fourth birthday in Keighley and just three months after that, the circus returned, a lot sooner than expected. Robbie was on the doorstep before he had even got his feet planted firmly on Keighley Moor.

Although Dory had heard endless stories about Robbie, she had never actually met the boy and was surprised to see what looked like a handsome Romany man in the hallway; he was now 15, nearly six foot tall and dressed in gypsy style.

Adam and the boy greeted each other like father and son, both readily throwing their arm about each other with the sheer delight of being together again. Dory felt a pang of envy knowing how badly Adam wanted a son.

"How long do they plan to stay this time, Robbie?" the earl asked.

"Just a couple of months, I guess, until the queue gets shorter," was the reply. "We came to Keighley Moor a lot sooner than I expected, our last stop off was flooded so we came here first."

"That explains everything. I thought it would be another six months at least before we saw you again," said the earl with a smile.

Dory was thrilled at the thought of taking Seraphina to the circus; she had never been to one herself, so she thought they would both enjoy the experience equally.

After an evening of listening to stories about the circus' travellers life style everyone was looking forward to actually going to the moor and watching the performers. Robbie was now a juggler, he picked up three apples to show Adam his newly acquired skills. Cleverly, he tossed them up into the air one by one, catching each one in his right hand before throwing them upwards singularly again.

"Of course, it looks a lot more exciting with the clubs we use," Robbie explained, "I work with a partner and we throw them to each other. I am only learning but others use flaming torches."

"That sounds a bit dangerous, boy, stick to the clubs," was Adam's reply.

Robbie laughed, "The circus is a dangerous place, it is the danger that excites me."

They sat down to eat Mrs Frost having cooked everything she could remember that Robbie favoured. The chatter around the table was only interrupted when someone took a mouth-full of food.

"Sitting here with all this fine linen and silverware is quite strange now," said Robbie smiling. "Do you remember, my Lord, when you first found me in the sitting room, raggedy and skin and bone?"

"As if it was yesterday," was the reply. "It is nearly seven years past, where did the time go."

"You saved me from a life of misery and for that, I will always be grateful," continued Robbie, "And Kitty, so far away in Paris. I wonder what she looks like now."

"I often wonder, boy," replied the earl. "She had the potential to be a great beauty. Pierre saw that and he painted her a great deal as do other fine artists or so he writes and tells me."

"One day, maybe the circus will travel to France and we will meet up again," said the boy slightly sadly.

"You miss her, obviously," said Dory a little concerned and having been won over by the boy's open and loving manner.

"I do, Lady Southerly, but I know she is happy so I am happy for her."

"It is difficult when it is all the family you have," Dory continued.

"I am lucky, Madam, I have everyone here as well, and the circus is my family now also. I have a great many more people that I can call friends than most."

"I too miss my family and friends," said Dory looking a little saddened. "And I find the climate cold and damp here."

"We will visit the circus and then go to Wetherley for a while to see your parents," said Adam. "Maybe we will go down to Weston-Super-Mare as well and see James and Rosamond."

The mood immediately lifted. "I would love that," Dory replied.

Robbie left and Dory and Adam sat quietly by the open fire for a while before retiring to bed.

"He is a fine boy," said Dory. "Maybe next time, God willing, our next child will be a boy, I do hope so."

A few days later, the earl announced that he was going to ride up to Keighley Moor and buy tickets for the circus and also visit Robbie. Martin asked if he needed company but already knew the answer.

"Take care, Sir," said Martin as the earl was about to set off.

"Do not be afraid for me, Martin, I am settled now, I just need to lay a few ghosts," was the reply.

"Or open a few wounds!"

"Have no fear, I am stronger now," continued the earl.

"Why did you not ask Robbie for news of Jeanette?" asked Martin.

"I did, he said that she had a son now, so Georgiou must have got his way and she must have married a fellow traveller," answered the earl. "You see, I am quite safe, I will not be hunting her out, trust me. After all, she may be married to a knife thrower," he laughed as he spoke lifting Martin's spirits as well.

The circus was a lot larger than it had been on its last visit. There were a number of side shows, a bearded lady, a lady in a tank that was billed as a mermaid and a little tent that caught the earl's eye—a fortune teller. He decided that maybe this little tent might be worth the visit, not believing wholeheartedly in such things, but he wondered if maybe whoever was within might tell him if he would actually ever have the son he wanted and needed to pass his title on to.

He warily opened the tent flap and inside, there was a woman sitting at a table, her face obscured by a beaded yashmak that covered her nose and mouth, with small gold coin like objects hanging from it. She wore a similar beaded scarf round her head, very large hooped earrings and she sat behind a large glass fortune-teller's globe. It was all very theatrical, set to amaze and thrill any customer. She did not look up. Adam stood for a moment and then decided that maybe it was a mistake and started to leave. There was a heavy smell of lavender in the tent and a scented candle made shadows that looked like they were tiny dancers. As he was about to open the flap to retreat a small boy darted in on unsteady chubby legs, almost knocking him over. The child did not look like a Romany, his hair was fair and his skin quite light, though his eyes were very dark. Adam was struck by the look of the boy.

"Mummy," he cried as he ran behind the table to the woman who lifted her head at the sound of his voice.

Adam swallowed hard, it was Jeanette, he had not seen her since that fateful evening when he had loitered on the moor, having faked illness, to walk home alone and take in the night air.

She looked at him, her eyes as big and beautiful as ever, her lashes still the longest Adam had ever seem. She stood up, picked up the boy and unfastened the yashmak that hid her face. Adam could not believe that he did not realise it was her. She didn't look a day older and was still the most alluring creature possible. Once again, he was totally under her spell.

Jeanette walked round the table and handed the boy to Adam. "This is Georgiou Joseph," she said simply. "We call him Joe, he is your son."

Adam stood with his mouth slightly open and looked from her to the boy who was probably two years old.

"My son?" he said amazed.

"The results of our encounter. He is well cared for here, we do not carry the stigma that outsiders carry when presented with a child out of wed-lock," she said matter-of-factly.

"Why did you not get word to me?" asked the earl.

"Why did you not tell me of your wife and daughter?" she asked in reply.

Adam looked ashamed. "Because I needed to see you and knew I should not. I thought if I did not mention it, I could pretend it was not so."

"But it was so," she said, a tear running down her face.

"Does your father know that the boy is mine?" asked Adam.

"I have never disclosed who Joe's father is and my father has never asked me. But you would have to be blind, not to see that he is yours," was the reply.

"Robbie told me that you had a son and I assumed you had married amongst the gypsy group," said Adam. "He made no suggestion that the child was mine."

"Robbie is a total innocent, he would not have questioned Joe's parenthood, why would he?" was the reply. "It is not uncommon to have a child and the father not spoken of in my world."

"What now?" asked Adam.

"I do not understand the question, Adam," she replied.

"I cannot walk away now I know I have a son."

"You walked away from me, why not the boy?" she asked.

"I did not walked, Jeanette, I ran," he replied honestly. "I knew that my heart was lost to you but that it was not possible for us to be together." He placed the boy gently on the ground as he spoke. "I swore that I would never return to this place, it was the hardest thing I have ever done. I had spent years trying to undo the ills done by my father and now, I discover that I am as bad as he."

"Do not be foolish, Adam," replied Jeanette. "Our child was conceived of love, not lust or it was that way for me. Your father took what he wanted, I was willing."

The earl pulled the gypsy to him and held her tightly. "I do not want to let you go again but what can I do?"

"The child is yours, I will not stand in your way if you want to raise him," she said tearfully. "He is a wild, half-gypsy now but you could educate him. Is your wife a good woman, would she take the boy in to her home?"

"You would give the boy up!" said Adam amazed.

"Only to you and only if it was what you wanted," was the reply.

"My wish would be to have both, you and the boy. But I cannot see how that would be possible," Adam said. "I should never have come. My head is in a whirl, I cannot think straight when I stand so close to you."

Jeanette laughed. "We are safe here. See what your wife says, then return and we will talk about what is to be done. Will you tell her everything?"

"I have no idea what I will say yet, Jeanette. I fear another lie will not be good for my conscience. I am not sure how much my wife has mellowed over the years; I believe a short time ago, she would not have taken kindly to any suggestion of us taking in a young child, whatever the parenthood. She has, however, softened in the past two years," said the earl. "Had I told you everything this problem would not be have occurred?"

"I do not see Joe as a problem," she said.

"I did not word that well, I am sorry," he replied. "I meant that you would have walked away had I told you about Dorothia."

"I believe that you and I, both, know that this is not true. We were drawn to each other at first glance, I will not deny this even if you do," she said.

"What you say is true for me also," he replied. "I cannot deny that I would like to raise the boy if I could but what of you? I could not part you from the child."

"You can never part a mother and child in their hearts, that is an eternal bond, but for his better life, I would sacrifice my hold over him."

Adam looked down at the boy, who looked up at him with the same dark, soulful eyes of those of his mother. He felt immediately drawn to the boy, he looked at Jeanette and wondered how he could have been so foolish as to allow his life to take this path. Just as he was going to take his leave, Jeanette touched his arm and told him to tell his wife everything.

"No secrets must hang over our son. There must be no chance of any shame being brought to his head, he is innocent in this. If you cannot promise this, I keep him here where he is well loved," she said.

"I agree with you, my love," the earl replied and smiled at her.

He had intended to leave as soon as the boy tottered off out of the tent in search of adventures elsewhere, but he dallied and before long, found himself once more enfolded in his beautiful gypsy's arms. "You allow one so young to wander alone!" he said. "My daughter has a constant nanny watching her every move."

"That would not do for a gypsy's child. Birds are kept wrongly in cages, children should not suffer the same fate," she replied.

"But there are so many dangers out there," Adam said in a worried tone looking to where the child had been.

"And there are many wonderful adventures as well," she replied with a smile.

Adam kissed his beautiful gypsy with a pent up passion.

The earl left the camp and rode back to the manor, only to be confronted by Martin as he entered.

"Do not look at me like that, Martin, sometimes you forget that I am the master here," said the earl feeling guilty.

Martin apologised and walked away leaving the earl feeling wretched. He called after his man, who declined to hear and kept walking. The earl muttered under his breath that he had warned him that sometimes, the people who let you down are the ones you least expect. "I fight with my own conscience, please do not add yours to my burden," he called after him.

The earl waited until the following day to speak to his wife about the boy. He had been unable to sleep well thinking about the child, and how he could approach the subject. Martin had appeared at the door as usual to see if Adam needed anything before he retired, and this gave the earl a chance to apologise to his trusted aid.

"Martin, you always said that the gypsy would be my undoing and you were right."

"I thought that was all behind you, Sir," was the reply.

"And so did I," said the earl.

"You said Robbie had told you that she was married."

"He told me she had a child, he did not mention marriage."

"Maybe gypsies do not readily marry when they have children," replied Martin. "You know my views on their morals."

"They do not pass their sins onto their children, they put no blame on to someone who had no part in any shame. Children are simply enveloped by everyone and brought up by everyone," replied the earl.

"A rather nice sentiment, I cannot imagine it being encouraged outside of the confines of circus life."

"I have to agree with you there, Martin," said the earl. "I have not told you all."

"I suspected as much, Sir," was the reply.

"Do not judge me too harshly, Martin."

"It is not my place to judge anyone least of you, Sir," replied Martin. "I am happy to listen to anything you wish to share with me."

"You may change your mind after I begin. I foolishly went to the circus tonight and saw Jeanette, only to be confronted by a boy child that carries my blood line," he said.

"Are you sure, Sir?" was the alarmed reply.

"I am, Martin."

"And what do you propose to do, are you to be blackmailed?" asked Martin.

"You do have a very low opinion of these travellers," Adam replied. "No, there is no threat hanging over my head. But the boy is there and I long to be able to offer some assistance."

"Then give the girl some money and go back to Wetherley, Sir," Martin suggested.

"It may come to that, I will speak to Dory in the morning and see what she suggests," replied the earl.

"You are going to tell her about the boy?" Martin asked amazed. "You are a brave man, I wish you well with that."

The next morning, Adam approached Dory with the idea that there was a foundling in the circus that needed a home and wondered if she would consider the possibility of them taking him in. She was absolutely abhorred by the idea.

"You have given one foundling to the gypsies and now you want to take in another. How can this be?" she said quite annoyed by the idea. "I know you want a son but you cannot expect me to take in every ragamuffin to compensate. We will have our own boy given time. I am as sorry that I lost our boy, I wanted him more than life itself. It is not as if you are saving another who was begot by your wayward father, the problem is not yours and it will not be mine."

Adam asked if maybe they could find a home for the boy amongst their workers and just fund the boy's education from a distance but this did not meet with Dorothia's approval at all. "What is so special about this boy, Adam?" demanded Dory. "Why do the circus people not want him, does he have two heads? Oh no, silly me, he would fit in well then."

"I thought it was a way of thanking Georgiou and the circus people for their care of Robbie," replied Adam rather meekly. "He is not of full Romany blood so he does not fit in."

"He does not fit in here either, Adam," shouted Dory in reply. "Robbie is not of Romany blood and seems to have been accepted, tell them to clean up their own mess."

Adam opened his mouth to speak but thought better of it. Dory was so angry that he would not have been able to persuade her to think differently if he argued all night. She had never been so annoyed by a suggestion in her life, though she wasn't sure herself why it distressed her so much.

Adam did not approach the idea of the foundling again, she assumed that he did not want to risk pushing her over the edge and seeing her depression return. Sometimes, she actually feared for her own sanity.

A few days later, Dory, Martin, Adam and Seraphina took the carriage up to Keighley Moor to watch the circus. Adam had wanted to take Mrs Frost and little Kate as well, but Dory had insisted on a family outing only, she was annoyed enough that Martin had been included in the group. It was even more spectacular that the last time the earl had sat and watched. Dory and Seraphina were mesmerised but he was unable to show any interest. Blaming illness, he left the big top for a while and looked for Jeanette. They spoke for a while and a plan was formed that would change both their lives forever.

Chapter 44
The Beginning of the End

The young earl arranged for the rest of the Keighley household to visit the circus one evening and there was a great deal of excitement about this outing. Mrs Frost was allowed to include Seraphina in their group so long as she stay holding hands with Olive and Kate. Most of the group walked but the carriage took and collected Seraphina and her protectors, this was the only way Dory would agree to her being included. How different Adam thought to the upbringing of his wild, half-gypsy child.

Robbie continued to call at the manor house when he had a free moment and Dory made a point of talking to him. She was interested in the details surrounding the proposition her husband had made about the foundling child, but Robbie appeared to be quite ignorant of the whole affair.

"Children out of wedlock are not unusual in the Romany world, there are quite a number around the circus," Robbie explained to a shocked looking Dorothia. "The child is just taken on by the whole group, each teaching it something that will help him or her in later circus life."

"The mother is not forced to marry?" said Dory in an amazed voice. "Surely, the girl's father would insist on the man making an honest woman of his daughter!"

"Why should that be?" asked Robbie. "Why would you marry if you do not want to?"

"In my world, there is an unspoken honour," Dory explained. "If you have even discussed marriage, you have made a commitment that must be honoured. Sometimes, people commit too early and regret their actions but because it is the way of the world, they still marry." She was thinking of Adam as she spoke.

"But surely as you age, your desires change and that would include your choice of wife or husband," said Robbie seriously. "Before I joined the circus, I would have thought one way and now, I have experienced life; I can reason better and think more carefully about life decisions."

"You are wise beyond your years, young man," replied Lady Southerly.

"The earl taught me a great deal in the time I spent with him," replied Robbie with a smile that looked as though he was reliving memories. "He improved my written work, adding up and my look at life. His Lordship always thinks so well of people and it is hard to purposely disappoint him. The child you spoke of, my guess is, it would be Jeanette's bonny lad, she might want more for him than a circus life. Jeanette is the owner's daughter, my lord probably wanted to repay Georgiou for his kindness to me and thought educating his grandson might be a way to do this. It might even have been his idea, I do not know."

"You do have his mind, don't you, Robbie? My husband suggested himself that it would be a good way to thank the circus people," replied Lady Southerly. "I believe you might be right but I did not think kindly of the idea at all. I do not think the boy should be parted from his mother, surely it would make her very unhappy."

"I agree with you on that point, my Lady," said Robbie still smiling. "You always miss your mother, I have never forgotten mine though I can hardly remember her face and have long forgotten the sound of her voice. Just to think of her, sometimes, gives me a warm feeling inside. The master has been like a father to me, this has helped me greatly."

"I have seen the bond between you, you are a good and kind young man. Who would not want a son like you," said Dory sadly.

"I do miss my sister, Kitty, and would like to think I would see her again one day," said Robbie. "Maybe the circus will travel to France, can you imagine how wonderful that would be to travel to another land?"

"That is not something I desire," replied Dory as she felt her own spirits sink. "But I, like you, miss my sister and parents."

Adam, being an only child and a father who he would rather forget than would miss, had not taken into consideration the draw of family on his young wife. It was her greatest desire to return to Weston Manor Lodge and to her parents, grandmother and sister, regardless of the undercurrent of disapproval from most the villagers, but she could see that with every month in Keighley, the likelihood was slipping away and it did not help her state of mind.

Dory started to become even more unhappy in Yorkshire and spoke to her husband often about how she felt. As the young earl had realised, a long time ago, that he did not have any great feeling for the mill and with the coming of steam engines and mechanical looms, he discussed with Dory the possibility of taking a change of direction and selling the mills and weaving sheds in Yorkshire if he could get a good price. Dory saw that she had a chance to go home and happily fed her husband's desire to sell Southerly Mill. She hated the cold of Yorkshire and thought the people far too familiar.

"I know people were cruel to you in Weston-Under-Wetherley," she said to the earl. "But here, everyone is disrespectful, they speak to you as if you are their equal, this cannot be right."

"I believe all men are equal, wife," replied Adam. "It is only money and title that sets the divides."

"Do not be so ridiculous, Adam," said Dory angrily. "You pay the wages, they should treat you with respect, you are an earl after all."

"An accident of birth," Adam replied. "I do not think many people who knew my father would agree with you that being an earl makes someone a better man, quite the opposite I would guess."

Dory decided that she was wasting her time pursuing this conversation so she quietly crept away to the garden to compose herself.

She noticed that her husband was looking tired and spending a great amount of time talking to his man, Martin, about business; she was not included in and her dislike for Martin grew because of this. She considered the degree of intimacy that Adam shared with this man, who she considered to be a mere servant, really annoying, and she often told her husband so. Adam, however, always defended his man servant, which made Dory even more resentful of him.

Dory started to be very snappy and treated the servant quite appallingly, she only appeared to be graceful and polite if someone of consequence called. Adam's fear was that a bout depression might be on its' way, and he was not sure if he could or even wanted to deal with that alone. Adam spoke to his doctor about his wife and the doctor agreed that Lady Southerly would be much better if she had her family closer.

When the pair were alone one evening, Adam approached the subject of moving back to Weston-Under-Wetherley. "Dory, I am seriously thinking about selling Southerly Mill, I have been considering the cost of improvement and introducing machinery and am not sure what I should do for the best," he said as he faced her across the table. "I am not a business man as you know, I like the country life and farming more, but we need an income and the mill has served us very well for two generations."

"Are there other forms of business you could invest in instead?" asked his wife.

"Obviously, there are numerous," was the reply. "I have looked into some and have not found anything as yet that strike my fancy. I would like to be involved but have not seen anything that I feel I would be able to really take an interest in, not since my old friend, Lang Fox's, business venture and that seems like a lifetime ago."

"Maybe simply running a farm like James and Rosamond would suit you," Dory suggested.

"I don't think so, James was born into farming. I would like to invest in the arts but think it is maybe not the solution."

"I should think not, Adam," was the reply. "Your new French friends have put that idea in your mind, or maybe Martin has suggested that a visit to Paris might lift your mood."

Adam just sighed and ignored the last remark.

"I do feel though, Madam, that you need the support of your family and our daughter should get to know her grandparents and cousins, I have selfishly kept you here long enough, I have no family to miss."

"We are your family," said Dory.

"You are, of course. We will all go back to Weston Manor Lodge if you so desire to do so," Adam said. "I would request that you take Seraphina and go on ahead, whilst I sort out the mill. It should not take too long to find a forward thinking buyer. I would like a week or so to consider whether I should set in motion either the upgrading of the mill or the sale; although I have no great interest in the running of the mill, it has given my family a very good income for a lot of years so it is not an easy decision to make."

Dorothia nodded in agreement.

"I will join you as soon as I have decided which path to take regarding the mill. I believe that I can get a buyer for Southerly Mill and weaving sheds, I am reliably told that it will be easy to sell at this time," Adam said to Dory.

"Martin and I have been discussing the possibilities and I have spoken to my advisors on the subject."

"Martin, again he knows things before me," she replied with venom.

"Of course he does, woman," Adam replied in a frustrated voice. "Who do you think I send to discover things for me? I do not tramp all over the county on my own, that is what I pay Martin for." This was not strictly true but the earl knew it was the sort of answer that his wife needed to hear.

"The circus will be packing to leave in another week or so, so I will see Robbie and tell him our plans," Adam smiled as he spoke.

Dory was more than happy to go on ahead to Weston-Under-Wetherley but only on the reassurance that her husband was not going to change his mind and want to be running back to Keighley.

"No more running away, Dory," he said. "I know where my future lies and I will make sure that everything runs smoothly towards that goal."

"In that case, Husband," replied Dory cheerfully, "I will happily pack the family treasures and organise their removal from here back to Weston Manor Lodge. I only hope that your business does not delay you too long and you can join us as soon as possible. I will write immediately to my father and tell him we are returning, he will be so pleased."

"Tell your father from me that I would ask him to take very good care of you and our daughter in my absence," said Adam. "Tell him that I cannot say for sure when I will see him again but that I always valued his advice over the years."

Dory was a little puzzled by the last comment made by her husband but assumed he was tired and had a lot of work to do negotiating a good price for his mill interests.

"You make it sound as though you anticipate a long absence for home, whilst you sell here," she said.

"I simply do not want your father to worry if I am away longer than I, at first, hoped; I need to know that someone will be looking to your aid if necessary," he replied. "Sometimes, weeks turn into months before we realise it."

"You must do what you feel is best for you, Adam. I know your heart is not in the mill trade but you could surely find someone to handle any updating necessary to keep up with the modern world," Dory said. "Surely your solicitor can handle any financial dealings for you, I assume that is what you pay him for."

"There is more to think about than just the selling of the mill, there are people's livelihoods to secure with any sale and training if updating is the way forward," replied Adam. "Most of my mill hands have worked the same way for years, they may not find it easy to adjust to new ways."

"Oh for goodness sake, Adam, if they cannot be retrained, then they will have to look elsewhere for work," Dory said exasperatedly. "Surely you do not mean to turn down a good sale if the terms mean your workers have to find other employment."

"I mean that exactly, woman," was the reply. "In fact, I have already crossed that bridge."

"You really are a very strange man," she continued. "You do not have to forever be seen as the opposite to your father, it is about time you laid that ghost to rest."

"George Southerly will never rest, he will haunt me forever."

"Only if you let him," she replied.

"What do you suggest I do then woman?" Adam asked in a quite frustrated tone. "Sell the mills and throw all my loyal workers onto the scrap heap if the price is right?"

"That is what a sane man would do, Adam," she replied.

"I am not sure you are the right person to speak of sanity, Madam," replied the earl surprising himself with his cruel answer. "I am sorry I said that, Dory."

"I am fully aware of the problems I have caused, I lost our son and could not cope, I nearly lost my mind."

Adam was so sorry that he had brought up the problem of her delicate mind. "Do not think on the child any more, it is gone, past, forgotten."

"Not forgotten by me, never forgotten by me."

"You have to move on, Dory," Adam said. "Life moves on, let it, don't dwell on the past."

"It is maybe a good job that we did not take in Jeanette's child, a constant reminder of my failings might have made me even more annoying," Dory said strangely.

Adam was shocked. "What do you know of Jeanette and her child?" he said looking astonished.

"I know nothing," Dory replied. "Only what Robbie told me."

"And what pray did Robbie tell you?"

"Only that he thought because you had asked me to take in a baby from the circus, it might be hers as she is the owner's daughter, and you might feel educating the child might be a way of repaying the debt," she replied.

"What debt?" he replied. He was now standing and looking quite disturbed.

"The debt you feel you own him for taking Robbie and looking after him," she replied. "Why do you look so annoyed, Adam? It was only in conversation that I had with Robbie, but it made me understand why you wanted to help this baby."

"What else did he tell you about the child? Does he know who the father is?"

"I did not ask the boy, he said it was not uncommon for gypsy women to bare children and not tell who the father is," Dory replied. "A strange life style young Robbie now lives in and he seems to accept every aspect of it. I cannot say I approve but there."

Adam sat back down looking quite relieved.

"Back to the sale of the mills," said Dory not noticing anything was amiss.

"Possible sale," added Adam. "I have not decided for sure yet which path to take. I have been looking into the possibly sale for a few months now, the coming of engines has spurred me on. I have been offered a glove making factory in part exchange, I know even less about that industry. Martin said that I could be jumping out of the fireplace into the fire."

"Do you still take advice from Martin, what would he know about business?"

"About as much as me, I would guess," Adam replied. "He will listen to me as I talk through ideas."

"I would happily listen but you do not bring your ideas to my door, you would rather take them to your servant," Dory said venomously. "Your first loyalty is to your family, not to your workers and servants."

"My loyalty is to whoever deserves it," Adam said exasperated. "I will not see my workers on the streets, I would rather starve myself than cause misery to others. I have seen enough of what people can do to others through selfish desires."

"And you question my sanity," replied Dory annoyed.

"Now we have it, you have helped me without realising it," he said with a smile. "People have thought me mad for a while, maybe I am. I believe my sanity will be doubted by a great many people in the near future. I feel a great weight has been lifted from me." With that strange reply, Adam left his wife to organise the removal of all valuables from Keighley Manor to Weston Manor Lodge.

Chapter 45
Paris

Dorothia was happily organising the packing of her most treasured possessions, believing it was her final move back to Weston-Under-Wetherley. She was more than happy to go on ahead and leaving her husband to either sell or simply re-organise his business interests in Yorkshire, however long it might take him.

Dory, Seraphina and the servants, they had brought from Wetherley, were soon ready for the long haul back to the property in the South.

Adam did, in fact, have a great deal of business to contract. His first visit was to his solicitor to draw up some papers for him. He made the Wetherley Manor Lodge and land surrounding it over to Dorothia and put the mill up for sale. He also tied up the loose ends surrounding a trust fund for Seraphina that would come to her when she was either 25 or married. The earl had fulfilled his promise to his friend, Edward Lang Fox, and helped him fund a project in Weston-Super-Mare in exchange for his aid with this fund for his daughter. It included shares in glass making company and the part ownership of certain canals amongst other things.

The earl put the manor in Keighley up for rent with the provisory that the old staff stay on. This was to fund his future life style.

The earl had already been without his wife in Keighley for nearly two weeks before word reached him of a buyer for Southerly Mill and weaving sheds.

Martin had stayed with the earl and was living as though in a dream, wondering what was to become of his friend and master. He feared that he had gone mad. His total loyalty kept his thoughts to himself.

Once, Adam was clear in his mind how things were going to be, he sat Martin down to explain.

"I have had to make life changing decisions and I have thought long and hard about them," the earl began. "You will think me quite queer in the attic, I know. I have a buyer for the mill, it needs upgrading and I do not have the inclination. I would have sold Southerly Mill, whatever else occurred in my life, I feel it is the right time. We all know that machinery is the way forward, machines that do the work of men and women are not well thought of. Ever since the Swing Riots, a couple of years ago, I have thought about selling the mill. All those agricultural workers destroying the new wonder threshing machines to save their jobs in Kent. Hundreds of once hard-working men sentenced to death or deportation, rioting because they were starving. It will happen in the mills, people do not like change and if change costs them their livelihood, they riot." The earl stopped for breath. "Pierre told me about France and the riots that break out there from time to time. We live in troubled times. I abhor child labour but know that they work to put food on the table when they should be learning their letters."

Martin started to speak but was stopped in his tracks.

"You and I know the mill needed updating, why else would all those injuries occur and I was considering selling anyway. Southerly Mill and weaving sheds have housed, Arkwright water frames and the spinning jenny, but the steam engine will bring bigger changes. New machinery is now coming into fashion, new-style engines to drive looms and I have no head for this sort of business. My grandfather lived and died for the mill; unfortunately, like my father, I have no interest in it. Time to hand the reins over to someone who will bring the old place up to date. Ever since they opened the Liverpool to Manchester railway, I have thought long and hard about the way engines will rule our lives. People will object but it will happen. I cannot fill my head with how I can find work for everyone. I want a little peace in my life."

"I agree, Sir, we have seen strange times and you could be right about the mill," was the reply.

"I insisted that Simon Gibbs stays on as part of the deal, I have made no such provisions for Matthew Morgan as I care nothing for the man," continued Adam.

"There is no guarantee that as soon as papers are signed and you are no longer close by that, Simon will not be dismissed. After all, when you sell the mill, you have no say in its operation."

"You may be right, Martin, do you have any idea how I can keep the young man safe?" asked Adam.

"He is good with figures, could he not find employment with an accountant? He could undergo training surely," was the suggestion.

"That is an inspired idea, better still, maybe I could set him up in his own practice that is maybe a bit ambitious. I have it, I will buy him into a partnership. I believe that he will be happy with this plan. Once I have something in place, I might require you to give him the news," continued the earl. "I have put this manor up for rent providing the new leaseholder retained Mr and Mrs Frost and the rest of the present staff. I am not sure if I will ever return."

"You mean to leave Yorkshire altogether, Sir?" asked Martin amazed. "Surely Lady Southerly is not aware of this."

"You are right, she is not," replied Adam. "I only decided upon this course of action for sure after she left for Wetherley, though I have had an idea forming in my mind for a while. I am telling you, Martin, because I value you above all other men."

"I am honoured, Sir, and I go where you go, if that is what you require of me," was the answer.

"You may not want to when I tell you all," continued the earl. "I have said on more than one occasion that sometimes, the people who let you down are not always the ones you expect, and I am about to prove this by letting everyone down badly."

Martin looked confused. "I do not understand, Sir."

"You will when I tell you that I am not returning to Weston-Under-Wetherley, in fact, I will never be able to return there ever."

"What have you done?" asked Martin alarmed.

"Nothing as yet but soon I leave for Paris and I am taking Jeanette and my son with me."

"The gypsy!" exclaimed Martin. "You have chosen the gypsy over your wife and child?"

"I know I have disappointed you, Martin, you are a good and honest man and this is a lot for you to take in."

Martin was stunned into silence.

"I foolishly returned to the circus as you know, you advised me against it but I went," explained the earl. "Quite by chance, I came across Jeanette, I did not seek her out. But it was during this chance meeting I discovered that I had a son by her, as I told you. There is something about the boy, I cannot explain. I tried to persuade Dorothia to take the boy in, telling her that he was a foundling, needing a home. I even asked if I could bring the boy and show him to her."

"I did not think she would accept that plan," replied Martin.

"She did not, I saw a fury that I did not know she possessed. Maybe it was too soon after the loss of our would-be son, the wound was too fresh."

"I know I asked you before but are you quite sure that the boy is yours, Sir?" asked Martin shocked.

"Times, dates, all add up and the boy looks like me. Anyway, Jeanette tells me it is mine and I have no reason to doubt her," was the reply. "Also, I felt drawn to him in a way I cannot describe to you."

"Could you not have taken the boy in as you did Robbie with the help of Mrs Frost?" Martin asked concerned. "Maybe because Lady Southerly would not have him, asked Mrs Frost to keep him for you, she would not ask too many questions."

"I did consider that and when I spoke to Dory about us taking in a foundling and she was adamant that it could not happen, I also asked if maybe I could house the babe close by and keep an eye on him. It just enraged her more," said the earl. "Also, the boy has the look of me about him. It would not take long before tongs wagged and people whispered behind their hands about him. Either way, it would be the end of me."

"So what is the plan?" asked Martin concerned.

"I see no solution that involves Dory, she refused to help with the boy as a foundling, and I guarantee that she would surely be even less inclined towards the child if she suspects he is mine," replied the earl sadly. "She told me that I should stop taking on other people's problems and concentrate on my own life, it was actually this statement that triggered my present actions. We are not long on this earth and maybe we owe it to ourselves to be happy as well."

"But at what cost?" replied Martin. "Do you think she suspected the boy, you spoke of, is yours?"

"I think not, her anger at the suggestion was directed towards the firm belief that she did not want a substitute son," Adam replied. "I have tried so hard, Martin. My Father has left his mark and it is one I cannot erase. When I see such unjust hate directed my way, it is hard. I am not my father. There are those that will think I am now I have chosen this path, but I cannot live with so much animosity surrounding my every move."

Martin felt a wave of pity for his friend and master.

"Jeanette understands," continued the earl. "She is a gypsy so she is used to people assuming that she is dishonest because she has Romany blood, though she has never acted dishonestly in her life. She told me straight away that Joseph was mine but she did not ask anything of me. She has ran the gauntlet of many a farmer, whose prize cow is not giving the milk they should, blaming it on a gypsy curse. People distrust her because she is a gypsy. She is a great beauty and women hate her for that. Away from the circus life will be a tough place for someone who does not quite fit in. I do fear a little for her if she tries to fit into a world outside of the circus, where she is protected. I believe she will be accepted in France for her exotic looks and charm in a way it would never happen here in England. From what Pierre tells me, there is much more acceptance of differences and it is a much more easy going life style."

"France, you are definitely going to Paris and join Pierre?"

"That is my plan, Martin," was the amazing reply.

"Surely though, Sir," began Martin. "You leave your wife and child to face the backlash of your actions, will she not be treated badly as you have, but she will also not have you to support her."

"I have considered this and believe, like my mother, the people will not blame her; I fear they will pity her, which she will not like," replied the earl. "She does have her family and her father, the vicar is well loved and respected. I am particularly sorry to let him down."

"He has watched you struggle, Sir," was the reply.

"He has and he has also defended me in the pulpit on more than one occasion," continued Adam. "I would like to have spoken to him before I left but could not bear to see the disappointment in his eyes. He is a great believer in the marriage vows."

"What will you do about marriage, pretend?" asked Martin.

"I am assured by Pierre that the French do not have the same high principles that we English support. That is why, he had no qualms about marrying Camille despite her past if it was ever revealed; not as if her past was of her choosing, once more, it was down to my father. I signed Wetherley Manor Lodge over to Dorothia without her knowledge to secure her life, just in case anything untoward happened to me, and I have made provisions for Seraphina when she is of age. I can do no more."

"Of course, you can, you can stay and be a husband and father," replied Martin shocked.

"No, I cannot," was the reply. "I cannot and will not live without Jeanette, I do not want to even try."

"I always thought you were a better man....." began Martin.

"Than my father, you were going to say," was the reply.

"Even he did not run away, he stayed with your mother."

"We will never know what he would have done in time," replied Adam. "I should never have married Dorothia, I had made up my mind not to ask her when she came to me. I had strong doubts about my strength of character having met Jeanette. I thought if I married, the old feeling I had for Dory would return. I had admired her for a number of years, her carriage, her looks, but then I met Jeanette and I realised that what I felt for Dory was contentment and comfort, whereas what I feel for Jeanette is a burning desire to be with her, a love I never believed was anything more than a fairy tale. I cannot explain. It is not if you can live with someone, it is can you live without them that you have to ask yourself."

"What of your daughter?" said Martin. "She will be heartbroken to learn that you chose a son over her."

"She will never learn the whole truth and I am ashamed of my behaviour to the child. I do not know if I would have gone with Jeanette without the child, God knows I wanted to. It was the boy that is making me take the action I intend," replied the earl. "My daughter is young and I will soon be a distant memory to her. If Dory's mother has her way, I doubt my name will ever be uttered in front of the child again."

"Does Robbie know of your plans?" asked Martin.

"Jeanette is going to tell him for me and ask him if he fancies an adventure and a chance to see Kitty. I would like the boy to come but the plan does not stand or fall on his decision."

Martin listened in silence, looking deep in thought.

"I understand that you do not wish to come with me, and I do not blame you for this. You have been my conscience and my friend and I have let you down very badly," said the earl. "I leave for Paris a week next Wednesday, if you decide to join us, I will be most pleased but understand if you choose to stay here."

"Who will take word to Lady Southerly?" asked Martin.

"I have arranged for my solicitors clerk to take the deeds to Wetherley Manor Lodge to her with a note. It is not good, I know that, but I cannot face her."

"I would have gone for you," said Martin.

"I know but it would be too much to ask of you. She would ask all sorts of questions and you would find it impossible to lie, I would not put you in that position," was the reply. "Also, you are not her favourite person though, goodness knows why she holds you in contempt. I fear that she would have spat a great deal of venom in your direction. You have been a loyal friend and I would not have liked that to happen. I know it is not what a gentleman of breeding should do, but if I stay, I will only hate Dorothia, the child will suffer as a result and all that will happen is that we will all be miserable for the rest of our lives."

"I can see you are right about that, Sir," replied Martin thoughtfully.

Tuesday saw the earl writing what looked like endless letters to all and sundry to explain his absence. He wrote to James and Rosamond apologising for his behaviour and explaining to James fully that how Jeanette had captured his heart. He knew that Sally had affected James in the same way and hoped that he would understand. He had already written ahead to Pierre Conte, who was to meet the party at Calais. He wrote a note to Mrs Frost to give her at the last moment and enclosed a year's wages; he would have liked to have spoken to her but he knew that he could not face her tears. He told her that Keighley Manor was to be leased out, but she was to remain if she wished and that he would write to her.

The last problem was arranging an accountancy appointment for Simon Gibbs, he was a little old for an apprenticeship as such, but the earl had persuaded a firm in Wakefield to take him on and train him. He was sure that Simon would not let him down. Martin went to seek Simon out and ask him if the arrangements made on his behalf were satisfactory. Martin explained that the mill was in the process of being sold and although a promise had been extracted to keep the present employees in situ, the earl was worried that once he had put his name to the deal, the new owners might not fulfil this obligation.

"The earl has always treated me so very well, I do not deserve this," Simon said. "Who will guard the children?"

"It is understood that engines will replace many hands, things will not stay the same," explained Martin to Simon. "My master just wanted to make sure that you were safe."

Simon looked very puzzled. "I am so very grateful but I do wonder at his kindness."

"He liked you from day one and he believes you to be an honest young man, that is all," replied Martin. "The earl is inclined to treat people, he care about, well as a rule. He also asked me to hand you this package. It is a small amount of money that you might require to help you find accommodation if needs be and a little for your mother."

Simon just stood with his mouth open, staring at the package, unable to speak. The two men shook hands and Martin left the young man to go to his home and tell his mother of his good fortune.

Adam left his solicitor to deal with his finances and was now settled in his mind that everyone would be safe financially without him. His mind drifted to his father for a moment and he smiled thinking of how foolish he would have thought his son was, worrying about anyone else but himself.

A week later and the earl was packed to leave. He had organised a ship in Hull to take his party privately, he had enough money not to have to book a passage like everyone else. He looked around the old house for what he assumed might be the last time. He walked slowly down the stairway and came face to face with Martin, luggage by his side. The two men embraced, nothing was said. Then the earl noticed a woman in her middle 30s and a young boy of about 14 by her side. They looked strangely familiar.

Martin took the earl aside. "You may remember the widow Sparkes and her young son, Tim, who you helped when he lost his fingers in your mill," he said.

"I remember, Martin, I believe she planned to marry a widower," was the reply. "But I have also tasted her wonderful cakes, which I believe are sold locally."

"Marriage was the original plan, Sir, but I have been helping her and Tim financially since that moment we met, and with the money she got from her baking, she no longer felt she had to take that path."

"Clearly, I have been over paying you," said the earl with a wide smile. "And now you plan to make an honest woman of her?"

"She is a couple of years older than I am and the boy is now nearly 15, but she is a sensible woman, hardworking, has fine bone structure, happy disposition and best of all, a wonderful cook and seamstress; you will need such a woman," was the reply. "Now I know that we are leaving for a place so far away, beyond my imagination, I felt I did not want to have to say goodbye to her."

"And why the devil should you, man, I am happy for you both," replied Adam. "Introduce me to her properly, Martin."

Martin walked over to the woman, who looked nervous, picked up her hand and led her over to where the earl was standing. She curtsied in a graceful way.

"Sir, this is Betty, my wife. Do not look so surprised, I too can make decisions in a hurry, we married by special licence two days ago."

Betty flashed the earl a brilliant smile and bobbed another quick curtsy.

"I believe we all leave on an equal footing now. I do not know if my being an earl will help me in Paris, I know my money will," said Adam. "Does Tim come with us?"

"Begging your pardon, Sir," said Betty with another curtsy. "He has the choice to stay with my brother and has not made up his mind. He has the problem with his hand and that may make working in a strange place harder for him."

The earl turned to the boy and asked him if he was considering coming on an adventure, sailing away with the runaways, and Tim replied that he was a bit scared of what may become of him.

"You will grow to be a fine young man," replied the earl. "That is what will become of you and in my service if you please."

Tim went to his mother's side and hugged her. "I will come with you if that is alright with you, Mother. Now you have married, you may not want me."

"Foolish boy," replied his mother. "I will always want you."

"I am more than happy to gain a son if you can accept me," said Martin gently to Tim.

"It seems we both gain a son," said Adam to Martin quietly.

"Robbie is making his mind up as to whether he wishes to come with us and join his sister, so a companion for him would be very much appreciated."

All that was needed now was to load the coach, which had the earl's finest mare tied to the back of it. Everything else, that Adam felt, was needed was loaded onto a series of horse-drawn carriages.

Adam had left instructions for the barouche and gig to be sent to Weston-Upon-Wetherley for Dorothia to either sell or keep along with the horses. The carriage with the family crest that was to take the runaways to the coast was to be sent to the nunnery for Sister Teresa to sell or keep as she saw fit. Adam looked at the house and hoped that he had thought of everything. He took Martin aside for a moment. "I know I will never be forgiven by a great many people," he said, "and nor should I be, but I have tried to do my best for everyone. Selfishly, I have put my own interests above all others, and I am glad that you have decided to stay at my side, I thank you for your loyalty."

"I can see that it has been a hard decision for you, Sir, and I cannot say that I think it is the right one, but you battled long and hard to raise the family name, only to see your efforts shot down time and time again," replied Martin. "I feel you deserve credit for your efforts and a happy future. Let us all pray that we have all taken the right path. As for loyalty, it is gained, Sir."

Adam smiled and sighed with relief as he climbed aboard the carriage.

Mrs Frost watched them leave, clutching a sealed envelope, very confused by all the activity and uncomfortable in her mind.

The runaways stopped close to Keighley Moor to pick up their last passengers, Jeanette and Joe, and as it turned out, Robbie and Daisy had decided to join the earl on this adventure. Robbie had been told that there were circuses in France that maybe he could join once he learnt the language.

"I can keep you all entertained on the voyage," said the boy producing his juggling clubs.

No one took a backward glance, the plan was in action and there was no turning back.

It was an easy passage to Calais and all went to plan the other end. Pierre was there, as arranged, to take the group and possessions on to Paris, where he had rented Adam a house. Robbie and Tim became firm friends and Robbie took a great delight in teaching the other boy how to juggle, not terribly well because of the lack of all his fingers. During the hours gathered together on board, Martin softened to Jeanette as the earl knew he would, and Betty seemed quite comfortable with her life's decision, although the thought of having to learn the French language and customs frightened them all to different degrees.

Kitty was delighted to be re-united with her brother and Pierre realised instantly that Robbie had a similar look to his sister and would also be wanted as an artist model amongst his group of friends, if they could get him to sit still long enough.

Very quickly, all thoughts of England were wiped from the earl's memory, only the news that Edward Lang Fox had died before they had been a year in Paris brought him back to earth.

Being an earl set Adam in good stead in Paris. He was financially stable having sold a great many of his family assets, he had bought shares in the new railway system so he was quite happy with his decision. After the revolution, that had taken the lives of many titled people in France including the royal family, came another revolution that reinstated the aristocrats as the leading lights, so Adam had arrived in Paris at the right time. Jeanette was introduced to all and sundry as the Countess Southerly, much to her amusement and slight embarrassment.

Adam had written to his good friend, Sir James Sheppard, at Weston-Super-Mare apologising for being such a coward and not going to see him face to face to tell him the fact. Sir James was one person that the earl regretted leaving behind and regretted even more deceiving him this way. He had felt compelled to tell his friend, in a very long letter, everything that was planned and hoping that he would understand why he had chosen the route he had. James was a very kindly person, who could always see everybody's points of view and always tried hard not to judge others. He sent Adam a swift reply via Adam's solicitor, telling him that he would keep an eye on Dory and report to him if anything happened that might be of relevance.

As soon as he was settled, Adam intended to send Sir James his address; this privilege would not be given to anyone else, but Adam trusted James above all other men, except possibly Martin.

Chapter 46
The Deeds Arrive

The first few weeks in Weston Manor Lodge were busy ones for Dorothia as she re-organised her life there. She hardly noticed that she had not heard from her husband. Then, as time went on, she began to worry. She sent messages to Keighley but did not receive any replies.

Weeks became months and still there was no word. Dory did not know what she should do. She did not want to bother her parents, she did not want them to know that she had not heard from Adam, knowing that her mother would have something caustic to say on the subject.

Dory woke one morning with a particularly bad headache and was about to retire back to her bedroom when she was informed that one of the senior work hands, Brian Locke, was at the front door asking to speak to 'the mistress urgently'. He had come to tell her that the earl's gig and the barouche along with the matching horses had arrived at the manor. Dory was thrilled as she knew how much Adam prized his horses and thought it was a sign that the master would be close behind.

She thanked Locke and told him to take good care of the horses as the master would be sure to follow quickly afterwards. She spent the rest of the day feeling quite light headed, her headache had disappeared and she was hopeful that she would be re-united with her husband very soon. More time passed, still without word. She still supposed that Adam would soon follow the horses and appear at Weston Manor Lodge as planned; she firmly believed that something in Yorkshire was causing him a problem making leaving Keighley difficult, she just wished that he would write and tell her what it was.

A couple of weeks later, Dory had been out riding and when she returned, she saw a strange, formal-looking young gentleman standing on the steps of Weston Manor Lodge talking to her housekeeper Mrs Warner. Dory dismounted and led her horse over to where the two were in heavy conversation. Mrs Warner looked up with a look that said she was very pleased to see her mistress.

"Madam," she said, "this gentleman is Mister Simon Harris sent from the solicitors Foster and Newman of York. He has been here for what seems like an eternity. He would not leave his parcel, he said that he had to hand it to you, Madam, and no one else."

"Good heavens," replied Dorothia. "What could be so important?" Fear shook her whole body as she spoke, fear that this man from York had come to tell her that her husband had died. She could think of no other reason for his presence on her doorstep. She suddenly felt herself slipping into a faint.

When Dory woke, she was lying on a couch in the drawing room being fussed over by her maid, Kate.

"Oh, Madam," Kate said in earnest, "you gave me such a turn when they carried you in, I thought you had taken a tumble from your horse."

Dory smiled at her faithful young maid. "I am so sorry to have worried you, Kate, I just had a strange turn. I imagined there was a solicitor to see me and I feared for the earl. Too much sun maybe."

"No, Madam, it was not imagination, he is here," replied Kate. "I do hope and pray you are wrong about the master though."

"Fetch the fellow, Kate," said Dory. "Let us see what horrors he brings us."

Kate hurried from the room and quickly returned with the Mr Harris, the young man from Foster and Newman, who looked like a very junior clerk and was clutching a parcel wrapped in brown paper and tied and sealed in a formal manner. He walked over to Dorothia and stood very quietly waiting to be asked to speak.

"Well, man," she said quite forcefully, "you have managed to scare me half to death, what do you want from me?"

The young man stuttered nervously as he spoke, "I have been charged with delivering this package into your hands and your hands only, Madam. I have ridden from York and have put up in the inn nearby but am told not to expect a reply."

"You have come all this way," said Dory, "and do not expect a reply! What is the contents of this package, why all the mystery?"

"I am au fait with the contents and am instructed to answer any questions you care to ask about it," the young man said as he handed Dory the package.

Kate stepped forward and handed Dory a paper knife, which she used to slit open the package. Inside were a great many formal looking papers and the deeds to Weston Manor Lodge.

Dory stared at the papers that were now sharing a large portion of the couch where she had been placed. "What does this mean? Had my husband met with an accident?" she asked in earnest.

"I believe he was well when he left our offices, Madam," was the reply. "If you look closely, you will see that the Earl of Wetherley has made the deeds to this property over to you."

Dory looked at the papers before her and, with wide eyes, looked up at the young clerk. "For what purpose?" she asked.

"I do not understand the question, Madam," he replied.

"Then I will speak slowly, young man," replied Dory, now quite annoyed. "Why has my husband turned this house over to me? Does he return or does he stay in Yorkshire?"

"I am sorry, Madam," replied the clerk. "I cannot answer that question. Sometimes, if a man goes bankrupt, he makes his property over to his wife to save it."

"Are you telling me that the earl has lost his money or anticipates that he might?" Dory asked, looking the young man straight in the eyes.

"I honestly do not know, Madam," was the reply. "I was told only to bring you the parcel and tell you that the manor was now yours to do as you wish with."

"What would I wish to do? Where is my husband?"

"I understand that he is negotiating a business deal in Keighley and wanted you to have this manor house and that is all the information I have," was the reply.

Dory sprang to her feet. "Then be gone, you useless item," she screamed at the frightened young man. "If you remember anything of use to me, you may return but if not, I do not wish to look at your silly face for one more second."

"I was told to say that the contents of the manor are also yours to do with as you see fit," the young man said with a quake in his voice. "Also, the horses and carriages that would have reached you previously are also now yours."

"And what of the earl, does he still live in Keighley?" Dory asked the young man. She stood very upright with her hands on her hips and looked quite formidable as she was at least two inches taller than the nervous clerk.

"I only know what I have been told, Madam, all that I mentioned is now yours," the young man said, wanting very much to be gone from the manor. "Where the earl now lives, I cannot say, I do not have that knowledge."

"It strikes me that you do not know a lot. I know that they have sent a boy to do a man's job, and I do not wish to converse with such an ill-informed person." She stepped closer to the clerk as she spoke.

With that, the young man fled the building.

With the arrival of the deeds to Weston Manor Lodge now in her name, Dorothia wondered if her husband had no intension of following her to their summer home. She was confused, angry and upset.

She had received just the one letter from Adam in all the time he had been absent, just a few weeks after she had left him in Keighley conducting business; it explained that there were a few problems, and repeated that he did not feel he had the inclination to move his mill into the present time and introduce new machinery and that he was considering selling the mill and weaving sheds but it was of no concern of hers and she need not worry. He explained that the new industrial age of machinery was making his mill obsolete, and he needed to either upgrade it or sell it to someone with more vision than him. She had such total faith in him that she just assumed that things were taking longer than planned. There had been no mention of Weston Manor Lodge and his intention to make the property over to her.

She thought long and hard about the events of the day and was very annoyed and stressed. After she had calmed herself, she went to see her father and face all the "I told you so, blood will out" comments from her mother, Bathsheba.

The mill had been sold, that much was obvious, Weston Manor Lodge had been signed over to Dorothia and Lord Adam Southerly, the Earl of Wetherley, had disappeared off the face of the earth for all intents and purposes, having left his wife and child well protected financially.

Dory hurried to the rectory leaving Seraphina in the care of Kate and Olive. Dory's father pointed out to his distressed daughter that it was obvious that the earl knew that Dory would not need to re-marry to be kept in the style she had become accustomed, he had at least seen to her safety financially.

"So I am safe financially from would be fortune hunters because I can afford to turn them away," she said to her father in reply to his observations. "But what of my mental health? Do I just sit and worry about where Adam may or may not be? Has he lost his money and cannot face us? Is he ill and does not wish to burden us? Has he in fact chosen to end his life, setting me free? What am I to think or believe?"

"Think, child," replied Phillip. "Did he behave strangely when you last saw him, was there any indication that something was amiss?"

"Not really, Father," she replied after a moment's thought. "He told me that he intended to sell the mills because of the changes taking place and his lack of knowledge and interest in the industry."

"That I can understand," said Phillip. "There is a lot of unrest at the moment, amazing machines are being invented but they are putting people out of work and making a lot of unease amongst farming folk as well as mill people. Adam could be right, maybe his family may have outstayed their time in the mill industry; after all, it was his grandfather who started Southerly Mill and his father took no interest at all. Obviously, he never told Adam anything about the running of such a business."

"I doubt George Southerly knew or care so long as the revenue reached his pockets," said Dory with a smile. "He hardly spoke to Adam, least of all discuss business matters. No doubt, the old earl thought that he would live forever, he certainly had no fear of the here-after or he would have lived a better life."

"That is true, child," replied Phillip laying his arm gently across his daughter's shoulders as he spoke. "Let us, at this time, give Adam the benefit of the doubt, there could be a very straight forward explanation for his present behaviour. The young clerk could have been right, maybe the mills are unsalable because they are out of touch and he fears a great loss when he sells. Sensibly, he would send his most valued assets to you here, his horses and his home in Wetherley."

Dory smiled widely and agreed with her father that maybe he was right, and she should put more trust in her husband and give him time to organise himself and return to her. She left the rectory a lot happier than she had arrived.

Poor Dory could not understand why the months dragged on and she still had no word from her husband. As another winter approached and she was alone with Seraphina in Wetherley, she was now starting to really worry. Letters that she wrote were never replied to or returned. She began to fear that Adam was dead, she could see no other explanation.

Regardless of anything that came before, as far as Dory was concerned, she and her husband were happy enough and his disappearance came as a great shock. She had suffered from depression on two occasions, after giving birth to Seraphina and secondly, after her miscarriage of a near full-term still born boy. She wondered if these happenings contributed to the earl's disappearance.

Chapter 47
The Hunt Is On

Dory's father, the Reverend Phillip Mountjoy, could no longer sit back and watch his daughter worry and listen to his wife telling him that she had been right all along and that the earl was a 'bad lot'. He organised a visit to Keighley Manor to find out for himself why the errant earl seemed to have disappeared. They had, he thought, been friends and he was beyond disappointment that he may have been wrong in that thought.

Phillip arrived in Keighley in a flurry of snow and was greeted at the door by Clarkson, who was extremely amazed to see the vicar standing on the doorstep alone in such terrible weather. Phillip explained who he was and where he had come from and that he was seeking the where-about of the Earl of Southerly. Clarkson was not sure what to do, so he asked the vicar in but was unable to get advice from his new master as he and his family had gone down south for the winter. The house was all but closed, dust clothes were covering the majority of the furniture.

There was nothing to do but to take the vicar down to Mrs Frost in the kitchen, at least he could be given a hot meal. Mr and Mrs Frost ran Keighley Manor previously for Adam and now for the new people who rented the manor. Mrs Frost was willing as usual to help anyone and a man in a dog collar would have been top of her list.

"My dear Sir," she said, "please be seated. I have a pot luck boiling on the side here. I think a bowl of the hot pot and a glass of sherry might be just what you need."

"An explanation of what is happening here is what I need most," said the man wearily.

Mrs Frost placed a bowl of stew like substance, a large chunk of bread and a spoon in front of Phillip, whilst she went to look for the letters that the earl had left when he departed so suddenly. Phillip muttered grace almost under his breath before he dunked a piece of the still warm bread into the steaming bowl. After a short time, Mrs Frost returned clutching several letters.

"The earl left unexpectedly, I thought that he was going to Weston-Under-Wetherley to join his family but the letter he left told a different story." She handed a letter to Phillip, it had obviously been read many times as it was quite crumpled and there were a few smudges; later, he was told that they were from tears shed by Mrs Frost.

Phillip read the letter quietly to himself, whilst taking spoonfuls of the much appreciated food, asking occasional questions. "How come the man was able to tell you more than he told his own wife?"

"I do not know, Sir," was the reply. "We were as amazed as you. I had no idea that the master intended to let Keighley Manor and move away. He was always so open, it has upset me greatly, I can tell you."

"Did he not show any signs of distress or worry?" Phillip asked, trying to think of reasons for such behaviour.

"On the contrary, he seemed very happy. The circus came to town and we all went to watch Robbie, you know about Robbie, of course, a foundling taken in by the master," said Mrs Frost almost proudly.

"Yes, I have heard about the boy. My daughter told me that the earl had asked her to consider taking in another such boy from the circus," said Phillip. "She had refused."

"I know nothing of that, Sir, but it would be like the master to feel sorry for an unwanted foundling."

"He is no saint, Mrs Frost," said Phillip angrily. "He appears to have deserted his own wife and child."

"There will be a good reason, of that I am sure," replied Mrs Frost. "I only ever saw the master do good things. He even went into the brothel to rescue Robbie's sister, Kitty; he bought Lizzie from a mill owner to save her life."

The Reverend Mountjoy was amazed by these revelations. "Who are Kitty and Lizzy?" he asked.

"The old earl had bought Kitty and Robbie, we do not think that he wanted Rob but the girl was very beautiful, very young as well, and he hid her in a brothel and the master discovered where she was and rescued her."

"And where is the girl now and Robbie for that matter?" Phillip asked almost bemused by these heroic stories.

"Robbie joined the circus with the master's permission and Kitty has gone to Paris with Mr Conte, who is an artist, and his wife who, was also rescued from the same brothel by the master."

"My goodness, and the girl called Lizzie?"

"Ah Lizzie, she had nothing to do with the old earl but when the master was searching for Kitty and was told of a young girl working in the mill who fitted her description, he thought it was Robbie's sister," Mrs Frost explained. "It turned out to be a young, orphan girl, very delicate and alone in the world. The master allowed the publican of the Dorchester to take her in as they did not have any children of their own. He had to pay the mill manager to let the girl go."

"My daughter has never told me of any of these events," said Phillip confused.

"This all happened before the master brought Lady Southerly to Keighley as his wife."

"That would explain that then," replied Phillip. "Is there anything further you can tell me that might help explain the earl's disappearance?"

"I have two more letters, Sir, one from Robbie and one other from the master," said Mrs Frost, retrieving other missives from her pocket and handing them to the vicar. "The master even left us all a year's wages in advance, just in case the new people did not pay promptly."

Phillip was amazed. He opened the first letter and it was from Robbie. His writing was a scrawl and hard to decipher but Phillip got the gist of it. "Am I to understand that the boy, Robbie, has gone to France to join his sister?"

"It would seem so, Sir," said Mrs Frost.

"He does not say if the earl is with him, just that 'they' were met by Pierre at Calais. Do you know any more?"

"That I do not, Sir," was the reply. "I took they to mean Robbie and his dog, Daisy, who he would not have been parted from for anything."

"So you believe that the earl has paid to reunite the boy with his sister," asked Phillip.

"That I do, Sir. The master likes neat and tidy endings."

"And do you foresee him returning to my daughter and his child any time soon?"

"I am sorry, Sir, but I thought that was where he had gone. The barouche has gone and the gig and his favourite horses, where else would I except him to be?" Mrs Frost said matter of factually.

"Where else indeed, Madam," was the reply. "Now I am confused, I cannot make up my mind whether the man is a saint or a sinner. If a saint, where is he, is he safe? If a sinner, the same question comes to mind, where is he?"

"I pray he is safe, Sir," added Clarkson, who 'til then had remained silent.

"We all do," added Mrs Frost.

"So let us look at the facts," suggested Phillip. "The manor is leased to some gentleman or other so the earl does not intend to return for some time. Do you know the length of the lease?"

"I am told by my husband that the new master has an option to buy in one year's time," replied Mrs Frost.

"Right, so we know the earl does not intend to return here," said Phillip. "He has told my daughter that he has sold the mill and weave huts, so he has severed all ties to Keighley."

With that, Mrs Frost burst into uncontrollable tears.

Ignoring the woman, Phillip continues, "He has not returned to Wetherley and yet his horses have. Strange! He has made the property in Wetherley over to my daughter making her financially independent, even stranger. I wonder if he has got into debt with all this rescuing of young women, maybe bankruptcy loomed and he has made Dorothia safe."

Clarkson said that he had considered the fact that the earl might be in debt—that seemed a good explanation. Worse, still he could have been kidnapped but there has been no ransom note, so he dismissed that.

Phillip then remembered that he had one more unread letter in his hand, and he opened that hoping for more information.

"Did you keep the envelope, it might give us a clue as to where it was sent from?"

"No, Sir," said Mrs Frost between sobs. "I did not think to."

It was a brief note from Martin saying goodbye and telling Mrs Frost that he had gone to take care of the master so she was not to worry. It also contained the name and address of the earl's solicitor, in case there were any problems that needed sorting out. There was no clue to their where-about or suggestion that they would return.

"Martin is the earl's man, he has taken care of him for many years, he is a good God fearing man. I know the master is safe if Martin is with him," said Mrs Frost dabbing her tears on her apron.

"So he may be but it does not help us find the earl," replied Phillip. "Had I not read that this Martin was with him? I would have supposed dealing with his father's mess had driven the man insane or to an early death."

"That thought did cross all our minds, Sir," said Clarkson.

"Widow Sparkes and her son, Tim, have also disappeared," added Mrs Frost, almost as an after-thought.

"Who is widow Sparkes?" asked the vicar alarmed. "You are not suggesting that my son-in-law has run away with a neighbour surely?"

"No, of course not, utter foolish talk," was the reply.

"So why did you mention her?" Phillip asked.

"Betty Sparkes has a son, Tim, who lost a few fingers in the workings of the earl's machinery at Southerly Mill," Mrs Frost explained. "The earl was there when it happened and was so alarmed by the event that he employed a lovely young man called Simon Gibb to trace all the children maimed in his mill so he could check that they had enough to live by."

"Now I am getting more convinced that Adam had lost all his money on good causes," replied the vicar. "Please continue. Where has Mrs Sparkes gone, do you know?"

"Not exactly," Mrs Frost said, re-starting her tale. "Betty was all set to marry old Mr Brown from the village, he had been after her for some time. A wonderful cook is Betty, anyone would want to marry her."

"Your point is woman, please get to the point!" by now, Phillip's head was about to explode with all this information.

"It seems, or so she told me, that Martin persuaded her to try selling her cakes before she entered into a marriage that she did not want to undertake. As I said, she is a wonderful cook, surpasses my skills twice fold. We bought cakes from her regular like as did all the big houses and boarding houses here about."

"And?"

"And my dear vicar, suddenly the cakes stopped arriving. It was the same time as the master disappeared. I thought Betty might be sick so I sent my hubby, Mr Frost, round to check that she was alright."

"And?"

"And, she and the boy had gone., Mrs Green next door said that she had married by special licence and gone away all sudden like," concluded Mrs Frost.

"Can I assume that she did not marry old Mr Brown from the village?" asked Phillip, confused but interested.

"No, heck as like. She married a younger man and by the description, I thought it might have been Mr Martin, the earl's man. I could be wrong, but as they have all vanished as one, you must draw your own conclusion."

"Did Martin, in your opinion, show a fancy for the widow woman?" asked Phillip, almost amused.

"Betty told me that he helped her out financially from time to time, whilst she was gathering together her cake buyers, and it was he who persuaded her not to marry in haste," was the smug reply.

"Could this be something else funded by my son-in-law, do you think?"

"I got the impression it was a bit of a secret between the pair of them, Sir. So I think not," was the reply.

"Right, so now we think that maybe, and only maybe, Martin has married widow Sparkes and they, along with her son, are in hiding with the earl," said Phillip rather pleased that he had at last discovered something, however tentative.

Another voice from the room suggested that it sounded to reason that taking a good cook along on an adventure was a good idea.

"I do not consider a man running out on his wife and child to be undertaking an adventure," replied Phillip crossly. "I cannot believe all I have learnt and I thought I knew the earl rather well. Rescuing girls from brothels, saving maimed children, finding homes for some of them, sending the boy, Robbie, to France to join his sister and now, encouraging his man servant to marry a good cook—all to what end, I ask myself. With all this new knowledge, I am no nearer finding out where the Earl of Southerly has taken himself off to or why."

"You are right, it seems that we have reached a block end," replied Mrs Frost.

"Would I be able to stay a couple of days Mrs Frost?" asked Phillip. "I can put up at an inn if necessary. I want to speak to the earl's solicitor to try to clear up his disappearance."

It was agreed and the vicar stayed three full days but even after speaking to the earl's solicitor, who would not tell him anything other than the fact that Dorothia had been left well cared for, Phillip was no nearer to finding out where Adam had gone at the end of his stay. He had concluded that Adam had gone, for whatever reason, and was not likely to return. With that information, Phillip went back to Wetherley the following day, before the weather got too dreadful.

Dorothia, by now, was firmly convinced that her illness whilst Seraphina was very small had been the catalyst to whatever was occurring now.

Phillip returned to Wetherley and spoke first to his wife, Bathsheba, who had been busy telling all and sundry that she had been right all along and blood will out. He told her that he did not consider that to be a very Christian way to behave but was finding it hard to excuse his son-in-law himself.

He told his wife, with slight amusement, all he had discovered whilst in Keighley; she too was finding it difficult to acquaint all the good deeds done with deserting a wife and child. Neither could decide if Adam Southerly, the Earl of Wetherley, was a saint or a sinner.

Dory had, by now, decided that she was alone and as such had to learn the running of the estate and that life must go on.

Chapter 48
James Returns to Wetherley

Sir James appeared at Wetherley a few weeks after receiving Adam's letter. He had read it over and over to himself, trying to decide which parts he could share with Rosamond and Dory without compromising his friend's faith in his secrecy. It began:

Dear James,
You have always been a good and faithful friend and I know you will be shocked when you hear that I have deserted Dory and the child. You are one man that I know that does not jump to conclusions or judge people unfairly without a hearing, so I am going to explain fully why I have done what I have done. My name would, I believe, be on a level with my father's if the story got out. You, my true and trusted friend, are the only person I have decided to give all the facts to.

I should never have married Dory, my heart was not fully in it. When I was younger, I believed that she was the woman for me but several occurrences in Yorkshire, before I married, opened my eyes to life. I have made you privy to the majority of them through previous letters, of course, you know about Robbie and also Martin and my efforts to trace his sister resulting in several adventures. These were just happenings that had shown me that life could be exciting and that I was not ready to settle down to a dull, domestic life style. I had already decided not to propose to Dory when she came to Wetherley on the day you and Sally came to give me your news. As you know, Dory proposed to me and I was like a rabbit in a snare. If I had rejected her, I would have been the lowest of the low, so I agreed, hoping that her parents might object and it might not come about.

We did settled down quite well together for a while, that was mainly thanks to you and our visits to Bleadon Farm, that is true but there was no fire. I could see when I observed my sister and you that there was a real love between you, your eyes gave it away. Sally was so warm and loving whereas Dory is and always was formal and cold. I know this is a poor excuse for what I am about to tell you, but I need you to have all the facts.

The circus came to Keighley Moor and with it, a young woman of exquisite beauty and charm, very young at first and I resisted her charms. I am not yet my father. Robbie decided that he wished to join the circus and as I have no hold over him, I agreed. The woman I spoke of earlier is the owner's—Georgiou's—daughter, Jeanette, and she has proved to be my downfall. My man, Martin, warned me but I did not heed him.

By the time the circus returned again, Jeanette was 18 and her beauty was breath-taking. I am not going to go into too many details but all you need to know is that I sold my soul for one night in her arms.

Now, the circus has returned and I discovered that I have a son, a beautiful boy, who has stolen my heart at a glance as did his mother. This is not a whim, James; in a way, I wish it was, I could buy my way out of anything. The woman haunts my dreams, I see her face everywhere I look, her eyes are the stars at night. It is a feeling that I cannot and do not want to dampen. I even asked Dory if we could take in a foundling from the circus, I wanted to keep both the children that was selfish of me, I know. It was a foolish idea. She flatly refused anyway, so I moved on to another selfish plan to secure my future happiness.

We are away to join Pierre in Paris, I wish there was some other way but I cannot think of one. I have to either desert my daughter or my son, I cannot have both. It is hard to desert either. As for the women, that is easy; I would chose Jeanette in a heartbeat. This is obviously what I have done.

I have left Dory well provided for as I have Seraphina when she is of age. My major regret is that I will probably not see you or Rosamond again in this life or see my daughter grow up. I hope you will stay in touch with Dory and if there is something I should know, please inform me immediately. I trust no one else with the information I have given to you, least of all my address.

I am sorry that I have proved to be a disappointment to you, James, you have been like a brother to me and I love you as one. Take very good care of yourself, Jasper and Rosamond and be happy.

Yours friend always, A.S.

James had waited for the dust to settle before showing his face in Weston-Under-Wetherley, not being sure if he would be welcome. Dory was very happy to see James and hoped that his arrival meant he had news of her missing husband.

James had not even told Rosamond the contents of the earl's letter to him, and he had no intension of disclosing it to Dory; in fact, he had burnt it to secure that it did not fall into the wrong hands.

"Have you heard anything?" were Dory's first words to Sir James, he had hardly time to step over the door step.

James took Dory's hands in his and looked sadly at her worried but hopeful face.

"I had a very short letter telling me that Adam would not be returning but the details of his whereabouts were not revealed," he said, not quite truthfully. "I am so sorry, Dory, I came to offer any help I can to you and little Seraphina."

"You had a letter, did it have his seal on it? Did he give an address? Have you brought it with you, can I see it?" she asked in earnest. "I have not had a single word from him since his initial letter to tell me that he was selling Southerly Mills and weaving sheds and telling me not to worry. How can I not worry? Where is he? Is he dead? Why has he done this?"

James took a deep breath and felt relieved that he had burnt the letter he received from Adam, in case he weakened and showed Dory. "I can only tell you what I know and that is not a lot. The letter had his seal but it gave me no clue of his where-about, and I did not bring it with me, I am sorry that was very remiss of me. He just told me that he had done something out of character and asked if I would look in on you and Seraphina from time to time. He indicated that he had left you comfortably off and would not be returning to Weston-Under-Wetherley in the foreseeable future. That was all."

"Are you sure the hand was his? Maybe he has been kidnapped and a demand for money will follow?" She cried.

"It was written by Adam, I would know his hand anywhere. People are not kidnapped and kept for months, a demand for money comes swiftly," he said. "You have to accept that he has chosen to go away, no one has forced him to take this action."

She just nodded.

"I have heard from Adam's solicitor and it seems that I am a very wealthy woman in my own right, just as Adam told you, so money is not a problem," she said softly. "I have no idea how to run the estate but I have good men about me who do."

"I will speak to them all before I return home if you so wish, Dory," said Sir James. "Just to make it clear that I will be back if they cause you any grief. Some men do not like taking orders from women."

"Do not worry, James, I can be firm if I need to be," was the reply. "I think that most of the men feel a little sorry for me, at least they do not show the animosity they showed to Adam, even when he was good to everyone."

"Unfortunately, they were expecting his father to reappear in the son at any moment," replied Sir James with a smile.

"And maybe rightly so," said Dory. "Do you think he has run away with another woman?"

"She would have to be some woman to take him from you, Dory," Sir James replied with a pang of guilt. "Rosamond and I would like you to continue your visits to us at Bleadon Farm, nothing needs to change."

A tear ran down Dory's face, and she tried to smile. "You are a good and kind friend, James, and I would love to come to Weston-Super-Mare quite soon if you would not mind too much," she said. "I have not been able to explain to Seraphina what has happened, I do not know myself so how can I. A visit with Rosamond might be what we need right now."

"Then it is decided, you will pack and leave with me," replied Sir James. "We need not rush away, you can take time to speak to your men and family."

Sir James and Dory went into the sitting room followed by Kate, the little maid, who was waiting for instruction. Soon, they were sitting comfortably with a glass of sherry and Dory was telling Sir James that her father had gone to Keighley searching for the earl, without success. She told Sir James of several stories that her father, the Reverend Mountjoy, had been told by Mrs Frost, the Keighley housekeeper, about rescuing young woman from brothels and mills—Kitty, Robbie, Lizzy, the fingerless boys and Camille.

"My father could not decide whether Adam be a saint or sinner, time will tell, I guess," said Dory with a little smile that made Sir James feel a little less guilty about with-holding information. "I feel I may have rushed Adam into marriage, maybe his heart was not really in it, though he never gave me reason to doubt him before. He used to write to me in Brighton, nothing too personal, just telling me what he was doing. Maybe I read too much into the letters and when I approached him and almost threw myself at him. Did I force him to marry me, James, is this my fault?"

"I believe that Adam always intended to marry you, Dory, he gave me that impression anyway, so do not worry on that part," was the kind reply. "I wonder if he has not fallen into a state of depression, not unlike the one that struck you soon after Seraphina's birth. The mind is a strange thing."

"I did wonder that myself, James," Dory replied. "The death of his sister was very hard for him."

"As it was for us all," replied James looking sorrowful.

"I know you loved her, James, we all did, it was impossible not to," said Dory. "You are happy now though I hope, James."

"I am happy enough. I would never have swapped Sally for Rosamond, of course, but I have been lucky enough to have found contentment a second time round," James replied thoughtfully. "Finding true love once is a wonder but twice is a miracle. They are two very different people, I do not compare them, that would be foolish."

"You deserve to be happy, James, you are a good man," replied Dory.

"Everyone deserves to be happy surely."

"Not me, I do not deserve this privilege," said Dory, a tear running down her cheek.

"Don't be foolish, woman," came the stern reply. "What could you have done to be undeserving of anything?"

"I will tell you, James, and only you. You are the only person I know who never judges anyone, I could not bear for Rosamond to know my secret," she replied.

James looked astonished, he was starting to feel worn down with secrets. "Do tell me, Dory, I will listen."

"I know you will, James," she took a deep breath before starting to relate her tale. "When I came to see Adam before we married, I told him that I had helped with a little of the research he was doing. I told him that I had found Freda, the laundry woman, made pregnant by his father."

"I remember he told me," said James. "He was very pleased, it was one less problem for him to solve."

"I lied to him," she continued. "I knew that if I told him the truth, he would spend another couple of years righting another wrong, and I was not getting any younger, I wanted to marry, I wanted to forget all his father did. I knew Adam would not forget until his race was run."

James moved his chair closer to Dory and picked up her hand, which was visibly shaking. "Go on."

"I did look for Freda, she was not hard to find. She was in the work house with her small son. I went to visit her. The child was so small and thin but he looked so much like Adam, it scared me. If Adam had seen his half-brother, for that is what the child surely was, he would have taken both, he and his mother, under his wing."

"So what did you do?" asked James, quite shocked.

"At first, I did nothing, I just left them there. I paid the workhouse to provide extra food and warmth but I just walked out, to be more truthful, I ran out."

"And yet, you told Adam they were all gone, Freda through grief and the child miscarried."

"That is exactly what I told him," she said grimly. "As soon as we married and he kept talking about his sister, Robbie and sons, I knew how much he would have cared for his brother. But what could I do, I had already dealt with the problem, I could not tell him then!"

"What did you in fact do if you actually did anything?" asked James.

"Oh, I did a great deal, believe me. I went to the workhouse again, they were still there, where else could they be! I could see that Freda looked reasonably well considering but the boy still looked small and frail."

Dory stood up and walked about the room, wringing her hands; Sir James followed her with his eyes but did not speak. "I took a goodly amount of money, it was from Adam for the poor, I paid to have the mother and child released, paid their debts and arranged to have them move to Hampshire."

"Why Hampshire?" asked James a little confused. "Why not simply tell Adam that you made a mistake, the woman lived after all."

"I could not do that. I had told him a story of how her father's death had shocked Freda so much that she lost the child. I could not simply turn round and then say, oh dear, sorry, I made a mistake, they are alive and well in the workhouse, I saw them there. He would never have married me."

"I can see that, Dory, but why Hampshire?"

"My sister, Everline, married a travelling vicar and they were at this time in Hamble-le-Rice in the New Forest. I asked her if she knew of any positions for a young widow, who was trying to bring up her son alone. She found Freda a job in the laundry, cleaning and general duties for a nobleman nearby; not a well-paid position, of course, but one that offered a room and board in a large house, as well as work for the boy. You must see, I wanted the woman and her son far away, I did not want Adam to come across them by accident."

"That does not sound too bad, Dory. What else?" asked James.

"It all ended well as it seems, Freda married a fisherman and he took the boy in as his own," continued Dory. "I received a scribbled note from Freda telling me of her good fortune and thanking me for my help. But still I did not tell Adam."

"That was wrong of you, Dory, but there is no need to fret about it now," replied James.

"I have worried ever since if maybe the boy will realise his birth and make demands on the estate."

"He might, but as none of us know where the earl is, it will not get him very far."

"I wondered if maybe Adam found out about what I had done and that is why he has deserted me," said Dory.

"That is not possible, he would have told me," was the reply.

"True. When I had a girl, Seraphina, I felt it was a punishment for what I had done, and then when I miscarried the son, I so longer for I was convinced," Dory said.

"You sound like Adam, with his sins of his father's," replied James.

"I am beginning to believe Adam's theory about blood ties and sins. I have not finished yet, there is more, James. Adam came to me with a story of a foundling at the circus that he wanted me to take in," she said. "I knew it was not Freda's son, that was impossible, but I had this vision of him appearing one day to claim his rights and to show what sort of low person I was. I was so mad at the suggestion. I could have helped, it would not have done me any harm to have done so, but I could not bring myself to be kind. I drove Adam away. He was trying so hard to be the opposite of his father. I could not and would not take in the child, although he begged me quite forcefully to re-consider."

James had to bite his tongue and not tell Dory what he knew about the child. Adam's letter had obviously told James everything, about Joseph, Jeanette and how he had asked Dory to take in a baby, not telling her that he was actually the 'foundlings' father. He could see that the truth would only make Dory more miserable.

"What has happened is over, it is in the past. You must let it go," said James kindly. "You and Seraphina must come with me to the sea side and you will feel like your old self again. Do not fall into despair, the child needs you."

"You are the kindest of men, James," said Dory tearfully. "I do not deserve such a good friend. You will not tell Rosamond how wicked I am, please do not, James, I could not bear for her to hate me."

"I do not believe Rosamond had the capacity to hate anyone, but I will not share your secret with her, it is your secret to share or keep as you see fit," was the reply.

Dory and Seraphina travelled to Weston-Super-Mare with James for a rest, the start of many visits without the earl.

Chapter 49
Bleadon Manor Farm

A week later and Dory, Sir James and Seraphina were back in Bleadon Manor Farm near Weston. The farm was always a welcoming place and Dory was happy to be back there and have Rosamond's shoulder to cry on and talk things over with her. If anyone ever asked Dory who Rosamond was, she used to refer to her as her cousin, it saved long explanations.

Dory was surprised to find that Rosebud, the lamb named at birth by Sally many years before, was still a family pet. Sir James explained that he did not have the heart to send the now aging sheep to the abattoir, Rosebud being the last link to Sally. Rosamond did not mind at all, she was a gentle soul with a kindly disposition.

Sir James was what might be called a gentleman farmer. He liked animals and was very reluctant to part with any, even when they grew old. Luckily, his financial well-being did not depend on the farm, farming was more of a hobby than anything.

Seraphina had often been confused by the fact that she lived in Weston-Under-Wetherley and Rosamond and Sir James lived near another Weston, this time Weston-Super-Mare. Dory explained many times that there are several places with similar names throughout the country and how a descriptive additive is usually placed before or in front of the town to mark the difference. Weston-Under-Wetherley was mentioned in the Doomsday Book, Weston once being West Stone is situated under Wetherley Wood and usually shortened to Wetherley; whereas Weston-Super-Mare is in Somerset edging on the Bristol Chanel and is usually referred to as Weston. It was such a confusion that had made Sir James' representative purchase a property in Wetherley for his mother-in-law instead of Weston-Super-Mare.

Seraphina was an inquisitive child, like her father; she liked to find out all there was to know about things that interested her. Dory often told her stories about the history of where they lived. She told her about November 1605 when a group of riders, including Robert Catesby, who were involved in the gunpowder plot rode through Weston-Under-Wetherley, pursued by the king's men. She also told her what she knew about the Weston in Somerset.

There had been a settlement in Weston-Super-Mare since the iron ages. In 1565, the mineral calamine was discovered on Worle Hill, this type of zinc ore was crucial in making brass. The last of the mines can still be seen alongside the spoil heaps on Weston Hill.

Rosamond's husband, Sir James' father was a life-long friend of the owner of one of the larger manor houses in the region and it is because of this that Sir James Snr bought what he refers to as a small holding nearby in Bleadon.

By the middle of the 18th century, doctors had started praising the virtues of bathing in sea water. King George had tried it in Weymouth in 1789 and started a fashion.

For people living in Bristol and Bath, Weston was the nearest coastal village within easy reach and it became a very popular resort. The secluded cove at Anchor Head was Weston's first bathing place for ladies, whilst the gentlemen often just stripped off on the sands and ran into the water. It was the custom originally to bathe naked, which is why the women used Anchor Head Cove.

As the popularity of taking the water grew, so did the desire to cover up so families could swim together.

Bathing machines were introduced at Glentworth Bay. These are huts on wheels, people climbed into them, changed into their bathing attire and then were drawn down to the sea by horses. Women could then just walk down the steps into the water unseen by anyone. Weston had started to be an up and coming place in the early 1800s and Sir James Snr realised this. He invested in several ventures in Weston and made a fortune doing so, which passed to his son, the present Sir James. Seraphina's errant father also had interests in the Weston Area in partnership with a friend of his, Edward Lang Fox. Lang Fox had planned to buy Knightstone Island just off the shore of Weston with the earl's financial assistance, Dory had no idea if this venture had ever actually taken place. She knew that the island had originally opened in 1810 as a get-away for invalids; in 1820, there were also refreshment rooms, a reading room and a spa, a place for peace and quiet away from the bustle of everyday life; originally reached by being ferried over by a local boatman, Aaron Fisher. The earl had been delighted when a few years later, a low causeway was built to the island. Before the earl disappeared, he had spent a great many happy weeks in Weston with first Sally and then later Rosamond and Sir James, so he knew the financial benefits of investing in anything to do with the new trend towards spas. Lang Fox had acquired Knightstone Island in September 1830. Dory assumed that her husband had probably lost interest in the project and it was now presumable on hold as the earl had followed a very different path. But she was wrong on one account at least, wherever the capital came from, Doctor Edward Lang Fox from Bristol had purchased the island and was using it in his work as a pioneer in the treatment of the insane.

Sir James' small holding, as he calls it, is actually a considerable property on Bleadon Hill, on the edge of Weston-Super-Mare with several acres of pastoral land and large stable facilities. Although he owns a large house near Weston-Under-Wetherley, his preferred residence is definitely Weston-Super-Mare believing that the air is clearer and it is an extremely healthy place to live and bring up a family. He owns other property near the front and was quick to realise the benefits of letting out such properties to families of the wealthy, who want to escape the smog of large cities.

Jasper is much the same age as Seraphina, but unlike her, he is considered to be delicate and this increased Sir James' idea that Weston-Super-Mare is the better place to reside. The house in Westerley was really only a retreat, there was very little land attached and James enjoyed being a gentleman farmer.

Whatever reason Weston had been chosen over Wetherley, which is itself a beautiful clean country environment, Seraphina and Dory did not really care. The opportunity to spend time by the water appealed to them greatly and they accepted every offer of accommodation from Rosamond. James always made everyone very welcome. They had been there many times with the earl as well, before he decided to disappear.

There was always something to see or do in Weston-Super-Mare. Artists could always been seen painting and sketching along the water front. There were reading rooms, boats for hire and dances in the assembly rooms and for those more pious, a Methodist Church as well as a Parish Church.

Dory preferred the life in Weston to that of Brighton, even though they are both popular sea side places, things seemed to move at a slower pace in Somerset.

It was simple life in Bleadon, all the servants were genuinely fond of Sir James and his wife. Dory felt a little sad that Adam had never managed to totally gain the trust of every one in Weston-Under-Wetherley, though he had faired a lot better in Keighley. This also played on her mind as a possible cause for his disappearance.

During one of their visits to Weston, Seraphina decided that she too would like a more simple name, after all her mother had managed to change from Dorothia to Dory. They went through a great many shortened versions of Seraphina but none of them appealed to the child.

"Why don't you just call yourself Agnes, your middle name," suggested the ever practical Sir James. "It was your grandmother's name and she was a fine lady."

This, of course, opened a flood gate of questions from the ever curious Agnes, who wanted to know about the grandmother she had never met. Dory managed to distract the child by telling her about her other namesake Seraphina, her own grandmother, and no more mention was made of any kin connected to Adam Southerly.

"Agnes is a fine name child," said Dory. "It is a Greek name meaning pure and holy, what could be better."

"I like that, Mum, what does Seraphina mean?" asked the inquisitive child in reply.

"I can answer that," said James with a smile, "because we discussed it when choosing your name when you were born."

"I thought I was just called after grandmother," said Agnes confused.

"You were dear, but it is always good to know meanings of words," continued James. "Your grandfather looked up the meaning and it is from the Latin word Seraphinus, which is taken from the biblical word Seraphim, which means fiery ones."

"I do not like that very much, Uncle James, I much prefer to be pure than fiery, that sounds scary."

"I do not think that either you or your grandmother would scare anyone, little one," James replied with a smile. "And anyway, the Seraphim were an order of six-winged angels spoken of by Isaiah in the bible so they must be good."

Agnes smiled her contagious smile and was satisfied with all the information she had been given.

Chapter 50
More Changes, Great Losses

Then one day, everyone's world was turned upside down. The happy, although lonely, life that Dory and Agnes had built together without the missing earl came to an abrupt halt. Sir James was given to spending time in London on business, he had interests in Ceylon that gave him a considerable income, and his overseers and solicitors all gathered in London from time to time to keep him up to date with his affairs. He returned from one such trip with a slight cough, which was very quickly transferred to Jasper as he was always said to have a weak chest. Rosamond employed the best of medical aid but insisted on nursing her family herself. She sat night and day by the side of her loved ones and amazingly, the illness overlooked her and she stayed strong. The family had, what the doctor called, 'the White Death' and were in isolation, even the sea air did not help. Despite Dory's pleas to be allowed to go to her friend's aid, she was told not to go to Weston until the drama was over one way or another. This pained Dory greatly, although she did not relish the idea of bringing consumption back to Wetherley and her own child. Sir James struggled to survive and he was a strong man so everyone expected him to recover; unfortunately, when Jasper was finally taken, he blamed himself so heavily that many thought he died of despair and guilt. Whatever the reason it was seen fit to take a strong man like Sir James, he died and Rosamond was now alone and discovered that she was in the early stages of pregnancy. Now she needed Dory and went to Wetherley to stay, whilst the family solicitor sorted out the legal ramifications of Sir James' unexpected death.

Unfortunately, Rosamond was only early into the pregnancy, possibly three months, and the grief at the loss of her son and husband affected her greatly. She did not eat well and Dory worried continuously about her. It seemed inevitable to Dory that unless Rosamond perked up, the baby would be lost.

One Saturday, Dory found a stranger standing on her doorstep in the shape of Miss Bella Stokes. She was a trained nurse, who resided in Southampton and had been paid to call on Lady Dorothia to offer her assistance in nursing Rosamond back to health. Dory was dumbfounded and invited the woman in to explain herself fully. Miss Bella Stokes was a well-built woman of about 35, she was quite tall, articulate and neatly dressed with an easy smile. Her employee was a gentleman of means called John Henry Bridges, who ran a lucrative business empire in Southampton. John Henry dealt in the import and export of mainly leather goods from his base in Southampton. Dory had met him several times in Yorkshire and again in Weston-Under-Wetherley, not long before her husband disappeared. The earl had made a point of keeping his wife well-informed of where he bought his goods and who she could trust. John Henry Bridges supplied leather pelts for the making of boots, shoe, saddles and anything else that might be needed. He was known to have good connections in Spain, where the best leather was imported from. Dory always found John Henry to be polite, respectful and above all, business like and as her husband thought highly of him, so did she in the business sense. She had not really taken a great deal of notice of him as a person outside of business but obviously, he had taken a lot of interest in her. She was newly deserted and was just feeling her feet as lady of the manor living alone.

She kept a low profile as a rule but had been talked into judging a flower and vegetable show in nearby Hunningham by a member of the village of good breeding, who had offered assistance to her on more than one occasion. This is where she met John Henry again, he was staying locally on business and offered to assist her in the judging. She was grateful for his input. She always made a point of inspection the fruit and vegetables that were delivered to her door but a connoisseur she was not. Whereas John Henry was a business man who dealt with imports and had a good eye for quality goods. They made a good team and she found it easy to make small talk with Mr Bridges. But this is where their communication ended, she thanked him and he went on his way, whilst she gave out the prizes.

Dory was fully aware that as a beautiful and wealthy lady, she would raise a lot of interest but until she could reconnect with her errant husband or obtain a divorce, she intended to stay out of the limelight. There had already been several men of means that had shown an interest in her precarious position, and she was fully aware that if the earl did not return, she might have to re-marry, though the thought scared her. And now this John Henry Bridges had shown his hand and she did not know what to do. Dory was not insensitive to the fact that the scandal connected to her name, though not through any fault of hers, would make a very lucrative marriage out of the question. It was more likely that an adventurer would try to woo her for her money.

Bella explained that John Henry had heard through a friend in the village that Dorothia had been alone now for 18 months with no sign of her husband and the talk was that he had died abroad. He had also heard that she had returned to the family home with a sick friend. He merely wanted to help a damsel in distress and was offering Dory the opportunity to make use of a trained nurse with no obligations. Dory talked the situation over with Rosamond and it was decided that Bella would stay until the end of the next month. They felt that they could hardly expect the poor woman to turn round and head straight back to Southampton without a bed for a few nights at least. Bella proved to be a God send. She was calm, tidy, helpful, organised and above all, very caring.

Regardless of all the care taken, Rosamond lost her baby at seven months and was inconsolable. Her finances were starting to untangle and she was now a very wealthy woman; once she regained her strength, Rosamond returned to Weston-Super-Mare to decide what she wanted to do with the rest of her life. She was only 32 and not terribly worldly. Bella returned to Southampton with Dory's gratitude to be passed on to John Henry.

A further year passed and no news arrived regarding the young earl. Then one day, a letter arrived at Wetherley from Adam's solicitors in Yorkshire. The letter was very formal and was just to inform Dorothia that Adam Southerly, the Earl of Wetherley, would be calling at Wetherley Manor Lodge to discuss matters that would be of mutual interest to him and Lady Southerly within the next fortnight.

Much the same time, Dory received news from Rosamond that she intended to marry a local Weston-Super-Mare business man. Dory wanted to hurry to Weston and see for herself what sort of man her friend intended to marry but as her husband was due home, that was impossible.

Chapter 51
The Missing Earl Returns

The first couple of years in Paris were exciting and trouble free. All the runaways worked hard at learning their new language and settled in well. Then Adam had news that his friend, Sir James Shepherd, had been struck down by the white plague, and he felt compelled to return to England and see his friend and once brother-in-law. It turned out that the information was a whole year out of date, so he arrived in England far too late but sent word to Dory that he was around and needed to see her. Adam was grief stricken to have lost such an honest and true friend. They had kept in touch but the letters became less frequent. Adam had considered returning to seek out his friend when the letters stopped altogether. Then he received the terrible news of the illness that had struck Sir James and Jasper down.

Another tie to England had been Edward Lang Fox, who had also died so the Knightstone project was now in different hands and being extended as a general spa. Adam found that he was not very interested in the workings of Knightstone Island any longer, and he also considered selling his shares in the production and use of the granite that had been mined in a quarry near Falmouth and used to heighten the causeway out to Knightstone Island. The granite was also used to make fine fireplaces. All these interests tied the earl to England and he needed to be free. The details of all his dealings with the Weston-Super-Mare projects were with a solicitor used by Dr Lang Fox and who he had recommended to the earl.

As soon as Dory was sure that the earl was about to visit, she sent Agnes to her parents, away from any unpleasantness.

The next weekend was the embarrassing meeting of deserted wife and errant husband. He sat down and they spoke in a very civilised way about what had happened and why he had chosen to desert his child, though he did not give out very much information. Once he had made it clear that he would not be returning, Dory asked for a divorce. Adam said that he would admit to adultery to make the process simpler, making it clear that this was not a confession, just a plan to ease the path.

"Another woman would have made sense at least," said Dory. "Was I really that terrible a wife that you needed to run away?"

"The fault is not yours, it never has been," he said reassuringly.

"Then why?" Dory said in despair. "Why did you run away like a thief in the night? I know life was difficult for you, I watched you struggle, I have been difficult as well but we could have worked through it together."

"I didn't want to work through it any longer," was the reply. "Every turning gave me a new challenge, I dreaded waking up in the mornings some days."

"I was led to believe that you enjoyed your adventures of righting your father's wrongs, you seem to have put a great deal of time, effort and money into it," Dory replied quite unsympathetically.

"I did to a degree but as I solved one problem, another slapped me in the face."

"But surely, all this was before we married, I wasn't privy to the details of the children you saved and housed," Dory continued. "My father, during a visit to Keighley to seek your where-about, discovered much more about you than I ever knew and I was your wife. That hurt, Adam."

"I never set out to hurt you, Dory, believe me on that score," replied the earl. "I fought my demons and they won, it is as simple as that."

"I am not going to pretend that I understand what you are trying to tell me, Adam," she said. "I only know that if you had run away with a bit of flimsy, as was suggested by many, I would see a reason but to go for no reason, it is not the business of a sane man."

"I have doubted my own sanity on many occasions, Dory, that is true," Adam replied. "I have no doubt that my father was totally without conscience and that could be a way of describing madness. Maybe I am more like him that we all thought."

"Now you are being ridiculous," replied Dory. "My father came back from Yorkshire with the idea that you are bordering on sainthood, the direct opposite of your father."

"Your father always was a kindly soul, I regret very much having let him down," said Adam. "I once told my man, Martin, that sometimes, the ones who let you down are the ones you least expect."

"I can say that is true for sure, I never imagined you would let me down in the way you have."

"I had choices to make, Dory. Some would say I made the wrong ones but they were mine, and I am solely to blame for any misery caused," replied the earl.

"So the fact that I was not easy to live with and did not produce a son, these did not push you into any direction?" she asked.

"Do not be foolish, woman. I will not pretend that I would not have wished you to be of a softer disposition that would be a lie," he replied.

Dory sprang to her feet as she replied, "I guessed as much, you would have been happier if I had taken in every waif and stray you came across and we had all lived in harmony and contentment." She started to laugh hysterically.

Adam shook her, his hand on each of her slender shoulders. "Stop this foolishness, Dory," he shouted. "I expected too much of you, I know that now. My father's sins were not yours."

They stood close to each other, tears rolling down Dory's face. "Adam, surely you could forgive me, I know I can forgive you, for the sake of our daughter, come home."

Adam took a long look at his wife before he replied. "Things would never be the same, Dory, I have sold the mills and weaving sheds, our life would be very different."

"I would be willing to try, Adam, if you were," was the reply.

"Dory, I simply do not want to try. I am going now and I will return tomorrow afternoon. I would like to see my daughter, I won't make life difficult, I just wish to see her," he said and turned to leave.

"She may be here, she may not, I will make no promise to you, Adam. You do not deserve any courtesy," Dory replied acidly.

Dory was calmer when Adam returned the next day and had made up her mind to remain so.

Seraphina was a very confused little girl, she had not seen her father for nearly three years, and when he had left, she could barely talk but now she was a little girl who wanted to ask questions. Dory explained that Seraphina had chosen to use her middle name now and so she was to be Agnes to them all. Adam was pleased as it had been his dear mothers' name.

The earl asked his wife if he could take Agnes away for a couple of days, he wanted to spend a short time with her before he left forever. It was agreed, although Dory had an underlying fear that Adam might just take the child and she would lose her as well. Also, she did not want the child confused and told of their blood ties. If he was to go again, she did not want the child to know her father only to lose him again.

Adam readily agreed to Dory's demands and the earl and Agnes went to Weston-Super-Mare, first to see the work that Doctor Lang Fox had done and the changes since his demise and then to visit Rosamond, who was not entirely happy to see him. Adam felt he could not leave again without saying how sorry he was to hear of the loss of his good friend, he also wanted to be assured that Rosamond would stay in contact with Dory despite who ever she married. He needed to know his wife had one good and loyal friend to call on.

Adam's involvement with Dr Lang Fox had always been on a business level. Many years earlier, the two men had agreed to form an alliance and work together on a business venture. It had always worried Adam that there may have been a degree of madness in his family. He could not easily explain his late father's extraordinary and debauched way of life and wondered if it was a hereditary illness. He, himself, could not explain why he had chosen to run away with a gypsy to a foreign land and leave a beautiful, loving wife and adorable child. It was not the actions of a sane man in his eyes. A few years earlier, Dr Fox had spent a great number of hours with Adam going over his childhood and then present life and had persuaded the earl that the madness was purely in his father. This had, of course, aroused an interest in mental health in Adam; he not being totally convinced that Lang Fox's evaluation of him was quite without flaws, and he had agreed to help fund Lang Fox's work on Knightstone Island. In exchange, the good doctor was going to organise a trust fund for Agnes that would mature when she either married or reached the age of 25, whichever came first. It was to be kept a strict secret so no unsuitable young men would come looking for an easy life at his daughter's expense. The details of all transactions were kept under lock and key with a solicitor in Weston, and Adam went to see this firm to have everything transferred to his man in York, so all his British business was in one place and easily assessable to him if needs be.

Agnes just thought it was a couple of days back in Weston-Super-Mare, where she loved to visit; she was not even sure who the handsome man was that was taking such good care of her. She thought he was maybe an uncle. He was tempted to just grab his daughter and run, taking her to join his new family abroad, but he could not bring himself to be so hard hearted.

Earlier, Adam and Agnes had made their way to Bleadon Manor Farm, the atmosphere was at first quite frosty but very soon, with the help of Agnes' cheerful disposition, the ice melted and Rosamond began to talk freely.

Rosamond told Adam how bravely his friend had clung onto life and how the loss of Jasper had made him give in. Adam was greatly saddened to think such a kind a gentle man as Sir James Shepherd could have been taken so young and when his life had started to be happy again after the loss of Sally. He was convinced that it was the curse of his father hanging over all their heads.

Rosamond had always been very fond of Adam, his easy charm made it difficult not to be. She found herself forgetting for a moment the sorrow he had caused his wife when he vanished so unexpectedly. She always suspected that her late husband, Sir James, had more knowledge of the events leading up to the disappearance than he had disclosed to her.

Adam and Agnes stayed for two nights at Bleadon Manor Farm and between telling Adam briefly about the possibility that she might re-marry and talking about James and Jasper, the three of them—Rosamond, Adam and Agnes—went for walks in Weston Wood, took afternoon cream tea at Reeves Hotel and walked along Weston sands.

Adam reluctantly returned to Weston-Under-Wetherley and returned Agnes safely to her mother's care. They had been gone longer than she anticipated, and she had feared that she would never see her daughter again, even after Adam had sworn on the Bible that he would return her safely. She would have readily accepted that as a punishment, still feeling that she had to take a lot of the responsibility for Adam's unhappiness.

Adam explained why they had been longer than expected and apologised for worrying her. "I wanted to spend a little time with Rosamond and let her know how sorry I was not to have been there for James when he needed me. She was very forgiving and asked us to stay on a couple of days. I was so glad that you have a special friend to rely on in Rosamond, she promised to keep closely in touch with you."

"If you do not mind, Adam, I will choose my own friends. I do not need you to put in a good word for me. Sometimes, I wonder who you think you are," said Dory furiously. "Looking out for everyone with one hand and letting down the most important people in your life with the other."

Adam swiftly left, returning to his lodgings.

The Reverend Mountjoy had chosen not to seek Adam out, even though Dory sent word to her father to say that he had returned, much to Dory's disappointment. She wondered if her father might have actually persuaded the earl to stay. She did not, however, want him to stay through guilt, she wanted him to stay because he had made a mistake in leaving and wanted to be forgiven but unfortunately, Adam showed no signs of this. Then out of desperation, she decided to tell him about his half-brother with the hope that he would search for him and so stay a while. She sent a note to his lodgings asking him to call as soon as possible as she needed to give him some important information.

Adam had taken a temporary room in lodgings close to Wetherley Manor Lodge. He intended to stay as short a time as possible and was packing to leave when he received Dory's missive explaining that she needed to tie up a couple of ends before he left again. He was travelling light as he had not expected to stay very long at all.

Adam was not keen to return to Wetherley Manor Lodge, expecting a verbal onslaught from his wife; he felt a little tired of all the bad words that had passed between them, but he knew that he owed it to her to reply to her plea. He decided that he had to do as requested as it would definitely be the last time he would have a conversation with Dory in this life time.

He was greeted very politely by his daughter, who was as pretty as a picture and the image of her mother.

Agnes had still not been made aware of who the strange man was, though she felt drawn to him in a strange way. Adam had decided not to make her privy to his identity, agreeing with his wife that when he left her again, it would be like walking out on her twice.

Dory invited Adam into the sitting room to take a glass of sherry with her, whilst she told him something that she felt he needed to know before he left again, this time for good. It was very strange for Adam, being invited into what was once his own home. The servants were most confused and spent a great deal of their spare time wondering if their master had returned, most of them hoped that he had and some were not sure how to address him.

Adam entered the room cautiously, almost expecting to be confronted by Dory's father in high dudgeon and was almost disappointed not to have had to defend his honour.

Once they were comfortable with a glass in their hands, Dory began, "Adam, I need to tell you something before you leave. I assume you will not be making regular visits to Wetherley."

"No," was the reply. "I doubt I will ever return here, unless some real drama occurs."

"If this drama does occur, how do I contact you?"

"I will leave a forwarding address, my solicitor's, he will get in touch if needs be. Though he was very slow in informing me about James and I would have liked to have seen him one more time."

"He would not have allowed you to risk your life by visiting him, I tried and I was rejected. He loved you like a brother, despite your wreck-less behaviour," was Dory's reply.

"I know and I he." said Adam sadly.

"Not enough to keep you here, of course, as are any of us," was the caustic reply. "It is the subject of brothers that I wish to talk about."

"Brothers? Do not tell me others have come forward to claim kin."

"No. I am going to tell you something that I intended to take to my grave, but as you have dealt so badly with me, I have decided to share some information with you."

"Carry on," replied the earl looking fascinated.

"Do you remember when I came to ask you to marry me all those years ago?" she began, Adam nodded.

"I told you that I had found Freda, your father's dismissed and dishonoured laundry maid."

"I remember it well, she had died sadly after losing the baby," replied Adam interested.

"I did not tell you the whole truth of the matter," said Dory.

"Go on, I am intrigued," replied the earl.

Dory was quite enjoying causing him pain, something she never imagined she would ever do. "I did find the woman, she was not, however, deceased; she was very much alive as was her son."

Adam sprung to his feet, the look of fury on his face.

"Madam, why would you lie?" he asked.

"So you would stop searching and settle down with me," was the honest answer. "I did not want to spend years putting right things that were not of your making. I wanted us to be happy."

"Happy, by pretending that I did not have a half-brother when clearly I have. Where is the boy?"

"I sent him and his mother to Hampshire, Freda married a fisherman and settled there."

"How did you contrive that?"

"They were in the workhouse when I discovered them," she said. "I paid to have them released and I sent them to my sister, Everline, in Hamble-le-Rice. Her husband is a vicar, who goes from church to church when the appointed vicar is sick. They were at St Andrew's, Hamble-le-Rice, at the time I discovered Freda and little George."

"Freda named her son after my father!" he laughed. "That is the last name I would have expected. So they are in Hamble still now I assume."

"Close by in a little fishing village called Netley on the Solent," said Dory. "Originally, I told my sister that Freda was an old friend of mine, widowed and struggling to bring up her child alone."

"At least I am not the only person you spun lies to," replied Adam caustically.

Dory just sighed and continued. "Everline found Freda a position in a large house as a laundry maid, something she had experience with. She met a fisherman, married him and the last I heard was that the husband had taken the boy willingly and was planning to teach him to deep sea fish."

Adam's mind drifted back to his talks with Pierre about teaching a son to fish, and he found himself smiling despite his anger.

"So I could seek the boy out and he would be well?"

"Yes, Adam, he would and probably happy. I cannot see why you would wish to seek him out and complicate his life," said Dory. "He is probably very happy with his lot in life. Better he does not carry the stigma of your family name."

"That is one thing I must agree with you on," replied Adam sadly.

"What do you intend to do with this information, might I ask?" requested Dory.

"I wish you had the decency to have given me this information before I went to Weston-Super-Mare," said Adam firmly. "I would have been quite close to Southampton, whereas I have to travel back in that direction again."

"Why would I want to help you?" was the reply.

"What happened to you, Dorothia?"

"You happened and then you deserted me without a word, you could have been dead, how would I ever know?"

"You are right, of course, what I did was inexcusable," replied the earl. "You will probably not believe this but Martin tried very hard to talk me out of leaving."

"Much as I would wish to thank Martin for trying on my behalf, I also find it deplorable that he knew your mind before I did."

"Martin is a good and loyal man and as I have already said that as far as I am aware, has never lied to me," said the earl.

"Whereas now you know I have. What do you intend to do about this news I have given you?"

"I am not sure," replied Adam. "I will go to Hampshire before I return to my new life and decide once I am there. If, as you say, the boy seems content, I will probably walk away."

"And if not, will you take him with you on your vanishing act as well?" asked Dory rather ungraciously. "My father tells me that you took Robbie and his sister, and now I know Martin is also with you. Quite a little crowd, is it not?"

"Your father, how would he know?"

"He went to Keighley to seek you out. Mrs Frost told him all about your heroism—saving young woman from whorehouses, the children in the mills; he came home wondering if you were a saint or a sinner," she replied. "But still, he could not discover your whereabouts."

"He is right, I do have a large entourage and am happy with that," Adam said. "I am sorry James has gone and your friends have depleted because of this. Don't make the mistake of driving Rosamond away, she has always been a good friend to us, both."

"I won't. I just hope if she re-marries, he will allow our friendship to continue. Did she tell you anything about the man?"

"She only touched on the subject, we spoke mainly of Sally, young Jasper, James and the evils of the white plague," Adam replied sadly. "She has had a hard time of it."

"And I have not, I suppose," replied Dory. "Always thinking of others before your wife. Rosamond intends to re-marry, I think, in haste. Her new husband might not take kindly to old friendships."

"Oh goodness, I only wish I had brought Martin with me," exclaimed the earl.

"I am amazed you have not, he always seemed more important to you than your own family," replied Dory.

"He would never have spun a web of lies like you have done, Madam," was the reply. "In fact, he would willingly uproot himself and follow me to the depth of hell if called upon to do so, even if he did not approve of my actions—that is unquestionable loyalty."

"And how could you ever know if maybe I would have done the same, I was never asked to make such a sacrifice," came the reply.

"True, Madam, but I doubt it," the earl said. "I do not believe I know you at all or even want to anymore."

With that, the earl left Wetherley, started to leave Weston Manor Lodge for the last time, feeling a little guilty that he had withheld information from his wife that was probably less easy to forgive than that which she had kept from him, namely the fact that he was the father of the foundling he had asked her to take in.

Adam decided that he had out stayed his visit and as he left, he turned and spoke one more time to Dory. "I will set about the divorce proceedings before I go completely from these shores. I will admit to adultery to speed things."

"Adultery, so there is another woman," Dory said venomously.

"I said to speed things up, not as a fact."

"You also said that you will be leaving these shores, so I take it you have gone abroad. Might I know to where you have fled?"

"I will not be giving you that information, Dorothia," replied the earl.

"No doubt, you are with the odious artist friend of yours, so you must be in France somewhere."

"No doubt," was the reply and the earl left Wetherley Manor Lodge for the last time.

Adam felt obliged to find his way to Netley. He hired himself a valet for his journey and wished he had taken up Martin's offer to accompany him back to England. He found a young man of good parenthood, who was seeking employment as a gentleman's gentleman, explained that he would pay well but he would only need his assistance for a short time. The man, in his early 20s, was called Thomas and they hired a carriage and livery men to drive them on their search. It was a long and arduous journey through parts of England neither the earl nor Thomas had ever been before.

Netley is situated on the Hamble Peninsula and consisted of several small fishermen's cottages and very little else, so it did not take the earl long to locate the tiny cottage that housed his half-brother. He could see instantly that the boy was happy, looked like him and it would have been easy to make the boy believe that he was a relative. He watched the young man for a while as he walked with his 'father' towards the fishing boats. They seemed to have an easy way about them, Adam was pleased about that. He decided that enough was enough, he had done all that could ever have been expected of him, he would leave the boy where he was and go home.

Regardless, he contacted his solicitor as soon as he was able and made over his shares in the granite quarry near Falmouth to the boy, when he struck 20 years of age. Adam realised that Freda would make the connection and there might be a possibility that she would encourage her son to claim kin. This was a chance he was prepared to take.

With a heavy heart, he made his way to Alvestoke in Gosport for the night, dismissed Thomas, paying him well for his trouble, watched him ride away back to Wetherley and then took passage to Calais from Portsmouth. Adam had not wanted to see Dory for the last time and leave with anger in his heart. He had considered taking Agnes with him but felt that would have been too cruel. He had often imagined the last encounter with his wife, for he always realised that he would have had to see her again if only to gain a divorce, which would be in both their interests. He had prepared himself for anger and tears but not for the venom that came from her once genteel mouth. The thought that she had told him so many lies hung heavy on his heart.

Getting back to Paris was now top of his priority.

Chapter 52
The Divorce and Bad Choices

Dory got her divorce very easily. Adam put everything in motion before he disappeared again. Of course, as she and he had suspected, there was an array of eager gentlemen after her money who offered marriage.

She was struggling with the ins and outs of the running of the estate and knew that one day, she would feel obligated to accept one of these offers. She did not set her sights too high knowing that the scandal her husband had invited would go against a really good catch.

In the summer of 1836, John Henry Bridges reappeared in Wetherley. He paid a visit to Weston Manor Lodge on business and to re-new his acquaintance with Lady Southerly. Brian Locke was his first point of call as he dealt with the over-all running of the estate. He then asked to be allowed to pay his respects to Lady Southerly. Mrs Warner opened the door to him and was quite surprised that he had not used the tradesmen's entrance. He explained that he was acquainted with Lady Southerly, handing her his private card instead of his business one and charmed the woman into allowing him into the hall, whilst she went to see if the lady of the house was in to visitors. Because of his kindness towards Rosamond when he had sent a wonderful nurse to them for much needed assistance, Dory felt obliged to accept this visitor and he was shown into the drawing room. Having ordered a glass of sherry, they sat and talked and she found him remarkable easy to converse with. She realised how lonely she was and with Rosamond about to re-marry, she found the company of a good talker very comfortable. He told her about his travels to Spain to inspect leather for import before she realised the time they had been sitting for almost an hour. She told John Henry that she had never travelled overseas and wondered at the experience. Dory found herself inviting John Henry to dinner a couple of days later, swept up by her enjoyment of intelligent and amusing conversation. He had taken lodgings in the next village and had hired a horse for a few days. The dinner went well and Dory had invited a couple of local dignitaries to make up a small group. The food was simple but charmingly prepared and arranged and John Henry had taken a great deal of care about his appearance, he looked like a man of considerable means. After a very short courtship encouraged by his kindness in the previous year, they married. John Henry showed a willingness to live in Weston-Under-Wetherley, although he said that he had a fairly fine house of his own near Southampton. Dory suggested that he let his own house out for a while and see how that worked out, but he explained that his business was conducted from Southampton so he would need to return there regularly so that was not possible. He promised to take her and show her the Hampshire property at some stage.

All seemed well between them. John Henry was charming, a good listener and equally good talker. He liked to play cards and soon, gathered a group of like-minded friends together. John Henry always encouraged Dory to write to her so called cousin, Rosamond, and her new husband in Weston, which Dory found quite endearing. Rosamond had married a very brusque sort of a fellow, very unlike her previous husband, Sir James Shepherd, who had been a kind and gentle, golly man. Rosamond had realised her mistake in rushing into marriage but was now trapped in a loveless arrangement. Dory had tried to dissuade her cousin from marrying, what everyone considered to be below her, but loneliness can make you do silly things.

"It is alright for you, Dory," Rosamond had once said to her cousin. "You have looks, education, poise and confidence, I do not have any of these things. I need a strong man to take care of me. I will not get the offers you receive, although I do have a great amount of wealth which can make even the plainest woman attractive."

"It is your wealth that worries me, Rosamond," came the reply. "Please, be certain that any man who asks for your hand has money of his own and is not just after yours."

"I cannot even give a man a son," continued Rosamond, "or any child for that matter. There will not be the callers you expect because of this and I will not lie."

Unfortunately, Dory realised her cousin was right on this account. Sons seem to be a big want for most men of property.

When Sir Alfred, a widower with two teenage sons, came into Rosamond's life, she thought that he would take care of her and her business interests. He seemed a caring sort of man and his boys were very polite, that was until after the wedding. Very soon, the property empire built by Rosamond's late husband, Sir James, had been carved up in favour of Alfred's sons, who instead of being grateful, treated Rosamond like a skivvy. They were wastrels who were gambling and drinking heavily from the moment it was legally possible. Their father indulged them and encouraged their every outrageous action. Rosamond wondered if maybe they were all slightly insane as there was no reasoning with them. She had to sit back and watch as the money, her husband had so carefully and cleverly built up, was wasted on lavish trips, clothing, horses, carriages and loose women. No attempt was made to maintain the life style, it was a live for the day attitude.

Very soon, Rosamond realised that she was going to eventually end up alone and poor, because it was obvious that once the bulk of the money was gone, so would Alfred be. She prayed that he spent the money fast as she was continually being emotionally drained by her now unwanted family. She was so happy that Dory kept in touch and seemed to have made a better match than herself; not what Rosamond had anticipated, however, she thought Dory would at least marry a titled gentleman. Unfortunately, they no longer visited each other, Alfred would not allow it.

Before long, Rosamond and her new husband, who was as disinterested in her as she was in him, decided to share out the inheritance and go their separate ways. All of Rosamond's property was now under the control of her hateful husband but she managed to persuade him to allow her to keep the house in Weston-Under-Wetherley and receive the income from one of the Weston-Super-Mare lettings, both of these properties were legally passed over to her. Rosamond felt that at least she had saved some of Sir James' fortune, resenting deeply the fact that she had ever allowed herself to be married to such a brute of a man after being married to such a gentle one. Alfred readily agreed to the divorce terms as he was keen to get on with his own debauched life style and was happy to see the back of Rosamond. She moved to Wetherley so at least she was safe and in familiar territory and could once more visit Dory. Alice and Jake had been amongst the first of the once loyal servants to leave Bleadon Farm, they had taken Rosebud with them and gone to work for a neighbouring farm that provided them with a little cottage to live in.

Chapter 53
New Family, 1837

Just a year after the wedding, Dorothia gave birth to a healthy son which they christened Robert but was always called Robin. He was christened Robert John Bridges, John after John Constable, who died that year and not after his father as suspected by most people. As she looked down at her new bundle of joy, she was a happy, contented woman.

She had already decided that if the child was a girl, they would have called her Victoria after their new, very young queen. William 1V had died that year and this tiny, little woman was now unexpectedly queen—much to everyone amazement and delight. Victoria was the daughter of Prince Edward, Duke of Kent and Strathearn, the fourth son of George III; both the duke and the king having died in 1820, leaving Victoria as heir to the throne at the tender age of 18 after her father's three elder brothers had all died, leaving no surviving legitimate children.

Not long before Robin's birth, Dory received a letter from Lady Mary in Brighton. She usually wrote once or twice a year and gave Dory any family news or stories of happenings in Brighton. Dory always replied with very scant details of her new life, giving the impression that nothing had really changed for her.

Mary had written ever since Dorothia had stayed in Brighton with her. She had been unable to go to Dory and the Earl of Southerly's wedding because she could not leave her ailing husband. Her husband had been ailing for a number of years and did not seem to improve or get any worse, so Dory had guessed that although Lady Mary had always been charming and was still writing to her, there was certain feeling of the wedding in Weston-Under-Wetherley being a little low brow for her. Not that she actually ever said such a thing to Dory. In fact, the letters to and fro had always been informal and very informative. Dory had told Mary of the disastrous marriage her 'cousin', Rosamond, had made and how she was back in Weston-Under-Wetherley. The Bradbury's had known Sir James Shepherd many years ago but had lost touch; they had heard that he had married, had a son and that they had both died of TB. Lady Mary remembered Sir James as a charming young man and had been sorry to hear of his demise. She had taken an interest in what had become of his wife and was sad to hear that she had rushed rather unseemly into an uncomfortable marriage. Dory did not want to write and tell Lady Mary that she was now a divorced woman; that was very frown upon in high circles, better you be beaten black and blue than divorced.

When the earl disappeared, Dory decided that as she was unlikely to ever go to Brighton again, she would not mention her change of circumstances. News of that type reaches all important people's ears, so Mary was fully informed from other sources and chose not to embarrass Dory by mentioning it. Mary liked to talk and she liked to write, and Dory kept all her letters, reading them again from time to time when she felt a little down.

Mary had written a few years earlier to tell Dorothia how she had introduced her eldest brother, Henry, to a good friend's daughter, being concerned that he did not seem to have found himself a bride and was 30 years of age. She had contrived to arrange for the young woman, Amy, to accompany her to a party being held in Falford Hall in Somerset, the family home of the Fitzroys, which was her surname before she married. Henry was immediately attracted to Amy, who was vivacious and very pretty, though he considered her too young. Henry then inherited the family fortune in the same year that his parents both died on one of their foreign excursions, and two years later, he married Amy, who was very mature beyond her years and a capable woman despite her youth, she was considerably younger than Henry.

Lady Mary reminded Dory how she had sent a bound book of poetry for her daughter, Seraphina, when she was born and told her she had sent the same to Amy when she was expecting her first child and she had loved it. Mary really was very fond of Amy as she enjoyed a great many of the same interests. Unfortunately, Amy had died in childbirth, delivering a daughter, Esme, and her brother was heartbroken.

At the time, Dory had written a little note to say how sorry she was at the news. It had taken her back in her mind to the death of Sally in childbirth. She added that the book of poems would be treasured all the more for knowing that Amy had loved it and how much Amy meant to Lady Mary.

The latest letter was telling her how her grandchildren were progressing and any changes in Brighton since Dory had been there. It made Dory very happy to know that she had people she could write to and hear all about the outside world; she didn't travel very far herself now that Weston-Super-Mare was no longer an option. She had noticed that Lady Mary's letters were less informative than they used to be and guessed it was because she was now married to a man of business instead of an earl. She knew the way the tom tom's worked and was sure that Mary would have been fully informed. She had not invited anyone from her previous life to the wedding, which was very low key, not wanting the embarrassment of each refusal she might get.

Agnes was starting to grow into a pretty little girl, she loved her little brother and spent many hours just watching him. She never once asked about her real father and as time went on, seemed to forget their previous life; she had, after all, been very young when Adam made his choice in life. John Henry spent a great deal of time away from home in Southampton so Dory took the opportunity to teach her daughter to read and write and even ride a horse occasionally. John Henry was not interested in the arts, opera, poetry, horse-riding or any of the other interests that Dory missed since the earl had left.

Sometimes, Dory would take Agnes up into the attic and there, she would open a large trunk and take out beautiful dresses to show her daughter. Dory would hold the dress up against her and waltz round the room, whilst the dress twilled out around her. Agnes would clap out a tune and laugh with sure delight watching her mother. It was never made clear to the child why these magnificent dresses were hidden away in a trunk in the attic. It was Dory's secret world. Sometimes, they would sit cross legged on the floor and read copies of the Literary Gazette. Dory had taken trouble to teach Agnes how to read and write and subsequently, the child developed a passion for poetry. Dory would read passages from the gazette to her eager daughter, her favourite writer being a young woman called Letitia Elizabeth Landon. Letitia had chosen to publish poems in the gazette under the initials L.E.L and there was much speculation about the author, who was still very young. The young poet had quite a following and, with the financial help of her grandmother, had a book of poems published which Dory had a copy of and treasured. One day, she presented Agnes with a beautifully bound book of poems by the aforementioned young woman called 'The Fate of Adalaide', that had been sent to her from Lady Mary in Brighton to be given to Seraphina when Dory thought she was old enough to appreciate it. It was to become Agnes's greatest treasure and she became determined to read well enough to fully appreciate the book and works of other poets, which she thoroughly enjoyed.

One day, Agnes found her mother crying on her own in their attic hideaway.

"What is the matter, Mother?" Agnes asked.

"It is nothing, child," was the reply. "It is just something in this letter from a friend in Brighton."

"Do tell me," implored her daughter.

"It is silly really, Agnes, it is just news of someone I didn't even know but it touched my soul," replied Dory. Agnes sat cross legged on the floor in front of her mother and took the letter that hung loosely from her hand. It had a clipping from the gazette inside an envelope.

"You can read it, child, if you wish," said Dory.

Agnes took the cutting out of the envelope and carefully unfolded it. It was about the poetess, Letitia Elizabeth Landon, and she read the contents slowly, then looked up at her mother.

"What does it all mean, Mother?" the child asked.

"It seems that the wonderful Miss Landon married in haste and sailed to the Cape Coast with her new husband looking for a life away from her critics," Dory explained.

"Why would she have critics, Mother, if she was so wonderful?" asked the child innocently

"My dear child," continued her mother, "when you grow into a woman, you will learn that being a woman is hard. People expect you to fail and some even wish you to fail. Do not ask me why, it is just the way of the world. Letitia had a delicate mind and body and she could not take unfair criticism. You will find that poets have a very delicate ego, not that I expect you to meet many."

"I do hope I will one day, Mother," was the reply. "Wouldn't that be wonderful to write and listen to poetry every day? I would love to marry the greatest poet ever born and he would write just for me."

"I think you would soon tire of that life, my dear," said Dory with a slight smile. "Poetry can take you to places you can only dream of but it rarely make you rich."

"Do tell me more about Letitia, Mother," Agnes begged.

"Well, she married and went to distant lands," Dory continued. "But it seems that her constitution was not strong and after a very short time at their destination, she died. There is talk that she took her own life and that would be very sad."

"So you are crying for her loss," said Agnes, a tear appearing in her own eye. "I can understand that, Mother."

"My child," said Dory, "you are much too young to have to worry about loss. The thing is that I read a story about Letitia a while ago, also sent to me by my friend, Mary, in Brighton; she had once found true love, or at least thought she had, a man called John Forster. But he had believed stories about her virtue or lack of, that may or may not have been true. He did not give her the benefit of the doubt and Letitia felt that was no basis for a marriage, so she broke off the engagement and married instead the first man who asked her."

Agnes looked puzzled at her mother.

"I truly believe that there is one true love for everyone and when you find him and maybe lose him, you should never try to replace him, whatever high-minded reason you may have," concluded her mother, still looking tearful and obviously thinking about the errant earl and poor Rosamond.

"Will we go to Brighton one day, Mother, and visit your friend?" asked Agnes.

"Who knows what is round the corner, child. I would like to see Mary again, I like her very much but we are worlds apart now, I doubt our paths will ever cross," replied her mother.

"And she likes poetry as well," added Agnes.

"That she does, Agnes. In fact, I told her in a letter that I had given you the set of poems she had sent to me for you some time ago. When she sent the book, just after your birth, she told me that she had purchased a bound copy of The Fate of Adalaide for herself and had sent one to her brother, Henry's, young wife, some years ago and could understand why we both love it so much." Dory was looking quite pensive, thinking about poetry and her past life.

When Rosamond moved back into her little house in Weston-Under-Wetherley, Dory was so pleased to see her and made sure she was her first visitor.

"I have been a great fool, Dory," said Rosamond. "I allowed myself to be won over by a false charm; Alfred turned out to be brute and I will never mention his name again. My only consolation is that I had very little when I met my dear James and so I am at least in a better financial position now than I deserve."

"I am so glad you are here, Rosamond, I have missed you so much and so has Agnes," said Dory smiling broadly. "You must come over to the lodge and meet my husband and our dear little Robin, he is adorable."

"The child or John Henry?" replied her cousin laughing.

Rosamond became a regular visitor to the lodge, especially during the periods that Dory was alone, whilst John Henry was away on business.

Dory was heavy with John Henry's second child when she and Rosamond met up for afternoon tea at Rosamond's little house on the edge of the village. The house was not really small but seemed so after the lodge. It had four good-sized bedrooms, as well as three attic rooms, a dining room, spacious sitting room and very pretty withdrawing room with a study off. The kitchen was in the cellar and enormous part of the lower floor was also a wine cellar. A great deal of Rosamond's time was taken with sewing, painting with water colours, reading and gardening—gardening was her real love. James had taught her to appreciate the colour and the smell of a well laid out garden. When she painted, she painted water colours of the garden. James old retainer, Pernell had travelled with Rosamond and she relied on him greatly. Pernell could not bear to stay in Bleadon Farm after the changes as result of Rosamond's unfortunate marriage choice. She had found a cook in the village, who proved to be a very accomplished cook, quite adventurous for a county person.

"How our lives have changed," said Dory. "Who would have imagined that we would be here like this. I am so glad you are close by."

Life went on and Dorothia miscarried what would have been a daughter, 18 months after the birth of Robin and again a year later. John Henry did not seem unduly distressed by these occurrences. As the years passed, he showed less and less interest in Dory and spent more and more time away. When he was in Westerley, he seemed to have a great many hangers on in tow, and he showed off a great deal about his wealth to them. He gave his so called friends gifts that actually were Dory's by moral right if not by law. Unfortunately, she had not realised before she committed herself that when she re-married, all her property became her husband's property to do with as he will. She was sure that the earl had not considered this when he put the estate in her name to keep her and his daughter financially stable. She thought that the earl had probably not expected her to ever re-marry anyway; there had been no financial reason for her to do so, and she often wondered herself why she had.

John Henry was always very proud of his wife's looks and paraded her around like a prize heifer in front of his so called friends. She was constantly feeling uncomfortable when he was at home.

Then she found that she was with child again and this time, she felt that she might actually carry it full term; she had none of the sickness that she had endured with the last two pregnancies.

Dory's strength had been drained by three miscarriages in the five years of marriage to John Henry. He still appeared to be a caring man at times, though he spent more and more of his time in Southampton looking after his business interest.

Dory was starting to believe that John Henry was losing interest in her, though he seemed to be very fond of his son, Robin, who was growing into a strong and capable little boy.

Robin spent a lot of time visiting Rosamond at her house nearby and he was a happy child. Dory taught Robin to read and write and Rosamond taught him the fundamentals of arithmetic, which he enjoyed; in fact as he grew, he became more and more fascinated by numbers. When Rosamond was married to Sir James, he encouraged her to take an interest in the financial running of Bleadon Manor Farm and she became a competent book keeper, these skills she was passing on to young Robin.

John Henry was at home when Dory gave birth to their daughter, Florentine, in 1842. Agnes was now old enough to be able to help her mother with the new baby, which Agnes loved.

Agnes took a keen interest in everything around her, when she didn't have her nose in a book; she liked to groom her own pony, take cuttings from plants and try to grow more and she was turning into a competent, knowledgeable and practical young girl. She even liked to watch the cook in the kitchen preparing food and often offered to assist, much to the amusement of the staff. She used to help her mother with her hair. Dory was always particular about her appearance and her daughter thought that she was secretly a princess in hiding. They used to try different styles and Agnes became quite competent at the art of hair sculpture. Dory often looked at her eldest daughter and felt content in the fact that she would be able to look after herself if needs be.

Agnes and her mother spent as much time as they could together reading poetry and short stories. Dory was pleased when William Wordsworth, one of her favourite poets, became poet Laureate in 1843, and she explained to Agnes the importance of the role he had undertaken.

Dory noticed that Wetherley Manor Lodge was starting to look a little run down and started to worry where all the money was going. She knew that her husband was a gambler but he had taken to drinking heavily as well. He found country life very dull and found any excuse to go to Southampton without his family.

Slowly, things started to change around her. She had noticed that the stables were no longer all occupied and quantity of livestock seemed to have depleted recently. Something she intended to discuss with John Henry when he was home next.

Dory did not realise that her life was about to slip into the same sort of abyss that her friend and so called cousin's had.

Dory had never told Lady Mary that her husband had vanished; when she wrote, she always talked about the house, the garden and village life. She made up her mind not to communicate with Mary again now that she had a new life, she felt their lives were now on a different plateau. It was fine whilst she was the wife of an earl but a common import and exporter's wife did not have the same ring to it. She felt it would save the embarrassment of Mary feeling obliged to write for old time's sake and maybe, even offer to help her and her husband financially, that would be too much to bear. Better to end the friendship now.

John Henry went to Southampton on business and was gone longer than usual. It was at this time that Brian Locke, the foreman of the farm, came to Dory in an agitate way looking for her husband. When she explained that he was away on business, Mr Locke asked if he could speak to her, which she readily agreed to.

Brian Locke, cap in hand, stood in front of Dory looking most embarrassed. "Madam," he began, "when your husband, the earl, took me on many years ago, this farm and surrounding land was very profitable."

"So I believe," she replied. "Please continue, speak freely."

"Madam," he twisted his cap in his hand as he spoke, "the earl made me promise to keep a close eye on you and Miss Agnes and keep this place running well for you both."

Dory showed a little alarm at the fact that the earl had obviously taken an employee into his confidence and obviously talked with him that he was leaving before she realised herself.

"If I can be blunt, Madam?" he said. When she nodded, he took that as a sign to do so. "The present master does not have a farmer's mind. He has sold all the best and strongest horses, goodness knows how we are supposed to mow the hay or pull the carts or take livestock to market."

"Have you spoken to him about this?" asked Dory. "What horses do we have left?"

"We have an old nag that can barely pull herself along, your stallion, the coach horse and Miss Agnes' pony," was the reply.

"Then you must sell them, Brian, and buy a work horse immediately," she said.

"I can do that for you, Madam, but the farm hands have not been paid for many a week and if we lose them, we lose everything," Brian replied. "They have youngsters of their own to feed, they will start looking elsewhere for work."

Dory was appalled. "Why I was not informed?" she demanded.

"I was told on pain of dismissal not to tell you, Madam," was the reply.

"I will go to the kitchen and see what supply we can offer to help," she said.

"I do not believe that it will be enough for the amount of people we need to feed, Madam," was the reply.

She put her hand on her stomach and felt the new life inside her move and was sickened by the thought that maybe after the life she had lived, she might find herself and her children hungry as well.

Dory looked about the manor for items to sell to rescue the situation. She found herself wishing that Sir James was still around to offer support and sensible suggestions, but he was gone and so she had to think for herself.

She had considered selling the dresses but decided against it and clung on to her old life as long as she could. There were silver items that could be sacrificed first.

Dory miscarried yet another tiny life, this time she was not too upset as she knew that she would have struggled to feed it.

Dory's grandmother, Seraphina, who Agnes was originally named after, passed away after a long illness. Dory took this loss very hard as her grandmother had always been an unbiased ear, who would always listen without judgement and she would miss that cushion. Dory had even told Seraphina about the lie she had told Adam connected to Freda and the half-brother; she was the only person she ever told besides Adam and Sir James, and she knew that it would stay with her until she died. Dory could unburden any evil thoughts by sharing them with her grandmother without fear of outrage and condemnation. It would be hard to replace the void left by such a person in anyone's life and her passing saddened Dory greatly.

A lot had changed since the disappearance of Adam Southerly, the Earl of Wetherley. William 1V had died and there was a queen at England's rudder, a very young one at that, Victoria. The queen had already produced a healthy daughter, Princess Victoria, Princess Royal and a year later, a much wanted son and heir, Albert Edward followed by Alice Maud Mary and now, she was expecting yet another baby. Dory was in awe of the queen's breeding capacity and also, Sir Robert Peel was the Conservative Prime Minister, all amazing changes.

Dory sat for a while thinking about what she should do for the best. She decided that she would have to tell her father, she had no option. Phillip Mountjoy was a very proud man and the thought of his daughter living under threat of bankruptcy upset him greatly. He was, by birth, from a wealthy family so he was able to arrange for a small amount of money to be passed to his daughter to cover the wages of her servants and field hands. It was made clear that it was a one off payment to avoid any embarrassment to the greater family. Dory accepted the money, she did not care about embarrassment caused, she just wanted to know that her people were going to be fed.

Chapter 54
A Move to Southampton, 1843

John Henry was now on the verge of bankruptcy, having gambled and drunk away a small fortune; his temper was now very short and life was becoming very uncomfortable. When he was in Wetherley, he was usually in his cups so he was no longer the stimulating company he once had been.

A great many of the treasures that Dory had inherited, when her first husband made the manor lodge over to her, had been sold to pay wages and other debts and the house was looking far from grand.

Debtors had started knocking on the door and it was quite clear to Dory that her life in Weston-Under-Wetherley was about to come to an end.

One morning when John Henry was recovering from an unusually heavy hangover, Dory took the opportunity to confront him about his extravagant ways and put forward the suggestion that they sell Westerley Manor Lodge, which he readily agreed to.

John Henry owned what he referred to as a considerable property near Southampton, which was still as yet unvisited by Dory. She had always thought this strange remembering how Adam could not wait to take her to Keighley and meet everyone as soon as they married. It was several years now and still Dory had never visited Hampshire, let alone the house that it seems she was now bound to end her days in.

John Henry had operated out of Southampton and Portsmouth when his business was lucrative, before money went to his head, and he allowed his business interests to slide into near bankruptcy. Southampton and Portsmouth are both very large ports and perfect for running an import business from. Marrying Dory and gaining the finances that came with that venture had made John Henry lazy. He had quite quickly changed from a wealthy and respected business man to a drunken ruffian.

It was quite an upheaval for Dory, Agnes, Robin and Florentine, none of which wanted to give up their present home and move to a strange part of England away from friends and family.

Rosamond asked Dory if maybe Robin could stay on with her. She promised to keep teaching him the fundamentals of accounting with the hope that he might be able to buy himself an apprenticeship when he was old enough. The boy was seven, coming on eight and an apprenticeship could be gained by the age of 12, sometimes even younger if you have the right connections.

Dory hated the idea of her family being split up but also did not want to drag her children into an uncertain life.

It was not difficult to find a buyer for Weston Manor Lodge. Dory used the solicitor that the earl had used and they started packing up everything they could for the move to Southampton. She assumed that the solicitors, Foster and Newman, of York would send a message to the earl out of courtesy so she did not bother to write to him herself as any missive would have gone via the solicitors anyway, account of her not having the earl's address to send anything directly.

Carts were packed to the gunnels, Dory's precious trunk from the attic being the first thing to be loaded.

John Henry explained that the Hampshire house was fully furnished but that maybe some special pieces might not look out of place. There was no room for family portraits or large pieces of furniture.

Unbeknown to John Henry, Dory gave several pieces of silver to staff members to repay them for lack of wages and loyalty; she also arranged for her father to house a few items safely, just in case all did not go well for her and the children in Southampton. Family portraits were placed in store for safekeeping.

Soon, the family was on the move. Dorothia had taken Agnes and Florentine to her parents to say goodbye, and there were a lot of tears shed and a lot of angry word spoken about the Earl of Southerly by Dory's mother, Bathsheba, who blamed Adam, rightly or wrongly, for all Dory's misfortunes.

The trip was long and tedious, especially with a young baby in tow. Agnes had noticed that how tired her mother looked and took over the caring of Florentine.

They travelled down the Fosseway, past Banbury and Bicester. Agnes was charmed by the scenery, the thatched cottages they passed on the way and ruddy complexions of the bemused villagers, who seemed to line the streets to watch the passing of the line of heavily laden carts. They had hired a carriage to take the family and it caused quite a disturbance when they pulled up outside The Bear Inn stands on the corner of Alfred Street and Blue Boar Street, opposite Bear Lane in the centre of Oxford. It is not a very large inn but it has a very good reputation. The servants that travelled with the family and took care of the carts of furniture lodged in a less salubrious place for the night.

The Bear Inn, being right in the centre of Oxford, gave Dory and Agnes an opportunity to see a little of Oxford before moving on the next day. It was not very practical stopping in the centre of Oxford, usually when on the move, an inn is found on the outskirts for convenience but John Henry had arranged to meet a gentleman in Oxford, Dory assumed it was to do with business. When he arrived back at the Bear Inn, very worse for wear and with signs of a black eye, she guessed that the meeting had not gone as well as hoped. Later, she discovered that John Henry had met up with one of his creditors, someone he owed a lot of money to. He told Dory that he had booked into the Bear Inn instead of a larger inn, so no one would be aware that they were moving lock stock and barrel and try to claim any money due through goods and shackles. The whole scenario was a great worry to Dory.

The inn keeper kept a good cellar and the food was excellent so they all spent a comfortable night as regard to food. The pork pies and boiled leg of lamb were particularly pleasing. Agnes enjoyed the pancakes and roasted chestnuts more than anything else and John Henry ate anything and found pleasure in any food or drink.

The sleeping arrangements left a lot to be desired, especially for Dory, who was used to a better style of living.

Agnes had slept on a slat bed that pulled out from under the main bed, which John Henry and Dory used, and baby Florentine slept with Agnes. Agnes hated sleeping in the same room as her mother and father as John Henry snored very loud, especially when he had too much to drink, which was nearly always. Dory found herself cursing Adam, the Earl of Wetherley, for putting her and their daughter in the position they now found themselves.

Dory and Agnes had taken the opportunity to explore a little of Oxford, there was not a lot of time for too much of this activity. The inn keeper had given the women an insight into the history of Oxford and offered a man servant to accompany them and keep them safe when they venture outside the inn.

Oxford fascinated both, Dory and Agnes, the beautiful English architecture was breath-taking for people who had spent most of their lives in the heart of the country. The young poet, Matthew Arnold, had referred to Oxford as the city of dreaming spires.

The Oxford canal connects the city to Coventry and there is also a link into the Thames at the Isis Lock. The Great Western Railway has just finished their link from Oxford to London via Didcot and Reading so Oxford is a very busy city.

Early in the morning, after breakfast, the family gathered their things together to join the rest of their entourage outside the Angel Coaching Inn. When they arrived at the inn to pay for the night, they discovered that two of the men, hired to accompany the family and deliver them safely to Southampton, had taken to their heels and left. The lure of a big city had taken its toll.

This meant that John Henry had to ride with one of the carts to secure the contents. This pleased Dory no end, she did not want her husband breathing his stale beer full breath in her face.

The carts and carriage travelled on to Faringdon near Newbury before stopping again to rest the horses and people. This time, they all stayed together. John Henry did not want to risk losing any more hands, so they stayed at the Old Crown Coaching Inn, which was equipped for such a large amount of people and horses. As usual, the work force slept where they could, whereas the family booked into a large room for the night.

The food was basic and the room was clean so everyone was satisfied.

After three days of travelling, the entourage arrived at the outskirts of Southampton on the Portsmouth Road and stopped for the last time at the White Horse in the market town of Romsey. The white Horse is situated right in the centre of Romsey and used by many travellers, especially ones coming from Bristol to Portsmouth. It wasn't until they reach this point in their journey that John Henry told his wife the actual address of his property and it was Boldre—deep in the New Forest, quite some way from the lights of Southampton.

The tired travellers moved on the next day, past Ower, across Netley Marsh, down to Lyndhurst, on to Brockenhurst and finally, they reached their destination, Boldre near Lymington, deep in the forest. The first fear that struck Dory was that she was dangerously close to Netley, where she had housed Adam's half-brother, George, and his mother, Freda. What if they bumped into each other, the possibility was horrifying to Dory.

Dory's sister, Everline, and her travelling vicar husband no longer lived at Hamble, he had been transferred to the village of Biddistone in Wiltshire, many miles away, so Dory knew she could not rely on seeing her for a long time, much to her disappointment.

Dory had expected to be living in the large city of Southampton as she had always been told but the property was actually a long way from there. She had never been to Southampton so it really made no difference to her if she lived there or not. She knew that her life, as she had known it, was over and that she had to make the most of what life threw at her for the sake of her children. She was not, at first, displeased as Boldre looked to be a very pretty little hamlet set amongst the trees of the New Forest. Years ago, she had disliked the idea of Brighton as a long-term place to stay because of its size, although she had enjoyed the facilities offered in such a vibrant place, so a small settlement appealed to her greatly. It was usually easy to make friends in small community once you become accepted, and it was far enough away from Weston-Under-Wetherley that no one would ever have heard of the Southerly's.

It was, undoubtedly, a beautiful part of the world but not what Dory had expected. She had expected to be taken to the industrial side of Southampton as John Henry did most of his business in or around the docks, either Southampton or Portsmouth. The idea had not appealed greatly but she had no choice but to follow where he lead. Boldre was, in fact, a pleasant surprise.

The Southampton Docks Company had been formed just over 10 years earlier in 1835 and in 1838, the foundation stone of the docks was laid and the first dock opened in 1842. Until then, John Henry had spent the majority of his working life in Portsmouth or nearby but had migrated to the Southampton Docks in recent years.

The house owned by John Henry Bridges is in shadow of the Parish Church perched high on a hill. St John the Baptist Church, Boldre looks down upon the village like a huge reminder of what was to come. Dory thought it very appropriate that the church be on such a high hill, she felt it was nearer to God. It has an enormous churchyard full of gravestone. Walking round the church, you would think that families never moved far away; there are so many grave dedicated to people of the same surname. Dory did think this might be a good sign that it was a pleasant place to live your life out.

When Dory first encountered the house that was now to be her home, she was appalled. The property, although detached, was very rundown. She looked at the outside of the property and dreaded the work she would have to undertake to get the house looking in any way acceptable.

It looked like a good size, obviously very tiny as compared to Weston Manor Lodge or Keighley Manor and very neglected. It bore no similarity to the property John Henry had described to her.

It was a detached house, but it did not stand in very much land. There was a slightly battered wooden gate, a small front garden and a path with three stone steps at the end that led to a very wide wooden front door that had a faded green hue. She smiled as she managed to make out the name of the house, Far End, carved into the stonework above the door. She thought it described the house perfectly. Either side of the door were very large bays with three very wide sash windows in each that reach down to a stone section that marked the bottom of the windows. On either side of the house, there was a huge red brick outer chimney stack that looked like book ends. The roof was of charcoal coloured slate tiles that were covered greatly in moss, giving the roof a green look. Ivy grew up one side of the house, taking over that chimney stack. A wooden fence went all around the house and Dory walked to the side and could see that there was a small garden enclosed by tattered fencing on two sides only and a stream running across the far end forming a boundary. Most local people work on the land, in Lymington or other fishing towns, or travelled as far as

Portsmouth or Southampton to the docks. Lymington is an up and coming town with gas street lighting and a police force, there is also the baths and open air swimming pool to use. The paddle steamer travels between Lymington and Yarmouth so a lot of people are moving to Lymington looking for work. The poorhouse was re-built in 1836 to accommodate anyone seeking help, and Dory imagined that might one day be her destiny.

There were several elegant villas that had been built in the past few years on the edge of the forest near Boldre and the neighbouring village, Sway, which made John Henry's older property look even less inspiring. The surrounding area had been virtually untouched by the Swing Riots of November 1830 because there had been only non-violent protests in nearby Shirley and Millbrook by labourers demanding an increase in wages, this means that all walks of life live side by side there about without too much resentment. There had been no rioters hung or shipped off to Australia from the immediate area causing friction amongst neighbour, which made the forest a pleasant place to live.

John Henry unlocked the front door and the family stepped inside. There was a heavy layer of dust in every direction. Happily, the majority of the furniture had been covered by dust clothes and the carpets had been rolled up and placed to the side of the rooms. The net curtains that hung from every window and once presumable had been white, were a distinct colour grey. The velvet drapes looked saveable. Dory sighed a large sigh of relief that she had brought some of the Weston Manor Lodge servants with her, including the little maid, Kate, though the majority had chosen to stay on with the new owners, not wanting to be up-rooted and away from their families.

There was a central hallway, either side was a large wooden door, to the right was the sitting room and behind that a small drawing room. To the left of the hall was the dining room and behind that a large kitchen and butler's pantry. There was a large range for cooking that looked as though it would take quite a lot of effort to get clean and working again but it pleased Dory to see it. The butler's pantry had enough cupboard and shelves to supply a large household, let alone their meagre one. All the rooms were very full of furniture. Apparently, John Henry had not been able to throw anything of his mother's out when she died so even her clothes were still in situ.

The stairway at the back of the hallway was quite imposing for small house and led up to four large bedrooms, there were also two small, windowless attic rooms. As John Henry was rarely at home, Dory shared a room with Florentine and Agnes most of the time, which meant that Kate and the female servants could all sleep in one room and the men in another. This also meant that they could concentrate on cleaning fewer rooms immediately and then the others could be dealt with in due time. If John Henry was at home, everything changed and Agnes and Florentine moved into the spare bedroom.

Dory asked John Henry why he had told her that he used the house when working in Hampshire as clearly the place had been closed up for many years.

"It was my family home," he explained. "I was brought up here. I didn't want the bother of keeping the place clean, so I closed it up and took lodgings instead."

"But it could have given you an additional income," she replied sensibly.

"I did not want strangers living in it," was all he would say on the subject. Dory actually did feel a sort of empathy for this sentiment and it made her determined to make it into a home again.

The first month of arriving at Boldre was full of cleaning, scrubbing and sweeping out the old house to make it fit to be lived in. Curtains had to be washed and carpets beaten. Dory found herself quite enjoying the challenge. House work she could understand a lot easier than running Weston Manor Lodge. John Henry seemed quite unbothered by all the activity and was rarely to be seen in Boldre. Dory discovered that when he used to go away on business, he always stayed in lodgings in Lymington with a woman known locally as widow Brown, who had three young children which is why the house was so full of dust and cobwebs; it had not been lived in since John Henry's parents had died—first his father in an accident whilst fishing and then his mother. Dory learnt more about her mysterious husband from neighbours than she had ever been told by him. He had, apparently, been devoted to his mother and worked very hard to keep her living in the manner that he felt she deserved. She discovered that John Henry had been quite a leading light in the village at one time, having risen to quite a man of means. His import and export business had thrived and he became rather wealthy operating out of Far End with his mother, acting as housekeeper and accountant. They had employed quite a few young people from nearby to attend the house inside and out, and there had been talk of him moving his mother to a larger property. She died suddenly so this never happened. John Henry had become quite inconsolable when his mother died but suddenly seemed to pick up and resume his business ventures. Dory assumed this was when he met her and guessed that he planned to make her his wife and use her as a stepping stone to his ambitions. John Henry had never told her about his growing up years but a lot about his foreign travels, which she now wondered whether they were actually true or fantasy.

Money was short, one by one the servants left of their own free will, unable to or unwilling to work for nothing.

Dory, who is very good with a needle and thread, started to work as a seamstress from the sitting room of the Boldre house.

Despite John Henry spending less and less time in Boldre, Dory found that towards the end of 1844, she was pregnant again. Something she did not want or need. He had arrived at Far End, full of the joys of spring with talk of work and hope for the future; Dory was hopeful for a moment that he had turned a corner and the move to Boldre and her making the house a home might have shook him up and re-kindled his old work ethics. Very soon, she realised that she was wrong; he was sliding into a deep hole of drink and despair and looked likely to drag his whole family down there with him.

When John Henry arrived at the house, he was usually drunk and was becoming more and more volatile. On one such occasion, he struck Agnes across the face with such force that she totally lost her balance. He screamed at her that she was too expensive to keep idly and she needed to find herself a position in a fine house somewhere and help bring in money. When Dory said that the girl was too young, John Henry insisted that they pretend the girl is older by a couple of years.

"Who would be able to tell?" he slurred. "She is well advanced for her age, we will say she is 13 or 14 and we will have no trouble finding her a position and there will be one less mouth to feed."

Any amount of protesting came to nothing. John Henry had made up his mind, Agnes must go into service. He even went to the trouble of taking Agnes to one side and telling her that he had found her birth certificate and now realised that she was older than he had imagined or she believed. Agnes never questioned anything told her by the man she thought was her father, John Henry Bridges; she had felt the edge of his belt too many times of late to argue.

Dory was too embarrassed at her fall from grace to write and tell her parents about her change of circumstances. She had written a jolly letter when she first arrived in Boldre to tell her mother how pretty the house was and about the stream at the end of the garden that attracted ducks and other wild life. She tried to make her life sound idealist so no one would worry about her. She did wonder if maybe she should have sent Agnes back to Wetherley but knew that her husband would not approve, he wanted her to help with the family finances.

Dory noticed an advertisement for a scullery maid in the local paper and decided that for Agnes' safety, it would be better if she actually considered applying for the job. Agnes wrote her own letter to Mr and Mrs Keeping, who were searching for a suitable candidate to work as a scullery maid in their rather fine property on the edge of Sway Village, which was about two miles away from Boldre. Mrs Keeping was, at first, put off by the fact that this young, possible servant girl could read and write, something not overtly common. They decided to give the girl a chance and she went for an interview one Saturday afternoon in January. Both, husband and wife, were absolutely charmed by the young woman standing in front of them. Agnes is a particularly pretty, young woman with bright eyes and clear skin, she very closely resembles her mother. Her knowledge of plants, cooking and general house duties was far beyond the dreams of the Keepings. Usually, they employ simple souls and spend a great deal of their own time going over things done inadequately by servants. The fact that her mother was a seamstress seemed to impress the couple, they assumed that Agnes possessed some of these skills as well.

Agnes started work as ladies maid and general dog's body, part of her duties were to work as a scullery maid. All these things were far from the life she had been born into but happily, she did not remember much about.

With the job went a bed in a very small room at the top of the stairs in a dark and airless attic room. She could easily have travelled the short distant home but the Keepings wanted someone who was on call, so it was necessary for Agnes to live in. She had one afternoon a month off and every Sunday so long as she went to church. There is a virtually brand new church very near to the Keepings property, Saint Luke's; it was only built in 1839, so Agnes went regularly to that church. Mr and Mrs Keeping preferred to take their carriage to St John the Baptist in Boldre. The other servants told Agnes that it was because of the rivalry between the Keepings and the Bond family, who live in a very large manor house also in Sway. The Bonds use St Luke's and have seating reserved especially for them, as most wealthy families do; after all, they are more likely to put something worthwhile in the collection box than a mere servant. Agnes smiled to herself thinking of rivalry extending to church, she could not believe that God would approve of such nonsense. She did, however, feel that St John the Baptist, being older, did feel more spiritual to her.

Agnes soon settled into this new unexpected life style. She could feel at ease and not have to worry about upsetting her father, though she missed her mother desperately. She had taken a couple of her favourite poetry books with her to make the evenings go by quicker.

Not knowing her history, her reading poetry amused the other servants, who thought she had allusions above her station, most of them could barely read at all. She started reading little piece out loud to those who were interested and enjoyed watching their faces when she read something that struck a nerve. Most of time, it was just work, eat and sleep.

Chapter 55
Life in Boldre

Meanwhile, back at Boldre, John Henry Bridges became more and more unpredictable because of his alcohol dependency. All his business ventures toppled one by one and he, once again, faced bankruptcy; this time, there was no escape, no wife's inheritance to fall back on, he just had his house and contents. All of Bridges' business acquaintances started to avoid him like the plague, he no longer had a following of card playing friends, just debts.

Dory found herself actually praying that she would lose the expected baby as she was finding it difficult enough feeding her and Florentine and felt very guilty that she could no longer afford to send occasional monetary help to Rosamond for looking after Robin. Dory had changed quite quickly from the robust young woman that first went to live as Lady of the Manor in Wetherley. She was now the shadow of her former self, thin and looking drawn, as if all the cares of the world were upon her shoulders. She thought often of Adam and wondered how she could have been so stupid as to allow her life to change so drastically and what she could have done to prevent it. She used to lay in bed and wonder why she could not have been more giving and caring, maybe the earl would have stayed. She also thought a lot about her error of judgement in marrying John Henry.

John Henry appeared to vanish into thin air. Dory knew that he was in Lymington at the widow Brown's but had no idea where that was or had any intension of seeking him out. She found it hard to comprehend how she had managed to marry two men that would chose to desert her and wondered what she had done to deserve such treatment. She worked very hard at her new profession, her needlework skills brought her plenty of customers. She used the sitting room as a sewing room and she worked there from morning to dusk. Happily, sewing is done sitting down so her pregnancy did not slow her down. Mostly, she was taking in or letting out dresses; occasionally, she had the pleasure of starting anew with a rough pattern and fresh material. She took pride in her work and often said a little thank you prayer to her grandmother, Seraphina, for insisting that she learn the art of needlework from a very young age. Dory also having been instructed to move all of John Henry's mother clothes into an attic room, had sorted through them when he was absent and used a few to create new clothes for Agnes, Kate, Florentine and herself, taking material from one, a little lace from another. She amazed herself how clever she was.

A week before the expected date of the new baby's delivery, Agnes had managed to talk to Mrs Keeping into allowing her to take a week off to help her mother at the birth. She arrived home in Boldre just in time, Dory's water had broken and the local midwife was already in situ. The local midwife was not an actually trained midwife but few could afford the expenses of a real one so they used Hannah Goodfellow, a nurse who gave up nursing when discovered to be involved with illegal abortions. In Dory's previous life, she would have considered Hannah to be sent by the devil, but now she was on the other side of the blanket; she understood how some women would not have any other choice than to abort an unwanted, unaffordable baby and was starting to believe that she may have done so herself if she had thought of it sooner.

Regardless of Hannah Goodfellow's back ground, she was a gentle, soft-spoken woman, who commanded a lot of respect from her clients.

On return, Agnes noticed immediately how run down the house had become. There were only two remaining servants in the house—the cook, Mrs Payne, and Kate, the little maid who had come with the family from Weston-Under-Wetherley; neither had anywhere else to go so stayed regardless of lack of wages. There was no way Kate could keep the house spotless, even though she tried her hardest.

When Agnes arrived, her mother was having frequent contractions and Hannah assured her that it would not be long. Having already produced three healthy children, Dory was quite use to the process and showed no outward signs of distress.

24 hours later and the baby was stubbornly still resting in the womb instead of showing itself to the world. Dory was having contractions, one after another with hardly a breath in between. It was quite apparent that something was amiss and Hannah sent for the local doctor, who did not rush but turned up a few hours later. After he looked about the house and was secure in his mind that he could be paid in kind, as there were a few valuables left if not in actual money, he went to examine his patient.

Dr Banks was alone with Dory for about half an hour before he came into the room where Agnes stood holding little Florentine and talking to Hannah.

"Where is the father?" the doctor asked abruptly.

"We do not know, Sir," Agnes replied polity. "We haven't seen or heard from him for three days now. We believe he is boarding in Lymington but do not have an address."

"Well, you need to get word to the man," said the doctor shaking his head in despair.

"What is the problem, Doctor?" asked Hannah with a worried look on her face.

"Mrs Bridges needs a caesarean, in fact she needed one several hours ago, it is probably too late now," was the reply.

"What do you mean too late?" cried Agnes. "You are a doctor, you can do this surely."

"I can but I won't," the doctor replied. "It isn't that I don't want to, I just know it is too late and I might save the baby but not the mother. I need the father's permission to do what I need to do."

"Do you mean you would let her die if the father does not appear soon?" said Hannah shocked.

"I mean I will follow the law," was the reply.

"Good God man, this is my mother we are talking about. Surely, she can give permission," said Agnes in tears.

"I am afraid that your mother is delirious and she is not capable of making a rational decision."

Agnes sat on the floor, baby on her lap and cried so hard that the ground shook.

"Enough," shouted Hannah. "Are you saying there is no hope for Mrs Bridges?"

"I am," replied the doctor matter-of-factually.

"Then I will use all the skills I gained through abortions to get the baby out alive. Will you help me, Doctor?" pleaded Hannah.

"Certainly not, Madam," was the reply and with that, the doctor picked up his hat and coat and left the property as quickly as he could, slamming the door behind him.

Agnes suddenly came to her senses. "I will help you, Hannah," she said.

"No, but you will run to my friend, Susan, at the other end of the village and fetch her for me, she has helped me before," was the reply. "She is in Dog Rose Cottage, tell her to hurry."

Kate, the little maid, and the cook were the only paid servants left in the house at this time, not that they very often actually were paid, so Agnes gave Florentine to Kate to take charge of while the drama unfolded. She was a sweet child so no one minded such a chore.

Hannah gave Agnes full details of where to find Dog Rose Cottage, and she ran as fast as she could to fetch Susan, who returned with her within half an hour. Agnes was sent out of the house again on a false errand whilst the two women looked after Dory as best they could.

When Agnes returned, before she even got through the front door, she could hear the sound of a baby crying. She entered with trepidation, not knowing what to find. Amazingly enough, her mother was still alive, very weak—her clothes were stuck to her in a combination of blood and sweat; her hair, which she prized so much, was soaked and unkempt—but she managed a very feeble smile for her daughter. Hannah and Susan stayed long enough to help Agnes bath her mother. It took the combined strengths of all three women to fill the bath and lift Dory into it.

Hannah held Dory's head above the water, she was too weak to support her own weight, and Agnes washed her mother very gently and as much as was possible in the circumstances. They managed to dry her and once they had dressed her in a clean night dress, they placed her into the now clean bed.

Hannah took all the bedding and Dory's blood-stained nightdress out into the back of the house and burnt them.

"They would never have been clean again, best be rid of them," she said matter-of-factually. "We are going now but I will tell the doctor that your mother lives and so does the baby. He may call but I doubt it,"

Agnes was absolutely beside herself with worry, she had Florentine to look after and now this new little sister and her mother did not look capable of helping in any way. She had no idea where her father was so she was alone.

Kate came into the bedroom carrying Florentine and sighed a large sigh of relief when she saw her mistress was still alive.

"Katie, I do not know how we are going to manage," said Agnes. "I have no idea where my father is and I am not sure if mother has enough strength to feed the new baby."

"I have asked cook for some chicken broth for the mistress," replied Kate. "What else can I do for you?"

"Katie, you are a God send," replied Agnes. "I need to go to the Keeping's and tell them that I cannot go back to work for a while. They will probably not allow me to continue my employment with them."

"You do what you have to do, Miss Agnes, I will wait for the master and give the mistress some broth," was the reply.

Agnes placed her cloak around her shoulders and hurried from the house.

Agnes arrived back at the house in Boldre in the late afternoon having secured a couple of weeks' unpaid holiday to sort out her family dilemma. The Keeping's are not an unkind or unfeeling couple, they just have no idea of the problems that less-fortunate people face each day.

Hannah had, meanwhile, secured the assistance of a wet nurse, a kindly lady in her 30s called Brenda—an unmarried woman from Lymington, who had been a prostitute and given birth to a daughter that she had given up to a couple who were unable to have children of their own. It was not what she wanted but she had no way of providing for the child. She was, however, happy to help and had already taken charge of the newcomer when Agnes got back home. Brenda owed Hannah a debt for some reason so this was her way of repaying it. Agnes thought it best not to ask details, she did not expect to like the answer.

Mrs Payne had managed to get Dory to sup a little of the chicken broth, though she did not consider it to be enough to keep up her strength. Everyone was exhausted by the end of the day.

Chapter 56
Another Upheaval

Everyone woke to sunshine the next morning. No one in the house had slept well, sleeping wherever and whenever they could. Agnes had chosen to sleep on a chair next to her mother's bed.

Agnes woke with a jolt, the noise of the front door opening made her leap to her feet. She heard what she guessed to be her father's footsteps coming up the stairs.

The bedroom door flew open and John Henry was standing in the doorway with a look of thunder on his face.

"What the devil is going on here? Why are you here?" he said to Agnes.

"The baby, it arrived yesterday, mother is not well," was the reply.

"She will recover," he said simply and started to leave.

"Don't you want to know what it is, a boy or a girl?" asked Agnes.

"It is another mouth to feed, that is all I know and I cannot afford it," he replied.

"Mother nearly died," said Agnes tearfully.

"Better she had and the brat with her," he replied with venom. With that, he left the room slamming the door, which woke the household including the baby, who started to cry down in the sitting room where it had fallen asleep on Brenda's lap.

Dory gave a little shiver in the bed and Agnes felt her brow, which was burning up. She hurried down stairs to try to defuse any difficulties that John Henry might start.

John Henry opened the sitting room door to find Kate asleep in one corner with Florentine and Brenda and the baby on the settee.

Agnes appeared behind him. "Brenda is a wet nurse looking after your new daughter," she said.

"More cost," was all he could say. He stepped over to Brenda and looked down at the little squirming bundle in her arms. Then he stood and looked at Brenda for a few moment. "I know you, don't I, woman?" he asked Brenda.

"I do not think I have had the pleasure," she said sarcastically. Instinctively, he struck her across the face but she hardly moved.

"Get this lot out of my house," he said. "I only came to fetch a few things. I will return to my lodgings, in a couple of days when I get back, I want everything as it was."

"Not possible, Father," said Agnes. "We have a new addition, I have a new sister, you have a new daughter."

"Not wanted," he said simply. "Look for a place for the child, take her to a nunnery or some such place of sanctuary. Do not look at me like that, girl, I mean what I say. Get rid of the baby and go back to work. I have enough to worry about."

Agnes wanted to cry but she did not want to give her father the satisfaction of seeing her broken.

"Where can I find you if I need you, Father?" she asked.

"You won't need me, you have managed very well without me," he replied.

The women stood in stunned silence, whilst John Henry went about the house picking up bits and pieces, presumable to sell and stuffing them in a sack. They did not speak until he had left the building.

As soon as the front door slammed shut, everyone got to their feet.

"My God, what a man!" said Brenda shocked. "How could anyone be so cold and unfeeling?"

"He wasn't always like that," said Agnes. "It is the worry lack of money brings and the drink." With that, she went to fetch a bowl of cold water to bathe her mother's brow.

Hannah was a welcome visitor that morning. She spoke quietly to Brenda, who told her about the encounter she had with Mr Bridges. Hannah could see clearly a mark on the woman's face.

"He recognised me, Hannah," Brenda said. "He was a regular customer for years before I got big with child, possibly even his, that is a terrible thought, don't you think?"

"Is he coming back?" Hannah asked.

"Who knows, he said that he will when we are all gone including the baby," was the reply.

The whole house shook with a scream from Agnes in the room above. Hannah ran up the stairs to find Agnes glued to the spot, a shallow bowl in her hand, standing like a statue. She was near to the bed where her mother was lying, and it was obvious at a single glance that Dory was gone. Hannah lifted the sheet that covered the woman and her nightdress and bed beneath her were bright red. Hannah knew that Dory had haemorrhaged and died because of this. She had not expected her to live as long as she had, so she was not surprised. She gently took the bowl from Agnes and led her from the room.

Having told everyone what had occurred, decisions had to be made immediately. After an hour or so of discussion making, it was decided that Agnes would take Florentine, the new baby—which they decided to call Franchesca, one of Dory's favourite names—and go to Rosamond in Wetherley. Agnes had already written to her grandfather to tell him that Dory was near her time and that John Henry was nowhere to be seen. She had now written another letter to update him and warn him that she intended to try to get the family back to Wetherley. Kate and Mrs Payne, the cook, asked if they could accompany the family to Weston-Under-Wetherley and it was already decided that Brenda would go with them, she was more than pleased to be given the chance to start life a new elsewhere.

Dr Banks arrived in the early evening having been asked twice to attend. He is a robust looking man, about five foot eight inches in height and wears built up heeled shoes to appear taller. He was dressed very formally and carried a very large black leather medical bag, one that he takes everywhere he goes. He has a round face and wears half glasses perched at the end of his nose giving him a slightly comical look. He does, however, lack humour, a bedside manner and any charm.

He pushed past Kate, who opened the door, and came into the sitting room. After examining Franchesca, who he declared to be fit and healthy despite several bruises round her head and shoulders where she had been delivered rather roughly, he almost ran up the stairs giving the impression that he wanted to spend as little time in the house as possible.

The doctor reappeared in the sitting room after about 10 minutes and sat down without being asked.

"It beholds me to say it, woman," he said directing his comment to Hannah. "But you saved the baby's life without a doubt, a pity the same could not be said for the mother."

"You said yourself that Mrs Bridges was not saveable," replied Hannah.

"Quite so and I was right," The doctor replied sternly. "I will write you a certificate to say that Mrs Bridges died from complications after childbirth. In my opinion, something ruptured inside causing blood loss. What are you intending to do with the body? Has Mr Bridges been informed?"

"I do not know the answer to the first question, Sir," said Agnes politely. "I would like to take my mother back to Weston-Under-Wetherley but I suppose that is not possible. As for my father, he called in yesterday, noted the situation and abruptly left, I do not know where he lodges."

"You could get the body embalmed, I do not know the cost of such an action and it should be done very quickly, then you could take her wherever you saw fit," replied the doctor, almost kindly.

Agnes sat for a while and then asked the doctor if the certificate he had given her was all she needed to make arrangements regarding her mother's body and he said it was, so she showed the doctor to the door and returned to the group of woman to ask advice. Everyone had their own opinion but it seemed that generally the best idea was to bury Dory in or near Boldre; after all, Dory had liked the St John the Baptist Church, she thought its location was as close to heaven as you could build a church.

"Do you know where your mother was happiest?" Hannah asked Agnes.

"I do not remember her being happy at all for a great many years," was the sad reply. "Maybe when she walked in the forest or borrowed a pony for an hour or so."

Hannah, in her line of work was used to losing patients so once Agnes had decided to bury her mother locally, took charge. The ladies made Dory look respectable, clean her up, put on a pretty flowered dress and Agnes did her hair in the way she had liked, whilst they waited for the funeral director to arrive to measure for a coffin.

Agnes then returned to the Keeping's to tell them the latest; they were most sympathetic at first but when Agnes said that she would be taking the new baby to West-Under-Wetherley to her aunt, they said they would have to find a new maid and were sorry to have to let Agnes go. Agnes was not too upset by this action as it gave her a chance to travel to Wetherley and Rosamond without any time restrictions. By the time she arrived back home, arrangements had been made to have a coffin delivered the next day. Agnes shut the bedroom door where her mother lay and cried until she had no more tears to shed.

Hannah Goodfellow, Brenda, Kate and Mrs Payne had all proved to be of great strength to Agnes. Hannah seemed to know everything and everyone and always knew what to do in any situation.

Agnes took Hannah aside and explained to her that there was no actual money available and asked her if there was anything obvious that she could sell or pawn to provide for a decent burial for her mother and to get the entourage to Wetherley.

Hannah looked about the house before she replied, "I think your father took most of the valuable items when he visited the other day, but my guess is there is something still to be found in some of the rooms."

There was an unexpected knock on the front door and Kate hurried to answer it. It was Doctor Banks, still with his bag in hand.

"Excuse the interruption," said the doctor, sounding almost friendly and addressing Agnes. "I have traced your father and he is lodging with the widow Brown in Lymington as you thought."

"That is most kind of you, Doctor," said Agnes surprised.

"Kindness does not come into it, young lady," was the reply. "I need paying and it is Mr Bridges' job to pay me."

"Has he done so?" asked Agnes.

"He gave me a candlestick that I think will suffice," was the reply. "So that is one less debt for you to worry about. Let me give you a little advice. I will give you your father's address and you must have all the bills sent to him at the widows' address. No one would expect someone as young as you to pay her father's debts."

Agnes found herself wanting to actually hug the formidable doctor but restrained from doing so.

"Could I really do this?" asked Agnes, a little taken aback.

"You can and you must, how else will you survive," was the reply.

Hannah went with Agnes to speak to the vicar of St John the Baptist and was amazed to discover that the Keepings had also been to see him, they had gone as regular members of the congregation and landed gentry. A good many of the graves in the churchyard contained ancestors of the Keepings and they had offered a plot close to an ancient distant relative to be used by Agnes to bury her mother. Agnes was overwhelmed and as soon as she could, she hurried to the Lower Sway Manor to thank her benefactors.

The funeral went ahead and Dory was buried in a grave next to someone called Betty Keeping, who had been sleeping in the churchyard since 1788 and appeared to have numerous brothers and sisters close by, all buried fairly close to the actual church on the edge of the New Forest, an area she loved. Although a letter was sent to John Henry to tell him of the details, he chose not to attend the funeral.

Agnes had not had time to write to her grandparents and wait for them to arrive. She wanted to get the remaining members of her family safely away from Boldre and John Henry, before he followed through with the threat to have her new sister, Franchesca, left on the steps of the nearest nunnery.

The funeral was a quiet affair. Kindly, a few of Dory's customers showed up to pay their respects and make the church not look quite so empty. But it was a very sad day and Agnes found herself thinking that life had ended for them all. She knew that if she could get to Weston-Under-Wetherley and the protection of her grandparents and Aunt Rosamond, she would be fine, but it seemed so far away and so great a responsibility on her young shoulders. A marker was organised and the bill sent to John Henry. Hannah found a man who dealt with buying and selling items of value, and he came to the house and removed several pieces for sale.

The women began to pack to move to Weston-Under-Wetherley and two carts were hired for the journey. Agnes was determined to take her mother's secret trunk if she took nothing else.

Agnes' grandfather arrived in Boldre just a day before they all planned to leave for Wetherley. He was sorry that he was unable to get to the children earlier, but he had started for Hampshire the moment he received Agnes' letter about Dory's demise. Agnes was so happy to see her grandfather; she had a lot of support from the women who had assisted her so nobly but to have her nearest relative standing on the doorstep was a great boost.

The Reverend Phillip Mountjoy was now quite an elderly gentleman and it had taken a lot of determination on his part to make the journey to help his granddaughters. He was much amused by the collection of women in the house and the parts they had all played in the dramas of the past few days.

Just as Agnes was about to tell Phillip about John Henry's whereabouts, he turned up, a little worse for wear, having obviously drunk copious amounts of alcohol.

"What the devil is this all about?" shouted John Henry, waving a handful of bills about under Agnes' nose.

Phillips stepped from the shadows and formed a barrier between father and 'daughter'.

"Oh, so you are here," said John Henry, slightly alarmed.

"I have come at my granddaughter's request to take her and her sisters back home with me, unless you have other plans for them, Bridges," Phillip replied.

"I have no plans, they can go to the devil for all I care," was the reply.

"I think that place is reserved for you, Sir," said Phillip calmly.

Bridges look at the carts, now quite heavily laden for travelling. "I hope you are not taking anything of mine," he said.

"It is mostly the property of my travelling companions and some bits of my mother's," Agnes said bravely.

"The house is still yours, Bridges," said Phillip. "And all the furniture there in."

"I should hope so," Bridges replied. "What about these bills, I did not sanction any of these payments."

"They are relating to the death of your wife and delivery of my sister, Franchesca. I am told that you are legally obliged to pay such debts," said Agnes defiantly.

"Don't you get high and mighty with me, young lady," he replied, raising his hand to strike the girl.

From no-where appeared a ruddy-faced man of about 25, very muscular with a good head of curly hair who caught hold of John Henry's arm just as he was about to bring it down and strike his daughter.

"We will have no bullying here today," said the man in a loud, clear voice. "I would knock you down myself but I can see you are in your cups and I hope not aware of your actions."

"This is a private matter," shouted John Henry, "between father and daughter, none of your concern, whoever you are."

"Who I am is irrelevant, no one strikes defenceless young woman if I can prevent it."

"They will all be on their way tomorrow so I suggest you go back to the widow woman you chose over my daughter," said the Reverend Mountjoy.

John Henry reluctantly staggered away, still waving his bills and shouting that there had better not be any more in his name.

"I thank you, young man," said Phillip, holding his hand out to the saviour of the day. "I am the Reverend Phillip Mountjoy, Agnes' grandfather."

The young man took Phillip's hand and told him that he was called Mark and a friend of Hannah's, who had asked him to sell some property for Agnes so they could afford to travel.

"For whatever reason God sent you, I am grateful," was the reply.

Mark smiled and turned to Agnes and held out a roll of bank notes. "Take these yellow boys, they will see you to your destination and beyond," he said.

Agnes stared at the roll of notes for a moment and told Mark that she wanted him to take some for his trouble, to which he replied that he had already done so.

Hannah was standing behind Mark and Agnes could not help herself, she pushed past Mark and flung her arms about the woman who smiled widely. "This is your doing, I know," she said with a tear rolling down her face.

"I wish I could have done more," replied Hannah.

After everyone was introduced to the Reverend Mountjoy, water-proof covers were tied over the carts, and Mrs Payne announced that she had made a spread like she had not done for a great many months, all thanks to John Henry. She had been to the grocers, the fishmongers and the butchers and given them each a promissory note from Bridges. She also suggested that they all ate their full and that they be gone early in the morning, before they received another visit from John Henry.

Agnes and her grandfather walked the short but steep distance up to St John the Baptist Church so she could show him where her mother, his daughter, was buried—thanks to the kindness of Mr and Mrs Keeping.

Early the next morning saw a lot of activity. Phillip had ridden all the way in a small cabriolet, one he had adapted to make more sturdy but remain light enough for him to handle on his own if neccessary; something he had not done for a long time and did not really enjoy, so he had brought a villager, Bill Pope, with him who knew the area and had a relative in Lymington. Mr Pope was more than pleased to have reason to visit, what turned out to be his cousin, for a couple of days. Reverend Mountjoy hurried off to retrieve his pair of horses and carriage from the nearby stabling yard and then paid a quick visit to the Keepings to thank them and promise them a special place in heaven for their goodness, something that made Mrs Keeping smile.

When Phillip had left home, he had thought only to collect Agnes and the two youngsters, he did not know that Agnes had managed to collect a following that intended to travel with her—little Kate, who was now in her 20s but very short in stature; Brenda, the wet nurse, who didn't appear to have a second name; and Mrs Payne, the cook, who was a widow of about 50 years of age, were all intending to make the journey to Wetherley.

Agnes had hired drivers for the carts and there was room on them for the women travellers as well. Mrs Payne had packed a considerable picnic hamper and everyone was ready to leave; she was the first to climb on board, closely followed by Kate.

It was decided that Brenda and baby Franchesca should travel in the cabriolet with Phillip and Florentine. Agnes chose to climb into the first cart with Kate and

Mrs Payne. Bill Pope was ready to leave, having enjoyed an unexpected visit to his relatives. Happily, John Henry did not pay them a visit that day. Agnes assumed that he had probably drunk too much, drowning his sorrows over the promissory notes in his name and was hung over. She looked for the last time at Far End and smiled. It now looked like a respectable property and her only regret was that John Henry would probably now be able to sell it without much difficulty, thanks to their hard work cleaning it. Even the garden looked pretty.

The little group of travellers stopped several times, not always in salubrious places and sometimes, just in fields en route, money not permitting any luxury.

They made just one comfortable stop overnight at Oxford and then travelled on to Wetherley, stopping by the side of the road like gypsies where they could.

Chapter 57
Back at Weston-Under-Wetherley

There was quite a gathering waiting to greet the carriage and carts. Agnes' grandmother stood open-mouthed at the arrival of such an entourage; she had expected her granddaughters, Bill Pope and her own husband but all these other strange faces were baffling to her.

Florentine could not wait to get down from the carriage and was soon running on sturdy, chubby legs to be greeted by Bathsheba, who swept her up in her arms. Both grandparents had not been allowed any access to the family since they moved to Hampshire, mainly by reason of cost and distance. Everyone was happy to be together again. Robin was now beginning to look and act like a proper gentleman, he had missed Agnes and Florentine very much but had been happy with Rosamond, who treated him like a son she never had.

Agnes climbed down stiffly from the cart she had travelled in and went to collect Franchesca from Brenda to introduce the latest addition to the family to her grandmother. Robin was equally thrilled to meet his new sister. A great many tears were shed over Dorothia and there was a general sadness that she could not have been brought home to rest. Bathsheba and Phillip understood the logistics of such an action and the costs involved, so they tried to seem happy and content with the burial in Boldre.

No one asked after John Henry Bridges and it was decided that his name would never be mentioned again, although Agnes did give a brief outline of past events to her brother.

The rectory is reasonably large but many of the rooms are taken up with a study and rooms for parishioners to air any grievances, and for this reason alone, Rosamond's offer to house the children of her old friend was accepted willingly. Rosamond was also very pleased to allow Mrs Payne to live with her. She had lost her own cook to a wealthy gentleman in the village, who offered larger wages. She was happy to cook for herself and Robin but did not relish cooking for a houseful, so Mrs Payne was a welcome addition. Brenda was also accepted without question as she was Franchesca's life line, although the young woman made it quite clear that as soon as the baby was weaned, she would be off to seek a living elsewhere. Agnes thought it best to withhold the information that Brenda had been a prostitute in Hampshire, allowing the woman to receive a degree of respect from the villagers in Weston-Under-Wetherley. She was always introduced as Mrs Brenda Jones, a newly widow friend of the family.

Agnes never actual discovered Brenda's actual name and chose not to dig too deep into her new friend's background.

This was greatly appreciated by Brenda, who quickly made friends locally.

Agnes felt the necessity to get employment so she could help feed her brother and sisters, and her grandfather came upon the idea of contacting Lady Mary Bradbury in Brighton and asking her if she would take in a distant relative from Hampshire, who had fallen on hard time. He knew that Agnes would be safe with Lady Mary and he did not relish the idea of sending his young granddaughter off to strangers, where she might be worked to death. He did not disclose Agnes' real identity as he did not want Lady Mary to know how low Dory had fallen before her demise. He did tell Lady Mary in the letter that Dorothia had passed away due to complications of childbirth. This made Mary very sad but she had assumed something had gone wrong with her old friend as she had letter returned unopened from the Weston Manor Lodge address and was informed that the manor was under new ownership. Dory had decided to break the friendship rather than have to tell Lady Mary how foolish she had been in marrying John Henry and had returned the last couple of letters that she received from her before leaving for Hampshire. The new owners of Wetherley Manor Lodge were not privy to John Henry Bridges forwarding address so they could do nothing more than inform Lady Mary that they had taken over ownership of the property and could not help her locate the previous owners. Lady Mary could have traced Dorothia through her father, the Reverend Mountjoy, if she had chosen to do so, but after all she was a busy woman and they were after all only passing friends that had kept up a connection through letters only.

Phillip relied on Lady Mary's old connection with his late mother-in-law, Seraphina, it was through this that he had managed to talk to Lady Mary into taking his daughter in many years ago. Lady Mary had readily taken in Dorothia and her sisters when the old Lord Southerly, the Earl of Wetherley, had made it known that he had noticed Dorothia and planned to use his power to secure her as a mistress, willingly or not. They had all gone to stay for several months in Brighton and were treated most cordially. If Dory's sister, Everline, had not married the travelling vicar, Allun Parton, they might have prolonged their stay in Brighton. Sensibly, Phillip should have told Mary that Agnes was Dorothia's daughter but family pride stood in the way so he said that she was a cousin's daughter, who had fallen on hard time. He used Agnes' chosen name so the connection would not be made too easily. He wasn't looking for charity, he was offering the child as a servant of some sort, giving a long list of the girl's accomplishments, such as reading, writing and needlework.

Lady Mary answered positively telling Phillip that even the most distant relative would be more than welcome, especially if they were as delightful as she remembered his daughters been and how sorry she was to hear of Dorothia's demise. She had an opening for an under maid and she offered to house Agnes and see if she would fit the position, stating that if not, she would find her something suitable.

So within a couple of months of being home with her family, Agnes was once more on the move, this time to Brighton to work as an under maid.

The younger children all stayed with Rosamond and Rosamond was very happy to have a family around her again, even if they were not blood kin. The children all called her Aunt Rosamond and no one ever questioned why she had suddenly taken in three children. Robin was growing up to be a delightful, studious young man and Rosamond had done a good job of teaching him accountancy.

When Agnes was packing her case to take to Brighton, she found amongst her mother's papers a card from Lord John Fisher; she had no idea who he might be but asked her grandfather to make enquiries about the man. She seemed to think that she might have heard the name mentioned sometime in the past. He, unfortunately, put the card aside and only re-discovered it after several months. Once he had done so, it did not take him long to discover that Sir John was Lady Agnes', the Countess of Southerly, estranged brother—a man of considerable wealth and consequence, who lived fairly locally.

Phillip took it upon himself to contact Sir John and tell him of Dorothia's demise at the age of 37 and then tell him of the unfortunate circumstances that his relatives were now facing. Guilt that the gentleman felt, having left his only sister to live with the monster she married and never offer her or her son a safe haven, brought him to Reverend Phillip Mountjoy's door one Saturday afternoon.

Phillip was in his study when his wife, Bathsheba, showed a very distinguished looking, elderly gentleman in his late 70s into his presence. Although he had a slight stoop, he still had a dignified air. The vicar leapt to his feet immediately realising who the stranger must be.

"I am Lord John Fisher and I believe we have relatives in common," said the booming voice, standing and looking very imposing in the doorway—coat open, displaying a very elaborate embroidered waistcoat and carrying a gold-topped cane, his servant closely behind him.

Phillip was silent for a while, the man before him had considerable presence that made him feel quite inferior; Bathsheba, who had no idea that her husband had contacted any relatives on Agnes' behalf, looked very confused.

"Bathsheba, please take this gentleman's man to the kitchen and offer him refreshments, I would very much like it if we are not disturbed until I request it." Seeing her confused face, he added that he would make her acquainted with everything later.

Being a very forceful woman, she was not keen to leave but did as requested, dipping a quick curtsy to their unexpected guest as she left. Phillip smiled to himself imagining the questions that the poor, unsuspected servant would face, once his wife got him out of earshot.

The door closed and the gentleman stepped deeper into the room.

"I have looked closely into your claim of kinship, Sir, I am a very cautious man," said Sir John, taking a small leather pouch from his pocket and taking from it a small pinch of snuff. He held the pouch towards the reverend, who declined to share this habit. "And I find it quite amazing that I have allowed close members of my family to slide so low without my knowledge. I only pray that they will forgive me this indiscretion."

Phillip was quite lost for words. He beckoned the gentleman into his study and offered him a seat next to his desk. Phillip nodded towards the decanter of sherry on his desk and placed two glasses in close proximity of his visitor. The smile suggested that a glass of sherry would be acceptable so Phillip poured out two glasses and handed one to Lord John.

"I realise that my nephew has been lacking, as was his father, but that is no excuse for me to desert kin," Sir John continued, sipping the sherry and nodding approval of the taste.

"My dear, Sir," said Phillip, "I cannot place any blame at your door. There is no possible way that you could have foreseen my daughter's husband deserting her, none of us saw that coming. He was a good man despite what you might now think. He tried very hard to escape the shadow of his father's evil ways but one day, it all became too much for him and he vanished; I do not know where to or the full details but I would like to believe the best of him."

"As would I, Sir, of course," replied Sir John. "My nephew, Adam, who I never actually met, was blood kin as was my poor, ill-used sister, Agnes, but I never had the privilege of meeting your dear daughter or, in fact, my grandniece who, as you tell me, is named after my sister. I am now to believe that there are other children, not directly my responsibility but ones that I would like to help in some way if possible."

Phillip smiled a very broad smile. "I was so hoping that you would think in this way and that my beautiful daughter, Dorothia's unfortunate and ill-advised second marriage would not totally close your mind to the situation that your grandniece, Agnes, finds herself in, though no fault of her own."

"Is the child around so I can acquaint myself with her?" asked Lord John.

"No Sir, I am afraid that circumstances did not allow me to wait for an answer from you before I took things into my own hands," replied Phillip sadly.

"In what way?" Lord John enquired.

"I am acquainted in a very casual way through my late mother-in-law with Lord and Lady Bradbury of Brighton. Lady Mary Bradbury married the son of a friend of my mother-in-law quite some time ago," explained Phillip. "Lord Bradbury married Lady Mary Fitzroy of Somerset and my mother-in-law was friendly with Lady Mary's mother when young."

"I have heard of the Fitzroy's, an eccentric group I believe but of good stock, I do not actually know the family though."

"My mother-in-law, long gone now of course, thought highly of them," replied Phillip.

"And?" said Lord John confused.

"And I sent my daughters—Dorothia, Everline and Elizabeth to Lady Mary in Brighton using this tentative connection to my benefit. Your brother-in-law, George Southerly, the late Earl of Wetherley, had shown an unhealthy but not totally unexpected interest in my eldest daughter, who was particularly beautiful, and I needed to remove the girls from his presence and proximity as quickly as possible. A local land owner and my son-in-law to be, Adam, both warned me of Sir George's desire to add Dorothia to his list of ill-used and later, cast off women."

"Good God, so the stories I heard were true after all," said Lord John in dismay.

"If, in fact, you ever heard a bad word against Sir George, you could double it one hundred fold and then you would only touch on the tip of the man's depravity," said Phillip, now starting to feel his feet. "I am a man of the clothe and as such, hear many stories from parishioners begging forgiveness from the Lord. Everyone, however sinister, would not shine a light to the way that man behaved. Luckily, he did not seek forgiveness in my church or any other I would suspect."

"I am ashamed to say that I started to no longer listen to stories coming from Weston-Under-Wetherley regarding my poor sister's husband," said Lord John quietly. "I did not want to believe them. My parents had known George's father, also called Adam, and I believe he was a good and respected hard working man. They chose my sister Agnes' husband for her. He was an imposing, handsome man with a great deal of money and charm if he wanted to use it. My parents liked his father very much and assumed that the son was of the same metal. This proved not to be the case, of course. I did hear later that the marriage had been arranged when the couple were very young children and there was an obligation to fulfil the promise. The man turned into a monster, he abused my sister and his position in the world."

"Did you not try to help the poor woman?" asked the vicar.

"You know full well, no one can come between husband and wife once the wedding vows have been spoken," replied Lord John. "My sister came to me, she showed me bruises, she told me stories, I confronted my brother-in-law and only made things worse for Agnes. I was banned from Wetherley Manor Lodge and I crept away like a dog with my tail between my legs. Do you have any idea how powerful his friends were?"

"Everyone here-about was fully aware of the man's power. He could rape, imprison and even kill and no one could touch him," was the reply. "Not a tear was shed when that man died."

"I realise that," said Sir John. "I crept into the back of the church at Agnes' funeral and learnt a great deal about what she suffered by listening to the congregation. I left my card with Adam's man, hoping that he would get in touch but he never did. I even attended the inquest into the devil's death. I had never heard so much venom spoken about a human being as was directed at my brother-in-law. I was not keen on anyone discovering any link I might have with the beast."

"And yet, here you are now," said Phillip.

"Yes, too late to help my sister or your daughter but maybe not too late to do some good," was the reply. "You have not explained where my niece is?"

"Oh, no, I am sorry, I digressed," Phillip replied. "Because Lady Mary had been so kind to my daughters, I took it upon myself to ask if she would take Agnes into her household in some capacity. I sent my granddaughter, Agnes—her birth name is Seraphina, after my late mother-in-law but she chose to change it—to Lady Mary Bradbury in Brighton as I did sent her mother once; only this time Lady Mary is not aware of any blood connection between Agnes and my late mother-in-law," Phillip started to explain. "Agnes has gone as a distance relative, who has fallen on hard times to work as an under maid."

"Good heavens, my great-niece an under-maid!" replied Sir John in a shocked voice. "What can I do?"

"Agnes has no memory of her father. She believes her father to be a ne'er-do-well called John Henry Bridges, who married my daughter after her divorce from your nephew. Agnes is a strong and independent young woman, who wishes to keep a roof over her three half-siblings, as she has been doing for nearly a year now," Phillip explained. "Obviously, I did not know that you would appear, so I had to do what was best for the girl with the knowledge I had. I did not tell her that she had an errant father, who deserted her mother and maybe caused her early death by doing so. As you can see, Sir, I am touching 70 years old and may need to retire very soon."

"I can see the difficulty here," replied Sir John. "I believe Agnes has two half-sisters and a brother. Where, might I ask, are they?"

"They are all here in Weston-Under-Wetherley," was the reply. "They live with a cousin—not an actual cousin but they call her aunt—Lady Rosamond who was, at one time, married to your nephew's best friend, Sir James Shepherd. Lady Rosamond was Sir James' second wife, his first being Adam's half-sister, Sally, who died in childbirth. Rosamond, herself, now being widowed when Sir James died of the white death along with his son. Her story is a lot more entwined but not mine to tell."

"Good heavens above, half-sister, I knew nothing of this niece," replied Sir John, alarmed. "So many twists and turns to every tale, your life appears to be very complicated."

"Sally was no blood kin of yours, Sir John, she was the result of George Southerly's wickedness, discovered by your nephew, Adam, and brought into the fold. A sickly but charming, young woman died in childbirth, weakened by the ravishes of tuberculosis," replied Phillip, trying not to overload his visitor with too much information.

"Dead friends, half-sisters, the story is quite complex and involved and difficult to follow," said Sir John, confused.

"I realise this, Sir," said Phillip. "If you would kindly stay and take a bite to eat, I would very much like to enlighten you to all the details. It is a long and sad tale."

"A tale I would like to be fully aware of and I would like to know also how I can lighten the burden of all concerned," replied Lord John.

"I would not ask much of you, Sir," said Phillip. "Agnes has the desire to help financially her brother and sisters, though Lady Rosamond has not expressed any desire for her to do so. She has some income of her own and loves the children."

"How old are these children?" asked Lord John.

"The girls are but little: Florentine, Florry, is four coming on five; Franchesca, Franny, is just a small toddler, not yet two years old. She had a very good nurse found by Agnes when the baby was born, who has now gone away; Agnes made sure that the woman had some small sort of payment for her kindness to Franchesca. There is also the elder brother, Robin, who is a fine lad of 10 coming up to 11, who is very good with figure taught by Lady Rosamond, who was always very good at accounting. She tells me that the boy has a natural aptitude to figures. Agnes is now herself 15, touching 16 years of age and has the look of her mother."

"In that case, I can see now how I can help without letting my grandniece know," was the reply. "I will visit Lady Rosamond soon and ascertain her needs financially. I feel I should meet such a fine woman, who would take on so much."

"Rosamond and her late second husband, Sir James Shepherd, who was Adam's greatest friend, both loved Adam like a brother. Rosamond took on Sally's child, Jasper, when Sally died which led to Sir James and her marrying; she has a great kindness towards children," Phillip continued to explain, even though Sir John was looking more and more confused.

"So many names, so many dramas. The boy, Robin, if he is good with figures as you say, I will send him to my accountant in Oxford as an apprentice; he may be a little young as yet, but this will be my plan for the boy, maybe next year. No, I think this will be top priority, they will take him now if I pay enough and he will eventually earn a good living. I will source a room for the boy in Oxford, a safe and secure place for a boy in a strange city," said Sir John forcefully. "I will not waste another day in planning, action must be taken. I am touching 80 and only God knows how much longer I have on this earth so time must not be wasted."

"You look very healthy to me, Sir," said Phillip, replenishing his visitor's glass of sherry.

"I will write to Lady Mary in Brighton and enlighten her a little to why I have an interest in her maid, I will not tell her too much. You will understand that Agnes may not be accepted in higher circles now, though I hope to elevate her above the roll of maid. I will take the financial pressure off my niece, she need not know how

Lady Rosamond has come about her good luck. Better still, maybe you could keep any money Agnes sends to help the children and keep a fund for the girl when she reaches an age that she might need the money herself."

"Agnes is an educated girl, my daughter saw to that. You should see the amount of books she took with her to Brighton."

"My guess is that Lady Mary may have guessed herself that the child is not the usual maid material, that will make my task easier. My guess is also that Lady Mary already has an interest in Agnes, women like mysteries."

Phillip did not know quite how to reply to all this generosity. "If you would pardon me, Sir,", he said, "I would like to go and tell my good wife that we have one more for dinner and then as we eat, I would like very much to fill you in on all the details."

Lord John nodded in approval.

Chapter 58
Lord John Fisher

Lord John Fisher is the older brother of Adam Southerly's, the Earl of Wetherley's mother. Lady Agnes had died in 1826 along with her greatly feared husband, George Southerly, leaving Sir John to feel that he had let her down.

Sir John is a very private person, almost a recluse. He lives in a moderately small but stylish property, just outside of Princethorpe, near Weston-Under-Wetherley in Warwickshire. He has never married and he keeps himself to himself. Occasional trips to Oxford, where he has business interests, afford him the opportunity to dress in the latest mode.

As a young man, he was very much top of the ton. Many young and beautiful women hung onto his coat tails but he never married. Rumours abounded that Sir John loved a woman that his parents thought inappropriate, either because she was already married, because of her birth, lack of breeding or even some thought her age; the truth was never made public and Sir John kept it close to his heart. The truth being that it was because of Sir John's blood ties to the Southerly's, his chosen love's parents had banned their union.

It appears that his only vices are an occasional pinch of snuff, a glass of ratafia or sherry and the races. He loves horses and likes to watch them run; he was never, however, a gambler. He is also a lover of poetry, the arts, theatre and fine wine, all of which his wealth allow him to experience. When young, he was considered a very fine dancer, light and nimble on his toes, but as he aged, he enjoyed crowds less and less; in later life, avoiding gatherings of any sort. He is now considered to be an eccentric and lonely figure when seen walking on odd occasions near Wetherley Wood with his faithful wolfhound, pretty well unnoticed and unrecognised by most of the locals.

Sir John's sister's unhappy arranged marriage to George Southerly affected him greatly, both in respectability and embarrassment. He did not chose to be related to such a man as George Southerly and despaired of his parents' choice for his much loved sister. Agnes was quite a plain young woman and certainly did not enjoy being the centre of attraction in any way. When she was forced to marry the flamboyant earl, she was thrown into the lime-light and did not enjoy the experience. The earl was a very handsome man with more wealth than any man needed, much of it was squandered on wine, woman and any other vices he felt attracted to. He was into any and every vice known or so it was wildly believed. As time passed and the earl became infamous for miles around, he used his money and status to do the most outrageous things. He kept company with like-minded men, some in very powerful positions; he felt that as an employer, he owed every aspect of his employees. Good men were sacked or falsely accused of petty crimes if they did not allow George

Southerly access to their wives or daughters. Despite her husband, Agnes was greatly liked. She was a timid creature but she regularly visited the workers' cottages and would stand up to her husband on worker's behalves if there was a problem that she felt he could easily fix, such as a leaky roof. This, sometimes, cost her dearly as George was always quick to strike out if affronted. Agnes found just being seen outside of her home incredibly hard to deal with. Sir John was affected in the same way. He did not want people to know there was any connection between him and the evil earl and so he visited his sister only if absolutely necessary. When she had come to him with bruises inflicted by her violent husband, he simply sent her back home with a promise that he would speak to George and tell him of his disapproval. One day, Sir John called at Weston Manor Lodge to carry out the promise he made to his sister. Raised voices could be heard for a great distance and John was literally ejected from the property with the cry of "I will beat my wife with a metal bar if I so wish". John feared for his sister and it is commonly believed that the earl did, in fact, take out his anger on his poor, gentle wife. Although Sir John knew that he was a coward, he never ventured near Weston Manor Lodge again. He spent the last 30 years of his life hoping that people would forget he had any connection with the Southerly's.

After Agnes produced a much needed son, she found her life was a lot easier. George left her in peace and pursued other woman instead, often wives of his cronies or unsuspecting servant girls unable to defend their honour. More than one such affair ended in pregnancy and the ruined woman ejected from their job to fend for themselves.

Sir John had a great deal of sympathy and understanding towards his nephew, Adam Southerly; both, he and Adam, had run away from their relationship with George Southerly. John had chosen to hide inside his home and live unnoticed, whereas Adam had physically ran away.

John did not totally approve of Adam deserting his wife and child, but he understood the pressure of having such an evil relative. Adam found the late earl's notoriety harder than Sir John because he had the same blood flowing through his veins. John was particularly impressed with Adam's treatment of his discovered half-sister, many would have ignored her plight.

Sir John felt that now, maybe it was his chance to make a few things right before he dies. He is nearly 78 years of age and in good health, except for a slight back problem and age-related aches and pains on occasions. The new challenge was actually a new lease of life that he was looking forward to.

Four days after the visit of Lord John Fisher to the rectory at Weston-Under-Wetherley, his magnificent coach pulled up outside of the abode of Lady Rosamond, who was busy dead-heading her roses when it swung into her drive. Lady Rosamond's home is what you might call a country house; it is larger than an average house in Weston-Under-Wetherley other than the actual manor houses and country lodges of noblemen. It is a rather pretty, double-fronted house on three floors, the attic was originally for servants. Rosamond is not one to have servants as such. Because she came from lower stock herself, she could relate to everyone. She had kept little Kate on as a maid servant but treated the girl more like a friend and companion. Kate would happily do any job asked of her because she loved Rosamond and liked living with her and her family.

Rosamond would happily have kept Brenda—the one time prostitute who accompanied Agnes to Weston-Under-Wetherley acting as a wet nurse for

Franchesca—if she had wanted to stay, but the young woman had escaped a terrible life and wanted to see a bit more of the world, so she moved on with a promise to return if life got difficult. Rosamond had kept Mrs Payne, the cook, who travelled with Agnes, even though Rosamond was a very adequate cook herself. Her house was now full of children so she did not have the time to cook so she was allowing herself the luxury of being waited on and cooked for. Although she hired a general gardener to prune the trees, cut the grass and who also acted as a mole catcher, she enjoyed doing some of the gardening herself and could be often seen pottering about in her garden, which was not huge but certainly adequate. In the front, she grew roses, lavender, lilac and other flowering plants. She had a great love of butterflies. At the rear of the property, she had space to grow enough vegetables to feed the household and chickens to supply eggs. Kate and Mrs Payne attended to the vegetable patch and saw that the chickens were fed. The only other employed person at Shepherd House, named after Sir James Shepherd's father who had originally bought the property for his mother-in-law, was a man called Harry Ingels, who worked alongside a now ailing Pernell and acted as butler and general dog's body. She did not need a house keeper as she was very adequate with figures herself so she kept her own accounts. Rosamond was reasonably self-sufficient and very happy with her life; she was not extravagant so she managed to afford the extra mouths to feed, though sometimes, she felt a little more would be helpful.

To say she was surprised, to receive such a visitor as the one who had just rode up her drive, would be an understatement. She watched from a distance as Sir John's man climbed from the coach and approached the front door. Only then did she step from the shadows and make herself known. She approached the coach with trepidation and as she got near, a finely gloved hand could be seen resting on the open carriage window; Rosamond immediately knew she was dealing with quality.

Rosamond stood back as the visitor's servant opened the carriage door, lowered a step and helped what looked like a gentleman in his late 70s from his carriage.

Sir John pretended that they had lost their way and requested directions to a nearby village. Although Rosamond felt that the man was faintly familiar, she could not be sure if she had ever seen him before.

Sir John complemented Lady Rosamond on her well-kept garden and told her how amazed he was to see that she appeared to be working herself instead of employing a gardener.

Rosamond smiled as she replied and bobbed a small curtsy. "I enjoy the garden. I do have a man who attends to the grass, trees and the weeding but the actual planting and pruning, I love too much to pass to others."

"I can see that the love you have for your garden blooms in your flowers," Sir John replied with a gentle smile.

Sir John and Rosamond strolled round the garden for a few moments, whilst Sir John's man pretended to take note of directions being given to him by Ingles, the butler. Being normal children and full of curiosity, Robin was soon in the garden inspecting the fine horses that had pulled the carriage to their door. He was closely followed by Florentine held on a ribbon by Kate, who had stayed with Rosamond to help with the children after Brenda was no longer needed as a wet nurse and moved on. With the ribbon's tightly in her left hand, Kate carried little Franchesca on her right hip.

All the children were delightfully pretty and well behaved. Sir John had used the lost excuse so he could see the children for himself and understand fully what and who he was dealing with. He managed to cohere Robin into a conversation about the joys of mathematics by counting flower beds and discussing the angles chosen to display the plants. Rosamond was quite taken with this delightful stranger, who had happened upon them and was speaking to her and her charges as if they were long lost friends. She was not privy to his relationship with everyone and he was not intending to make her so.

As they strolled back to the coach, Sir John asked Rosamond if maybe her son had considered being apprenticed as an accountant as he obviously had a leaning in that direction. Rosamond laughed and explained that the children were merely in her care, much as she loved them like her own. She went on to ask if the gentleman had time to partake of a cup of tea and maybe a slice of homemade cake before he continued his journey. Rosamond was quite amazed herself by her own forwardness. She was not one to invite strangers into her home but this gentleman made her feel comfortable and like a long lost friend.

A few moment later found everyone in the garden room and Kate hurrying off to find Mrs Payne, the cook, and tell her that they had a distinguished visitor, who required tea and her delicious cake.

Sir John had not envisaged himself being so taken with this little family as to feel the need to stay any longer than necessary but he was enraptured by them. Rosamond, he found, to be a delightful woman, very articulate and knowledgeable. He introduced himself under a false name and felt very badly about doing so as he felt that he was abusing their hospitality.

"I am serious about the boy, Madam, do you think he would wish to be an account's apprentice?" asked Sir John between bite of cake and sips of tea.

"It would be his dream, Sir," Rosamond replied. "But I am afraid, my finances to not run to such a luxury."

"No, Madam, but mine do," was the reply.

Rosamond looked most confused and embarrassed. "But you do not know us, Sir, why would you be interested in the wellbeing of my ward?"

"I am not a total stranger in these parts, Madam," Sir John said. "I have a tentative connection to the Mountjoy family, who I understand share a lineage with your wards."

"Why did you not say as much, Sir, when you arrived?" asked Rosamond, confused.

"I wanted to see the children unprepared for my visit, natural as they can be," was the reply.

"So, Sir, you did not come across us by accident?" replied Rosamond, surprised.

"No, Madam, I am afraid I was not wholly truthful when I arrived. I know my way about these parts very well but I had a desire to see Mountjoy's grandchildren."

"To what end, might I ask?" enquired Rosamond.

"I have it in my mind to assist slightly with your financial burden if you will allow me," was the reply.

"I do not think it would be proper, Sir, we have only just met. Maybe if I speak to the Reverend Mountjoy first," said Rosamond.

"I would much prefer that that did not happen. I would like you to indulge an old man with no kin to care for and allow me to help Robin into a life that I believe would be the making of the boy." Sir John continued, "I would like to buy Robin a place in the accountants I use in Oxford. I have already set the wheels in motion, it will only take your trust in me; a stranger, I know, but someone with your best interests at heart and I will fulfil my promise."

"I need to introduce you to Robin as his benefactor and see if he truly would wish to take up your amazing offer," was the reply and she left the table to seek the boy out, who still was in the garden.

Young as he was, he was fully aware of the honour and opportunity that was being offered to him and he was absolutely thrilled.

"It will mean being a long way from home, boy," said Sir John kindly to Robin. "I have sourced you excellent lodgings, where you will be well fed and cared for."

The boy's only worry was leaving his little sisters but once Rosamond assured him that they would always be safe with her and his room would remain untouched for his visits home, he was totally in favour of this new adventure.

When Sir John left, Rosamond stood for a while watching the coach until she could no longer see even the smallest sign of it. She was not convinced that it had not been a dream but just a few days later, the official paper work arrived that Robin would need to start his new adventure. It was agreed that Robin, now aged 10, needed to reach another birthday before he started off for Oxford; even then he was very young but all was in hand, and Robin was very mature for his age and ready to face the challenge. Children a lot younger than Robin were doing manual work all over Britain—down mines, up chimneys, in service, in the mills and factories—so the thought of the boy working with numbers, which he found so pleasing, did not upset Rosamond too unduly.

It did not take Rosamond long to establish her gentleman visitor's actual name and she then understood a little of his interest in the children. She only regretted that he had not been contacted earlier, before so many dramas had taken everyone over. She kept a promise made to him not to disclose anything about the transactions about to take place to anyone. He felt very embarrassed about his lack of protection over his late sister and needed to make amends in his own way, quietly, without thanks.

Chapter 59
Brighton and Secrets

Agnes was treated very well in Brighton and had settled into her new way of life quite easily. Lady Mary is not a strict employer, so long as everyone pulls their weight and does their job, she allows a lot of free time to her servants. Agnes spent most of her free time either in the library or reading quietly in her room.
One day, Lady Mary received a letter from Sir John Fisher and Agnes suddenly elevated from under maid to ladies maid, without any explanation other than Lady Mary liked her. Another letter arrived in Brighton, this time from her grandfather which Lady Mary read to Agnes. Lady Mary was still unaware of the close blood links between the Mountjoys and her young maid. Her understanding was that Agnes was a relative, possibly a black sheep of the family, although the letter from Lord Fisher suggested that the girl was more important than she looked. The letter from Phillip Mountjoy was telling Lady Mary that Robin has managed to be taken on as apprentice in accountancy. Agnes did not understand why her grandfather had not written to her directly instead of through Lady Mary but she was pleased all the same. Life seemed to have turned a corner for Agnes. She was now nearly 17 and in good employment, where she was treated extremely well. She enjoyed working for Lady Mary and loved Brighton. She had enough spare time to read her precious books and visit the library. The library in Brighton is well used, it acts as a social epicentre for visitors to Charles Street. Another gathering place being the public house, of course but the library is more for the refined and elite. People used the circulating library to announce their arrival in town and Mr Tuppen runs a library that allows the residents and visitors in surrounding streets to meet and intermix leaving their calling cards so everyone is aware of who is in town. Although Agnes is only a maid, she has the ability to compete in any conversation or discussion, especially if it is about poetry; people actually find her quite fascinating. She is careful to not to lose sight of her humble birth, still unaware that she is in fact of better lineage than a great many of the upper classes that used the library as a literary meeting place.

Agnes kept her feet on the ground by volunteering to fulfil the task of collecting the newly cleaned items from Thomas and Sarah Rose, who are dyers and scourers by trade operating from number 20 Charles Street. The Rose's dye and scour domestic items, not just clothes, any item that cannot be cleaned at the laundry such as woollen dresses, bonnets, feathers, fancy shawls, lace frills, furnishing fabrics, gentlemen's clothes and a lot more. It is a family concern with some of their six children working in the business. They had recently added calendaring to their list of services that they offer to customers. Calendaring, as Agnes discovered, is a process that is used to flatten cleaned or washed wool with the help of large rollers, similar to mangles used in most houses, only on a much larger scale. So as not to make it look as though she favoured Agnes and annoy her other employees, Lady Mary agreed to allow Agnes to take on the job of collecting items from the Roses'. The Roses are in the same street as the library, so Agnes could indulge in her love of books before carrying out her given task. She occasionally had to push a hand cart to carry heavy items back to the house on. Lady Mary found her little maid quite amusing and often read her pieces out of the paper to see her reaction. Mary knew that one day, all would be revealed and Agnes will come out of her cocoon and suddenly become a social butterfly; she had no idea how this would come about but she felt sure that it would be something to do with Lord John Fisher. She even wondered if Agnes was an illegitimate child of his, though she thought it quite unlikely. A mere maid would not walk so upright or be able to quote such obscure poetry. Mary also felt that there was something very familiar about the girl, her face her colouring. She put this down to the fact that Phillip Mountjoy had said that Agnes was a distant relative so she probably has the look of his daughters, who Mary remember so well, even though it was a good many years ago that they visited her and Sir Gerald. For this reason, she guarded the girl closely and made sure that she was happy in her work, being afraid that one day, the truth might come out and bite her. Better to be safe than sorry.

Sir John's sudden death in 1850 stopped any further financial or moral assistance but Lady Mary was still convinced that Agnes is special in some way, so much intrigue seemed to surround the girl and she is so highly educated. Lady Mary half expected a visit from Lord Fisher's solicitors with news of an inheritance, it did not happen.

Robin's apprenticeship was safely paid for and an allowance in Sir John's will keep the boy safe but not wealthy so Agnes was happy. Agnes was never made aware of who Robin's benefactor might be and suspected that it might be Lady Mary herself, though she did not know of a reason for this.

Life went on, Agnes blossomed and her personal library grew. At first, she had shared a room with two other young women, but after Sir John Fisher made himself known to Lady Mary, Agnes was moved into her own room. It did not make her very popular with the other servants but because she is intellectually superior, Agnes found them quite draining so she was not too worried about having to spend a lot of time alone. So long as she has her precious books, she is perfectly content with her life. She particularly treasures 'The Fate of Adelaide', the poetry book by Letitia Elizabeth Landon that her mother had given her many years ago. Because of that book and her mother, Dory's connection to a Lady Mary in Brighton, Agnes wondered if she could introduce herself as Dory's daughter and possibly be received like a long lost friend, but having been told by her grandfather that she was going to Brighton as plain Agnes Bridges and that she was not to disclose any connection with Dory or even that he was her grandfather, she did not do so. Dory had been careful not to tell Mary of her disastrous second marriage, wanting to be able to keep in touch without feeling inferior. She never intended to visit Brighton again so did not think that her little white lie would ever be discovered. After all, they only ever exchanged a couple of letters a year. Dory had stopped the correspondence as soon as she realised that she was going to move to Hampshire. Agnes thought it was highly probably it was the same Lady Mary, she was now working for, that her mother kept this tentative contact with but without breaking her promise to her paternal grandfather, she could not find out for sure.

Lady Mary had once added to the confusion by asking Agnes if she was in contact with any of the Southerly's in Weston-Under-Wetherley, wondering why she had not been sent to them seeking employment. Agnes answered truly that she did not know anyone of that name, which of course she did not as her memory of that period in her life was now wiped clean. In fact, there were large gaps in Agnes' memory in general. She remembered that she used to ride with her mother but could not remember for sure where they were at the time and sometimes wondered if she just imagines some of the things that came into her mind. She felt an affinity to Weston-Under-Wetherley but also to Weston-Super-Mare, which confused her greatly.

"You have never heard of Lady Dorothia Southerly?" asked Mary, quite surprised.

"Dorothia is a very common name, my mother was also called Dorothia, though we always called her Dory," replied Agnes with a smile, now convinced that she probably was staying with a different Lady Mary than the one her mother knew as Mary is quite a well-used name as well.

Lady Mary thought that Agnes probably spent so much time with her books that she did not take a lot of notice of her surroundings or betters. She also wondered if maybe the girl had only ever visited Weston-Under-Wetherley from Hampshire and maybe not ever lived there. Had she asked if Agnes' mother had ever visited Brighton, she would have discovered Agnes' secret immediately, but as it was not her usual practise to converse in an intimate way with her servants, the subject of Agnes' lineage was never taken up again.

Agnes spent some of her spare time trying to teach any other servants who desired to learn their letters; most only want to be able to write their name so the task is not too demanding. The thrill on the face of the little laundry maid, Ellen, when she finally managed to write her name unaided, Agnes thought, was worth all the hours spent.

Agnes did not go back to Weston-Under-Wetherley as it was a long and difficult journey that did not lend itself to being made regularly. When she was given a week's leave, Agnes chose to go to Boldre and look for her friends that had helped her so very much when she needed it, Hannah Goodfellow and Susan.

It was fairly easy to follow the coast road round from Brighton to Southampton and not too long a journey. She told Lady Mary that she was hoping to discover the where-about of her father, John Henry. She arrived in Lymington and found a farmer, who allowed her to ride on his cart to Boldre. She first went to the house that she thought was owned by John Henry, the old family home, only to find that he had sold it to the present occupants. She then wondered on into the village and knocked softly on Hannah Goodfellow's door, wondering to herself what she would do if the young woman was either not in or had forgotten her. She need not have worried because the door was opened by a heavily pregnant Hannah, who had married Mark, the candlestick and small goods seller, who had made it possible for Agnes and her little group to go to Weston-Under-Wetherley on the death of her mother. Hannah was so pleased to see Agnes that you would have thought they were actually related. Agnes stayed a few days, long enough to discover that John Henry was long gone and no one knew his where-about or cared for that matter.

When Agnes arrived back in Brighton, she seemed very refreshed and told Lady Mary that although she had not managed to discover where her father had disappeared to, she had stayed with friends and visited her mother's grave, which was the main reason she had wanted to go to the New Forest. She had not seen the erected headstone and wanted to do so. Lady Mary was very pleased that the girl had managed to travel so far unattended and safely. After Agnes described the headstone and lettering to Lady Mary, Mary was convinced that it was a different Dorothia that she had known all those years ago; the one she knew would not be buried in Boldre and would not be called Dorothia Bridges, she had been the Countess Southerly.

Agnes, obviously, wrote copious letters home but as was the way of things when in service, she was never allowed to be handed her letters from home without them passing through Lady Mary or Sir Gerald Bradbury's hands first. She longed for the day when she could actually pick up a letter addressed to her from the stand in the hallway and take it to her room, unbeknown to her employers. Anyone writing to Agnes was very careful not to say anything that would confuse the situation, knowing it would be read by Agnes' employers first. So Agnes always considered that she did not actually ever receive any letters herself, they were actually, though addressed to her, for her employer to read and pass on to her if deemed necessary. Some employers just tell their people roughly what was said in letters; others were more polite and handed them over. The majority of maid and general servants would not have been able to read any letter clearly anyway, so it was thought to be doing them a service reading their missives to them. Agnes, being well read, considered the fact that if anyone other than herself even opened a letter addressed to her, it was an insult but she did not speak out. She could not wait to write and tell her grandparents how fine the headstone was that the Keepings had kindly arranged and John Henry had reluctantly paid for. Agnes did not know that the cost of the marble headstone had been the straw that broke the camel's back for John Henry and that he was now greatly in debt and destined for debtor's prison. She knew Bathsheba and Phillip would have approved of the black marble and bold gold lettering.

Before she left Boldre, Agnes had left a posy of wild flowers on the grave and said a quick prayer to herself.

Agnes managed to write a note to the Keepings thanking them greatly for their help and left it with the vicar of the beautiful church in Boldre, which she knew they attended. She promised these kind people that one day, God willing, she would repay their kindness.

Chapter 60
Secrets and Deaths

Agnes was just 18 when she heard that her grandmother, Bathsheba Mountjoy, had suddenly passed away, struck down by a fever. The letter that arrived in Brunswick Square did not refer to Bathsheba as Agnes' grandmother, just as a close relative. Lady Mary called her to the sitting room and sat the girl down. Agnes could tell immediately that she was going to be told very bad news. Although it had never been made clear to Lord and Lady Bradbury that how tentative the link between Agnes and the Mountjoys was, they knew that Agnes was obviously beholden to Bathsheba and Phillip in some way, or he would not have sought Lady Mary's help when it came to employing the girl. Lady Mary had always assumed that Agnes was probably the daughter of a black sheep of the family or someone who had made an ill-advised marriage. Phillip had only described the girl as a distant relative.

Sir Gerald made one of his rare appearances and told Agnes that he had arranged for her to go Weston-Under-Wetherley to see her relatives and attend the funeral. Sir John Fisher had left with the Bradburys a small contingency fund to be used at their discretion to help Agnes, especially if it was something to do with any member of her family. This seemed like the right time to use this money.

When Sir John Fisher had written to Mary, he had told her that he was Agnes' patron along with her two sisters and a brother. He did not explain why and Lady Mary wondered if maybe it was something to do with a secret family of his. It was not unusual for a wealthy gentleman to have a secret mistress and take care of them and any family they produced together but keep it very discrete.

Obviously, Sir Gerald had looked into the background of Lord Fisher as much as he could and discovered that he was the brother of George Southerly's wife, Agnes. Once he heard the name George Southerly, the Earl of Wetherley, he dropped the inquiry. Anyone who bore that name was suspected of being a little shady and Sir Gerald was completely convinced that Agnes, their little maid, was the result of either a dalliance by the late, disliked earl himself; maybe the daughter of a servant he had ruined or even more unlikely, a child of Lord John Fisher. Either story, he did not chose to pursue but told his wife, Lady Mary, to be very careful how he treated the young woman.

Within two days, Agnes was on a coach heading to Weston-Under-Wetherley. It is a long and tedious journey and she stayed at three overnight stops— Southampton, Reading and Oxford—which broke the journey rather nicely, arriving on the very day of her grandmother's internment. Having been given as long a leave of absence as she felt she needed, she was able to not only comfort her grandfather but spend a few days with her sisters, who were growing up fast. Robin had not been able to have the time off to come to the funeral so there was a hole that sadly could not be filled. Rosamond had regular letters from Robin so she was fully aware of how he was managing, the letters always seemed positive and full of enthusiasm.

Rosamond never told Agnes about the visit a couple of years before from the stranger, who changed everyone's lives, she had been bound to secrecy. Sir John Fisher had left a small legacy to Rosamond on his death, arranged for Robin to stay in comfort and left the remainder of his wealth to the orphans and the church.

Agnes loved being in Weston-Under-Wetherley and hearing about things that are close to her heart. In Brighton, being a reasonably short distance from London to travel comfortably, the talk is always about happenings in the capital; whereas in Wetherley, people do not show the same interest, they just worry about everyday life where they live and Agnes liked this. Riots and discontent in London seem a million miles away to Agnes, whilst back home under the shadow of Wetherley Wood.

Bathsheba Mountjoy was buried next to her much loved mother, Seraphina, Agnes' great grandmother, in St Michael's churchyard in Weston-Under-Wetherley. The grave is to the left of the church, up the steps that lead you to the front door and over a slight hillock, where the ground flattens again. Bathsheba had often sat on the hillock and looked out towards the end of the village daydreaming, so it seemed a very appropriate place for her to be buried. The funeral was well attended and Agnes' Aunt Everline had managed to attend with her husband, who kindly carried out the service himself, which Agnes felt was very appropriate. Bathsheba's other daughter, Elizabeth, had married a local man and was heavily pregnant so she stayed in the vicarage, away from the crowd. Agnes watched her grandfather and worried over the pain she could see etched on his sad face. At the end of the service, Phillip announced his intention to retire and said that on next Sunday, he would be introducing the new incoming vicar to his parishioners. It was a very sad day for the village of Weston-Under-Wetherley.

Agnes was preparing to return to Brighton when she was alerted by her grandfather's man that he had been taken ill. Before Agnes had a chance to return to Lady Mary in Brighton, she lost her grandfather as well as her grandmother. People told her that it was a blessing that they should go together but Agnes did not see it that way. Her trip back to Brighton was a very tearful one and she was greeted with open arms by Lady Mary, which Agnes found unexpected but appreciated. Mary had felt a slight loss herself as she had known Phillip Mountjoy through letters for many years, although they had never actually met.

Agnes had found it difficult to leave her family at such a sad time, but she knew that there was nothing she could do for anyone. Her siblings were all well cared for by Aunt Rosamond and she had seen very little of her mother's sisters as she grew up so as not to miss them. Agnes would lay awake at night, sometimes trying to remember her childhood but it was such a muddle. Weston-Under-Wetherley and Weston-Super-Mare kept reoccurring in her dreams and she knew that both places had been important in her life, but the two places were intertwined and she could not remember which Weston was the important one in her young life. Did she horse ride with her mother in Weston-Super-Mare or was it Weston-Under-Weatherly? Was the handsome man, she half remembered, who took her to Weston to visit Aunt Rosamond on a farm when she was very young, her father before he turned to drink? She had remembered somewhere in the back of her mind that her father, John Henry, being a kind man once. She believed that her mother must have felt some tender emotion towards him once as they had produced four children together or so she thought. It was hard to shake the memory of the many years of drink and violence that overshadowed any pleasant thoughts about her youth.

Chapter 61
Esme and More Changes

Life went on as usual for Agnes. She never heard from her father, John Henry, ever again and although she did try from time to time to contact him, the only information that she received was to tell her that he had married the widow Brown and he did not wish to hear from her ever again. This had come in the form of a very short note address to her grandfather and forwarded to Sir Gerald Bradbury, who read the letter and passed it on to Agnes. The content of the letter were enough to convince Lady Mary that she had been mistaken in thinking that Agnes had any connection to the Dorothia that she knew. Agnes was the daughter of John Henry Bridges, someone she doubted that she would ever wish to encounter.

Agnes scanned the newspapers from time to time expecting to read that her father had been arrested for some crime or other but didn't see or hear of him or about him again. She felt no love for the man or real desire to ever see him again; after all, the way he had treated her mother and his children, in general, had been shameful.

She knew her sisters were safe enough, Rosamond looks after the girls very well and they are greatly loved. They were learning their numbers and letters and she felt they would grow to be reasonably worldly with Rosamond's help. But the sudden loss of her grandfather and grandmother made Agnes realise how delicate a thread all their lives are hanging on. She also wondered if maybe Aunt Rosamond might marry again one day, she was still only in her 40s after all and a very pretty woman. Would she still want the children?

One spring day, Lady Mary came to Agnes to inform her that they were to have a young visitor. She did not give any real details, only that the visitor was her niece, Esme Fitzroy, who was 17, touching 18 and needed shelter for a while.

"Agnes, I have assigned you to take very good care of my niece," said Lady Mary. "She needs a friend as well as a maid and I feel you will foot the bill, being of a similar age. You are only a year or so older than Esme so she will feel comfortable having you attend to her, I am sure,"

"I would be honoured, Lady Mary," was the reply.

"My dear brother Henry has been a widower a good many years, ever since he lost his dear wife, Amy, in childbirth, and he feels it is time for the girl, who is fast approaching being a woman, to have the chance to come out in society," Continued Mary. "My brother assures me that Esme is a country girl and is not enamoured of the honour he has bestowed upon her."

"Begging your pardon, Madam," said Agnes, "I do understand, I found it very difficult to adjust to such a large place having come from a small village."

"There, I knew you would be the right person for the job, Agnes," said Lady Mary with a broad smile. "You can accompany her to your beloved library if she so wishes. I will appoint you to be her personal maid and dresser."

"I am honoured," said Agnes really pleased, she bobbed a quick curtsy as she spoke.

One sunny spring afternoon, a very smart coach baring the Fitzroy coat of arms pulled up outside of Lady Mary's beautiful house in Brunswick Square. And so, it was that Esme Fitzroy arrived in high dudgeon with a distinct lack of fashionable clothes, obviously not happy to have been shipped off to Brighton.

"Well, my child," said Lady Mary to her niece as she kissed her on her cheek, "I do not know what has made my brother suddenly decide that you need to see a bit more of England and meet a few more people than those in your tight circle in Falford Hall, but I am happy to have your company. I have assigned Agnes as your personal maid and companion, she is a bright girl, very well read for a country girl."

"We do have books in the country, Aunt," replied Esme, rather caustically. "We are not all country bumpkins."

"I am sorry, child," was the reply. "I did not mean to sound condescending. I know your father to be a very well-read man and our parents were certainly well travelled; as for your late mother, she was delightfully informed for one so young."

Esme's mood softened immediately on hearing these words. "You knew my mother?" she said. "Of course, you must have."

"I knew your mother from a babe in arms and in fact, it was I who introduced Amy to Henry, your father, when she was of age," was the reply. "She was the daughter of a very good friend of mine. My eldest daughter is named after her."

"Maybe you could tell me about her sometime, Aunt," said Esme eagerly.

"I will tell you all you want to know, child," replied her aunt.

Esme smiled one of her brilliant smiles.

"I knew you would be a pretty young woman, Esme," began Lady Mary. "You have your father's eyes but the look of your mother. You will cause quite a stir hereabouts, of that I am sure. There will be suitable beaus knocking our door down."

"Oh no, please, Aunt, I have come for a quiet life," replied Esme. "And as for a beau, I do not seek any such person. I cannot image that Brighton will have anything to offer that will enrich my life in any way. I have only come on my father's insistence and he has promised me that I need not stay any longer than I wish to, whatever Uncle William thinks."

"What has William got to do with anything?" asked Mary puzzled.

"It is he that has persuaded my father that I need to see Brighton or London, the hateful man. I beg your pardon, Aunt, I know he is your brother," said Esme with a tear appearing in her eye. "My uncle and his horrid son have ruined my happy life, I cannot believe that my father allowed them to do so."

"My goodness child, you must tell me more," said Lady Mary, now very curious. "What influence could William hold over Henry?"

"None any more, I believe," was the reply. "My father is shipping my uncle and his son back to their home in Bath, they do not want to go but father is adamant, they have caused enough trouble at Falford Hall."

Mary laughed. "I told Henry it was a bad notion of his allowing William and Robert to move in with him. I know he felt they had a common bond besides being brothers of course, by both being widowers. Henry and William are so different in nature, always were."

"You are so right, Aunt," replied Esme. "The moment Uncle William moved into Falford Hall, everything changed. My father has an easy way with everyone, everyone loves him. My uncle, on the other hand, thinks anyone who is not of the best noble blood is so far below him that there is no need for him to even be polite to them."

Mary laughed again. "He was always that way, Esme. He always thought himself superior. So what has opened Henry's eyes and made him send William back to his own house in Bath?"

Esme realised that she had probably said too much already. "It was a great many things that combined to annoy my father enough to find Uncle William a housekeeper and give notice to the people who were renting the Bath house so uncle could return forthwith."

"And is my nephew, Robert, to go willingly with his father?" Mary asked.

"The plan, as I was leaving, was that they both go, willingly or not," Esme replied.

"And does the boy still write poetry?" asked her aunt.

"He does little else," was the reply. "Have you never read any of his work, Aunt?"

"No. I would be telling you a lie if I said I was desperately interested in what I might think is amateur poetry. I enjoy good poetry by fine writers but could not imagine that Robert could ever give me reason to read anything of his. I have seen snippets of what Constance calls his genius from time to time. My sister is very taken with him," replied Mary.

"He does have a certain following," said Esme reluctantly.

"Nevertheless, William must have been as proud as punch, he never thought Robert would come to much in the literary world," said Mary.

"I do not believe that neither my father nor uncle classify poetry as something very worthwhile," replied Esme. "Robert has enough pride for everyone, no need for others to feel any."

"I assume from that comment that you and Robert are not the best of friends," said Mary looking concerned.

"Friends, I hope I never have to see Robert again ever," replied Esme looking almost furious. "He ruined my life, he thought that he would marry me and keep the family money so spoilt everything that might have prevented it."

"I look forward to hearing more about that, child," said Mary, realising that she had struck a nerve. "Meanwhile, I have kept you standing about in the hallway long enough. Agnes will show you your room and the servants will follow with your baggage. As soon as you have settled in, please come down. Your Uncle Gerald is not very mobile, that is why he is not standing here greeting you."

Esme was glad to go to her room, she felt she had told her aunt more than she had intended. She walked up the stairs behind Agnes and into a room that was very light and airy, decorated in delicate pastel colours. Esme smiled.

"It is a pretty room, don't you think, Miss?" said Agnes with a short curtsy.

"Before we go any further, Agnes, I must ask you not to curtsy to me. My aunt says that you are a companion, I hope we might also become friends, I really do need one right now."

Agnes was quite taken aback by this pretty, young woman's upfront attitude. "I too hope we might be, Miss Esme, it would be an honour."

"Oh tosh, no honour intended," replied Esme. "Do they treat you well here, Agnes?"

"Your Aunt is a delight to work for, Miss," was the reply.

"How long have you been here?" Esme asked genuinely interested.

"Over three years now, Miss," replied Agnes. "I worked for a family in Sway in the New Forest before I came here."

"You must have been very young when you went into service, Agnes," said Esme amazed.

"A lot older than some," was the reply.

"And where do your family come from?" Esme asked Agnes with interest.

"I believe, originally, a place called Weston-Under-Wetherley, you have probably never heard of it," was the reply. "Although I am not completely sure of my origins."

Esme laughed at the thought of someone not being sure where they came from. "You are quite right about Weston-Under-Wetherley, I have never heard of it but you can tell me about it someday."

Esme liked Agnes a lot and found it a lot easier settling into life at Brighton with a young woman of similar age to talk to.

Agnes and Esme sorted out a suitable day dress and Esme changed from her travel clothes and went down stairs as requested to meet her Uncle Gerald, who she had only ever heard about before and never actually met because he suffers from severe pain caused by a particular bad fall from a horse many years before and now has gout to contend with amongst other things so he does not travel far.

This was the start of a firm friendship that developed over the following month between Esme and Agnes.

Within days, Mary had written to her brother, Henry, and told him that she felt he had made the right decision sending Esme to Brighton. Saying she felt that she was too bright a light and far too beautiful to keep hidden in the country. She went on to tell her brother of the plans she had made to introduce Esme into society in Brighton and of all the young, eligible men that she planned to introduce to her. She had done very well with her own girls and was going to relish the chance to show Esme off.

Very soon, Agnes was privy to all of Esme's secrets, she knew who her frequent letters from abroad were from and Esme's hopes and dreams for the future. The two were much the same size and height so any clothes that Esme decided were not quite the mode for Brighton, she gave to Agnes, making Agnes suddenly a very well-dressed young woman and a suitable strolling companion. Agnes had already utilised a number of her mothers' old dresses that were not too fancy and had given the rest to Aunt Rosamond to use.

Esme was kept well amused in Brighton. Her two cousins, Mary's married young daughters, Amy and Margaret, called often to take Esme to the shops or for tea with friends.

Amy was quite a way into her first pregnancy so it was more often Agnes, Esme and Margaret. They walked along the beach and strolled out on the pier. Esme found herself beginning to enjoy her stay in Brighton much more than she had imagined she would, but she could not see that Brighton held a light to the countryside around

Falford Hall. When not with Amy or Margaret, Esme could be seen in the library with Agnes or helping her collect items for her Aunt Mary. Esme was fascinated by all the local businesses. Like Agnes, she had never seen so many all in one place. Esme did, however, make it clear to her aunt that she did not wish to stay too long into the year because she missed her horse, Thunder, and even more so, her father and the Hall.

Aunt Mary had done her best to introduce Esme to as many young people as she deemed proper and was heartily disappointed in the times Esme turned down invitations to tea or such like. She had written to her brother, Henry, to inform him of her concern that the girl showed very little interest in town life.

My Dearest Brother,

'I thought I should put pen to paper and inform you of how your daughter has settled in Brighton. I have no doubt that she has sent many a missive to you already.

Esme is a sweet child but she only seemed happy when she was reading letters from home or out horse riding across the chalk hills on the South Downs. The only real conversation she appeared to enjoy was when a young man, who was a friend of my son-in-law, called and told Esme about his long trek along the South Downs Bridle Path, following the entire length of the chalk ridge from Winchester to Eastbourne. I do not feel that this is healthy for a young woman approaching her 18th year. I am, however, very happy that Esme has bonded with her personal maid, who is acting as a companion for her, so she always has someone much her own age to talk to. The maid, Agnes, is very well read and perfectly suitable as a companion, I hope I have not over stepped the mark by appointing the girl in this role.'

Your loving sister as always.

Mary.

Sir Henry had smiled when he received Mary's worried letter. All was as Sir Henry had expected it to be. He felt that Esme would not easily fall into the ways of city dwellers. He did thank Mary for being so thoughtful as to appoint Agnes and did, however, ask Mary to continue her efforts to make Esme meet young people and with good luck and a fair breeze, she might actually start to really enjoy herself.

Back in Falford Hall, Sir Henry, Esme's father, was already regretting sending his daughter away to Brighton. He had not been disappointed when asked if he could fetch Esme home earlier than planned along with her new companion.

Chapter 62
Meanwhile in Paris

Lord Adam Southerly, the Earl of Wetherley, settled down to a happy and contented life in Paris. Martin remained an important person in his life and he, in turn, enjoyed married life with Betty, who had proved to be a great asset, as Martin had predicted, cooking and mending for the household.

It was not until Joseph was 16 that Adam even allowed himself to think about England and his previous life. He started receiving letters from England, there were three in all and he didn't even open the first; the second, he glanced at and the third, he felt compelled to open and read fully. He rather assumed that they would be from someone helping Freda trace him, and he did not want any ghosts from the past destroying his new life. It was actually from a Daniel Foster, a solicitor in Brighton, England, and was asking probing questions about a young woman called Agnes Bridges. The young woman had worked in Brighton for Lord and Lady Bradbury before leaving to live in Somerset with the Fitzroy family. Agnes had seemed to all to be a very upright and well-educated young woman and out of place as a maid. Daniel Foster had been employed to discover all he could about the young woman and shed some light on her history. Agnes Bridges, herself, had a very scant memory of her childhood but everyone, who came in contact with the young woman, felt that there was a secret to be told. Daniel made it clear that his job was not to put Miss Bridges in an embarrassing position; it was to discover if she was in fact someone of consequence and use this information to her advantage. Daniel added that there appeared to be a connection with Sir John Fisher of Weston-Under-Wetherley and the Mountjoys according to Lady Bradbury.

The earl replied to the latest solicitor letter and apologised for not doing so earlier. He explained that he believed the young woman to be his long lost daughter, Seraphina, and that her mother, Lady Dorothia Southerly, previously Mountjoy, had remarried, further details he did not have. Adam posted his beautifully written letter and enclosed the two miniatures that Pierre had painted of him and Dorothia as a wedding present as well as his daughter's birth certificate that he was not quite sure why he had kept. The family seal was carefully placed on the missive and it was sent on its way back to England post haste. Although fascinated, the earl thought no more about it for a while.

Another letter followed and the earl, being very content with his chosen life and did not relish anything changing this, returned it unopened. When a second arrived from England, he felt obligated to open and read the letter. It was from a man he had not heard of, Sir Henry Fitzroy of Falford Hall, near Bath. It was imploring him to make contact as his daughter was about to marry. The request was that he came to England. The letter did not give many details other than that Agnes had come into the care of the writer, having lost her mother and he felt it would be advantageous all round if the earl returned. It ended by saying that if he did not get a reply to this last letter, he would send a representative from his household to give the earl full details and try to persuade him to do the right thing by his daughter. This was the first indication that Adam had ever received that Dorothia had passed on, her life had changed so dramatically after she re-married and all contact had been lost.

Thomas Garson, the young representative from England, stood waiting nervously for the earl at the appointed place with no idea what the man looked like or his disposition. He need not have worried, as soon as the earl approached, Tom knew instantly it was him. He walked upright, a gold topped cane in his hand, with shoulder length grey hair tied back and a neat pointed beard. He was wearing a tall, stovepipe top hat, long fitted cut-away morning coat over a linen shirt and Brocade waistcoat. His trousers were checked and his shoes had a high shine. This very impressive outfit was finished off by a plain white cravat. He looked every bit a fashionable Parisian gentleman of standing.

The earl greeted Tom like a long lost friend, shaking his hand warmly with a wide grin on his face. It was an encounter that he had been, both, expecting and dreading for a great many years. He always thought, even hoped, that one day, he would have word of his lost daughter. Once Tom had fully explained how Agnes had come to be living in Falford Hall and how Sir Henry's daughter, Esme, had chosen her as a friend despite her being a ladies maid and how, in turn, Sir Henry's family had taken her into their hearts, the earl was captivated by the whole romance of the tale. Tom was somewhat taken about by the ease in which he completed his task. He had expected to have to persuade the earl, who by this time insisted that Tom call him Adam, to come back with him to England and be reunited with his daughter.. Adam was, in fact, the first to suggest that he should return with Tom. He had been genuinely moved by Tom's description of the poor girl's life after the loss of her much loved mother, having believed that he had left them both financially stable. He was embarrassed that he had allowed his own life and happiness to take precedence over that of his daughter's and was determined to right that wrong.

Adam was the jolliest man Tom had even encountered. He found himself quickly drawn to him in a strange way. He expressed no outward airs and graces. Although he had been born into the aristocracy, he spoke to Tom as an equal, he reminded Tom of the man who had sent him on this errand Sir Henry.

Adam explained that he had arrived in Paris with no home and a gypsy in tow, not the recipe for joining the higher ranks of society. But he had been happily surprised by the acceptance of his position, knowing that he had a fine title did help, of course. He had been very humbled by his reception in Paris and soon fell in with like-minded noblemen that had blotted their copy books and for one reason or another, had chosen to slip quietly out of English society. No questions were ever asked. So long as you could pay your way, hold your liquor and tell a good yarn, you were quickly included in the life Paris offered. Even Adam's beautiful wife, Lady Jeanette, was accepted. She was considered an exotic beauty and her company much sorted after amongst this band of runaways. They had lived as a married couple with their son and as soon as he was released from his obligation to Agnes' mother, married secretly.

The earl put an arm about Tom's shoulder and led him to his home to meet his wife and family. The pair were already making plans to return to England and face the music. Adam's wife and son were both enthusiastic about visiting Britain; Joe had been born there but left as a baby and he was interested in his roots, and Jeanette was happy to accompany her husband wherever the wind blew them. Robbie had married by now and was a father himself. Kitty had married well as was expected and Pierre and Camille were two of the most compatible people that the earl knew. They had a son and daughter together, much to everyone's delight. Martin and Betty were still in Adam's employment but they had decided that England no longer interested them so they would stay put until the earl's return. Betty's son, Tim, had married and was also a father so everyone was settled in their chosen lives. Martin had fathered a daughter with Betty and was very content.

To be continued...........

If you wish to know how Agnes fairs in Falford Hall, you need to read 'The Poet's Trap', which explains why Esme was sent to Brighton.

Reviews

Obviously, my first novel *The Poet's Trap* had a lot of reviews, none negative, I am pleased to say, and I decided to include a few of my favourites in the introduction of this new novel.

1. *I can't honestly dismiss this as full-on 'chick-lit' but (provided I've got this right) I think it can be called a 'period drama'. Characters are well-developed (Sir Henry – honest, even if 'to the manor born', thoroughly likeable from the off. Esme – such a sweet, loyal heroine and her beau, Tom, maybe a stable lad but capable of so much more as is later proved. The last of the 'good guys', Tanner, the faithful and trustworthy footman, who's wisdom and advice is welcomed by Sir Henry. Then we come to the villains of the piece. What insufferable snobs are William and his despicable son, Robert!)*
   Enough of the cast. You have blended in so much history, not only of Falford Hall itself but of each of the main characters and you achieve this whilst maintaining interest, rather than creating a boring ramble. Great stuff! I will skip over the storyline for no other reason that there are so many plusses it would take me all day to single out and give praise to each element—suffice to say that the tale's end is more than satisfactory.
   I was fearful when Robert 'hit on' Agnes, wondering when he would resort to type. Not just a case of 'how' but 'when' would he do the dirty on her? But then you amaze when the leopard does indeed change its spots and he ends up likeable?
   So, there you have my appraisal of your first work of fiction—a darn good read, indeed, one of those 'difficult to put down' novels. Well done!
   Wishing you every success. Pete Foxworthy (1947–2017) (Baldock, Herts.).

2. *A delightful story that gently but firmly guides the reader to see the injustice in society without even being aware of it. SUBLIME! Esme and her father live harmoniously in middle England. Their values on the mark of a man differed from the materialistic, pompous society they lived in. They held true to their belief that manners maketh the man. Society at that time revolved around money and the belief that money maketh the man. An added joy is the exquisite poetry that Gallimore decorates the book with. I read the book three times and was immersed each time. Phenomenal.*
   Tracey Causer (Birmingham England).

3. *The story deals with Sir Henry and a father's love for his daughter, Esme. His brother, William, whose son, Robert, a young man who can't get his*

own way, decides to create upset and mischief within the family, after being rebuffed by Esme, in favour of Tom, the stable boy. The story also depicts Sir Henry's support of trusted employees and their families.

I find it well written of its time with well described scenes. The author takes you into the location as if you are actually there.

Well done, Sylvie Gallimore! May we have some more, please? Maybe a sequel and, or even a prequel? John Vickery (Bristol, England).

4. I was given a copy of this book (The Poet's Trap) in autumn 2016. Before I finished reading it, I decided that it would make a good Christmas present and I ordered two more copies. Both recipients were very pleased with their presents.

This is a simple, clearly told story of a wealthy family living on a country estate near Bath in the early years of the reign of Queen Victoria. It is easy to read a few pages at a time, put down and pick up again without losing the thread. An ideal book to have on your bedside table or to take on holiday with you. As a retired headmistress, I found the historical and geographical information of the 1850s seen through the eyes of Tom, one of the characters, and written in his letters home during his travels abroad, particularly interesting. Congratulations to Sylvie for undertaking this extensive research. I did find some of the characters annoying, too good to be true in their ability to forgive and even reward great wrongs. However, others might not agree so why not read the book and start a discussion. Looking forward to learning more about the family in the next book.

Judith Banfield
(South Gloucestershire).